Copyright © 2025 by Debra Anastasia

All rights reserved.

No part of this book may be reproduced in any form or by any electronic or mechanical means, including information storage and retrieval systems, without written permission from the author, except for the use of brief quotations in a book review.

copyright (c) 2016 Debra Anastasia

All rights reserved

Published by Debra Anastasia

Editing: Jessica Royer Ocken

For All The Evers is a work of fiction. Names, characters, places, and incidents are all products of the author's twisted imagination and are used fictitiously. Any resemblance to actual events, locals, or persons, living or dead, is entirely coincidental.

Except as permitted under the US Copyright Act of 1976, no part of this publication may be reproduced, distributed or transmitted in any form by any means, or stored in a database or retrieval system, without the prior written permission of the author.

ISBN-13: 978-1540335777

ISBN-10: 1540335771

Always for T, J and D
In Honor of Thomas McHugh

TO MY UNCLE TOMMY

Uncle Tommy,

I wish I had known you. I know that you died in World War II. I know you had no wife, no kids, no descendants other than your brother's children. I've often wondered how life would have been different if you'd lived.

My mom never met you, but you're talked about a lot. My poppy, your brother, told us your stories. He was hilarious, and I guess you're together now. That's a good thing. I know he missed you. And I was proud of the stories I heard about you.

I've felt helpless because there's no fixing the past, but now I realize maybe I can. This letter is to thank you for your sacrifice, but I went further than that. I finished the book I promised your niece I would write.

After people read this, you will be known. You will be remembered. And you will be loved. Your niece found your grave, and this book brought you to life again. We haven't forgotten you.

And we love you.

Deb

PROLOGUE

"Don't close your eyes. Please, stay. Just stay." Fallen held on to him as tightly as she could.

He tilted her face toward his, lips smiling but eyes sad. "I won't. I can't stay."

"You can." She climbed up him until he held her, her legs wrapped around his middle. "I believe we can stay here. Just don't wake up. Don't go back." She ran her fingertips down his handsome face. "I know what's going to happen. I'm begging you. And I've never begged anyone for anything. Ever. Please, Thomas."

He put his forehead against hers. "I'm going to miss you." His eyes teared up a little, but his determination shone through. "So, so much. Forever."

Her own tears were free now, coasting over her lips and into her mouth. She wrapped her arms around his neck and spoke against his mouth, the salty emotions painting his lips as well. "Love me enough to stay."

He shook his head infinitesimally, refusing to break the contact. "Don't say that."

She had to play dirty. He was her everything.

"If you loved me, you'd stay." She gripped his wide shoulders.

"Dream girl." He sighed his nickname for her for one last time. "I love you enough to die for you."

She panicked in his arms, hearing the finality. "No. No. No! Please. No."

He held her closer as she struggled to get away. If she didn't say goodbye, he couldn't leave.

"Stop. Don't. Be still." He set her on her feet and stroked her hair from the crown to where it ended at the middle of her back. "I need this. This one moment with you. It makes me brave." He began to nod. "It's happening. It's going to happen. I can't desert them."

His voice sounded less commanding. He was scared.

They weren't going to get to have this life together, but she could try to help him with his death.

"Okay. Okay." She wiped her tears, centering herself with a strength she hadn't possessed until this very second. "Look at me."

They looked into each other's eyes. Despite all she had done—the hoping, the praying—it had come to this. He began to fade, his lids getting heavier.

"Remember this. Remember us," she told him.

He put his arms around her. She made sure they maintained eye contact.

He's leaving.

Superhuman strength welled up in her as she focused instead of dissolved.

"Know that I love you more than time." She kissed his lips, his nose, his lips again.

"What if I'm a coward...in the end?" He voiced his unspoken fear.

"I swear on this, on our love—I know you will be remembered only for your valor."

She'd seen his Purple Heart. His legacy was bravery.

"Dream girl."

He grew quieter; this was how it went, the way it ended in all her waking nightmares.

The pain of not saving him would crush her soul.

"Yeah?" She put her hand on his heart, feeling it thump against her hand.

"Live. And that flag?" Even in his last moments, pride and commitment.

"It'll fly every day." Her heart performed a wedding here, in this place, only to that piece of material instead of to him.

"Love. Don't give up on that." He held her face and kissed her.

Beneath his gentle lips, she couldn't lie—even if he wanted her to. "There's only you. There will only ever be you."

"Okay." He ran his knuckles along her cheek and jaw. "Yours is a face worth fighting for. Don't worry. I'll make your future safe."

"When I die, I'll come here. I'll find you."

Thomas nodded. He was almost gone now, barely in front of her.

She wanted him ready for battle on the other side.

"I love you forever, Fallen." He was just a ghost of a shape.

"You give them hell, Thomas McHugh." She went to her tiptoes as he took his last kiss.

In the wisp of his silhouette, after the kiss could go on no more, she sensed his stunning blue eyes on her, like she was his talisman.

"I'll love you for all the evers I get." She blew a kiss, and the wisp of him washed away with the sentiment.

Then he was gone. She'd sent the man she loved to his death.

A sound as close to the soundtrack for hell as she'd ever heard ripped though the quiet. It wasn't until she put her wrist to her mouth, blocking her airway, that she realized the noise had come from her.

She bent at the waist, hugging her middle as she gasped.

Was it now?

Was it now?

Was he dying right now?

She cried herself to a prone position, and desolation found her like a rogue wave.

It had all been for nothing in the end.

A little while later, when she felt the heat, she opened her eyes. She was awake, back in her world, and it was on fire.

Engulfed in flames, Fallen felt a small hope. In death she could see him again. In death she could triumph.

1

MILK

Fallen Billow looked at the list of her brother Fenn's 11th grade school supplies and fees. She'd just paid the electric bill the day before when the man from the company had appeared on her front door step. There might have been some change from her car's cup holder involved. And now the rough total in her head for what Fenn needed to start his junior year at White Plains High School was enough to make her cry.

The list was yet another reminder that her decision to leave college and her part-time job there had been necessary—and unavoidable. Fenn needed a full-time income, not to mention a full-time presence in his life, to support him. Her classes had been too expensive anyway, and she'd been turned down for another school loan. But above all, things here at home were more than desperate. She hadn't been back long, but that much was abundantly clear.

Just then Fenn popped into the kitchen, his dark blond hair flopping over his eyes. He proceeded to pour the largest glass in the history of milk and guzzle it down like he did that very thing for a living.

She tried not to parse out how much money he'd just swallowed, but she smiled at him a second too late, and he wiped his mouth with regret in his eyes.

"I'm sorry. Is it really tight this week?"

She tried to shield him from the worst of it. And thankfully, he was so easygoing that he accepted some of her lamer excuses. For now, Fallen went along with his belief that their mother, Nora, would come back. Even though she'd taken every red cent they had and left her kids behind, she might come back. She might be able to kick her addiction and be an adult for Fenn.

"We're cool," Fallen told him, mustering a more genuine smile. "You're allowed to drink milk."

She turned her back on her brother and went to her room. Her eyes went automatically to her textbooks gaining a layer of dust in the corner, but there were no tears, no sadness. She'd wanted to be a teacher, but for now she was shelving her hopes for her brother's dreams. And those dreams cost money. To that end, tomorrow she would start the new job she'd miraculously found in housekeeping at an old hotel in downtown White Plains, a walkable two miles from their home, and just 40 minutes from New York City.

J ust after seven in the morning, Fallen accepted her new uniform from what appeared to be the oldest woman in the world. Desta, she'd said her name was.

"Wear this every day. You'll have two. Put this one on now, and there's another in a bag with your welcome packet."

It was a classic look: black with white details.

"Get yourself a pair of the white sneakers with the Velcro down at Payless. Buy one get one sale going on now. Stock up. And get bleach at BJ's in bulk. You will not believe the stains you'll have to get out of the shoes and the uniform. You'd think we were working at a hospital."

The oldest woman in the world started laughing at her own joke, before segueing into some really wet-sounding coughs. Fallen had started to panic at the woman's wide eyes and blue lips when she made a loud, popping noise in the back of her throat and began breathing normally.

"I smoked for twenty-five years," Desta explained with a shrug. "It did some damage."

"When did you quit?" It seemed the obvious way to continue the conversation.

"Who said I quit? No end in sight for this lady." Desta started laugh-coughing again, covering her mouth with a weak wrist.

"Well, you've got a firm commitment there," Fallen offered.

"Anyway, you've been assigned to the fifth floor. That's yours. If you're not here for work, that floor doesn't get cleaned. And we pride ourselves on clean." Desta gave Fallen a hard look over her thick glasses.

She nodded. Desta seemed to come to work dead every day, so Fallen guessed sick days weren't much of an option.

Desta led Fallen to the elevator. It looked original to the hotel, and instead of a moving room with secure, solid doors, it was more like a huge birdcage. They stepped on, and Desta jammed an old key in under the buttons, then hit five.

"Do this; it takes you right to your floor."

Sure enough, the terrifying bird cage ground to a halt on the fifth floor. Fallen stepped out into the hallway, relieved to be on solid ground again.

It was pretty, the hotel. But desolate in a way. The wallpaper seemed vintage and had peeled in some of the corners, bubbling in other spots. The rooms were spacious, but strangely configured. On the whole it was elegant, but odd.

Desta was going on about charm and original finishes. The floor had fourteen rooms, she explained. Each needed to be cleaned after the guests had checked out, or during a moment when they'd stepped out.

"Most important of all, room 514. That one you have to clean every day. Do you understand? Every day. Never skip it." Desta repeated that particular direction four more times during their tour of Fallen's new workspace.

She learned she would shadow Desta for the first week, and then be on her own. After that, they got started.

Old or not, Desta was a little dynamo when she cleaned. Every two rooms, she took a smoke break. She tossed hints and tips at Fallen as they went, but when Fallen attempted tasks on her own, they were always just a little under par.

"Practice, practice!" Desta assured her.

By the end of the day, Fallen's back ached, and her hands were red from the stiff bleach used on the sheets. But the good news was more time she'd spent with Desta, the more she liked her. The care of the old hotel was obviously very important to her. She had a pride almost like ownership, even though she wore the same uniform as Fallen.

One week later, when Fallen got home after her first day of solo cleaning on her very own floor, she'd worked three hours of unpaid overtime to get her rooms done. Desta told her she hadn't even done that great a job either.

She had just settled on the couch and closed her eyes, trying to think of something for dinner, when her brother walked through the door, sweaty from playing football with his friends.

"Hey. How'd work go?" he asked.

She smiled and nodded by way of an answer.

"So I overheard one of the teachers talking today," Fenn began. "Her husband is getting back surgery, and she's allergic to pollen. Me and the guys were thinking of taking turns mowing her lawn until he gets better. You think it's okay to use our mower?"

Apart from cleaning instructions, Fallen felt like her head only held math these days. Her mind was fully occupied with deducting things from the paycheck that wasn't even due to be deposited into her account until next week. The thought of a bunch of teenagers throwing their mower into different trucks had her concerned. But Fenn had great impulses. She rested her head on the back of the sofa.

"You okay?"

"Just tired. Of course, use the mower. That's awesome of you to help them out." If it broke, it broke.

Fenn was mature for his age (nearly 17)—a product of growing up fast without reliable parents—and Fallen was downright old for hers (a recent 21). She had never known her father, and part of her wondered if her mother knew who he was either. Same for Fenn's dad.

Their mother, Nora, was an alcoholic. She'd been a largely functioning one when the kids were little—only forcing Fallen to fend for herself when she'd had way too much to drink. And for many years that hadn't been every night. Fallen still had memories of her mother reading to her and Fenn, tickling them before they fell asleep. But as Fallen reached her teen years, Nora had seemed to take her daughter's growth and expanding capability as carte blanche to let alcohol overwhelm her. Fallen still remembered when suddenly she'd spent a straight week picking her mother up from the couch, the bathroom floor, and once the bar two blocks over. It was then Fallen had realized she was the only real adult in the situation.

At fifteen.

She'd cried the whole night through, but in the morning, she was ready. She had taped the list of her new chores to the fridge:

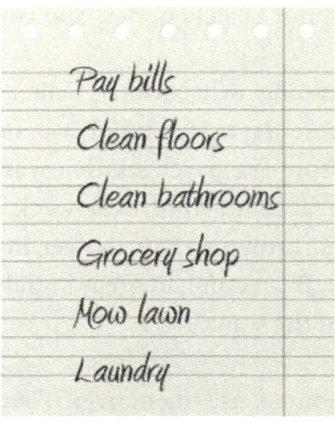

It was an overwhelming list. And she hadn't even put her personal chores on it.

When Fenn woke up, he'd read the list and pointed to the lawn and the bathrooms. "I can do those."

She'd patted him on the shoulder. They were in this together. So they'd worked around Nora's headaches, her bitchiness when the alcohol bled from her system. Fallen had driven her mother to work on more than one occasion without a driver's license.

These days Fallen did the bills after her brother went to bed. All the chores she'd lined up required cleaning supplies, and those had their own costs attached to them. That was the rub. Fortunately, a few years back Fallen had hit her mother up on a good day, at a good moment, and had talked her into getting an extra debit card. Now Fallen could pull money for groceries and the bills.

She'd always watched the balance carefully, and she'd noticed that on payday, as soon as her mother was done with work, she would extract hundreds from the account at an ATM.

So as a junior in high school, Fallen had begun leaving school grounds in the middle of the day to pull money before her mother could get the chance, hiding it in her locker.

That might have been the end of any semblance of responsibility for Nora, if she'd really thought about it at the time. Once her mother had figured out Fallen's trick, she'd yelled for hours, eventually crying about her need to have a drink to keep it together. Fallen had had to promise to create a budget for her mother's alcohol.

After that she drove Nora to the liquor store herself. Her mother would fill a box with wine, demanding the storeowner carry it to their car without even a thank you. Fallen hated thanking the man for bringing her mother's vice to the trunk, but it wasn't his fault, so she did it anyway. Fallen knew then that her mother would never offer hope or comfort to her or Fenn again as a parent. So she decided not to think of her as Mom. Her mom was gone. To protect her heart, Fallen tried to think of the woman as Nora after that.

She had gotten through high school that way—as the Band-Aid holding Nora, and her family, together. Before Fallen left for college, she'd coached Fenn on the finer points of the budget and keeping a tight watch on the bank card, and she'd lectured her mother on making sure she went to work.

And then the guilt marched in because she'd accepted a place at a school on the other side of the country, taken on loans and debt of her own because she wanted a life for herself. She'd left Fenn, knowing in her heart of hearts that he wasn't ready to be the adult yet. She had escaped. And she'd called home, sure, but she had disconnected emotionally from him. She had to.

Of course their mother had a way of convincing Fenn she was okay. She called him her angel. Nora took back the bank card, eventually. She lost the car, eventually, and then in the end, Nora left.

Fenn had finally called Fallen shortly before she was to start her third year of school and told her how desperate he was. She packed up, and when she got home after his phone call, she'd realized he'd been going hungry. He was embarrassed that he hadn't been able to keep tabs on their mother the way she had.

Fallen had tracked down her mother after talking with the bartender at Nora's favorite spot. It seemed Fritz was her new love, a fellow alcoholic, and the man she was now living with. Nora was still employed, but barely. The bartender said she'd told him just the other day that her hours at the call center had been cut, and she was taking unpaid leave for her frequent absences.

So now Fallen and Fenn were here, fighting to keep their heads above water—without any help from or hope for Nora, though that was to be expected by now. The mortgage on the old brick rambler with the failing roof was in arrears, but luckily they hadn't been asked to move out yet. Fallen dreaded every mail delivery and suspicious truck that drove by, wondering if this was the moment the bank would reclaim the house.

But damn it, she was determined to get Fenn through high school. And they would stay in this house until they were forced to leave. After that? Fallen's stomach dropped when she thought about it. After that she had no clue what she would do.

A few days later, Desta found Fallen in room 510 just after her lunch break. Though slightly out of breath, she immediately stepped to the other side of the bed Fallen was making and began to help. Fallen had wanted to kiss her for the kindness until the woman started in with her telltale cough. Amazingly, Desta was able to continue to tuck in corners while covering her mouth.

When she was finally able to catch her breath, she delivered her news: "Big boss is coming in a two weeks. Got to make sure everything is as good as can be."

Fallen nodded. Not quite two weeks in and she was barely getting the hang of this housekeeping thing, which was so much harder than she'd ever imagined. There were smudged windows, toilets that seemed to have been used by something other than humans, and random bloodstains on sheets she tried not to think too much about. All were difficult to clean. Her Payless Velcro sneakers were indeed getting the workout Desta had told her they would.

She'd been hired by Desta, and for a few days had thought the woman was in charge of everything. But now she knew that while Desta knew all the ins and outs of the building and staff, she didn't have a fancy title or office.

The manager in charge, Melanny, was a woman who seemed about the same age as Desta with the personality of a rock. She handled scheduling, and apparently also scowling. As a result, Fallen usually came in the back door of the hotel with her master key and avoided the lobby as often as she could. She used a workplace iPad to communicate with management and update the rooms she'd finished cleaning. Morning meetings were mandatory and used to update all housekeeping and maintenance staff and check their uniforms for infractions at the same time.

When Fallen met the housekeepers for floors 8 and 9, she got excited about the potential for friends closer to her own age. But when she introduced herself, instead of responding with their names, they'd just snickered.

After that, since Melanny called out issues to be addressed by floor, Fallen just dubbed them 8 and 9 in her head. She didn't need their names. Or their friendship.

"What does the big boss do here?" Fallen dug the TV remote out from the crack between the headboard and the mattress.

"Welp, he owns the place. So he sort of makes sure it's still standing. He'll meet with each of us and tour the floor. It's supposed to be a time to show him where there are repairs needed. But really, he's checking to make sure you're doing your job. If you see something that can be fixed with glue or a little paint before he gets here, let me know, and I'll show you where I keep that stuff." Desta grabbed a rag and started on the mirror above the dresser. "You're still doing room 514, right?"

Fallen was frankly a little sick of Desta being so specific about the always-empty room. "Yup. The ghost who lives there is real neat. Just moves the dust around."

Desta paled a bit, like Fallen mentioning a ghost was bad luck or something, before busting up with another round of coughing. She held on to the dresser for a second, so Fallen stepped closer, worried the woman was feeling dizzy.

She held up her hand. "No. I'm fine. I just need to actually get out there and suck on one of these. Eases the coughing." Desta pulled a package of cigarettes out of her pocket.

"I don't think it works that way. Good luck, though." Fallen waved at Desta as she left the room.

Actually, room 514 was Fallen's favorite; it was so easy. She was in and out in fifteen minutes. She dusted, made sure everything was still there, and once a week she freshened up the linens. As she thought about the impending visit from the owner, Fallen made a mental note to try the tap and shower to make sure everything was in order there as well.

She did room 512 next, the even side of the hallway being her path of choice before lunch.

A little while later she gathered her cleaning supplies and marked 512 down as clean and ready on the hotel iPad she had with her. Then she turned toward room 514, her last task before taking a break.

2

HALLUCINOGEN

Fallen opened her eyes slowly. The last thing she remembered was falling backward onto the bed in room 514. She'd been so tired all of a sudden. And now she looked up at twinkling stars and could hear a crackling fire nearby, along with murmurs and a little light laughter.

The air was crisp, and she sat up to find she was still wearing her maid's uniform, complete with her name tag, though her surroundings were entirely different. She pinched her arm. It hurt and left a red mark.

Fallen got up in a hurry when she felt a creepy crawly on the back of her thigh. She attacked her legs with her hands until she was sure whatever had been there was gone.

As she looked around at the trees, she felt panic rising. Had she been drugged and dragged into the woods somehow? Fallen let her eyes adjust to the dim light offered by the night sky. Then she carefully stepped through the woods to hide behind a tree. Her horrible work sneakers seemed to glow, and she cursed silently as she tried to stay camouflaged.

Her heart pounding, she waited like that for more minutes than her nerves were ready for. Finally, when nothing had pounced on her and no one came looking, the happy murmurs coming from the direction of the fire seemed the logical place to start poking around.

Fallen tiptoed through the night, drawing closer. Soon she could see tongues of flame dancing between the trees, promising warmth. Maybe her attackers were there, waiting for her to wake. Maybe heading toward them was the exact wrong thing to do. Still, she came to the edge of a clearing and peered around a large oak that towered over her like a canopy.

She got an eyeful, and then hid again while she tried to figure out what she'd just seen. She struggled to make it make sense. Fallen was pretty sure she saw nicely dressed couples toasting marshmallows and drinking wine. Digging her fingernails into the bark, she let the bite remind her she was actually awake. And then she looked again.

This time she watched a man turn on the radio in a car parked close by. An old song replaced the crickets and crackles of the fire as the background for the evening.

Fallen shook her head. This was so out of her realm of expectations, she wasn't sure how to classify it.

"Fallen!"

The sound of her name nearly made her pee her pants.

"You made it! Come on over."

Through the shadows, the tall man was silhouetted, except for his glistening white smile, a friendly smile. He waved her over like she was a stubborn child.

She stepped forward, because hiding when people knew she was there just seemed stupid. The man grabbed her hand and pulled her into the circle. The people there welcomed her by name. She did not recognize a single one of them. They weren't even vaguely familiar.

After a moment she accepted a glass of wine from the tall man. The couple closest to the car began to slow dance. The mood was far from captors at a kidnapping. It was more like friends celebrating the start of a weekend.

Fallen looked down at her uniform. She felt very out of place. She tried to catch bits of conversation, but it was as if she had water in her ears—everyone sounded just a little out of her range.

Maybe I'm on drugs?

That actually made the most sense. As she cleaned she'd somehow stepped on a drug needle or ingested a hallucinogen.

She sat on one of the logs that circled the fire. The flames had such vibrancy. They burned blue towards the middle, each one clearly defined.

One hell of a drug.

The man who'd handed her the wine came and sat next to her, and she could understand him when he addressed her directly.

"Is your drink not to your liking? I can get you something else." He touched the edge of her glass.

She shook her head no, responding as if she'd been invited to this party, not awakened in the woods like an alien ship had dropped her off.

"It's good. Just enjoying the atmosphere. Do you know how I got here?"

The tall man had an air of authority and deep brown eyes. He was older than she was. His hairline was receding a bit, but he wasn't unattractive. He wore jeans and a button-down shirt.

He narrowed his eyes. "Don't you remember? Do you feel okay?"

Fallen gave him a smile and a nod. She decided not to say any more, pretending to listen to the music while she sipped her wine instead.

The man stood and offered her his hand. He pulled her into his arms when she set her glass on the uneven ground and stood.

"So glad you made it." He directed her in a little twirl, following the music still drifting from the car radio.

She hummed by way of response. Her mind scrambled in her head. Nothing made sense. This dream, this crazy dream, was so real. Her sneakers shuffled through leaves as they danced.

Fallen held on to the man's shoulder and hand. He clearly had a plan for the song. She tried to get a better look at the people around them, but they seemed a bit out of focus. She couldn't figure out the color of the car.

When she looked over her dance partner's shoulder, just past the ring of the campfire, she saw another man, this one sharp and clearly focused. He looked as confused as she felt, and he locked his gaze with hers. She watched as he put his hands though his thick, dark hair, messing it up. He was distressed. She understood the feeling.

He blinked repeatedly and ran his hand down his face. He seemed to acclimate more quickly than she had, and soon he was looking at her again.

"Is this real?" *he mouthed.*

Fallen patted her dance partner on the shoulder. "Excuse me for a minute."

She didn't give a reason, but to her relief he merely nodded and stepped back to allow her to walk past him. He then turned to talk with a woman sitting on a log, and Fallen backed carefully into the woods to meet up with the man who seemed as stunned as she was.

She ducked under a low-hanging branch and moved some ivy out of the way. He waited between two trees. She looked around, but didn't see anyone else.

The sight of him was a visceral punch to her heart. His deep blue eyes and stunning face made her stumble a little. He was the kind of handsome that made a girl long for a mirror to check her makeup.

He stepped forward and held out his hand, but he didn't touch her. He was tall—even taller than the other man—and easily a head taller than she. His shoulders were broad under the plain white tee he wore over khaki pants held up with a canvas belt.

It was a uniform, like what she wore.

He spoke first. "Are you real?"

"Normally I'm very real," Fallen replied. "Not sure about the last thirty minutes or so." She stopped in front of him.

He put his hand on her upper arm, looking around at their surroundings. "Are you in danger?" He pulled her close, prepared to protect.

"I don't think so. Over there is a group of people dancing and drinking wine. The man you saw me dancing with—he knew my name." She rested her hand against his hard stomach.

He looked down at her. "God, your beautiful face is such a pleasure. May I touch it?"

Fallen nodded and swallowed. Maybe he was the bad guy after all.

He grazed her cheekbone with his knuckles, then used his fingertips to lift her chin. He looked at her face like she was a jewel in a case. The chill started at the base of her skull, trickled down her spine, and ran all the way to her toes.

"That's a face worth fighting for." He moved his hand away, setting it behind his back like a gentleman who didn't want to take too much.

He looked like a mix of Superman and an old-time movie star. Of the two men she'd encountered here—while she was either on a crazed drug trip or in a kidnapping scenario—the one in front of her made her feel safe.

"I'm scared because I don't remember how I got here, and all of those people seem to know me," she told him. "Do you know me?"

"No, sweetheart. And I don't know how I got here either." He pulled her behind him as the noise of a person approaching filtered through her confession. Superman went for his hip, like there should've been a gun there.

The man she'd danced with called out to Superman. "Thomas! You made it. You and Fallen want to join us?" The dancing man still had a welcoming smile.

Fallen went on her tiptoes and whispered. "See?"

Thomas turned his head a little and whispered back, "Fallen's your name?"

She nodded at his profile.

The dancing man stepped around Thomas, making a big show of pulling Fallen out from around him. "Little lady gets away from me all the time."

Fallen allowed the dancer to take her hand, but she gave Thomas a look that she hoped clearly conveyed that this was all complete bullshit. She could feel sweat from the man's hand on her palm. Thomas followed as the man pulled her back to the circle.

"Hey, Russ! Can you get Thomas a beer? He looks spooked." Dancing man waved at a log close to the fire and motioned for Thomas to sit.

"Incoming, Lad!"

Russ tossed the beer to the dancing man, who seemed to be named Lad, based on the way his head snapped up. But Superman Thomas was holding the beer before Lad could catch it. His reflexes were amazing.

She then noticed that Thomas' uniform had changed. He still wore a white T-shirt, but now he had on jeans and hiking boots, a plaid shirt tied around his waist. While she watched Thomas with her mouth hanging open, he looked her up and down with an equally shocked face, though he quickly recovered and thanked Russ by name with a little wave.

Fallen looked at her feet, and instead of her white Velcro sneakers, she found cute black flats with little red roses embroidered on them. Her dress was vintage, a tea-length black-and-white masterpiece with a soft, white sweater tied around her shoulders.

She felt the tears rush in then, making the roses as blurry as some of the voices around her. She turned and found her wine glass on the ground. She kept her back to the crowd as she lifted it and attempted to wipe away the physical manifestations of her fear. Her wine rippled as her hand shook. She couldn't make it stop.

Thomas' shadow appeared next to hers as he whispered, "Don't let them see you upset." Then in a louder voice he asked, "Can I ask Fallen for a dance, Lad?"

Fallen turned to face Thomas.

"Sure. But finders keepers, so don't get too attached," Lad called from the circle.

She looked up at Thomas, and he took her glass, setting it on a folding table near the car.

"You Send Me," another golden oldie, came on the radio, and Thomas pulled her into dance position.

She squeezed his hand as it held hers.

Thomas led her easily through the slow dance, nodding and smiling. "Is that right? Nice. That's great."

He pretended they were having a conversation, and he leaned down as if to hear her. Instead he spoke.

"Sweetheart, we're going to get out of here. Okay? Figure out what the hell is going on."

She nodded. At least he seemed to have a plan in place.

"Are you a good guy?" Her intuition was so sure of him, but she was completely confused, so she had to ask.

"I hope so."

His simple, seemingly honest answer soothed her. Lad had a predatory gaze that seemed to be judging her as she looked over at him. And why was he acting like they were together?

"Okay, I'm going to stop dancing with you and say I'm

heading out. If they let me go, you do the same in a few minutes. Head north. I'll be waiting. We'll figure this out together." He pulled her a little closer. He smelled amazing.

"Okay."

He seemed to know what he was doing, so she stepped away from him and let him go, even though watching him leave was nerve-wracking. Would he disappear just the way she'd appeared?

Lad smiled and waved when Thomas called to him. "See ya, buddy. Need one for the road?" He waved toward the cooler.

"Nope. All good. Thanks again." Thomas left the circle, and as soon as he was past the light of the fire, she lost sight of him.

It occurred to her, as the smile slid from Lad's face like skin from a snake, that she had no frigging clue which way was north.

She turned and tried again to see which way Thomas had gone. In an instant, Lad was there, tapping her shoulder and turning her around.

"Hello, pretty lady. Have I told you that you being here has made my night?"

She gave him a wary smile. No teeth.

She started to pretend-cough, inspired by Desta, and waved her hand in the direction of the fire. "The smoke's getting to me. I'm going to get a breath of fresh air."

"No." He said it like he was in charge of her well-being.

"Yes." Her reply to him was fast and sure.

He seemed to catch himself and forced a smile.

She lifted his hands off her shoulders. "I'll be right back." She added more coughing.

He tilted his head and gave her a very thorough glare. Maybe he was trying—and failing—to be sexy? Lad put his hands in the air like her leaving was a poor choice, but he made no move to stop her.

As she strode past him into the woods, he added fairly aggressively, "Don't go too far."

Fallen smiled, but she *was* going far. As far as she could get.

Moments later, someone grabbed her arm as she blindly pushed at branches. Fallen whirled as a hand came over her mouth. She turned to find Thomas waiting patiently for her wide eyes to register that it was him.

When she stilled, he put his finger to his lips, and she nodded. Thomas took his hand away from her mouth, and she immediately bit her lip.

He bent down and gestured until she understood that she was to get on his back. Once he held her, piggyback, he took off running. She clung to him, her skirts bunched up around her, and his strong back made it hard for her to concentrate.

Thomas moved through the trees, farther and faster, until finally he put her down. "You all right?"

His beautiful eyes searched her face as she nodded, smoothing her dress and looking back the way they had come.

He grabbed a limb from the ground and began sweeping, sending her in front of him. They finally reached a clearing where a spring rolled over some rocks.

"Why'd you do that?" She pointed to his Snow White-style cleaning.

"Covering our tracks, gorgeous. Thirsty?" He took to his knee and made a cup out of his hands, holding it up to her. She shook her head, and he nodded before taking a long sip.

Finished, he shook off his hands and sat on a rock. Fallen sat next to him.

"Why aren't I awake yet?" she asked. "This is the craziest dream. It's a dream, right?"

Thomas shrugged. "It's a very real-feeling dream." He twisted so he could stare unabashedly at her. "And dream girl, you have on far too many clothes for my usual dream preferences."

She blushed. She blushed and wanted to him kiss her. And maybe this was a fantasy, because that's exactly what he did. Well, he pressed his lips to her cheek and inhaled like she was a flower.

Fallen touched his face, running her fingertips down his jawline. "Almost time to shave."

He lifted a brow.

"Are you afraid we're being followed?" She scooted closer, and he put his arm around her.

"I'm always either chasing someone or being followed. I'm used to it. You have to take peace when it comes." He trailed his fingers down her arm. "Dream girl, can I have a real kiss?" Thomas leaned close to her shoulder. In this clearing, the moon had painted his hair with silver streaks.

"I'm not with that Lad guy," she began. "I don't have any idea why he was acting like we're a couple." She put her hands in her lap. "I like this dress. It's sweet. But how did I get it on?"

"Did you hear my question?" Thomas asked. "Or should I take this as a no?"

The kiss. "So you are one-hundred-percent sure it's a dream?" she asked.

"I'm eighty-five-percent sure. Because there's only one way out of where I am—either it's a dream, or it's heaven. And you look so much like an angel, it could certainly be heaven." He reached out and held her hand, bringing it to his lips. Goosebumps raised on her skin from his touch.

"I remember I fell asleep," she offered.

He picked up her other hand and gave it the same treatment. She shivered a little.

"Okay, Fallen. How about we just hang around until you wake up?" He put his hands behind him, propping himself on his elbows and looking at the sky. "These stars are off. Maybe... Who knows any more? Where I am now the constellations look far different than they did growing up in New York."

He looked back at her. "You're a sight for sore eyes. This beautiful hair, so long."

She clasped her hands together. "So it's a dream. I can do whatever I want?"

"Sure. I mean, it might've had a little nightmare in it with that Lad guy, but I think we're on our own now, dream girl." He tilted his head toward her.

Fallen stood up from the rock and shook out her dress. "So," she said, turning toward him. "When I saw you? When you looked at me? I felt like I'd been waiting to see you my whole life, that my soul was off center until you put your arms around me. I felt safe, and until then I hadn't even been sure what safe was. I never really knew it was an actual thing. But I can understand now why feeling safe makes people happy." She grinned at him. "Also, you are by far the sexiest man I've ever seen in my life. I'm so damn proud of my imagination for slapping you together."

And then Fallen, wearing her pretty dress, hitched up her skirt and climbed into his lap, placing her legs on either side of his. She put her hands around his neck and kissed the living hell out of him.

The kissing continued as they sunk to the ground, fall leaves crinkling until everything dissolved into blackness.

3

REALITY

Fallen opened her eyes and found a ceiling light instead of Thomas' face. Somewhere in her mind she registered that it looked a lot like a boob. Her disappointment was so great it almost had a taste. The end of her dream was something to mourn.

Somehow, she'd gone from cuddling against Thomas' chest in the woods to lying on the bed in room 514 where she'd fallen asleep in the hotel. As she sat up, she thought she saw a flash of white light, but when she tracked its source, it was just an antique mirror on the desk.

She longed for the comfort and companionship Thomas had offered—things she'd never really had and now felt desperate for. That had been the most vivid dream of her life. She stood and turned on the small light on the nightstand. She must have slept for hours. It was completely dark now.

In the dim room, Fallen smoothed the bedspread to remove the imprint her body had left on it. Her hand brushed over something rough and crinkly. A leaf. A random leaf... Just like the leaves she'd been lying in with Thomas as they'd kissed at the end of her dream.

She wandered into the bathroom, flicking on the light. Looking in the mirror, she plucked three more leaves from her ponytail. She hadn't even seen the mess on the bed before she'd collapsed on it. How could she have missed a pile of leaves? She wet her lips with her tongue and stared at her reflection in confusion as she tasted the wine from the dream there.

This was probably a whole heap of sleep deprivation that had finally short-circuited her exhausted brain. She opened the hotel room door and looked at her chart. Room 514.

The room no one ever stayed in.

She turned the overhead lights on and saw that the leaves she'd been pulling out of her hair had friends. A nice handful were scattered all over the normally pristine bedding.

"Must've been maintenance fixing something in the ceiling... or something," Fallen mumbled to herself.

As she cleaned off the bed, she felt the excitement Thomas had caused draining from her system. It had all felt so real. She hadn't realized how flat and two-dimensional her usual dreams were until experiencing this one.

It was crazy how hard she'd slept. She pulled out her cell phone to look at the time—almost 6 pm. That was pretty much all she did with the device, as she had a fairly measly allotment of prepaid minutes—no data, no internet, nothing smart about this phone. Her brother had one as well, and they used them just to keep up with each other and for emergencies. He was really good about texting to let her know where he was. Better than she was, evidently. Hopefully she hadn't worried him. She'd had to stay late in the past to get the rooms right, so she crossed her fingers that he'd just assumed messy rooms were keeping her. She sent him a quick note to say she would be on her way shortly.

Fallen shook her head at the empty room and turned to go, making sure to pull the door all the way closed behind her—sometimes it stuck. Clearly she had too much on her mind. The bills and her concerns for Fenn were all she'd thought about, until that dream, since she'd come home from school.

As she stole back downstairs, the hotel was a ghost town. Dinner hour was a great time to sneak out of the place without talking to anyone. After logging out for the night in the empty maintenance closet, Fallen walked home, pulling her jacket tight against the cold and the dark, which came earlier every day now. Two miles had never seemed so long.

With each step, Fallen missed Thomas. She practically grieved his loss, which was ridiculous. And though the dream had been incredibly real, now that she was awake and experiencing no adverse effects, her worries about being drugged seemed silly—just another part of the very vivid dream. Sleep deprivation and an available bed had ganged up to remind her of all the things her life lacked. Namely, any sort of real living. Fallen sighed and shoved her hands deeper into her pockets.

When she got home, she opened the door, but the warmth she'd been looking forward to was absent. Instead she found her brother on the sofa, all wrapped up in a blanket and wearing his winter jacket. His shadow vibrated slightly with his shiver in the candlelight.

"I made an electric payment to the guy on the doorstep right after I got back. What the hell?"

Fenn shook his head. "They came by again. Said there were insufficient funds in the account they draw from."

Fallen pulled her phone from her pocket, closing the door behind her for security, not to keep any kind of heat inside. She plugged in the numbers and listened to an automated voice tell her the bank account was in the negative by one hundred dollars.

Before she could even wonder how to get it fixed, there was a knock on the door behind her.

When she opened it, Nora—who she hadn't seen and had

barely spoken to in weeks—stumbled in, along with a wave of alcohol fumes.

Fallen's stomach dropped. Before she could stop herself, the little girl in her thrilled at seeing her mother's face. The way the woman's eyebrows curved and the familiar scent of alcohol represented the Nora-managed childhood for Fallen. But the part of her that was freezing cold? The part of her that hated having her brother wear a coat inside the house? That part was angry. That part had no time to deal with an alcoholic mother right now.

There was a slight slur to Nora's words. In someone else this would be a hint that she'd had a few too many glasses of wine. For Nora, it meant she'd had a few *bottles* too many.

There was no *"Hello."*

No *"How are you?"*

No *"Why is it so damn cold in here?"*

Instead her mother said, "So you're making a paycheck? How regular is that?" She used the coatrack like a handrail in a subway car to keep herself steady.

And after that Fallen knew she wasn't talking to Nora; she was talking to Addiction—the disease that had taken her mother's self-control, that had taken her mother from her kids.

Fallen hated Addiction. She closed her mouth, which must have fallen open at the shock of seeing Nora, and let her tense jaw keep it shut.

Fenn bridged the space between them, embracing his mother like the open soul he was.

Nora used one arm to hug him. The other white-knuckled the coatrack with the effort of keeping herself upright. "Your sister's got a new job, angel?"

Fenn came away smiling, not faulting Nora for being only half able to commit to the hug.

"Yeah. Downtown at the—"

Fallen held up her hand to stop him. "No. Don't tell her. Not when she's like this."

And then Fallen was the bad guy. Her brother listened to her correction, nodding, but Addiction was immediately on her. Her rebuke was blood in the water for a hungry shark.

"Don't be like that, little girl. All I want to know is where you work. And what your pay schedule is. Don't have to be all high and mighty." Addiction looked back, using Nora's eyes as laser beams into Fallen's guilt.

It might have worked a few years ago. But being the adult had made Fallen realize Addiction was a manipulator—a living being that sought to bring down Nora and everyone who loved her, a devil in her mother's clothing. It was unsettling, but Fallen held her chin high and stared hard at it.

Nora now needed another hand to steady herself on the tilt-a-whirl Addiction had created for her. As she reached for the wall, she dropped a plastic card, which fell to the ground.

And then it clicked. Her mother still had the bank card Fallen had left for Fenn, and Fallen had never even thought to change the PIN. Addiction had stolen her money out of the bank account and turned it into alcohol before the electric company had been able to get there.

Fallen bent and picked it up off the floor, tucking it into the pocket of her jacket. She knew she should rage. She should fight, or at least yell until her throat was hoarse. But that was pointless. Instead she would change the PIN number that accessed the bank account tomorrow. Because even if she had the card back now, Addiction was clever when it was craving.

Nora's grasp on the coatrack faltered, and Fallen caught her before she hit the floor.

Fenn came quickly to help, and together they pulled her to the couch. Once she'd blacked out, Nora's face lost Addiction's cruel animation. Fallen brought blankets to tuck around her mother, making sure she was propped on her side so she didn't choke on her vomit. And she placed the bucket she kept under the sink close by for just that purpose. The ritual came back to her as if she'd never stopped doing it.

Fallen promised Fenn their mother would be fine, and she shooed him upstairs with a sandwich to do his homework. She hoped his room's small window would mean fewer cold drafts. Fallen sat on the edge of the couch, by her mother's feet, and spoke quietly to the electric company's call department.

Maybe it was the desolation she felt, thinking of how it would be days before her next paycheck, but she told the representative exactly the truth: Her mother had stolen her money to drink, and was currently piss drunk on her couch.

The electric company was surprisingly willing to work with a payment plan, agreeing to stop by to turn on the electric in the morning.

Fallen hung up the phone and felt her feet aching. Tomorrow would not be a pleasant day at work. Especially since tonight she would stay awake, making sure her mother didn't choke and her brother was warm.

She touched her lips. Thomas' kisses seemed even more like a dream now. The feelings he'd awakened in her were about as far from her current concerns as it was possible to get.

Her mother's face was hollow in the morning. When Fallen was younger, Nora had always woken up apologetic after a bender. But this wasn't a bender any more. It was a way of life.

Fallen greeted the electric company man at the door, bright

and early. Nora stumbled around behind her, trying to navigate the house.

When the lights came on, Fallen waved her thanks out the window and blew out the remains of the two candles that had helped her navigate the stairs last night. The heat kicked on, but it would be a while before the old place felt warm again.

Though she had to be more sober now, Nora and her addiction seemed to be still thinking about the same thing as they had been last night. She started in right away on Fallen's paycheck.

Fallen ignored her mother, but the woman followed her into the bathroom as she fixed her hair in the mirror. Her long, brown required ponytail had stray tendrils sticking out. She used water to smooth it all into submission.

"So it's how much an hour?" Nora sat on the closed lid of the toilet.

Fallen continued to ignore her and looked for her toothbrush. As she grabbed it she mentally added toothpaste to the always-growing list of things she and Fenn needed. Her mother rambled on about work at the call center and how she was picking up hours whenever she could, coming back with a new angle to try to find out how much Fallen made and when the money was deposited. Adding this information to what the bartender had told her just after she got home, Fallen concluded that Nora's full-time spot was gone. Now she was just filling in as a sub for people who were ill or had vacation.

Fallen used the scissors she cut Fenn's hair with to cut open the toothpaste tube. There was easily enough inside to get them through a few more days.

It hit her that she tossed out tiny tubes of toothpaste all day long while cleaning the hotel. She needed to keep them instead. That would be a good resource.

Then, suddenly, the thought of the debt to the electric company, the money her mother had simply erased, made her sick to her stomach. The budget was so, so tight already.

"So, I mean, if we could just get a system going here—you slide me a little—I can get back on my feet. I'll help out here once I get more hours."

Fallen finally turned to her mother and looked her up and down. "Your children were cold last night because you stole our money."

Nora looked at her feet for what she must have deemed a respectful amount of time for that transgression before starting another line of questioning that had the same transparent goal.

"Did you see my bank card anywhere? I had it last night."

Fallen knew she was wasting her time. She left Nora on the toilet and went upstairs to wake Fenn for school.

She entered his room and murmured the bad news that it was time to wake, as his alarm would go off soon, but also added the good news that it was Friday. He nodded with his sleepy eyes closed. She liked to think waking up to a friendly voice was a nicer start to the day than the alarm on his cell phone. She couldn't give him luxuries, but now that she was here, she could put some thought into small things for him. Once she was sure he would continue to get out of bed, she left and closed the door. Nora leaned against the wall in the hallway, arms crossed as she watched her.

"You're his mother now?"

Maybe if Fallen had gotten some sleep, she could have had more compassion for Nora. Or maybe not. Maybe she was just finished.

"Fenn doesn't have a mother, Nora. He has a sister. Now please get out." She pointed to the stairs.

Nora's eyes went wide before she blinked back tears. "Fallen Billow! How dare you?"

Fallen came back at her, standing nose to nose as the fire of her anger drove her next words. "We were cold. You *drank* our money. How dare you? How dare you come in here and ask me what my paycheck is? Do we have to starve? Do we have to have nothing to make you happy? Drink the whole world, Nora. I don't care. But don't you steal from us again. You're on your own. You need wine so bad? Steal from strangers or from Fritz. He's already letting you live with him, right? What did you do to lose your full-time spot, anyway?" Fallen's hands shook as she put them in fists by her sides.

Nora looked torn, like she wanted to be angry too, but knew she had no ground to stand on.

Fenn's door opening broke the tension.

"Everything okay?" he asked.

Fallen wondered if it was like this for all children of alcoholic parents, if the burning desire to make everything seem okay fueled all their decisions.

Until today, Fallen had never yelled. So many times she had placated her mom just to smooth things over.

But today she could see the future clearly. If Nora got her way, she and Fenn would have nothing. Addiction took what it felt it was due, no matter how many people it needed to feed it. She wasn't willing to let it have Fenn.

"Great. You ready? I left the toothpaste on the counter for you. Your lunch is downstairs in the kitchen. I'm walking Nora out."

Nora went to Fenn and hugged him. No doubt she believed him to be the easier mark. He hadn't gotten angry—yet.

He smiled and seemed happy she was coherent.

As soon as he disappeared into the bathroom, Fallen grabbed Nora by the arm and manhandled her down the stairs and out the front door.

As she closed the door behind them, she pointed at the front steps and issued her ultimatum. "You won't come back here again. If we need you, we'll find you."

"You can't kick me out of my own house." Nora pulled her thin jacket closer.

"It's the bank's house. Not yours. Not mine. I'm trying my best to make sure Fenn has a place to live. Have some shame."

Mrs. Moji from next door opened her front door, looking over at the commotion. Nora waved, plastering a Stepford wife look on her face. "Good morning Betty!"

Mrs. Moji waved back, but her face looked stricken.

Fallen repeated her statement at the same volume. "Have some shame."

Nora looked over her shoulders, as if trying to spot any other neighbors who could listen in.

"Find a rehab that I don't have to pay for. Get in it. Get sober. I'll find you after that. Best of luck, Nora."

"But I lost my key! And I don't have my bank card." Nora tossed up her hands.

Fallen walked down the three steps to the sidewalk and made sure her mother was looking her in the eye before she spoke. "And you don't have kids any more either."

A little while later Fallen stood in the kitchen composing herself when Fenn walked in, his hair still wet from the shower.

"Mom's gone?"

Fallen had a lot of answers to that question. She turned and looked at her brother. She saw more knowing in his eyes than she gave him credit for.

She always tried to cushion the blows for him, but the way he nodded slowly without her having to say a word told her he understood the situation just fine. She cringed again, thinking how terrible it had been for him while she was away at school.

"Until she stops drinking so much, she is," Fallen finally said.

"We can't have her here. We can't support her. And I don't know if she can stop drinking."

Honesty shouldn't have hurt to hear out loud. But it did. Fenn whistled softly. Instead of being crushed under the reality of the situation, he held his arms open for a hug. Fallen waited for a second before stepping into his embrace. Fenn patted her back.

"It's going to be okay, Fallen. We've got each other."

She nodded into his chest. Her brother was strong, and she allowed herself to feel a moment of pride in his upbringing.

4

BEST OF HER LIFE

Every day she went to work, which most weeks was every day but Sunday, Fallen spent any extra time she could find in her assigned rooms, trying to fall asleep. Of course she also slept at night, at home, but she couldn't make her brain manifest Thomas again. If she dreamed at all, it was run of the mill stuff—falling off a cliff, arriving naked at the high school she no longer attended—no Thomas, no Lad, no hyper-real sensations.

While awake, she thought of Thomas more often than she should, particularly since he was a guy who didn't exist. Fallen wondered about his strong shoulders and deep voice. She kept trying to find things that matched the bright white in his teeth. His kisses had been the best of her life. The sparkle in his eyes when he laughed ran over and over in her mind, yet recreating the realism of her stunning dream world was impossible.

She had no real explanation for this, but she needed one, so she chalked up her inability to dream so deeply again to her drive and focus on the job she had to do. The money from this place was her only hope of keeping everything together for Fenn. That one dream had been a fluke.

Getting back and forth to the hotel, completing her work, and then maintaining the house and juggling the bills took all of her energy. She didn't have any socializing to worry about because her friends from college lived in their own bubble, and she was on the outside of it now, not to mention thousands of miles away. Her remaining friends from high school were off at college as well. She couldn't afford to use her phone minutes on them or the guy she'd been sort of dating when she left school anyway.

It was better to let the life she'd briefly inflated for herself wither up and die like the fiction it was.

Today, a full week since her dream, she was finishing her shift with room 514. She'd saved it as a treat for herself because it was so easy, and perhaps because something wonderful would happen there again. As she puttered around, dusting, she mulled over the hotel employees' excitement because the owner would be dropping by in a week. Every square inch of the place was being shined up, and her requests for maintenance were suddenly handled quickly.

In their morning meeting, Desta had told her the lobby would be part of her cleaning routine for the duration of this week and all of next. Everyone had been assigned a portion of the hotel's entrance to detail. Fallen was in charge of a batch of plants and the front doors, which were always getting smudged by people's hands.

This meant she would be even later getting home. She'd have to try to prepare meals in the morning, or have things on hand that Fenn could make easily on his own.

So far Nora had stayed away, which Fallen was thankful for, though she didn't think it would last. Addiction would be back. Fallen had changed the pin number on the bank account, and she kept her mother's bank card in her wallet.

She sat on the bed as she started to think about the options for Fenn and college. Maybe he could get loans, like she had, or even a scholarship. His grades were okay—not great, though. Fallen turned and saw that one of the pillows needed to be fluffed, so she stretched out on the bed to run her hand across it. Fenn might need to do some after-school activities to beef up his college applications, she thought as she closed her eyes. Actually, it was like someone closed them for her.

When Fallen came to, she was on the ground by the trees that bordered the field where she'd kissed Thomas the last time she saw him. Her heart began to race.

She sat up, hugging her chest as she looked around. It was night, and this dream was definitely in high definition. She heard the crickets and saw fireflies dipping low in their waltz celebrating the evening. After slapping at a sting on her hand, she realized a mosquito had bitten her.

So real.

She stood and looked around. There was no sign of Thomas, but she listened for a crackling fire, scanning her surroundings for the telltale glow. There was none.

Sighing, she'd just resigned herself to being alone in this dream when, from behind her, he spoke.

"Dream girl."

She whirled around, gasping. He hushed her and pulled her close.

"It's you!" she whispered, tossing her arms around his neck.

He hugged her back, lifting her off the ground. "It's you," he murmured in her ear.

"I didn't think I'd see you again," she said. "I tried and tried." She ran her fingers down his face, and he smiled, kissing them as they passed close to his mouth.

He was so handsome. His deep blue eyes were electric, with flecks of lighter blue embedded in them. His jaw could cut a box open, and he smelled perfect—a mix of fabric softener and musky cologne.

He wore his uniform again: white T-shirt, pants with a

canvas belt, and boots. She ran her hands down his chest, enjoying her ability to touch wherever she wanted.

He watched her do this before stepping forward, tossing her off balance with a kiss. She responded eagerly, trusting him to carry her as she lost her footing. He laid her on the ground smoothly, propping up at her side.

"It's like you've been choreographing that move for a week," she teased.

"I have," he responded with a smile and a self-deprecating wince.

"Well done, then."

Now he explored her without inhibition. With one hand he outlined her shape—first her cheek, then her lips before tracing down her neck, breast, and stomach. He circled her knee with his index finger before dragging it up her outer thigh.

"So soft." He spoke to himself. "So pretty."

Her cheeks felt hot.

"See? Now that's the part I think I would forget to do in my head—make you blush."

"You think you're making me up in your head?" Fallen felt as real as the stick jabbing her in the lower back. She yanked it out and watched Thomas toss it aside.

He nodded. "Could you take your hair down? I'd love to see what that's like again."

Fallen sat up and pulled at her hair tie. Thomas plucked leaves from her hair before rubbing her lower back.

She groaned. Her back was always sore by the last room of the day. She fluffed her hair, letting it cover her shoulders like a cape.

Thomas sat up then, touching her hair and pulling it forward. Then he gathered a handful and sniffed it, which made her laugh.

"What?" He dropped her hair and straddled her legs.

"You're sniffing my hair. It's cute."

"Cute? I'm a strong, manly guy. Nothing about me is cute." He made his best scary face and flexed.

She knew it was a joke, but she admired his arms anyway. "Strong. Love that right there." She touched his forearm.

"You know how to make a guy feel like he hung the moon, Miss Fallen." He leaned forward and nuzzled her neck.

It was wonderful to flirt, to be touched, to feel her concerns float away. She leaned into his lips and ran her fingers up his back before dragging her nails gently down.

He looked in her eyes, and she saw lust change their color a bit.

And then his demeanor changed as well. He pulled her hard against him, cuddling her in.

"Quiet," he whispered in her ear.

She did as she was told; from her peripheral vision she could see that his jaw was tense.

Fallen listened and soon heard cracking branches as someone's footfalls disturbed the sounds of nature in the night. They stayed huddled and quiet, her cheek pressed against his neck. She could feel his pulse race and finally slow as the footsteps disappeared.

When he seemed sure they were safe, he disentangled from her and stood, holding out his hand to pull her up. She wished she had makeup on and a nice outfit. It would be lovely to be dressed up for him. Her uniform had no place on a date.

As Thomas grabbed her hand and pulled her into the meadow, she pictured possible outfits for a second date. Maybe a dress with a sweater? Heels that buckled around her ankles? She'd leave her hair down and just do light makeup, fresh perfume, and matching underthings.

Fallen was thrilled as she looked down and saw the exact dress she had hoped for.

"Look!"

Thomas turned quickly, scanning everywhere but her body

as if waiting for danger, or running from the cops. She had to point to herself before he seemed to realize she was wearing something new.

"Well, that's a nifty dress." He brought her close and hugged her, tugging off her sweater to feel her shoulders. "So soft."

"You said that already."

"I mean it. There's nothing like your skin. It's satin and clouds and sin, and I want to kiss all of it."

He began to do just that, working from her neck to her chest to her shoulders.

"I hear water," she said after a moment, interrupting his delicious progress. It was clearly the sound of moving water in the distance.

"Huh... I wonder..." He pulled her along behind him and they worked their way through some trees before he started really moving.

"Wait!" Fallen worried she'd stumble, trying to keep up with his long legs.

He simply turned and tossed her over his shoulder like he moved people for a living. She shouted and started to laugh. He slapped her bottom playfully and then caressed it the way she would only let him do in a dream.

He set her down soon after. "Look! I'll be damned. I was just thinking about how I wanted to take you here, kiss you here. I love this place."

She stepped away from him and had a peek. The stunning, bright moon put a light blue tint over everything, and they stood at the edge of a cliff. Far below was a river, with a rocky shore edging it.

"So amazing. Tell me about it. Why here?" She turned back to him, always wanting his warm skin under her palms. She lifted the back of his T-shirt out of his pants and put her hand on his lower back.

He pulled her over to a rock and sat, gathering her on his

lap. She put her head on his shoulder and listened to his deep voice rumbling as he began his story.

"Well, first thing you should know is I love the hell out of my brothers. The trouble John and Eddie can talk me in to is without equal. And that's how we all ended up right there…" He pointed to the high outcropping of rocks. "…in our underwear. This place is called High Falls."

"Who's the oldest?"

"Eddie. Then me, then John. He's the tallest and the baby of the family."

"Taller than you?" Thomas was a tall guy.

"Six foot five, and every inch of it trouble."

Fallen liked how Thomas' eyebrows moved as he talked about his brothers.

"Tell me about the last time you were here," she encouraged.

"I told them, 'You dumbasses, this is how we die. Like a bunch of nosebleeds in our drawers.' Eddie pretended to push John off the edge.

"Then I said, 'Think of Ma. She'll have to bury all three of us.'

"Of course John said, 'Swell. Drag us all down, Tommy, with talk of a sad Ma. Just man up and get over here and throw yourself into the water.'

"They knew I would do it. Anything my brothers asked. So I inched out next to Eddie.

"Then John said, 'We go together.' Which is our motto, you know?"

Thomas looked at Fallen, and she nodded.

"It's a good thirty feet up," he continued. "And I'm afraid of heights. There was a handful of bathing-suit-wearing honeys sunning on that rock over there."

He stood, setting Fallen on her feet and holding her close as he pointed it out.

"I prayed I wouldn't accidently scream like a girl. And then we counted down from ten. 'three…two…one!'" Thomas acted out the jump, letting Fallen stand a little ways away to watch. "And together we jumped.

"After that the honeys on the rock spent the rest of the day razzing us, because we'd all screamed like schoolgirls with spiders on our heads the whole way down."

Fallen laughed at his description, and his smile widened as he took in the water and cliff.

"I got that memory right here—my brothers laughing their fool heads off as we all flailed in midair. God, we have so much fun together."

She moved closer to him, drawn in. "Honeys, though? I'm jealous."

"Don't pout, dream girl. You're everything I've ever wanted and more."

Fallen hugged him. "I feel the same way about you. Can you please come with me back to real life? I could really use a lot more of you in my everyday."

"I'd love to." He was kissing her again. She hardly noticed that he was backing her closer to the edge of the cliff because his tongue was telling her a lot about what she hoped he had in store for her.

He took a step back. "So what do you say?" He had a devilish glint in his eye.

She looked over her shoulder and screamed at the river below. She had a bout of vertigo and grabbed on to him.

"I've got you. No worries." His voice was hardwired to her heartbeat.

"Mmmmm. What do I say about what?" She tried to force him to spin her away from the edge, but his grip was like stone.

"Do you want to jump with me?"

"No." Her answer was out of her mouth before she could even process the question.

He laughed. "Come on, dream girl. We're not in the real world, right?"

"It feels real," she hedged. "How about we just kiss a lot instead?"

She offered her lips, and he sampled her for a few minutes before chiding her again.

"You scared, Fallen?"

"I'm fine. It's a dream. Right?"

Thomas pulled them both away from the edge and removed his shirt, boots, and socks.

"You strip quick," she observed.

"Where I am when I'm awake, I have to be quick." He stepped back to the edge after putting his clothes on a rock.

"What the hell? Why not?" Fallen pulled her sweater and dress off before unbuckling her shoes.

By the time she wore just her underwear, Thomas was biting his thumb, watching her.

"Beautiful. You are a beauty." He held out his hand.

His chest was sheer strength. She stepped over to him, feeling a shot of fear up her spine.

"You ready?"

"No."

"On three? One..." He stepped closer, and she inched out as well.

"Don't look down," he suggested.

She ignored him and tried to back up.

"It's not that bad, I promise. I've done it before."

She stepped forward again when he said *two*.

And on three, she jumped with him.

They held hands to start, but she let go to hold her nose soon after her feet left the cliff. He screamed, but the dropping sensation filled her with panic that took her breath, so she was silent.

They hit the water, and it was so brisk she froze for a second, forgetting to swim. He was all over her, pulling her up with him, and eventually she remembered how to move, kicking until they broke the surface in the moonlight.

She slapped his shoulders as he tipped his head back to laugh.

"Are you crazy? That was terrifying. We're never doing that again. Holy crap." She tried to swim away, but his arms encircled her.

"I'm sorry. Really. I forgot how horrible it was until we were halfway down."

They treaded water until she finally smiled.

"It's freezing in here."

"Let's go over there." He pointed at a large, dry boulder a short swim away. Fallen breaststroked over as he swam past her in a clean freestyle. He pulled himself out of the water and waited as she arrived, his big hands held out for her.

She put her arms up, and he drew her straight out. His strength was a ridiculous turn on, though she knew she shouldn't be such a cavewoman with her carnal desires. But it was just a dream, right? Decorum be damned.

He pulled her against him, and she wrapped her arms around his neck, trying to glean some warmth from his cold skin.

"Have you ever been chilly in a dream?" she asked.

"No. Never."

"Me neither. This is bizarre. Let's lie in the nice hot sun and warm up. Oh wait. We can't. It's night." She put her hand against his wet face. He had a bit of stubble. He was so real.

In an instant, she was blinded by clear, white light. He hauled her in closer. The next time she opened her eyes, it was easier. The sun.

"It's daytime now," he said, sort of as a question, as they both squinted.

Fallen closed her eyes and thought about sunglasses for them both, and plump towels folded at their feet. When she opened her eyes, they were shaded, and she saw herself reflected in his aviators.

"Great idea." He tapped the glasses with his finger.

She bent down and returned with towels, handing him one and wrapping the other around herself.

He grabbed her hand and helped her up onto the rocks. She shivered as she went from one temperature to another. The daytime they'd somehow conjured was hot. She took back his towel and laid it out on a flat boulder jutting over the river. Then she untucked her towel from around her breasts and laid it next to his.

Fallen looked down at her damp bra and panties. They left very little to the imagination. She shrugged, feeling comfortable and excited, and then settled onto her back, wriggling in the warm sunshine.

He stood for a moment, watching, before joining her on the towels.

"So is this where the honeys were in your memory?" she asked.

"I think they were down river. Actually, I barely remember where we were. 'Cause now, this whole place has you in it, and nothing else matters." He propped up on his elbow and slid his sunglasses to the top of his head.

"Tell me a memory of yours. Make it seem like you're real, too." Thomas put his big hand on her bare stomach, and for a few seconds his touch was all she could comprehend.

He was being patient, and a gentleman, considering all she wasn't wearing. She looked at his face and found his eyes obeying an entirely different call of duty. They skimmed her body like she was art on a wall.

Covering his hand with hers, she sighed. "I'm having so much fun with you. My memories might ruin the mood."

His face fell, eyes ending their sexual journey and fixing on her face. "No, that's not good. Tell me, dream girl. Just give me something."

She told him her dark secret.

"My mom's an alcoholic. And I'm working so my brother can finish high school, maybe go to college."

It was hard to put into words, this thing that infused her entire life but was so easily avoided in polite conversation.

"That's who I am. My memories are mostly of that—except for when I was really young. Back then, she was at least able to pretend." Fallen avoided his eyes.

"I'm sorry." He squeezed her hand. "Good on you for helping your brother."

"He's a great guy. Deserves better than he gets. I mean, the electricity was shut off last week. My mother took all the money out of our bank account." Fallen shook her head. "I don't want to think about that. Here with you I don't have to worry about that, right?" She turned on her side, letting the sun heat up her hip and back.

He scootched closer, spooning her with an impressive erection. "You get to think about only what you like. I get to do the same."

He put his arms around her, and she used his bicep as a pillow. He pushed her wet hair out of the way, whispering about her beauty against the nape of her neck. His other hand began reaching lower, and she was ready to let passion dissolve the memories of her mother's vice now tainting her dream world.

Then her eyelids became heavy, and she closed them.

In the next second she was on the bed in room 514, shocked back into the real world. Her skin was still alive with his touch, her heart full of anticipation, but he was gone.

A flash of light in the antique mirror again caught her eye as she sat up and punched the mattress.

Her dream had been as real as this very moment. She wanted him back. She wanted Thomas.

5

DOUBLE MIRACLE

Fortunately, with practice, after a few weeks Fallen's cleaning skills had improved somewhat, and she had a spare moment to breathe here and there. Unfortunately, the maids from 8 and 9 were still mostly ignoring her—and teasing her when they didn't. She mostly ignored them right back.

But another pattern of disappointment had developed for Fallen: Every day in 514, she would lay down and try to fall asleep. She tried at all different times of the day. Nothing. She was so frustrated by the following Tuesday, she was ready to give up the whole thing. Thomas had just been a dream, she told herself. A twice-in-a-lifetime miracle.

But the heartache was worse now that she'd been with him twice. She craved him. If it was all happening in her head, she should be able to force him into any of her unconscious moments. She tried her hardest at home, when she wasn't on the clock. However, her slipping off to bed earlier and earlier had finally caught Fenn's attention.

He was still doing homework at the kitchen table when she

faked a yawn and headed up to bed before eight, reminding him to turn of the lights on his way to bed.

"Seriously? Are you getting ready for your AARP membership to arrive in the mail? You have the schedule of a toddler. " Fenn gave her a slightly worried look.

She put him off by saying she thought she was getting a cold, but this wasn't a sustainable pattern. She either needed to find Thomas again in her dreams or give up and move on.

Back at work on Wednesday, the shining up of the hotel for the owner had reached a fevered pitch with only one day to go. Every employee could be found cleaning something. Everyone had a rag in their pocket, ready to eradicate fingerprints or stains at a moment's notice.

Desta's coughing had ramped up as well. She'd waved off Fallen's offers to take a few rooms off her plate, so Fallen had taken to coming up with invented questions so she could at least take over some bed-making and mirror-cleaning here and there while she asked.

"I know what you're doing," the older woman pointed out at the end of the day.

"I'm glad someone does, because I feel like that's not my forté." Fallen followed Desta out the back door and through the parking lot, inadvertently walking her to her car.

"Tomorrow's the big day." Desta unlocked her big, old, smoky—but clean—car.

"I know. It's as exciting as Christmas." She bounced a little as Desta lit a cigarette.

"Just play it cool." Desta nodded at her. "Don't admit to anything out of sorts."

"Like what?" Fallen tilted her head to one side, not quite sure what Desta meant.

"Nothing. Nothing." Desta looked like she wished she hadn't spoken as she ducked into her car.

"See you tomorrow," Fallen called.

Desta barely waved as she sped away.

Fallen's mind replayed the conversation as she walked home, curious if she was reading too much into the woman's words. Desta couldn't possibly know about her dreams, right?

It felt like mere minutes before Fallen was taking the reverse route back to work the next morning, even though she had done laundry, cleaned the kitchen, and vacuumed, not to mention slept a little, in the interim. Fenn had talked about a girl named Jessica he had his eye on while he cooked mac and cheese for dinner, and it had been good. They'd both packed leftovers as their lunch today, and Fallen had encouraged him to be bold as she'd headed off to work.

She crossed the parking lot and passed Desta's old beast, shocked to find the woman already at work. Fallen had taken a bit more care with her uniform, pressing creases in her sleeves and French braiding her hair neatly, so perhaps time had gotten away from her a little.

She walked into the team meeting already in progress in the maintenance office. Desta made wide eyes at her entrance, the expression magnified by her glasses. Fallen tucked herself sheepishly behind the crowd as Melanny ran through the last-minute checklist.

After a rousing speech that ended with "And if you screw up, you're fired," they were released to start their duties.

Another day of relentless cleaning began. Fallen didn't dare find Desta for a chat, never knowing when the owner would arrive. Desta was equally serious. Despite her usual need for a nicotine fix, she'd told Fallen she wouldn't be taking any breaks outside.

Fallen got updates from 8 and 9 as she passed them in the hall, the elevator, and the laundry. They seemed to think it was fun to watch her squirm as they gave a moment-by-moment countdown, as if the arrival of the owner was a shuttle launch. Other workers shared information with each other that Fallen overheard: Mr. Orbit was late. It would be a while. There was traffic. Maybe tomorrow. Possibly this afternoon.

Fallen had heartburn from thinking about it. This job kept Fenn (mostly) warm and fed. She needed it to work out for her. The fanatical Mr. Orbit needed to be pleased with her floor.

She pushed herself to stay focused and keep working, but room 512 almost made her cry. The guests must have been celebrating a birthday. In addition to the used condoms everywhere —even on the lampshades—all the mirrors were decorated with lipstick porno drawings and birthday greetings to a "Paul." Lipstick was such a bitch to clean.

Fallen cursed Paul under her breath, the room taking a full two hours to get back to rentable condition. At least 514, easy and quick, was her last stop, like usual. She barreled her cart down the hall, still hoping to finish before Mr. Orbit's impending arrival. Though she could hardly bear the pain of not seeing Thomas, she had no time to try her hand at a nap now. Her iPad sounded a chime, and when she looked, sure enough an alert from her manager told her Mr. Orbit was in the building. Melanny had also reiterated her all-call to be on point yet again.

Taking a deep breath and trying to calm herself, Fallen grabbed her duster as she spotted a cobweb near the overhead light next to the bed. As she reached up, she felt her world tilt. She landed safely on the bed, and even as she fought it, her eyes closed like an automated lock, sending her into blackness at the worst possible time.

She woke on the rock where Thomas had held her in the sun last time she was here, but stars twinkled in the night sky above her now.

It was chilly, but not freezing. Certainly not as cold as any of the walks she took to and from work in the early morning and afternoon. She sat up and curled her arms around her knees. She tried to wake up back in her real world by squeezing her eyes shut and gripping her legs to the point of pain. As desperately as she wanted to see Thomas, her job was on the line at the moment, and she was worried.

It was no use. She was here, in this dream. When she looked up again, Thomas was walking toward her, and she had to smile at his face. He started running when she stood, and they met in the middle, hugging hard.

He kissed her before she could get a word out at all, but she was happy to let him take the edge off her anxiety. After a few minutes of passion that almost made her forget the hotel, he put his head on her forehead.

"Dream girl, is it Thursday where you're from?" He rubbed his hands up and down her arms.

"It is. It's, like, the most important Thursday. My boss is coming to check on us, and I think I'm asleep." She let her hands touch his chest. He was solid. So tempting. "But now I'm here with you, and I feel grateful. I've tried to make it happen a lot."

He nodded. "Me too. They're getting worried I have migraines or something. I keep closing my eyes wherever I am."

"You don't, right?" She traced the inside of his forearms with her fingertips.

"No. But I ache to be here with you." He began kissing her again. "You're heaven." He added between little nips.

"I know. It's the same for me."

Thomas laid her down on the ground, and she enjoyed the welcome weight of his large frame on hers.

Instead of kissing her, he looked past her, and his eyes went wide. "The hell?"

She turned to follow his gaze. Instead of water behind her now, there was an abandoned street. "Wow."

"I was thinking about how I wanted to show you my house, and there it is. I'll be damned. Come on!" He stood and tugged her to her feet. She was swept up in his excitement.

He knocked on the door, hollering as he went in. "Ma? John? Eddie?" He stopped her in the cozy kitchen, pulling out a chair. "Wait here for a minute."

Thomas ran past her, and she heard him calling as he clomped around in the rooms above her.

When he came back he still had a smile, but it was a little smaller. "I was hoping to introduce you to them. But I guess that's not how this works."

He opened the fridge and pumped his fist. "Hot damn."

Fallen stood and peeked in. Inside the fridge were two plates covered in foil. He pulled them out and took them to the counter, setting the oven temperature with a dial before putting the plates inside.

"We got Ma's famous dinner, and you're going to love it. It's so good I want to eat it ice cold. It's been a long time. But we gotta wait for it to heat up. Tell me something—distract me so I don't waste the food by eating it cold."

He sat down and gathered her into his lap. It seemed to be his favorite move. She liked being able to run her hands through his hair. His dark waves were stubborn, and she couldn't get them to go in a different direction.

"I'm boring," she said. "Tell me about you. Tell me about the last time you had this meal."

"You're so far from boring it's not even funny. But I'll tell you. The last time I had it was at this very table." He knocked on it for emphasis. "My brothers and I were crowded around it. Ma had put heaping plates of food between us because her boys love to eat. It was the same roast beef, mashed potatoes, and sweet carrots we're going to have in about ten minutes. We always pretended to fight over the platters, and Ma scolded us, but she smiled a little, too.

She'd say, 'Boys, I made enough for all of you.' Then she'd swat Edward's hand as he took two rolls from the bread basket."

Thomas grinned. "I used to say Johnny was like a cow—four stomachs, I swear. And he would always say, 'I bet you could get a gallon of milk from me.' That night, the last time I ate this, I reached past Edward and grabbed three rolls.

"Anyway, when our mother finally came to sit down, we boys would stand until she'd settled in her chair. One of us always held it out for her. We dote on her, each in our own way, trying to compensate for the loss of our father. It's been ten years since his heart attack. Sometimes I would walk into the kitchen when she wasn't aware, and I'd catch her looking out the window, the look on her face the same as the day she learned my father had passed, mere minutes after arriving at work to put in the day."

Fallen held her chest, her heart hurting.

He put his hand over hers now, smiling when she met his eyes. "Ma has been strong for us from that day forward. I have no idea where she finds the resolve, but she's raised three rowdy boys on her own. It explains why two out of the three of us still lived at home when we last had this dinner."

The kitchen had begun to smell like the delicious meal in his memory.

"Who doesn't live at home anymore?" she asked.

Thomas ran his hand up and down her leg. "Well, Edward moved into an apartment down the street. Ma kept her chin in the air the entire time he packed. She only cries alone, in her room at night. I've heard her. Needless to say, I put off my own moving plans, as did Johnny."

"You're kind." She couldn't keep her hands off of him.

He seemed to have the same impulse, always finding new places to caress her or rest his hand.

"I think it's ready." Thomas lifted her from his lap and held out her chair.

She thanked him and sat, watching him as he pulled the plates out with an oven mitt.

"Can I help?" She felt awkward letting him prepare the meal for her.

"It's all done. Just be careful of the plate. It's hot." He set it down in front of her.

He filled two water glasses from the tap and set them next to the plates.

She held up hers and toasted, "To dreams that keep coming true."

"Here. Here." His blue eyes sparkled. They each took a sip before digging into their plates of food.

The roast beef was tender, the mashed potatoes like little clouds, and the carrots sweet like candy. As she ate, Fallen discovered her meal was actually still lukewarm to coldish in the center, but she wasn't about to stop. It was delicious.

Thomas made so much noise while eating, it was almost obscene.

"It's been so long since I've had home cooking," he mused between bites. "This is fantastic. Thanks, Ma—wherever you are in this crazy dream world."

He came up for air for a moment and watched her watching him. He swallowed and graced her with a most tender gaze. She put her hand on his arm.

"There's no home cooking where you are?" She wondered where her imagination had the man stationed.

He looked around, confused. "No... But I can't think of why not. So strange. It's all hazy, but right on the tip of my tongue."

"Don't worry. Just enjoy. It's fun to watch you."

Thomas rolled his eyes and groaned when he took his next bite. Fallen wanted to get up and look at all the pictures around the house, but she refused to take her hand from his skin, cherishing the chance to touch him.

Once he'd finished his plate, she pushed over the rest of hers, which he didn't refuse. Finally he rubbed his hard stomach as if it might be sticking out.

"So much food. So good." Thomas lifted her hand from his arm and kissed her knuckles before standing. "Come here, Fallen. You still look worried."

She stood and accepted his embrace. To be encompassed by him, with his magnificent, tall body arched around hers, was a lesson in faith. The energy that flowed through him to her was so vibrant, her eyes pricked with tears.

His full lips brushed over hers. "What's wrong?" he murmured.

"You're so right. How are you not real? I want you to be real." Fallen let him lift her into his arms.

He had to pull her closer to get through the doorway, his muscles contracting. The textures of the furniture, the colors of the room, the sound of his breathing—her imagination wasn't this good. Though she had no other explanation, she refused to give it that much credit.

She explored his face with her fingertips again, as if touching him might give her an imprint she could recreate when she was awake.

With her index finger, she traced a line across his long, black lashes and down his strong nose. His jaw had stubble again, and she tried to count a few of the coarse hairs there. She quickly gave up, but given the time, she felt sure she could do just that. He was reality.

"Your braid is fancy, pretty lady."

"The boss is coming today. I tried to look good. Professional." She touched it, finding it plaited exactly as she'd had it in the waking world.

He sat on the couch, keeping her on his lap. Fallen put her head on his shoulder, inhaling him.

"What do you do?" His lips kept skimming her forehead.

"I'm a housekeeper. In a hotel." She couldn't elaborate; her brain refused to form any more words for her.

He picked up her left hand and stroked her ring finger. "No husband?"

She shook her head, watching delight flare in his eyes.

"No boyfriend?" He lifted up his eyebrow.

She shook her head again, feeling a grin form on her lips.

"Good. Because the things I want to do to you wouldn't be fair to him at all. I want to be forward with you. Enjoy your body."

He gave her a sensual look.

"I'm totally okay with that."

"You would be, dream girl. In this dream, you would be. You'd be dressed to the nines, and we'd be at home here, in our own place, ready to spend the night recovering from an evening on the town."

Fallen closed her eyes, lulled by the sound of his voice. When she opened her eyes he wore a tuxedo with the bow tie undone around his neck, the jacket open.

She had on a long, black satin dress with an impossibly pinched waist.

She gasped, running her hands over her voluminous skirt. She kicked up a foot to find an elegant pump beneath her hem.

He chuckled. "Mighty fine, Mrs. Fallen."

She clapped her hands together, laughing as she found a wedding band on her finger. "We're married?"

"For what I want to do to you? We should be married." He winked.

He was too kissable to resist at this point, and she felt giddy.

He mumbled about her beauty, her perfection, and said it was truly the best dream yet, continuing to pretend they had a whole night to spend together.

He shifted her to the cushions and kissed her until she lay on her back. All of a sudden she had to struggle to stay present, conscious. Her mind was flashing, tired. In the blurry glimpses she now had of Thomas, his infatuated gaze looked sleepy too.

"Fallen...Thursday...I think it happens on Thursdays. Stay safe. Thursday..."

He was slurring, and it took all she had to nod and acknowledge that she'd heard him. Her lips were on his, and she tried to burn the feeling he gave her into her bloodstream.

Then suddenly she was awake, back in her world. She was once again in room 514, but instead of finding it a safe, empty place, she looked up to see a man hovering over her in the semi-darkness—a man who wasn't Thomas.

6

THE OWNER

Fallen found her lips in a terrified pucker, her hands on this shadow man's shoulders. Terror forced her the rest of the way awake.

"Oh my God," she managed.

"Are you okay?"

His voice was vaguely familiar, though she couldn't place it.

"I'm fine. Did I just kiss you?" Fallen took her hands from his shoulders and covered her mouth.

"You did. I was checking your pulse, and you pulled me in and kissed me."

The well-dressed man stood from the bed before offering her his hand. She took it and yanked at the hem of her uniform as she less-than-gracefully got to her feet.

Fallen was nose to name tag with him as she righted herself.

"Mr. Orbit, owner," she read. Her eyes grew wide as the reality of what she'd done in her not-quite-awake state set in.

She'd just kissed her boss. Well, her boss's boss's boss.

"I'm sorry." She was fired. There were no two ways about it.

She hazarded a look at his face, trying to gauge how much trouble she was in, and a realization hit her like a ton of bricks.

It was him! The dancing man from the first dream. The one who'd known her name.

"Lad?" she asked.

He started. "Uh, yes. Though to my employees, I'm Mr. Orbit."

"Of course you are. Sorry again." Her mortification was all encompassing. "Oh my God. I just kissed you, and now I've called you by your first name. I'm so sorry. This is awful. Please let me get out of here before I make it worse." She tried to scoot around him.

All of this was wrong. She was so disoriented. Seeing Lad from the dream world here was mind melting. What did it mean?

"Fallen, it's okay. I'm more concerned that you were unconscious," Mr. Orbit said. "Did you hit your head? Don't you remember? Do you feel okay?"

He'd asked her the same things in the woods in her dream. Had that been some sort of premonition?

She looked back at his deep brown eyes. There seemed to be none of the underlying unease there that she remembered from her dream.

"Maybe I hit my head?" she whispered.

He leaned down to hear her better before nodding. "If you don't mind, let me take a look."

Mr. Orbit put his hands gently on her head. He inspected her scalp carefully, using her shoulders to turn her and pushing aside her braid in places.

"I don't see any blood. Is there a spot that hurts? Maybe you should sit." He gestured to the bed. After she sat, he squatted in front of her, putting his hands on either side of her.

Her heart hurt; missing Thomas quickly and viciously seemed to be its only job of late. Her mind struggled to make sense of Lad in front of her in the waking world.

When it hit her, her jaw dropped: If Lad was here, while she was awake, perhaps Thomas was too. Somewhere.

Her heart picked itself up from where it had already started mourning the loss of him and jumped into her throat. In her haste to go find Thomas, she stood and put her crotch in her boss's face.

"I'm sorry. Again." She sat back down.

Mr. Orbit gave her a look that clearly stated that he was unsure what the hell was going on.

"You're Fallen Billow, right? Fifth floor housekeeping? New employee?"

"Yes. I'm all those things. And I kissed you, and all this…" She waved in the direction of her vagina and his face before hanging her head.

He was going to fire the crap out of her.

When he started laughing, she looked up at him cautiously.

"You're certainly an interesting lady. I just wanted to say your floor looks great, and keep doing what you're doing. If you're feeling okay, I'll be happy to escort you to your vehicle."

"I'm not…fired?" She waited until he stood this time before joining him.

"No, you're not fired. Lucky for you, I'm single, so I don't have to explain your lipstick to a lady at home. I'm concerned for you, though, and I want to make sure you're okay."

She smoothed hair that had escaped her braid away from her forehead. "That's super kind of you, but I actually walk to work, so that's not necessary."

His brow furrowed. "Hmm… I'm really uncomfortable with you walking a distance by yourself after you've been unconscious. Can I trouble you to allow me to give you a lift home? Do you have someone there who can watch you?"

He touched her shoulder. His hand felt heavy, and she wanted to shrug it off. He was a nice-looking man, but there was something off-putting about his demeanor.

"My brother will be home. It'll be fine." She brushed at her skirt. "Thank you for being understanding. I promise I'll work really hard for your company."

He finally removed his hand and put it in his pocket, jiggling keys there. "I'm driving you home; I won't take no for an answer."

She couldn't protest again; it would seem ungrateful. And she certainly didn't want to tell him she'd been asleep, not injured, when he'd found her on the bed.

She nodded her acceptance.

"That's a good girl."

His affirmation made her shiver. And feel a little like a dog.

He helped her gather her cleaning supplies and watched as she fussed with a few more details before holding the door open for her. Normally, she kept the doors propped open a bit while she worked. But in room 514, she let the door shut behind her so she could be alone with her hope of seeing Thomas.

The thrill of hoping she could find him while she was awake shot through her again.

As they walked to the elevator, she tried once more to get Mr. Orbit to abandon the idea of driving her home, but he was adamant. Fallen took her cart down to storage and emptied the dirty linens. After going through her end-of-day procedures and signing out, she turned to him. He'd made himself busy going through things in the maintenance office and checking for dust.

"Ready, Fallen?" He held open the door for her just as two other housekeepers entered. They were polite to Mr. Orbit, but Fallen saw the judgment in their eyes when they turned to her. She wondered if they knew he'd been alone with her in room 514.

He walked her through the lobby and out the back door, inspiring terror in every employee he encountered, each of whom then gave Fallen a questioning look. She hugged her jacket around her because the zipper was broken as they hit the cold.

"My ride is over here." He stepped up to the fanciest sports car Fallen had ever seen and held the passenger door open for her. She slid into opulence. Leather upholstery and cherry red highlighted the interior.

"Wow. This is some car." She touched the door as the engine began to purr.

"It's a Jaguar F-Type R. I love her a lot." He said this while looking into Fallen's eyes.

She nodded and hummed a bit. She noticed as he backed up that he'd been taking up two spots.

She found the seatbelt and clipped it into place.

"So how's your head now?" He touched the crown of her hair.

"Fine. Great. I'm just glad no one seems to book 514. It would have been horrible for a guest to find me." Then she bit her lip, wondering if pointing out her gaffe was poor form. She didn't want to give him any ideas.

"True. No one will ever be in 514, so you know."

He put on his blinker and turned toward the road to her house.

"Why is that? It's a nice room." She liked the little antique touches in the vacant space.

"Well, this hotel has been in my family for years." He came to a stop sign and made a left. "And my parents had an affinity for that particular room. After they passed, I asked that it be left guest free. In my heart it's always available for them. That's why I appreciate your efforts. Really, you're taking care of a space that's a memorial to my mother and father."

He made a right on Branch Road. It occurred to Fallen that she hadn't told Mr. Orbit where she lived. Uneasiness found a home with her again.

"You know the way to my house?"

He touched two fingers to his forehead. "Got it all up here. I checked the employee records from my phone."

"How...prepared you are." She wished she could crack the window. The thick smell of leather had started to overwhelm her.

"I wanted to know if you had any medical issues after finding you in distress." He shrugged, and with the next turn he drove up in front of her house. "So who lives here with you, just your brother?"

"Yeah. He's in high school." She tried to open the door, but it was hard to figure out the handle.

"Oh. Your parents?"

She stopped trying to escape and gave him her attention. "My dad is not around, and my mother's unavailable at the moment. Yes, we live here together." She finally thought she'd solved the handle and yanked on it just as Mr. Orbit hit the lock button.

"You're his *legal* guardian?" He tented his fingertips.

The way he said the word *legal* made her leery. Such a specific question. And she really wasn't. She had no money to take Nora to court for something like that, and anyway her brother was less than two years from being his own adult. Instead of answering, she changed the subject.

"Listen, I better get inside. People will wonder why there's such a fancy car here. Don't want them to think I won the lotto and come looking for handouts." She pointed at the door's lock.

"No lotto winning here. Just hard work. And staying loyal. Do you think loyalty is important, Fallen?" He lifted his hips and reached into his back pocket, pulling out his wallet as she tried to think of a good answer—the correct answer to give her boss's boss's boss after he'd found her sleeping and she'd kissed him and shoved her crotch in his face, and now sat in his car. Then she thought of Nora, and her abuse of her kids' loyalty to further her own selfish gain.

"I think you have to be kind in the world. And try to be a true person." She shrugged. That was the best she had. She was so goddamn exhausted, she honestly just wanted to get inside and shower. There was a ton left on her to-do list for tonight. And a huge chunk of that included developing a plan to stalk Thomas.

Mr. Orbit ruffled through an impressive stack of bills and pulled out a hundred dollars. He leaned forward, boxing her in the small car and held the money out between his index and middle fingers. "For you."

Fallen put her back against the passenger window, grateful for the console that kept Mr. Orbit's body away from hers. "No, sir. Thank you, but I'm good."

His lips were close to hers. Inappropriately close. "That was a real passionate kiss earlier," he said.

"Are you trying to pay me for accidently kissing you?" She looked around the car for other ways to escape. There were none.

"No." He shifted his position and scoffed like he hadn't just been so close to her. Like he hadn't complimented her kissing. "This is the tip—for room 514. It's not fair that you miss out on that. You have a room to clean that offers no hope of getting extra money from it. I want to put this in your tip jar, so to speak.

He held the money up again, so close to her left breast that they were both looking as he grazed it with his pinkie. She looked up at his face. He smiled and lifted his brows.

"Taking the money isn't an option, Fallen. You need this job. You need the money."

She snatched the bill from him, mostly to take away his excuse to touch her again. She felt clammy all over her body.

"I do need the money, but I'm not looking for a relationship." *Oh, please don't fire me. Please.*

"I never insinuated that. Actually, I think I've been extremely tolerant. Most business owners wouldn't tolerate you lying down on the job, let alone drive you home and give you money. After you kissed them." His neck looked flushed.

She didn't want to make him mad. "I'm sorry. I'm grateful. Thank you. Really. I appreciate the tip, and you're right. I can use it." Then she started to babble, trying to make the air friendlier between them. "My brother, Fenn, is a huge kid and an eating machine, so a bit more grocery money is always helpful." She reached for the handle again.

"That's better. You're welcome." He hit the unlock button as he reached over and patted her thigh. "Much better. Goodnight." She swore his fingertips had slipped under the hem of her skirt before she was able to get out of the car.

She slammed the door, and the willies caused her to shiver. Something slimy was going down in that car. In that man's head. And she'd kissed him. She didn't turn back as she heard the car pull away from the curb, just continued forward to unlock her door.

It was dim inside, so she knew she'd beaten Fenn home. Since their last round of fun with the electric company, Fallen and Fenn had decided only to use power when they had to, keeping the lights off until they got home. Fallen leaned against the door after she closed it behind her and sniffled a few times. She didn't let herself cry, but she had a feeling Mr. Orbit was going to be a serious problem.

When Fenn came home a couple hours later, Fallen had soup and grilled cheese sandwiches going. There had been a special on apples, so each of their plates had two. She knew he should eat more vegetables.

He grabbed a quick shower and told her about his afternoon. The good news was that his teacher's husband was back up and about and could mow his own lawn again—which was good timing because the grass had pretty much stopped growing for the impending winter. And the Billow mower had lived through the kindness it was party to.

He asked her about work, and she told him it was fine. Some days she had funny stories of guests or the things they left behind, but today she had nothing that she wanted to share.

"I think I might be getting a new extracurricular activity," he announced.

"Oh yeah?" Fallen tried to focus on the positive—it was good for him to have interests and activities—and not on the fact that almost anything he might decide to do would cost money. She nodded for him to continue.

"You know I like playing football, just messing around, and the season's already started, but the coach approached me today. He said he saw me messing around at lunch tossing the ball and really liked my arm, that they could use me on the team. But it's a ton of time after school, and weekends too. I wanted to see what you thought."

He had the worst poker face in the world. She knew he wanted to do it. She couldn't even begin to figure out what it would cost, but she wanted to give him everything he could ever dream of.

"The coach said if I have a good grasp of the game, it could help me out with college." Fenn took a huge swig of milk.

"That would be great. Sounds like you have a new activity!"

She took a bite of her apple. It was hard enough getting fruit into Fenn's everyday, never mind compression shirts.

"Well, thanks. I think that means I can sit on the bench at the game tomorrow. I, um, I do need some cleats, though. I outgrew my old ones. Is that a possibility this week?"

Fallen stood and got her purse, pulling out the $100. Though it felt dirty in her hand, she forced a smile as she passed the bill to him and sat down.

"Really? Wow. Thank you so much. How'd you get this? I figured I'd be cutting room for my toes at the end of my old cleats."

"It was a tip someone owed me. Glad it will come in handy. You'll be a huge asset to the team. Have fun!" She held up her glass of milk to him, and he toasted it with his own.

"To football."

"To money for cleats."

Fallen still felt slimy.

After she and Fenn had cleaned the kitchen, Fallen prepped for the next day while he did his homework. She'd bagged up another set of peanut butter sandwiches before she flipped off the lights.

After her shower and a quick check of the locks, she had a few minutes to herself to think about Thomas.

And then she felt guilty again for taking money from Mr. Orbit. Lad. Mr. Lad Orbit.

She knew he was the man from her first dream with Thomas, and he'd been creepy then too. She wished she had the internet at home so she could launch a million Google searches. But the internet wasn't essential, and that's where they were, she and Fenn. They only got what they needed. And sometimes they went without that.

The hotel had a business center; maybe she could pop in after her shift. That was probably against the rules. Maybe after work she could go by the library and use a computer there.

Thomas.

She would Google search the hell out of him, but she had no idea who he was. Without a last name, she'd hardly know where to begin. How many Thomases could there be in the area, let alone in New York City? He'd said he grew up in New York, but that could be anywhere in the state. She needed to focus less on his handsome face in the next dream and more on getting some useful information from him.

Still, the thought of finding Thomas in White Plains made her heart pound. Then she blushed, thinking about how she acted when she was with him. So unfiltered. So handsy. She would have to be much more guarded in her waking world.

And maybe he wouldn't recognize her here. Lad certainly hadn't shown any indication of recognizing her. Maybe her dreams were premonitions of things to come? It was confusing.

But Thomas had told her Thursdays, and as she looked at the calendar on her wall, she realized he was right. Every time they'd connected, it had been a Thursday. Which also meant she had a week to wait until she could see him again and get more information. In the meantime she'd certainly keep her eyes wide open, in case she spotted him.

He was so tall and protective, he would make her feel safe around Mr. Orbit.

She grabbed her journal and jotted down her dream from this afternoon, shoving Fenn's newfound football expenses firmly out of her mind. No need to panic until she had more information.

Just before she went to sleep, Fallen wrote Thomas' name over and over, the blue ink getting darker with each pass.

7

AS YOU WISH

Fallen got to work on time the next morning, despite feeling flustered about returning after her creepy ride home with Mr. Orbit. When she arrived, the staff was still gathering for their daily meeting. Fallen had left her hair down for the walk in, letting it insulate her neck from the brisk morning wind. As she took off her jacket, Mr. Orbit moved in behind her before she even knew he was in the room.

"I like your hair down like that," he told her. "You should skip the braid." He put his heavy hand on her shoulder.

She startled at his touch. "Uh, it's part of the dress code. My hair has to be up."

He laughed deep in his chest. "I think if the owner makes an exception, you can listen to him."

Fallen twisted the hair tie on her wrist with her index finger. Housekeepers 8 and 9 showed their disapproval by squishing up their faces. This was a great way to add more fuel to their fire.

She responded formally. "Of course, Mr. Orbit. As you wish."

He nodded and stayed behind her, perhaps intending to listen to Melanny's motivational speech.

As their manager began, it was clear she was pulling out all the stops and being extra strict for Mr. Orbit's benefit.

"We support all of the staff by enforcing the guidelines here," she said, surveying the room. "Like the dress code." Melanny pointed at Fallen's head. "And that is clearly an infraction, Ms. Billow."

Fallen opened her mouth to defend herself, but shut it when Mr. Orbit cleared his throat behind her.

"Melanny, Ms. Billow has special permission to wear her hair down today."

Fallen felt her hair being tugged gently. Mr. Orbit was pulling on it where it brushed the top of her rump. She held her breath.

"What is her issue? Everyone else manages to comply."

That was the wrong tone to take, but there was no way to warn Melanny. Not that she would have listened anyway.

"I asked her to leave it down because I prefer it that way."

During the awkward pause that followed, Fallen wished desperately to disappear. Melanny looked flustered as she started and stopped a few sentences before returning to her gaze to her iPad. She announced some special requests and reminded floor eight that Mr. Orbit's room was not to be touched during his stay.

After Melanny dismissed everyone, Fallen couldn't get out of the maintenance room fast enough. But she didn't make it all the way out before she heard Mr. Orbit raising his voice at Melanny. Everyone around her cringed and rushed to leave so Melanny could get herself berated in private.

Desta bumped Fallen's hip with hers as they hustled out and gave her a soft smile. But then she paused to talk to another worker, leaving Fallen alone.

The housekeeper from floor 8 pushed past Fallen, snagging her duster and her good bottle of cleaner from her cart.

"Wait! I need those." Fallen was surprised to see that the woman already had those exact items on her cart.

"Let's see how resourceful you are. You can obviously suck some rich dick, but let's see if you can clean a floor using just your spit and that shiny hair. Don't think you'll find any refill bottles in the closet either."

The maid from floor 9 snickered. "You're mean, Larissa. But brilliant too."

The two bumped fists before pushing past Fallen with their carts.

Mr. Orbit rounded the corner, forcing the women to part and steer their carts around him. They straightened up their walk as they went.

He had his eyes on Fallen, totally ignoring the fact that they had to scramble out of his way. When he got to her, he apologized.

"Melanny should have known better. I'm sorry that happened."

Fallen shrugged. "It was an honest mistake. Everyone has to put their hair up."

"Not you. Not today." He motioned to her cart. "Do you need help pushing this?"

She shook her head. "Thanks. I'll be fine. It's even lighter now that those ladies took my duster and cleaner."

Fallen got behind the cart and started to push, thinking she might be able to run up and down the stairs to floor 4 to borrow Desta's in between rooms.

"What? They took them? Were they out of supplies?" Mr. Orbit stopped her cart with his foot.

The look in his eye made her realize speaking in front of him had been a mistake. The veins in his neck had grown pronounced. He was angry.

"It's fine. They're fine." Fallen started to push her cart.

This was the worst situation. She needed this job. Mr.

Orbit's fancy for a few minutes could have long-lasting negative effects on her work relationships.

And he was older. Too old for her. Too rich for her as well.

"I'll need you to do up my bed," he announced, "before you get to your floor." He strode past her and held the elevator.

Fallen reluctantly followed. "I thought you didn't want it touched?"

He smirked and held out his hand after helping her situate the cart on the elevator. "Key?"

She unhooked her set from the cart and handed it to him. A few of the grounds workers walked by and averted their eyes when they saw who was in the birdcage.

"I said I didn't want it touched by housekeeping on the eighth floor. You are separate from that request. And I promise I just need my bed made." He pressed the button with the key in place.

She nodded and looked at her white Velcro sneakers. She missed Thomas. There were so many more days before next Thursday with him. If she got a next Thursday with him. Mr. Orbit was a complication.

Maybe he really just needed his bed made. Maybe she wasn't going to have to knee him in the nuts and quit her job in about four minutes.

He held the birdcage door open for her, and she maneuvered the cart out. He walked down to his hotel room and used the old fashioned key this hotel was known for to enter.

He grabbed the rubber doorstop off her cart and set it under the door to keep it open. That simple action gave her hope.

She left the cart in the hallway and followed behind him. "Just the bed?"

"Just the bed. I'm very clean, but I can't get beds right." He shrugged and gave her a boyish grin.

She walked in and saw that he was telling the truth. The

room was neat as a pin. Even the wastepaper baskets were empty.

He waved her toward the king-size bed. Even that wasn't messy.

"Do you want new linens?"

He shook his head as he picked up the phone, jabbing in a number.

She began straightening the pillows and tucking in the sheets, her hands shaking a little. Was this some sort of test for her? Like a bed-making exam for new hires?

"Melanny, can you explain to me why two housecleaning specialists stole a bottle of cleaner and a duster from Ms. Billow's cart?"

Fallen gasped and looked over at Mr. Orbit, still holding his comforter.

He held up a finger. "Well, I suggest you find out who has those things and see that they're returned to her floor by the time she's done making my bed." He set the phone down.

"I'm sorry they gave you trouble this morning. That's not how I like my employees to conduct themselves. I know senior staff members can try to haze new hires, but they've gone too far."

He rubbed his nose before winking at her.

"Okay."

He sank into the room's plush chair.

Fallen had a strong suspicion that the two women now likely marching her cart's things to floor five would have a lot more to say about it as soon as Mr. Orbit's visit was over. She continued to make the bed, tidying the corners and smoothing the fabric until it was textbook neat.

"You do a nice job. Who taught you?" He had his hands folded together, touching his chin in thought.

Surely the owner of multiple hotels had other things to do than watch an inexperienced housekeeper make his bed.

"Desta. She's amazing. Really loves this place." Fallen looked around the bed and was satisfied that it was done. She could begin working on getting the hell out of here.

"Desta's been with us a very long time." He stood as she made her way to the door, grabbing her elbow before she could pass. "I want us to be friends, Fallen. I want you to trust me."

Her eyes widened. "Of course. We can be friends. As long as that's not weird, with you owning the place and all." She grabbed her uniform skirt with both fists, desperate to take his hand off her arm.

"No. It won't be weird." He gave her a smile that didn't reach his eyes. "Be well." He let go of her.

She nodded again and forced herself not to run on her way out.

"Don't forget the rubber stopper!" he called.

She'd stopped and squatted to wiggle it loose when he corrected her.

"No, don't bend at the knees." She turned to see his face, to judge whether he was serious or not. He was.

She stood and bent at the waist, catching her reflection in the mirror on the wall. This request left her hemline exposing way too much of her thighs.

"Wait."

She was almost positive she heard the click of a camera.

"Okay."

She plucked the stopper out and let the door swing shut hard behind her.

Sure. It won't be weird at all.

The next morning Mr. Orbit requested that Fallen leave her hair down for the duration of his stay, and he wanted her to make his bed each morning too.

As he stayed into the next week, the snide comments from the housekeepers on floors 8 and 9 reached a fever pitch, but Fallen learned quickly to keep her mouth shut and not inadvertently snitch to the owner.

He always made her pick up the stopper the same way as she left his room, and she had no idea how to refuse. Resigned, she went from wondering whether he was taking a picture of her legs to knowing he was and waiting for the click before finishing the task. Luckily he hadn't touched her. Their conversations were brief and consisted mostly of weather commentary. She still wondered if he recognized her from the dream.

Even though she always left the rubber stopper in the door while she worked in his room, the rumors had started. The hair request combined with the bed making had marked her as his favorite, and that did not sit well with anyone. Only Desta seemed to have sympathy. She had taken to wearing nicotine patches during his visit, cutting down on her need for smoke breaks, but the withdrawal from her favorite vice combined with the extra work every day Mr. Orbit stayed in the building was easily seen on her tired face.

Fallen did find a moment to tell Desta that Mr. Orbit had spoken well of her and complemented her bed making. Instead of seeming happy, she'd just gotten a far away look in her eye and nodded. "I bet he liked it real good."

At home, on Tuesday morning Fenn had laid a packet of football forms on the table that were supposed to be signed by their mother. Fallen had looked through them while nibbling her toast. Forging her mother's signature wasn't a problem—she'd been doing it since eighth grade—but the cost of being on the football team was amazing, even though she'd braced for it.

Jackets, uniforms, camps, and special fitness classes added up to almost $1000.

Fenn must have been watching her reaction because he'd started in right away with a plan he was working on. "Coach said they've given out all the scholarships already since I'm joining after the start of the season, but I asked if there was any other way to earn some money—like, if I could clean the locker rooms or mow lawns or something."

Fallen had reached over and touched his hand. She hated that something as all-American as playing football had him on the defensive. If they had their parents, this wouldn't be a concern. The responsible adults would figure out a way to pay, right? Maybe pull from savings. Maybe they'd even have an extracurricular activities fund. But Fallen had only her meager and recently pilfered-from bank account.

"I'm not sure there is," Fenn continued. "But coach is going to think on it."

"I'll figure it out," Fallen had assured him. "We're doing okay." That had been a bald-faced lie. But there was nothing they could do to change it, so why make him worry? "Did you get good cleats? How do you like the practices so far?"

He nodded. "It's really fun," he'd said, a smile breaking over his face.

"Cool. Great. Tonight's spaghetti for dinner, and I'll be home by six."

"That owner still there?" Fenn asked.

"Yeah. He's still making me make his bed. I guess I'm some sort of bed-making protégée."

"You sure it's all on the up and up?" Her brother sat taller in his seat.

When did he get so adult?

She nodded. "I'll keep you posted if I need the football team to drop by and storm the castle."

She was rewarded again with his bright, white smile. He

loved being on the team, that much she could tell, and his joy had kept her going all day long.

Despite Orbit's constant lurking, Fallen had managed to get to the satellite library branch near her home last night after work. It was open until six on Wednesdays, instead of closing at the usual 4:30. As expected, without a last name, her Google search for Thomas had been fruitless and frustrating. There were far too many. She'd been on the third page of images when the librarian tapped her on the shoulder to tell her the library was closing.

She'd thought taking action might make her feel better, but now she just felt overwhelmed. She decided to focus on the action of praying for a next time with Thomas.

On Thursday morning, as instructed, Fallen left her hair down for the walk in and tried to stay away from 8 and 9 while listening in the meeting. After the first day, Mr. Orbit hadn't come to the staff meetings, but he always waited for her in his room: dressed in a suit, sitting in his chair.

She would knock and announce herself as housekeeping, and he would yell for her to come in.

Today, as she set the rubber stopper, he asked her to stop.

This is a first.

She looked up at him, but stayed in her position. He stared at his phone's screen, his tongue peeking out of his mouth just a little while he adjusted the focus. She glanced down. Her very modest uniform top had enough of a V-neck that her cleavage was visible.

"Move your hair to the side."

Facing him and taking orders was even more demeaning than the pictures as she left had been.

This was clearly sexual harassment. She blushed and shook her head, standing.

"No. Sir, I'm here to make your bed."

He looked from his screen and frustration washed over his face before it was replaced with what seemed like a forced pleasantness.

He waved at the bed.

She started to make it, as she normally did—tucking, fluffing, and smoothing. When she was all done, Mr. Orbit stood up, went to the bed, and yanked all the blankets off.

"Today I want a linen change." He turned and sat back down.

She swallowed her anger. Maybe she should have asked. She was so on edge about standing up to him, she hadn't thought of that. Was he punishing her?

Fallen went to the cart and picked out two precision-folded crisp, white sheets with matching pillowcases. She took the ball of old sheets out of the center of the bed before inquiring, "And your spread?"

"No, thank you. Just the sheets."

Fallen dumped the dirty sheets in the laundry sack before coming back. All of the pillows and the comforter now sat on the very edge of the bed, closest to Mr. Orbit.

It was odd that he'd moved them while she was briefly out of the room.

"Make the bed from that side. I don't want you on this one." He pointed to her side of the bed and then his.

She knew her face showed her confusion. And then she got it. If she made the bed from her side only, she would have to bend down over and over, giving him a great view of the gap in her shirt.

He thought he was being tricky. She wanted to cry because he was creepy. Fallen turned and went into his bathroom. Inside the vanity was a small sewing packet meant for guest clothing emergencies. She extracted a safety pin and pinned her shirt closed at the neck.

Fallen returned to the bed, lifted her eyebrow at him, and began to follow his rules.

He said nothing, but he shifted around in his chair quite a bit.

It took a lot to make the bed only from her side, and required tons of extra smoothing, but she managed. When she was finally finished, she nodded at Mr. Orbit. He stood, went to the door, and removed the stopper himself, letting the door slam.

Her mouth fell open. She should have run. She should have never even let him take pictures of her legs—so many regrets in the span of just a few seconds. He spun on his heel once they were in private.

Fallen's knees were weak, but she managed to stay standing from rigid fear.

Mr. Orbit walked right up to her so the tips of her breasts touched his lapels. She could hear her own breathing and feel her heart beating in her throat.

He reached for her, and she flinched, but all he did was release the safety pin and free it from her blouse. He closed it and slipped it into his pocket.

"I hear your brother's playing football. That's great."

Fallen watched him with wide eyes.

He ran a hand from her elbow to her wrist. "I've forgotten to tip you, for all this extra work."

He reached in his wallet and flipped through it. She took a step back, and he countered with a step forward.

"Please. You're making me uncomfortable."

"Am I? I'm sorry, Fallen. I thought we were friends." He pulled out money, and the outer bill in the stack was a hundred.

"We are. It's just, I have to get to my rooms and..."

Mr. Orbit carefully tucked the bills in the front pocket of her apron and left his hand there, pressed against her hip. "I've decided I'd like to sponsor a student on the varsity football team this year."

She shook her head. All her concentration was on the hand against her hip. His fingertips were starting to bite into her.

Fallen tried to take another step back, and Mr. Orbit stopped her with his other hand.

"And I think your brother would be a great recipient. It's a prestigious honor to have a sponsor. The colleges love to see that."

Fallen let her gaze slip from his eyes to his throat. *What did he want?*

"I'm not trying to force you into anything you don't want, Fallen. But as friends, I'd love to take you to a charity ball I have to go to this weekend in the city. Black tie. I think you'd make a great companion. And it'll show the other attendees that fraternizing with my staff in a friendly way is what makes my business thrive."

"Are you implying that if I go to this charity event with you, you'll pay for my brother to be on the football team?"

"No. No. Not at all. The charity event is only if you'd like to spend the night dressed up and listening to boring men try to catch a dance with you. Please. Relax."

He stepped closer and lowered his voice. "For the football, all I need you to do is let me take that picture I was trying to take. And maybe give me a kiss on the cheek. That's it. Real friendly."

Fallen stepped back again, and this time he let her. Her pride demanded that she storm out and toss his money at him.

Her brother's smile the other morning over breakfast made her stay.

"Okay."

Mr. Orbit clapped his hands together like a spoiled child. "Very good. Glad we have an understanding."

He stepped aside and allowed her to get on the bed. She got on her hands and knees and waited. Mr. Orbit came in front of her and squatted down so they were eye to eye.

"You made the right choice. This is a good thing." He tapped his cheek.

That was her cue. She leaned forward and pressed her lips to his skin. When she backed away, his eyes were soft.

"Lovely." He dragged her shirt lower with his index finger.

It was just cleavage, not even nudity. *It will be okay. It will be okay.*

He took the picture a few times from slightly different angles before declaring her all done.

She adjusted her shirt as she stood.

"Will you come to the ball with me?"

"I'm not going to have sex with you." Her shame made her brave.

"Of course not. Did I ask you for that? What do you take me for? I thought we were friends."

Fallen opened the door. "I'll think about it."

Her skin crawled. She'd helped this man indulge in some sort of fetish, and it felt terrible.

"Have a good day, Fallen."

8

ANTIQUE

Fallen looked in her pocket and found that Mr. Orbit had given her $200 as a "tip" for making his bed. She should've marched back up and left it in his room, but she needed it for Fenn.

After forcing herself to start her actual day and do her best in each room on her floor, she had finally made it to room 514 and the end of her work. It was just after 2 pm.

Maybe she could dream of Thomas anywhere on a Thursday, but to be as certain as possible, she felt compelled to seek out the same atmosphere and recreate the initial experience.

She neatened the room and was thrilled when her lids felt heavier and heavier. After pulling her cart inside, Fallen threw over the bolt bar, hopefully preventing any unwanted sleep-kissing from Mr. Orbit again.

She crawled onto the bed and felt a twinge of revulsion and regret over Mr. Orbit's pictures as she stretched out on her side.

And then she committed to the blackness. Fallen wasn't sure how much time passed before she opened her eyes again, but when she regained consciousness, she lay on the couch in the house where she and Thomas had eaten in the last dream. She sat up and called for him. Getting no response, she began to worry.

She got off of the couch and started nosing around. She picked up a picture of Thomas with two other men who looked like him—the brothers, John and Edward. She'd forgotten about them. In her next internet search, she'd include their names, especially if she didn't get to see Thomas today.

That possibility sent a wave of disappointment through her. She looked around again, only to realize the house was incomplete. The rooms she hadn't seen last time were walled off now. Fallen felt a little claustrophobic as she tried the front door, but it was open, and the empty street lay beyond.

She didn't want to leave, though. She would wait right here, surrounded in his memories, until Thomas arrived.

Fallen went through the house looking for mail or some hint at his last name. No luck. But with her careful scrutiny she realized the place was impeccably vintage. His mother must be a serious antique collector. Thinking of his mom made her think of the fridge. She went over and opened it, once again finding two plates inside. A peek under the foil told her the same roast beef dinner awaited them as last time.

"Fallen?"

"Thomas?" She whirled around, slamming the fridge door.

He stood in the doorway, relief and a smile on his face.

She ran to him. He braced himself and caught her.

"I was afraid I was here alone. Oh, thank God you're here." She kissed his chin and nose before he slid her to her feet, stilled her frantic movements, and centered her with his kiss. She melted into him, his hard chest, his sparkling eyes.

She stopped the kiss to hug him, and he bent to accommodate her.

"Are you okay? Where you are, is it safe?" She ran her hands over his chest again. This time instead of appreciating his solidness, she checked for injuries.

She'd had such important questions for him, and now she could not drum up a single one.

His eyes held trapped answers, but he revealed nothing.

"Cat got your tongue?"

He nodded, pulling her close and kissing the top of her head. "I missed you so much."

"Every day is a million days. It took forever to get to Thursday." She wrapped her hands in his, standing toe to toe with his boots. Her white Velcro sneakers got a chuckle out of him.

"Those are something else. Where are your laces? Are those buttons?"

White noise saturated their world. He wrapped her close to him, covering her ears while she covered his.

They waited, and eventually the sound tapered off.

But the interruption had made their dream world seem less safe. She watched as Thomas scoped out the windows with a searching gaze.

"That was unexpected. Did you wish for that noise to happen?" She couldn't stop touching him.

Thomas shook his head.

"I thought for a second it was an earthquake. I'd hate for any of these antiques to be damaged." She glanced around at the charming vintage decorations.

He gave her a confused look. "Antiques? This stuff is all new and—"

The noise was back again. They covered each other's ears and waited it out.

When it tapered off, he suggested. "Maybe we should go somewhere new?"

Fallen was about to agree, but then she remembered the meal in the fridge. She towed him over and showed him. "Do we have time for this? You loved it so much last time."

Fallen tried to make a microwave appear on the counter the

way clothes sometimes appeared on her in this world. Nothing happened.

Instead she focused on the plates and thought about them being hot enough to eat. "Careful, don't touch," she said. "Let's see if this worked."

She grabbed a potholder from a hook on the nearest cabinet and checked— sure enough, the meal was steaming. Thomas grabbed a potholder too and picked up the other plate.

She snuggled close to him, wrapping her arm around his waist as he tucked her in close. Fallen pictured her favorite boardwalk from the trip to Atlantic City Nora had taken she and Fenn on when they were kids, before her mother was completely non-functional as an adult.

Instead of flashy lights and cars, a desolate boardwalk and a few older buildings appeared. The waves crashed in the distance at dusk, and she was pleased to see Thomas still with her, holding his plate.

"Okay, let's sit down right here and eat."

He didn't have to be told twice and folded his legs to sit on the wooden boardwalk.

He held up a hand to her so she could sit as well, forced into being graceful by her uniform skirt.

"We forgot forks!" She laughed as he shrugged and picked up the slice of meat in his hand to take a bite.

She did the same. "Is this better than the last time we had it?"

Thomas moaned. "Maybe. Thank you for thinking about this for me."

It felt good to give him something. She used her finger to scoop up mashed potatoes and licked them off.

He stopped eating to watch her do it, and the next minute she was under him.

"Do that again."

Fallen was hesitant, but she licked her finger again. Being

ordered around made her think of Mr. Orbit, and she looked to the side when Thomas went in for a kiss.

"What's wrong? What did I say? This is too forward. I'm sorry." He eased off of her and helped her sit.

She felt terrible ruining the moment. "You're fine. I'm sorry. It's just, today was kind of weird, and that gave me flashbacks. Seriously. Stay close."

She scooted over so her shoulder touched his chest, his mother's food smooshed beneath them.

"Tell me, dream girl."

"No. It's nothing; it's reality. I didn't wait all week to be with you just to whine. Come back. Kiss me more." She touched his chin.

His lips were yummy—that was probably the wrong word, but she'd never seen a man's lips so kissable before.

"Sweetheart, if something made you pause, I want to know what it was. Let me be here—" He pointed at her heart. "—while I'm here." He pointed at the boardwalk.

"Okay. Remember the guy who was at our first dream date?"

His gaze softened. "I like that you think of it as a dream date."

She blushed. "That's what it was."

"Yes. I remember him. Lad." Thomas's eyes got stormy.

"Well, he's in my real world. He's my boss. And he's being weird. He makes me uncomfortable. Like, he wants to take pictures of me bending over." She looked out at the waves. They seemed real, as real as the carpets she vacuumed almost every day. "And he wants to give me money, and Fenn, my brother, needs money to play football. What's a picture in the grand scheme of things, and I—"

She stopped talking when she saw Thomas's face.

"I'm going to kill him."

The absolute certainty came from a place inside of him that

clearly could follow through. It wasn't just a vent of anger. It was a proclamation.

"I let him take the picture; you can't kill him. And besides, we're in a dream."

She wanted to tell Thomas about her theory that he might be in her real world too, that she needed his last name, his address, something to go on, but those words couldn't find purchase in her mouth.

Thomas shifted to face her. "You work for him. You need the money for your brother. In what way is any of this your fault?"

Fallen nodded. "I shouldn't have said anything. I just want to spend this time with you."

"Can I hold your hand?"

"Please."

He took her hand. "I want that too, but obviously you had a rough day. I promised to be here, and I need to do a better job of that. Come get a hug."

She sighed with relief when his deadly demeanor faded. She cuddled to him again and buried her face in his chest. "We're a mess. Look at the food we have all over us."

She pointed to her uniform skirt, coated in mashed potatoes. "Let's fix that."

In a blink she was again in the classy black satin dress with the pinched waist and the full skirt. The food was gone, and Thomas was a vision in an old-fashioned tuxedo.

He stood and held out his hands, which she took. She now wore pumps, so she was closer to his face when she stood.

"This is great." She picked up the hem of her dress and held it out.

"You're the most gorgeous thing in your uniform," he said. "But like this? I shouldn't even be allowed to stand next to you."

He was wrong. *She* was the imposter. He could carry the formal clothes like a model. But she was allowed to be boastful in her dream tonight.

"You *are* lucky," she teased, wanting to lighten the mood, get to the good stuff. Their time always seemed limited.

He smiled. "That I am. You have to tell me what to do here. Because I refuse to make a mistake where you're concerned. You lead. Tell me what you want."

She wrapped her arms around his neck, but he kept his hands in his pockets.

"Give me kisses that will make me forget to wake up." She put her lips against his.

In his arms she found comfort. She felt his strength around her and knew with absolute certainty that he wouldn't let her fall as he dipped her into a movie star kiss. The waves crashed, and the stars came to the party as well. Her dream man kissed her like he had a plan.

This time she felt no hesitation. She thought of nothing but his hands on her skin. His kisses were perfection, but she was eager for more and let her hands feel all of him. The ridges of his muscular body became a map of her desires. She wanted to feel his skin on hers. Fallen began to undo the buttons on his shirt.

He halted her hand. "Come walk with me. Pretend everyone I know can see us."

She looped her arm through his and began to promenade with him.

"Tell me more about your brother." He walked her to the steps that led to the sand.

"Fenn? He's the kind of person who accidently wins the lotto and donates it all to someone else. So giving, such a big heart—to go with the big rest of him. It's amazing he hasn't been playing football before now, now that I think about it. I worry that our mother has disappointed him a lot, and that I can't set him up well enough to get him all the opportunities he needs. But he's a great person, and that counts, I think."

Thomas nodded. "I agree. You can't choose the battlefield,

but you can choose how you deal with the enemy. What about you? Tell me about you."

He helped her navigate the sand, but eventually she had to kick off her heels and pick them up.

"I left Fenn to go to college for a few years, and I shouldn't have. I really should have stayed. He has such a soft spot for our mother, and managing everything was too much for him. He was reluctant to tell me they were in trouble." She squinted at the horizon.

"Maybe he was trying to protect you."

They got to the water's edge. Normally Fallen would have worried about getting her skirt wet, but here she just gathered it up and touched her toe to the water. It was warm enough to make her smile.

She stepped away as Thomas took his boots off and rolled up his pant legs. She dropped her shoes in the sand.

"Maybe. But I'm the oldest. It's my job."

"You sound like Edward. He always wants to boss Johnny and me around. It comes from a good place, but he pissed us off something awful when we were teens." He waded in to his ankles. "Only for you, Fallen, would I step into water voluntarily."

"You don't like the water?" She tilted her head to the side and stepped up next to him, letting her dress swirl in the waves.

He looked lost for a minute. "No, I do... I used to. I can't think of why I said that. I'm sorry."

It was one of those things. Certain aspects of their lives seemed to be protected, unreachable during the dreams. This fed Fallen's belief that Thomas was a real person somewhere.

"It's okay. And maybe you're right. But Fenn was hungry when I got back home. Hungry. My mother would rather drink than get him food." Fallen closed her eyes as she tamped down her anger.

"You're a fantastic sister."

Thomas put his arm around her waist as a set of particularly big waves came in.

She squeaked when the first one hit, soaking her up to her hips. She basically crawled up Thomas, who laughed out loud as they endured two more above-average waves.

"Pretty lady, do you even know how much this time with you means to me?" He kept her steady as the waves ebbed, her wet silk dress flowing like sea grass around their embrace.

"If it's anything like what it means to me, it's big." She kissed his lips again.

After letting her taste the touch of salt air on him for a bit, he returned to his sentiment.

"It makes me want to live tomorrow." He gave her a sad smile.

Alarm spiked through her as she searched his face. His eyes were wistful.

"Where are you? I want to find you." She put her hands on his neck, curling her fingers around it while gently kissing his jawline.

"I can't remember." He shook his head, seeming distressed a bit, frustrated too. "But I don't think I want you to find me."

She recoiled. She wiggled out of his arms and pushed until he let her free. The waves were getting bigger, rougher. She was tossed around as she tried to wade back to the shore. He was next to her before she could get knocked off her feet.

"Don't. Don't act like you care." She swatted at him, but never connected.

He didn't flinch. "Stay with me."

Her heart softened, but her pride was stronger. "Why? You don't want me to find you when I'm awake."

She sloshed forward. He stood behind her, and she noticed a wave broke around them. He was taking the brunt of the current against his back.

Instead of a dramatic, independent stomp-off, Fallen needed

Thomas to help her all the way back to the sand. Her dress was plastered against her, and he'd tossed off his jacket in their struggle to get back to the shore.

She crossed her arms and regarded him.

"For a dream girl, you sure are stubborn." He lifted an eyebrow.

His wet, white shirt was painted against his chest.

"For a dream guy, you're scaring me."

Concern took over his teasing demeanor. "What's wrong?"

"You sound suicidal. And then you say you don't want me to find you. What am I supposed to do?"

Thomas opened his arms. "Come here."

"No. Answer me." She pushed the wet hair out of her face.

"I don't want to waste a moment here with you not in my arms." He kept his arms open.

She tossed her hands up, but went to him, allowing herself to be wrapped in an embrace. She put her hands over his heart while she cuddled in.

With her heels off, he could put his chin on her head.

"I'm not suicidal. I want picket fences." He took his hands from her lower back and used them to tilt her chin toward his face. "And a beautiful wife, with a dog and a newspaper and picnics and late nights in bed. Don't get me wrong—I want all those things. It's just that where I am, I can't have them now."

The annoying white noise kicked up again, causing them to cover each other's ears.

It took longer to settle down this time. But when it finally tapered off, she took her hands from his ears and put them on his cheeks. "I'm going to find you. I'm going to fix this."

"So much determination. That's why you'll make it, Fallen, through all the challenges in front of you. And if anyone can find me, I bet you can." He took her hands from his face and placed a kiss in the center of each palm.

"Will you look for me, too?" She watched his lips.

"As soon as I can. If I get that lucky, I'll look for you until my heart stops beating. Because you're all I think about." He looked so sincere.

The waves pounded the beach now, and night had completely taken over the dusk, making everything seem urgent, ominous. Later she would perseverate on each word he'd said, and the comment about his heart stopping would cause her to fret, but in this moment it was tremendous and romantic and desperate.

She was forward with him in her imagination, and a four-poster bed appeared in her peripheral vision. The thin, transparent canopy was instantly torn and shredded by the wind.

"Come with me." She turned in his arms and pointed to the bed she'd imagined for them right there on the beach.

He growled in her ear, and she closed her eyes for a moment, relishing the corresponding shiver that hurried over her skin. Fallen led him then, pulling on his hand and lifting her soaking dress so she could get there sooner.

The cut of her gown was demure, and she was buttoned to the throat. In her head she changed it into a strapless black dress now—for him, for both of them.

There were dim, flickering streetlights on the boardwalk behind them, which cast a golden glow over their makeshift bedroom.

As soon as her shoulders were exposed, Thomas skimmed them with his fingertips. "Soft."

Fallen threaded her fingers through his hair, loving the messy, damp curls. She tried to memorize the lust that painted resolve in his eyes.

"For you." She wanted to give him comfort, passion, strength for wherever he was that made him sad. She tilted her head back, inviting him, daring him to take more from her.

He picked her up and laid her on the bed, tossing her a bit to get her to the center.

A warm, misty rain began to fall, but Thomas ignored it as he pulled his shirt off, buttons popping, and incited a giggle from Fallen. He tossed the wet mess on the sand and smiled at her laughter as he crawled onto the bed.

"I don't even know where to start. I want all of you." He ghosted her body with his hands.

Her giggle ended as he looked her over. She shrugged. "Wherever. For you."

He slipped an arm under her lower back, pulled her up a little, and chose her neck. He kissed and licked, going lower and lower until he teased the edge of the fabric that covered her breasts.

"Can I?" He paused to ask.

"Please," she breathed. He set her back on the bed, his knees on either side of her hips, and gently revealed her breasts. She curled her shoulders at this first sensual reveal, hoping he would be pleased enough to touch.

"May I?" he asked again.

Fallen picked his big hand up and placed it in the center of her chest, against her heart, which she knew was beating like crazy. "You already own this."

Then she took his other hand and placed it on her breast. "So these are yours, too."

"Thank you."

Such a gentleman. And then he enjoyed. Instead of a rush, he seemed intent on discovering. He wanted to learn what she liked, what brought her pleasure.

His lips around her nipple seemed to cause a rumble of thunder in the distance.

"Dramatic." He gave her a smile and then continued.

She needed more of him and pushed on his shoulders until he got the hint and rolled over on his back.

Fallen straddled him now and lifted her hair high. "Can you get my zipper for me?"

Thomas bit his bottom lip. "I'd be honored."

She smiled at him while he found the tab and slowly dragged it down.

Fallen scrambled to her feet to shimmy out of her dress, and the thunder rolled again in the distance. She stood on one foot to toss her long dress next to his shirt on the sand.

"Just stay that way for a minute." He propped himself on his elbows.

So Fallen compiled, waiting as he studied her. Instead of shame, she felt pride. So different than with Mr. Orbit. She pushed the thoughts of Orbit out of her head.

All she had on was a simple pair of white panties. She almost wished she'd dreamed of something more elaborate, but then he began commenting as his eyes traveled her.

"Your legs, that curve right there…" He surveyed her hips. "It's impossibly lovely. And the white, the contrast? It's one of the world's greatest treasures."

She felt a blush creeping up on her and went to cover her chest.

"No. Don't. Please. Prettier than any flower. Like this. And that look in your eyes? Pleased with me? How did I win this prize? My imagination isn't this good."

He held his hand up for her to grasp, and she took it. The mist had beaded up on his chest.

"I've said that to myself about you a lot since we met." She decided to taste the drops on him, licking her way from one to another.

Three claps of thunder came together, quickly.

His hands were all over her when she kissed her way back up, feeling the curves he had complimented earlier. Fallen sighed and lay on top of him. Skin to skin. She could feel the rain on her bare back now, a little harder, but still warm. The crashing waves had grown louder.

He flipped her again, hovering over her.

"I think you're wearing too many pairs of pants." She pointed at his legs.

He gave her a bemused look. "I'm only wearing one."

"Way too many." She snapped her fingers and was rewarded with his deep laughter.

Thomas slipped off his tuxedo pants and climbed back into the bed in his boxers.

All teasing faded to seriousness as their skin touched anew. He gazed down at her and then kissed her, this time adding the tip of his tongue.

Lightning flashed as she responded, wrapping her legs around him.

"I want you, dream girl."

"Take," she offered.

His fingertips glided over her, and she let herself feel the ecstasy he was intent on delivering. She turned her head to gasp some extra oxygen and noted that the waves were now lapping at the edge of the bed. Then one crested over the footboard.

More lightning. She dragged her fingernails down Thomas' strong back, which was slick from the rain. He put his hand between her legs, and she groaned.

The smile that spread across his face looked like home to her heart. Two dimples, full white teeth, and sparkling eyes.

It wasn't until she felt the waves at her shoulders, with the sheets sticking to her left arm, that she looked past him to the ocean beyond.

"Thomas?" She felt her eyes go wide as she realized the waves they'd been playing with were now serious, 8-foot nightmares.

He looked up and reacted before she could even formulate a plan. She was over his shoulder in a fireman's carry, which was a little painful and disorienting. She covered her face as he kicked up sand. Soon they bounced up the stairs to the boardwalk, where he set her down, checking her briefly to make sure she was okay.

Fallen nodded before hugging him around his bare middle.

Together they looked out at the tumultuous sea. The bed they'd been lying in rose like a boat, one, then two waves working together to crash it against the sand. It began to break apart, the last bit of canopy clinging to one post like a flag of surrender.

"Are you making it like this?" She looked at Thomas and found his jaw tight as he shook his head.

"You're not either?" He seemed to be calculating as they stood topless on the boardwalk. He hugged her closer.

"Not on purpose. You were making me feel things though." She turned to put her now-chilly breasts against his warm chest.

He glanced down and cupped her, thumbing over her nipples. "We should go somewhere else."

"I know. But I'm worried our time will end. It's lasted so long."

He let go of her breasts and leaned down to get two handfuls of her ass, pulling her up so they were face to face. She kissed him repeatedly.

"We should go somewhere with shelter. I don't want the ocean to take you from me." He turned and nodded at the old building next to the boardwalk. It was on risers, so the water would flow underneath it, if it got that far. And they wouldn't have to change locations.

But Fallen felt her eyelids getting heavier, which made her want to cry.

Thomas shifted her around and picked her up, piggyback style. She glanced over his shoulder and was very pleased with the sight of his arousal.

She leaned forward and whispered her praise in his ear. He moved faster.

At the building, he set her in front of him so she could walk up the stairs on her own, his hands on her butt until they got to the front door. When they turned to survey the view, the waves had started to reach the boardwalk.

"Let's go inside." He opened the door and looked around before waving her in.

The room was sparse, but it had a bed. Thomas closed the door behind her and frowned.

"What?" She hopped up on the bed and flopped over dramatically.

"I'm feeling sleepy," he confessed. He crossed to her quickly, crawled up beside her, and sucked on her breast like he was trying to get to everything she had to offer before they woke up.

"Me too. Tell me something about you... What's your last name?"

His hand slipped between her legs again, and she forgot what she'd asked.

He moved lower, kissing her ribs and then her stomach before laying his head there. "I'm going to miss you so much."

"Don't miss me. Stay." She put her hands in his hair.

"If I could, I would be the happiest man. Mr. Thomas Happy McHugh."

The white noise started again, and he crawled back up. Once again, they held each other's ears, nose to nose.

Through heavy blinks, she tried to talk. The noise had seemed to invade her mouth too.

She formed the words carefully, hoping he could at least see them on her lips: "Stay alive. For me."

And then, with his hands over her ears, she lost consciousness.

When she opened her eyes, Fallen still had her hands where Thomas' ears had been just moments ago.

"No!" She sat up as lightning flashed again.

She was briefly blinded; the hotel room was so dark. Then a

man clearing his throat scared the crap out of her. She screamed.

The light in the corner flicked on, and for a moment Fallen froze as she recognized Mr. Orbit. The realization that he'd been taking pictures of her while she slept made her want to vomit.

"That was some dream you had there, Fallen." He closed what seemed to be a pocket watch and put his phone in his pocket before clapping slowly. "And this is how you treat my parents' memorial hotel room?"

Fallen glanced down and was thrilled to see she was still fully dressed in her uniform. At least there was that.

She scooted off the bed and straightened the comforter. "I'm sorry, sir. I was all done with the rooms and…what time is it?" She had a moment of panic, thinking of Fenn. God, she was as unreliable as Nora. She needed to text him as soon as she could.

Mr. Orbit checked his expensive watch. "Midnight. I thought you might be here until morning."

He folded his arms while she rushed around to gather her cleaning supplies.

"Wait—how'd you get in here?" Fallen asked, glancing over to where she'd bolted the door.

"How'd I get in here? Into a hotel room I own in the building I own? I have my ways; let's just leave it at that. Gather your things. I'll drive you home. Unless you'd like to stay?"

"Here?" She pointed to the bed she'd just been on.

"No. Not here. That would be disrespectful. There's space in my room though." He gave her a smile that said she might be the lady to make his coffee in the morning.

She shivered at the thought of his king-sized bed. No doubt he had king-sized plans. "I can walk. Thank you, though. Sorry about falling asleep." She wheeled her cart out of 514.

He was close on her heels. "No problem. Like you said the

first time, at least there were no guests involved. That would be awkward."

"I bet," she responded, but her mind stayed wrapped up in itself. She had Thomas' last name. She needed not to lose it. He'd slipped it in with a joke, not even really aware he'd been telling her, it seemed.

Though her return to reality had found her again in an unpleasant situation with Mr. Orbit, all she could think of was the possibility in that nugget of information. Maybe she could find Thomas tomorrow. Or later today, technically. The day was young!

Mr. Orbit had continued following her closely. And talking. She had been ignoring him.

"...so you can take the day off Saturday, and I'll pick you up around seven?" He held open the supply closet for her.

She pushed the car in. What was he talking about? Oh. That's right. The charity ball. "Um...I really think the fanciest thing I own is this." Fallen motioned to her uniform.

She thought about the gorgeous satin gown she'd worn with Thomas. And how careless she'd been with it in her dream. Getting it wet...that had been amazing. She jerked herself back to the present.

"That's settled, then. I'll come a little early with a dress, and you can finish up getting ready while I'm there." Mr. Orbit smiled. He had his hand in his pocket.

She nodded silently. Agreeing was just easier. But she still insisted on walking home. It was freezing and dark, but she'd rather that than give him the opportunity to get her to do something else she didn't want to do.

Fallen wrapped up and started home, texting Fenn that she was on the way. The streets were desolate. After she'd been walking for about ten minutes, she heard a motor's purr in the distance. It crept closer until the vehicle was rolling along next to her. A furtive glance to her left told her all she needed to know. It was Orbit's flashy Jaguar. She gave him a little wave and continued on.

He doggedly followed her all the way to her street before he gave a little honk and roared off.

Fenn met her at the door. She felt awful. The concern etched on his face reminded her of her own when she was worried about Nora.

"I'm so sorry to be late, but what are you up for? You have school today." Fallen walked in and hung up her jacket as her brother locked the door behind her.

"I was worried about you. Was that your boss?" He motioned out the window at the now empty street.

"Yeah. I must be really tired. He found me asleep in one of the rooms. He's not my favorite person, but he made sure I got home." She offered her brother a hug, which he took.

"I've got great news," he countered.

She now realized Fenn was basically humming with poorly contained excitement.

"What's that?" She kicked off her horrible sneakers and headed into the kitchen.

"Well, the coach had great news for me."

"What was it?"

"So, I guess someone has been watching me work out with the team and decided they wanted to sponsor me. Full-on anonymous donor, like, big league stuff. The coaches were impressed."

Fenn's grin was the most infectious thing, but still Fallen had to force hers to stay in place. She turned and reached into the cabinet for a water glass so she had a second to rearrange her face into joy instead of worry.

After setting her glass on the counter, she gave him another hug, patting his huge shoulders as well. "You must be thrilled."

She smiled at him as she returned to her glass and began filling it up from the tap.

Orbit.

"So that's a relief? Right?" Fenn waited for the response she had to manufacture.

"Absolutely. Congrats! It's a huge help, because I want you to be able to do everything you'd like. You have to remember to keep your grades up, too, though."

"I will. Now that you're home and safe, I can stop freaking out and let this news sink in, you know?" Fenn drummed his fingers on the counter while wiggling his eyebrows.

"Yeah, well, let it sink into your dreams, 'cause school starts in, like, six hours." She held up her water glass in an impromptu toast. "To Fenn, the best, most talented baby brother in the world. I love you."

"Love you too, sis." He wrapped an arm around Fallen and pretended to give her a noogie. "Even if you *are* short."

He tromped out of the kitchen and up the stairs.

She set down her glass and watched the little ripples of water inside, thinking of the waves earlier with Thomas.

Thomas McHugh. Maybe she could find him now—and he could help somehow. Otherwise Mr. Orbit was going to get a lot of what he wanted out of her because of the happiness her brother deserved.

9

FOUR MILLION

Fallen sighed. The first Saturday she'd had off since she started at the hotel would be spent, at least in part, with her creepy boss's boss's boss. He was bringing her a dress and expected God knows what from her. But that was later. Later *today*, but still later.

Now, after having toast for breakfast and seeing Fenn off to do homework with a friend—a friend who was a girl!—she had some time just for her. She would spend it cyber-stalking Thomas.

Thomas *McHugh*.

She said his full name about a hundred times as she puttered around the house, getting her chores done before heading out to the library.

Having his last name was sure to be a help, right? And she'd guessed his age, maybe 26? Either way, she had a better starting point than she'd had before. She put her jacket on, locked the door behind her, and almost skipped her way to the public library.

The bank of computers was crowded when she rounded the

corner, but she was able to snag one with a wonky mouse. Her hands shook as she punched in her library number.

She went to the search engine and typed in his name. Fallen held her breath.

Four million results in .06 seconds.

The first images that filed on to the screen were dignified older gentlemen. No one looked even remotely like her Thomas.

"It's fine. I just have to narrow the search." She tented her fingers and touched them to her nose. She typed in *New York* because that's where she hoped he still was somewhere. It'd be a whole lot easier to find him if he was close to White Plains. Mr. Lad Orbit was certainly in her atmosphere.

Half a million. This was better, but still daunting. The last of the empty computers were now in use. Now they would start enforcing the thirty-minute time allotment.

She thought about more of the information she'd learned. Maybe she needed to add his brothers' names too. She popped them in.

100,000.

Her stomach dropped as she clicked through the images. Not a single one was familiar—older men, some pictures of women. She clicked through some of the articles and listings. The information was useless.

Fallen meticulously checked each page, looking for a trace of Facebook or LinkedIn. Nothing.

On a lark, she typed Lad Orbit into the search bar in a new tab. His image was everywhere. Apparently his family had run hotels since the beginning of time, or close to it. He was divorced. No children. So he actually was single right now, like he'd said (a small comfort), according to a blog that kept tabs on millionaire bachelors.

Fallen closed his tab; she knew all she really cared to about Mr. Orbit already. She needed to use her time wisely.

She scrolled down to a page ten deep from her original Thomas McHugh search page, feeling her heart start to pound as a lady came to stand behind her chair. Soon she would have to log off and give up her space. But listed on an obscure site, she now saw something hopeful.

Tom McHugh, 31, had purchased a property right here in White Plains. She clicked on the link, though the lady behind her began clearing her throat. She jotted down the address on a piece of scrap paper with a tiny pencil from the jar between the computers.

She copy-and-pasted the information into Google maps and memorized her way there. It was just two blocks out of her way on the way home.

She logged off and had to ask the woman behind her to back up so she could scoot her chair away from the keyboard. Normally Fallen might feel a little guilty for overextending her computer time, but today she was too busy flying.

Her feet flew, and her hopes went even higher—soaring. Thomas. Just blocks from her home. It made sense. They had such a deep connection; of course he would be near her.

And he was new in town, which totally explained why they hadn't seen each other out and about. Thomas. Today. Now.

She wanted to go home and dress up, put some makeup on, find a present to give him—but she didn't have time.

Fallen walked at top speed to his neighborhood. It would be perfect—they would see each other, and there would be no impending doom ruining their time together. They could be here, together, awake and forever. God, she was in love with him. She knew it, and just as she arrived at her heart's conclusion, she saw the little blue house in the midst of several home improvement projects. A small plank had been balanced to walk up to the closed front door where the steps were missing.

Fallen bit her lip and hazarded the climb, keeping the doorbell in her sights. Would he be home? She was crestfallen when she realized he might be out and about on a Saturday.

She turned and tried to see the driveway from the middle of the perilous plank, to gauge whether he was home, when she lost her balance.

Strong arms caught her as she shouted with the surprise of it. She looked up at him, tall, capable.

"Thomas."

He was silhouetted in the sun, but she heard him say her name, and that was all that mattered. Her heart soared.

It was awkward getting her footing, and she blinked once, twice, and then a third time to get her eyes to focus with the noonday sun as his backdrop. When they cleared, her heart sank.

It wasn't her guy.

"Thomas?" she asked.

"Friends call me Tom," he said. "What can I do you for?" He nodded once she was squarely on her own two feet.

"What did you say when you caught me?"

"I said, 'Watch out, you're fallin'.'" He scratched his shoulder. "I have that plank off balance a bit. Are you here to sell something?"

He was older than her Thomas—blondish hair with gray at the sides.

"I'm looking for Thomas McHugh. And I really need to see him." She shaded her eyes with her hand and squinted around him.

"Well, I'm the only Tom McHugh I know, but if you need something, I'm here to help." He stuffed his hands in his pockets. He seemed like a nice guy. Tom had cornflower blue eyes with crow's feet that crinkled as he smiled.

"I'm sorry I disturbed you." She backed away, reeling at the cruelty of a Thomas McHugh who wasn't her heart's desire.

"Well, that's okay. You should drop by when the reno's done." He pointed at the front of his little blue house.

"Good luck." Fallen turned and walked as quickly away from the imposter as she could.

She wanted to fall into a pile of sobs and stomping, but she couldn't be that girl in public. Tears slipped from the corners of her eyes as she walked, the wind painting them up like winged liner at the corners.

She'd wanted it to be him so badly. Believed it would be him. And now that it wasn't, reality just sucked a lot.

Except for Fenn, she reminded herself after a moment. He was her family, and that was important. Her brother was important.

She made it to her house and opened the door. After discarding her cold-weather clothes, she wound her scarf back into the basket by the front door where she kept it.

The depression of it all was a weight. She didn't realize how high her hopes had risen in such a small window of time. It was a long crash down. After trudging upstairs, she lay facedown on her bed. Then she stared at her wall. After running through the whole scenario with fake Thomas again, scouring for any possible meaning in any of it, she closed her eyes.

Hours later, she woke to find herself covered with the afghan from downstairs. Before she could even work out who had treated her so sweetly, she sat up, her hand hitting a crinkly note by her head.

F Didn't want to wake you. Spending the night at Bill's -F

At least her brother wouldn't have to see her get dressed for Orbit. She didn't want to start crying again and instead went to the bathroom to run a brush punishingly through her long hair.

She'd wanted to find Thomas, kiss the living hell out of him, and drag him to her house. Then when Orbit drove up they'd put on an endless game of tonsil hockey right in front of him. Instead she put on eyeliner and a ton of red lipstick to discourage kissing.

She was alone in her awake world. On her own. Getting in too deep with her boss and his freaky fetish issues.

She wrapped her hair into a bun on top of her head, remembering that Orbit liked it down, and cemented it in place with hairspray and a ton of bobby pins.

The doorbell sounded.

Fallen stomped in place a little, daring herself to ignore him. She had a job she could do. She didn't need to be this guy's plaything. Shame tortured her as she thought of the pictures on his phone.

It was too much. He was too much. It was time to quit. She looked at herself in the mirror and felt the day's anger and frustration surge through her. Invigorated, she went downstairs to confront Orbit. She didn't need Thomas to fight this battle for her. She would just tell him outright that what he was doing was sexual harassment, and if he withdrew his financial sponsorship of Fenn, well, she would…sue.

That sounded good.

Fallen pushed her shoulders back and opened her door.

Orbit looked expensive in a black-on-black suit and tie. Even his watch was black, not a hint of color to it. All the darkness really made his eyes pop. He looked younger than usual.

He held a bouquet of red flowers and a garment bag.

"Why, Fallen, I prefer your hair down." His smile slipped a bit.

"I know." She waved him inside. After she closed the door, she leaned against it, preparing to make her speech.

"Where's your brother," he asked suddenly. "I was hoping to get to meet him."

Fallen felt her head shaking a vehement *no*. "He's at a friend's," she said.

"Too bad. Perhaps he'll be around later when we return. Or even in the morning…" he added slyly.

"No!" Fallen worked to keep her voice even. She wanted Orbit's sleaze nowhere near her brother. "He's spending the night. Won't be back—" She stopped herself abruptly and took a deep breath. "Listen, I'll keep this brief. You know I'm not interested in dating. And I'm not going to let you take any more pictures of me. This ends tonight."

Orbit's smile stayed plastered on, but his eyes squinted. "Is that all?"

She had to say the next bit, even though it made her the most nervous. "I'd like to remain at the hotel, doing my job, and have you continue to sponsor Fenn. Or else."

She didn't elaborate. Her tongue felt thick. Her words were demanding. She tried to think about telling Thomas what she'd done. He'd be proud of her, she hoped.

"Is that so?" Mr. Orbit set the flowers on the old coffee table and draped the dress over the back of the couch.

She hummed her acknowledgement and wrapped her hand around the doorknob, ready to show him out.

"Well, Ms. Billow, I'll have you know that I already have papers drawn up to sue you for blackmail. You stole my phone and had Desta take compromising photos of you, trying to create a smear campaign against the hotel owner. It really was a dishonest thing for you to do. I also have time-stamped still shots from the security cameras, showing us leaving a hotel room together after spending hours in it."

He had his phone out in a flash and readied the camera before moving in next to her. "Smile, or your brother will have drugs planted in his football locker—ending what could be a lucrative career."

Fallen looked at her feet. He'd done this before. He was good at it. She looked up and smiled.

Coming at this man the honest way wasn't going to work. For now, she would play his game. For now.

She turned to him and nodded. "Well, I hope the dress fits."

"Good girl, Fallen." His eyes sparkled.

She took the garment bag and hefted it over her shoulder.

"Do you mind if I put these in water?" He held up the flowers.

She responded like he was a normal human visiting her home and not an awful excuse for a bag of skin. "Please! I don't have a vase, but there's a large plastic cup that should work."

Fallen took the stairs two at a time and closed her door, twisting the lock on the knob. He was the worst. Her hands shook, and her knees felt like water. She tossed the dress bag on the bed and tried to will away the doom she felt.

When she unzipped the bag, she was stunned. She had to be wrong. Just a mistake, a trick of her mind—similar color, similar fabric. But no. As she removed the dress, she could see it was the exact black satin gown—pinched waist and high neck— she'd worn in her last dream with Thomas.

Fallen hugged it to her chest. It was amazing to hold it in the real world. It gave her strength after a day of hard hits.

She took off her jeans and T-shirt and unzipped the side of the elegant gown. Thomas had dreamed it up. It was what he'd wanted her to wear. The connection had to be real.

Maybe he would be at the ball tonight? How very Cinderella. Going to this event with Orbit made her feel more like a dirty Cinderella, but maybe it was all meant to be. She hated to get her hopes up again after finding the wrong Tom McHugh already, but just in case, she touched up her makeup. In the mirror above her old dresser, she smiled. She looked ready for Thomas.

A knock on her door startled her, reminding her that horrible Orbit was still a part of this scenario.

She opened the door, and his gaze softened.

"I was here to tell you we were running late, but you've stunned me. You're beautiful." He nodded like she was royalty.

"Thank you." She took the hand he offered and forced herself not to grimace.

Orbit walked them carefully down the stairs and took her keys from her as she pulled them out of her simple black purse.

"You know what? Let's not ruin your dress with an accessory. I'll hold your keys in my pocket. Anything else you need?" He held out his hand.

"I need a fistful of tampons." She almost laughed as he startled.

"No need to be crude." He was flustered.

She didn't actually need any, but it sure was fun to watch him squirm. She wanted him uncomfortable. She needed to plant seeds that would keep him as far from her as possible during their evening.

"I'm just honest, Mr. Orbit. Maybe I should bring my purse. Please lock the door, though." She opened it and waited for him to walk through. She yanked it closed, and he locked it. Then she took her key ring from him and tucked it in her bag. She wanted to be in control of as many things as possible. And she needed this place to be secure if she had to make a quick escape, maybe with Thomas...

Mr. Orbit trotted in front of her and held the passenger door open. She slid inside and buckled up as he went around to the driver's side.

Once they were on the highway, he turned down the light jazz music to give her some pointers. "Tonight's charity ball has an auction, and I'll ask you to keep your hands still during the bidding. Even if you adjust your cleavage, they can count it as a bid."

The dress was not at all revealing, so his reference to her cleavage was unnecessary.

"Noted." Fallen wondered if she could put him in deep debt by picking a wedgie. She didn't laugh out loud, but she couldn't stop the smile that spread across her lips.

"Ah, yes. Talk of big money usually gets the girls happy."

She looked at him as he reached over and patted her thigh. She reined in a shiver of revulsion.

He left his hand on her leg, massaging as if it was his right to do so.

"Don't get too close to my tampon string." He snapped his head in her direction. She made her eyes wide before semi-yelling, "POP! Goes the weasel."

"I'll remind you that your job tonight is to be pleasant." He gave her a chastising look and withdrew his hand.

Fallen decided her period was about to be a chronic, unmanaged problem from this moment forward.

Half an hour later, Mr. Orbit drove his expensive car into a gated entrance and got in line behind other flashy cars. He started mumbling about traffic patterns and the parking attendants' lack of foresight like a ten-minute wait was simply horrible.

Fallen couldn't stop scanning the faces of the employees. No way Thomas would be at a swanky place like this as a guest. She pictured him helping people. Laughing, drinking beer maybe. Not warning his date to sit on her hands.

When Mr. Orbit finally reached the gate, he handed over two tickets to be scanned.

The guard checked his ID and waved them through. Fallen got out when the valet opened her door, taking his offered hand to get out of the low-slung car.

"Have a wonderful evening, miss." The man gave her a genuine smile.

"Hands off. Wouldn't want you to use her up before I get a chance." Mr. Orbit forced a laugh.

Fallen let go of the valet's hand, murmuring her thanks to him. "Mr. Orbit, please don't—"

He didn't let her finish. She'd wanted to ask him not to treat her like a possession.

"Call me Lad, while we're here. At work you can call me Mr. Orbit." His lips continued moving a little after he spoke.

He grabbed her hand and pulled her along, passing their invitations to the man at the door. The sprawling mansion opened up to present an ethereal, gem-themed party.

If it could glitter or sparkle, it did. The dresses around her were mesmerizing, and Lad whispered in her ear as he guided her through the crowd. "Do act like you belong, Fallen."

At their table, well-known blue boxes sat on each seat. Fallen had to pick hers up to sit, and Lad pulled out her chair.

He removed the one from his seat as well, setting it on the table. Two men in tuxedoes stopped him before he could sit, and Lad came to life glad-handing with them. Fallen surveyed the room. So many tuxes reminded her of the time just a day ago she'd spent with Thomas. None of the men in this room could compare to the way he looked dressed up.

She rubbed the satin dress between her index finger and thumb. She had to believe there as a reason she was in this dress. Fate was trying to give her hints. As soon as she could, she would excuse herself and poke around to see if Thomas was among the staff.

She'd had no idea the ball would be huge. In her head she'd pictured dances from high school, which was, she guessed, a fairly sheltered view of an event, especially one in New York City. Lad eased out of his conversation and joined her.

"Didn't you open your favor?" He tapped his box.

"Am I supposed to?"

He gave her a condescending look that conveyed how

adorable she was in her ignorance. "Well, you could take a look. The theme for the evening is gems, so it might be a nice surprise."

He opened his own box and removed an all-black watch with a single diamond marking the 12.

"Nice enough." He shrugged. He already had on a fancy watch. "Give it to your brother." He stuffed it back where it came from and dropped it on the table.

Fallen nodded. They might be able to sell it and get ahead on their bills. She opened her box and saw a delicate tiara. She touched the glittering jewels embedded in it.

"It's all right." Lad shrugged again and was up out of his chair, socializing.

Fallen glanced at the other women at the table. None of them would make eye contact with her, but they were all wearing their tiaras. Maybe she needed to follow suit? She didn't want to be uncouth.

She stood, and the men at the table stood with her. She nodded at them, tucked her chair in, and picked up her purse and the tiara.

As she tried to move away, Lad latched on to her upper arm. "Where are you off to, girl?"

"Just wanted to put this on." She held up the jewelry she had every intention of selling tomorrow.

"Okay." He waved her away, not introducing her to the men he held court with.

A chill ran through her with the relief of having his hand removed from her skin. Fallen picked her way through the large gowns and past waitstaff with trays of champagne glasses. She looked carefully at the faces of those dressed to dissolve into the ambiance. No one had Thomas' height combined with this dark hair.

She found a marble bathroom with a gorgeous chandelier. The light made her skin glow as she gazed in the mirror. She was pleased with what she saw, knowing this was how Thomas had seen her—imagined her, whatever. She set the tiara in her hair, pushing the attached comb into her hair-sprayed locks. She was lucky she got it on straight the first time, because pulling it out would make her hair the kind of angry and disheveled only a shower could fix. And she wanted to look her best for Thomas—if she got to see him tonight.

Fallen used the paper towel in the fancy basket to dry the sink in front of her and had started to shine the faucet before she realized what she was doing. She was unconsciously cleaning.

A woman stepped up to the sink next to her and started applying her lipstick. "So, you're here with Lad?"

Fallen cut her gaze to the right to get a better look at the statuesque woman. She didn't have the mental fortitude for a catfight in this peach-and-brown marbled bathroom, so she just nodded.

"Well, I hope you're ready for all that entails." The woman was the kind of darkly handsome that sold cars without a test drive. Men most likely stumbled on their words in her presence.

"I'm not. Not at all." Fallen had no idea why she was honest, but the words fell out of her.

"Wait…" The woman grabbed her forearm. "Do you work for him?"

Fallen was wary, but she again answered truthfully. "Yes."

"Which hotel? Which floor?" Now the woman seemed less intimidating and more desperate, like she had information to share.

Fallen's interest was piqued. She allowed herself to be dragged to the empty handicapped stall. The dark wood doors reached floor to ceiling, creating a little, private room. There was no lock, so Fallen just closed the door.

"So?" The woman's dark eyes, expertly lined and highlighted, waited for her answer.

"Hotel Revel in White Plains. The fifth floor." Fallen waited to see what the woman would infer.

"Listen, I'm Lad's ex-wife," she said. "And I was a housekeeper in that hotel, too. That floor. You have to get out of there. And never fall asleep in 514. Do you hear me?"

"Fallen?"

Lad's voice made them both gasp; it was out of place in the ladies' room. His ex-wife put her finger to her lips. Fallen nodded. If they stayed quiet, he wouldn't be able to see their feet.

Then he began slamming each of the stall doors open. The fear on his ex-wife's face sparked Fallen into action. She pushed the taller woman to stand behind the door and reached over to flush the toilet.

She motioned for the ex-wife to stay put and pulled open the door before Lad could get to it.

As she stepped out of the stall, more women came into the bathroom. They started in on Lad immediately.

"Sir, this is the women's bathroom. Where's the bathroom attendant?"

"I'm sorry," Fallen said. "He came looking for me. I've been fainting lately, and they aren't exactly sure why. He's just overprotective." Then she turned to Lad. "Let me wash my hands, and I'll meet you right outside this door. I'm fine, not even dizzy. I just got a little lost on the way."

Fallen stepped over to the sink and said a silent prayer that Lad wouldn't go into the stall she'd just come out of. He glanced in that direction. She went through the movements of cleaning her hands while watching him from beneath her eyelashes in the mirror's reflection.

After a moment he patted her back and accepted her saving of his face. "Sure. Good girl. Glad you're okay. I'll be right outside."

Fallen hated the way he spoke to her, his words conveying

control, rather than affection. She dried her hands and didn't risk walking back to the ex-wife, though she was desperate to hear more of what she had to say.

Instead, she walked out the door and found Lad waiting for her, just as he'd promised.

10

NOT A NICE MAN

*L*ad led them back to their table. He was full of great ideas.

"Next time I'll escort you. I don't want you wandering around by yourself. These men are sharks with smiles, and they have plenty of alcohol in their drinks. They'll eat a little thing like you alive."

She tried to smile while using her trip across the gigantic room as a scoping-for-Thomas opportunity, as well as trying desperately to process her encounter with Mr. Orbit's ex-wife.

Luckily, by the time they sat, the auction had started, so he couldn't talk about her indiscretion of staying in the bathroom too long. Fallen sat still and returned to her thoughts. That the woman in the bathroom had known, that she had guessed what was going on, was incredible. Had he cheated on his wife with other housekeepers? Was 514 kept empty for his affairs? Is that why he was clingy?

She scooted herself to the far side of her chair, too paranoid to move it overtly. Being around terrible Mr. Orbit brought into sharp relief all the things she swooned over with Thomas. As she scanned the room again, a dreamy sigh escaping her lips, she spotted his ex-wife. They locked gazes, but Fallen looked away. She hoped the woman would realize she still had questions, but was trapped at the moment. Fallen would have to Google the crap out of him again and find out who his ex-wife was so she could get the rest of the picture.

Fallen was pleased to be allowed to eat the miniature entrée she was served during a break in the auction. Whatever it was, it was delicious, and she wished she could have seconds.

When the auction drew to a close, Mr. Orbit hadn't bid on anything. One of his suited friends soon approached the table and pointed this out.

"It's a fundraiser, you know," the man said.

Fallen couldn't tell whether he was kidding or not, but Orbit had a quick answer.

"I did all my bidding online in the silent auction," he explained. "Listen for my name in the results; I spent a fortune." He laughed a little too loud before telling Fallen to stay put.

As soon as he'd disappeared into the crowd, a man walked over. The band kicked in with a song, and he asked, "Miss? Can I have this dance?"

He looked nice enough, but Fallen wasn't entirely sure what the protocol was here. He couldn't be any worse than dancing with Mr. Orbit, she supposed, so she nodded and stood, accepting the man's arm as he led her to the dance floor.

He didn't make small talk, just committed to the dance movements. She was lucky he was a strong leader, because she certainly didn't have any clue how to make herself look normal.

She'd concentrated on not stepping on his toes when she realized there was something between their clasped hands. She looked at him and expressed her puzzlement with her eyebrows.

He leaned down to her. "Please take this. She wants you to get in touch. And she told me to warn you to be careful."

Fallen glanced over her shoulder, looking for Mr. Orbit.

Her dance partner seemed to sense that she was nervous. "I'm watching for him. Just read it and give it back to me. I'll dispose of it."

Fallen took the paper from their hands and kept up the pretense of dancing as she unfolded it.

> *Please, he's not a nice man. If you can get out, do it. If he already has you email me and I'll try and help.*

Fallen nodded, noted the email address printed in block letters at the bottom of the message, and put her hand back in his. Somehow he made the paper disappear with just a little movement of his fingers.

She'd memorized the email address, and judging from the fact that she was even at this ball, she resigned herself to the fact that *he* did indeed have her. Fallen started as her dance partner turned and graciously offered his spot to Mr. Orbit.

He hauled her close. "What did he say?"

"I...uh...nothing. He just wanted a dance. And I wasn't sure if I should say no, because you'd mentioned staying put, but then all the other ladies at the table were asked to dance, so I didn't want to stand out. So I said yes. You want me to fit in, and not stand out. That can get confusing." She gave him a stern look.

"Well, pardon me, then. I'm glad he got you warmed up for me." He put an extra swing in his hips that seemed designed to tell her he was in charge of the dance and had probably had professional lessons.

She let him wiggle around, dragging her along as she inspected the crowd. A tall man in the distance captured her attention. The height was right, the hair color, too. She held her breath as he turned to accept an empty glass. She exhaled as her hopeful head registered that the profile was all wrong.

"Looking for someone?"

Orbit's voice felt like acid on her patience.

"Just taking it in. I've never been somewhere so fancy."

He pulled her even closer so they were chest to chest.

"I can show you things you've never seen before, Fallen. I'm a powerful man. A man of means." He smiled at her.

Fallen wanted to snap back at him, give him a dig about his ex-wife thinking he wasn't a good man, but she felt the need to protect her. Their connection had been one woman trying to help another. Maybe she was wrong, but her gut told her the ex-wife was motivated by truth.

"I did a great job with your dress," he added after a moment. "Or rather, my stylist did, but I'll take the credit. Do you know how many women would kill to be in your place tonight? Chin up and smile like a good girl." He lifted his chin to show her how to do it.

"Yeah. I bet a bunch of these ladies wish they were wondering how to pay their bills while protecting their brother and fending off unwanted advances from their boss's boss's boss." She huffed at him.

And then shook her head. The ex-wife had warned her to be careful, but that response had not been.

"Really?" Lad's eyed sparked with anger. "We'll see about that. How about you protect your brother right here, right now? Kiss me, Fallen. And my ex-wife is here. Let's make her believe you love every second of it."

Now she'd wished she'd kept her mouth shut. His lips curled in a cruel smirk.

"There's got to be something else. I'm not ready for that." She felt less strong than when her tongue had taken off with her common sense seconds ago.

"When you were panting on the bed in room 514, you seemed like you were more than ready for a whole lot more than a kiss." He pursed his lips meanly.

He'd seen her reaction to Thomas' dream touches in reality, and that was mortifying.

"I'm sure you can be a little less of a cowering virgin with me here and now." Orbit puffed out his chest. Fallen tried to spin out of his arms, but he held tight. "Now, now. I gave you a task."

She looked everywhere, but she was out of options. She could make a scene and flail around, but then she was fired, and her brother was framed.

"You're not nice, Mr. Orbit." She met his lips with hers.

He held her hard so she had to continue the kiss far longer than she wanted to. When the length had gotten way outside of appropriate, she turned her head.

"Not bad. All in a good day's work, Fallen." He released her, grabbed her upper arm again, and headed toward their table. "Get your stuff; we're leaving."

She grabbed the two boxes and her purse and stutter-stepped to keep up with him. His neck was red, the veins bulging.

A waitress caught up to them and handed Fallen a sparkly gift sack. She stuffed the boxes inside and tossed in her purse as well.

When they were outside, Mr. Orbit held his valet ticket between his first finger and his middle finger like he was calling a cab. The valet scurried over and was very polite, but he didn't respond. Fallen watched him fearfully.

"Where are we going?" She hazarded the question while they were still in public, because once in his fancy car, she wasn't sure he would answer. Hell, she wasn't sure he would impart any information now.

"Your house is empty, according to what you told me earlier. We're going there to work on your manners, and your respect." He bit off his words, and Fallen recoiled. She looked around, but everyone else was either smoking a cigarette or waiting for the valet and seemed not to have heard—or cared—what he said.

She jerked her arm from his hand and hugged herself. It was cold, and she should have had a jacket. He turned to give her a harsh look.

"I'm cold," she snapped. The Jaguar came around, and he hopped in on his side while the valet held open the passenger door.

"Everything all right, miss?" He looked at her as Mr. Orbit began to complain to the other valet about how long it had taken him to retrieve the car.

"Thank you," she said, though she desperately wanted to say *no. No, this angry man is driving me to an empty house, and his ex-wife just warned me against him.* But she settled for *thank you*, because there was nothing to be done, and she appreciated that he would check on her.

The ride to her house was silent, save the occasional blinker clicking and the rev of the engine.

Fallen didn't wait for him to open her door after he pulled the car to a stop in her driveway. She was out and striding toward her front door, thinking about how she could get in and close the door on him, when he wrapped her in a bear hug, pulling her back against his chest.

"Not so fast. I told you we needed this kiss to happen a little more explicitly." He was deadly calm as she struggled. "That doesn't bother me at all."

Fallen stopped trying to get free and waited for him to let her go. His hands had clasped together right under her breasts, and he used his thumbs to graze the underside of them through the fabric of her dress. She decided right then she wasn't on board with putting out for him because he demanded it.

Let him do what he would—fire her, try to frame Fenn. She and her brother would make something make sense.

"We're going inside, and you're going to smile at me the whole time. Do you hear me?" he said.

The tone of his voice was a mixture of professor and

attacker. She was about to tell him he could stick his dick in his own asshole because she was so, so done when her mother—of all people—interrupted them.

"Well, look what the cat dragged in," Nora called, stepping out of the shadows on the front porch.

She didn't seem drunk, which felt a little like a miracle in itself, and her timing had Fallen grateful for her presence for the first time in God knew how many years.

Fallen felt Lad release his hold on her.

"Is this a new boyfriend?" Nora prattled. "Now that's what I'm talking about."

She waltzed up to Fallen and gave her an air kiss on each cheek like they never did.

"I'm Nora Billow, Fallen's mother. And you are?" She held out her hand.

Lad took her hand and nodded. "Hello, Nora. Funny, Fallen's never mentioned you."

Nora gave her daughter a thinly veiled sneer. "We have some differences."

Nora touched the fancy bag Fallen held. "Presents? So thoughtful of him. With this car and these outfits, I do hope you went somewhere exquisite."

Fallen held the bag out of Nora's reach. Her mother went on her tiptoes and lightly touched the tiara on her head. "Jewelry already? Well, this relationship is moving along."

Lad put his arm around Fallen, and she shrugged it off.

Nora's eyes flashed. "Please excuse my daughter's manners."

Fallen decided to make the most of her mother's appearance and turned to face her date. "This is where our night ends, Mr. Orbit."

He looked her up and down, clicking his tongue. "Very good then. I'll see you at work on Monday."

Nora did her best to be charming and hopeful as she wished him a safe ride home. Fallen was already on her way upstairs.

She'd tucked the watch and the tiara away in an old backpack when she heard the front door slam.

After closing her door and punching the knob lock, Fallen left her mother to face the fake wood from the hallway as she complained immediately that Fallen was ruining the chance of a lifetime.

The zipper got stuck as Fallen tried to take off her gown. It was the simplest thing, but it broke her. She turned and slid down her door as her mother pounded on the other side. She let herself just cry.

By the time she had gathered herself and changed into leggings and a T-shirt, Nora had moved downstairs to the kitchen. Fallen walked in and folded her arms, leaning against the counter.

"Need money, Nora?"

"Really? Can't I come into my own home? Say hello to my children?" Nora had a tall glass of milk and a cigarette.

Fallen did the math in her head. She decided that the money for a pack of cigarettes and the milk Nora was drinking could easily have bought Fenn two meals.

"You could. But it's 11 o'clock on Saturday night—not the usual time for a drop by. Also, I've asked you not to, and you never do anyway. Did Fritz kick you out? You want money. And I'm just exhausted. Tell me how much it takes to get you out of here."

Fallen meant it. This day had dashed her hopes more times than she could count. Her dignity had been compromised far too much, and she was pretty sure she'd just started a war with a millionaire.

Nora took another drag and a sip of milk after she'd exhaled. The combination turned Fallen's stomach.

"Fritz and I are fine. He went to visit family in Virginia. Well, if you haven't screwed up your relationship with good ol' Lad there, how much are we talking?"

Addiction was here now too. It usually waited until Nora's defenses were down to take the reins. It must be getting stronger. Bolder.

"Your daughter was being molested against her will in the driveway. But by all means, if we can get a full bottle of vodka into your hands, let's do that."

"Against your will? How is that even possible?" Nora scoffed. "You were on a date. You accepted jewelry. You must have wanted him a little." She walked to the sink and poured the rest of her glass of milk down the drain.

Fallen bit the insides of her cheeks and lifted her chin. She was all cried out for today. The idea that Nora believed being on a date equaled consent made her grateful she wasn't her mother anymore.

"You need to leave." Fallen pointed at the front door.

"How dare you? This is my home." Nora became indignant.

"Okay. You pay the mortgage, then, so I can stop wondering if Fenn and I are getting kicked out." She stepped closer to Nora, backing her up against the wall. "Do you know that people are scoping out this house because it's in foreclosure? They're sizing it up for auction. And then where will Fenn and I go?" She threw her hands in the air.

Nora looked away, pouting, defiant.

Finally, Fallen stepped back and tried reason, even though she knew Addiction didn't speak that language. "If I give you the money I earn, I can't keep Fenn fed. I can't keep him warm. Have enough motherhood left inside you to respect that doing those things is important. Please." Fallen stepped back. "'Cause having to say no to you hurts me on so many levels. I miss who you're supposed to be. I need who you were before you drank. Sleep here, if you have to—on the couch, please. And be gone before Fenn gets home in the morning."

Nora hung her head then, at least. Fallen checked the front door and made sure to take her purse upstairs. She returned with a threadbare blanket and pillow for her mother who had sprawled out on the couch.

"Here. Sit up a little." She tucked the pillow under Nora's head before spreading the blanket over her mother's thin form.

"You'll make a great mother someday, Fallen. Even if that Lad isn't the guy for you." Nora patted her hand.

Fallen nodded and left Nora in the living room. She trudged upstairs and curled up in her bed with her arms through her backpack and purse. Nora knew how to pick the lock on her bedroom door.

The next morning, Nora was gone. No note, no explanation, but Lad was no doubt bait for Addiction, so she'd likely be back. Being Sunday, Fallen had no access to a computer because the library was closed. She just had to be a normal person, not someone searching for dream guys on the internet—which sounded terrible in her head when she put it to herself like that.

Fenn was home before lunch, and Fallen had just finished cleaning. She was shocked how much she resented doing it at home now that it was her profession. Well, she'd never been crazy about it, but she'd had pride when the place looked nice. Now she was methodical with the cleaning, and it just felt like more hotel rooms.

Fenn complemented the work she'd done and immediately

began to pitch in. She didn't bring up the ball or their mother, preferring to see a relaxed look on his face. For dinner they had ziti, topped with a jar of sauce and a side of orange slices. Although they didn't fit as a composed meal, she figured vitamins were vitamins, and it was okay if dinner didn't make sense as long as it accomplished her goal of getting some healthy stuff into Fenn.

Together they watched a singing competition on one of the three free channels they could get on the TV. They both loved listening to music, but neither could hold a note. Still, it was fun. Then Fallen asked about his homework, which sent him to his room for about an hour before he returned, holding a permission slip.

"Hey, can I get Mom to sign this? We're going to a mock jury demonstration at Poughkeepsie High School." He gave her a pen.

Fallen forged her mother's name, even adding the slight tremor the woman now had due to her years of drinking for believability's sake.

"I should have asked her to sign it this morning, but I forgot. I even had my backpack with me." Fenn took the paper and folded it along the line back and forth until he could rip it neatly by bracing it against the coffee table's edge.

"You saw Nora this morning?" Fallen wished her words hadn't sounded so accusatory.

Fenn cleared his throat. "Yeah. Sorry about that. She stopped by Bill's house." He fidgeted.

"And she said?"

"She asked who my sponsor was for my football gear and stuff." He folded the paper again and tucked it in the pocket of his jeans. She noted the action so she would be sure to check his pocket before doing the laundry.

"How'd she find out about that, I wonder? Did you tell her?" Fallen asked.

"No. I guess she saw it in the paper. Coach put it in there and had me write a thank-you letter. So they would see it." Fenn smiled.

"Oh, that's great to say thanks," she agreed.

"She also said she thinks she knows who it is—the sponsor." Fenn cracked his knuckles.

And then Fallen knew. Nora had put the rich man from last night together with the sponsorship. Her mother was crafty. Well, Addiction was.

"Hmm…" she said absently.

"Your new boyfriend?" Fenn rocked from his toes to his heels.

"Not my boyfriend. Just my boss from work. He likes to make it look like he cares about the employees." She stood, reluctant to put an end to the weekend and dreading seeing Mr. Orbit again.

"Everything all right?" Fenn squinted at her.

"Yeah. It's fine. No worries." She patted his shoulder on her way past him to her bedroom.

"Well, if he needs a beat down, remember you can always let me know. You've got a football player on your side now." Fenn locked the front door before loping up the stairs behind her.

"I know. It feels amazing to have you and your team at my beck and call."

Fenn flicked the lights off after they reached the top. "You know, Mom looked really good this morning."

Fallen turned to face her brother. "She wasn't drunk, which is nice." She searched his face. Too late. The hope had returned. He wanted a recovery for Nora so badly. She had to caution him, and that hurt.

"It's got to be more than a few days sober for me to be comfortable with her living here again."

"She slept here last night. That's something. You let her in, right? She's our mom. I mean, can we leave her on the streets? I don't think it's working out with that guy she was seeing." Fenn's eyes pleaded with her.

Nora had put him up to asking. Fallen would have bet her good bra on it. She wanted to say, *Well, she'd have you in the streets already if Addiction had driven you both on the deluxe crash course it had set when I had to come back from college.* But that would just be hurtful, and it wouldn't change anything. She didn't want to fight with him.

"How about we think about it. If she's doing good, let's not mess with that process. We'll see how far she can get, and if it continues to go well, we'll talk to her about coming back." Fallen didn't love the idea, but if Nora was really starting on a road to recovery, Fallen had to be a soft landing place, didn't she? But Nora hadn't seemed particularly serious about making a change last night. Sober or not, she'd just needed someplace to be.

"Sounds great. Goodnight, sis."

She nodded before closing herself into her room. On her next day off, she would go to the pawn shop and see what she could get for the party favors from the charity ball.

Tomorrow was another day closer to Thursday.

11

HONEYMOON IS OVER

Fallen got to work on Monday just in time to see Mr. Orbit discussing something furiously with Melanny. She hung up her coat and punched in her employee code to register as present for the day. She was just a few minutes late, having snuck into the business center in the hotel to email Orbit's ex-wife. The short message had basically said *tell me more*.

Now she settled in for the meeting and bit her bottom lip when Mr. Orbit pinned her with a glare.

"Ms. Billow? Hair up is policy." He pointed to her head.

"O...kay?" She dug in her purse and found a hair tie. He crossed his arms and watched as she gathered her hair into a ponytail for the first time in weeks.

The housekeepers from 8 and 9 abruptly needed to suppress the giggles.

When the meeting was over, Fallen left with the rest of the crew to get her cart.

"Honeymoon's over now, I guess." 9 elbowed Fallen as she pushed past.

Fallen waited until everyone else was out of the supply closet before getting her cart. She was relieved to find all her tools and chemicals still in place. As she rolled out, Mr. Orbit and Melanny waited for her. Fallen slowed her cart to give them her attention.

"Mr. Orbit wanted me to tell you that you'll need to work on Sunday, but you'll have Thursday off this week."

Her stomach dropped. *Not Thursday*. Her fear and disappointment produced a reply before her common sense could kick in. "Why?"

Mr. Orbit stepped forward. "I requested it. You'll be busy on Thursday. All day."

She nodded and looked at her cart's wheels.

Melanny was not thrilled. "And I get to work on Thursday to do your floor. I haven't had to clean in a room in about 20 years." She glared at both of them before stomping away.

Fallen felt a headache coming on. "What do you think I have to do all day Thursday?"

Mr. Orbit came close enough that she could smell his cologne. "You need some time away to think about what you've done. And how you can make it up to me. Also, today Desta's making my bed."

That got a rise out of Fallen. "You're adding to her work load? I'll do it."

"You like posing for our pictures, don't you?" He nodded with his words like he knew the answer already.

"Desta's a nice woman, and I don't want her involved in any of that."

"Desta can handle herself just fine. You should take notes. Tomorrow you can make the bed. But not today." He walked away like he'd broken her favorite toy and now reveled in it.

She understood now why it had been so easy for her to find this job when the market was tight and competition was fierce. Orbit was an unpredictable tyrant. No one in their right mind would choose to work here.

While cleaning, Fallen told herself repeatedly that Thursday would be okay. She would just have the date with Thomas in her own bedroom—which honestly, was safer anyway. By the time she got to room 514, she'd convinced herself this was a fortuitous turn of events. She hadn't had to bend over for Mr. Orbit today, and she'd get to spend a limitless amount of time with her dream guy on Thursday.

She did check in with Desta in the supply closet on her way out.

"I'm sorry you had to make Mr. Orbit's bed today." She touched the older woman's elbow to get her attention.

Desta coughed at the startle and had to finish her bout of hacking before she could respond. "You gotta snap your fingers or something. Damn near killed me to death right there."

Fallen squelched a giggle. "Sorry again. I can't get it right today. I didn't want you to have extra work."

"Don't you worry yourself over it. He and I had to catch up anyway." Desta topped off her cleaner bottle from the larger one before passing it to Fallen.

Fallen didn't say anything more. They needed to catch up? She felt a little betrayed, though she had no right to. She'd only known Desta a few months, and perhaps she'd misjudged her. Could she possibly be close to Mr. Orbit?

The maids for 8 and 9 went past and dumped their carts. Desta went through and added the cleaner she'd taken back from Fallen to the women's spray bottles and swapped out their rags for cleaner ones.

"Are you friends with those two?" Now Fallen was certain she didn't have a clue which way was up.

Desta looked around and crossed to the door of the supply closet to close it gently. Then she came close to Fallen, who could hear the woman's labored breathing

"Here, in this place? Keep your friends close and make your

enemies your friends, too. You can never have too many people to watch your back. Even if they are unkind, always be nice."

Fallen sighed. That wasn't what she wanted to hear. Nor could she believe it. Those two were evil, and Orbit was a pervert.

"I see in your eyes that you think you know more than me." Desta shrugged. "And you can be that way for sure. But take it from an old lady, every second you get to be with true love is worth all the shit you take elsewhere."

"True love?"

Desta gave her a soft smile. "514."

And with that, the supply door opened and a pair of maintenance guys rambled in, drying Fallen's questions in her throat. Mr. Orbit poked his head in next, waving for Desta to join him in the hallway.

Fallen messed around with her cart for more time than it required. Then she freshened up Desta's cart too. But she really was just stalling and hoping Desta would come back

When she could drag her feet no longer, Fallen got ready to go home. On the walk, she had to wait for Orbit's car to drive in front of her at a crossroads. She thought he would get out and give her hell, but he didn't.

Fallen tried to calm her racing heart. She would get to talk to Desta more tomorrow. She could wait for her at the end of the day, if that's what it took. The old woman knew something. The ex-wife knew something. It all had something to do with room 514. Excitement bubbled up in her. If all these people knew about the room, surely her feeling that Thomas was not just imaginary was correct.

On Tuesday, when Fallen showed up for work—this time with her hair tied up because who knew what the hell Mr. Orbit wanted—Desta was nowhere to be found. Fallen had checked her email at the business center again with nothing in her inbox to show for her effort.

Every person she knew who might be a lead on the secrets of room 514 was inaccessible. And Mr. Orbit's hotel room had a Do Not Disturb sign on it when she went up to make his bed after the morning meeting. Everyone pitched in and took a room on Desta's floor, though no one seemed to know where she was.

Wednesday was the same: no Desta, no email, and no Orbit. Fallen saved 514 for last, like always, and she lingered, changing the sheets and dusting the light bulbs to add to her time spent in the room.

It panicked her to think the room might be the key to the dreams. She hoped her bedroom would work as well, that it was her mind that transported her to the dream. Otherwise it would be a whole other week of waiting.

In the supply closet, she topped off 8 and 9's cleaners and replaced their rags. Desta's unused cart was still stocked, so she had nothing to do there.

Fallen asked Melanny about a way to contact Desta, but the woman just shook her head. She didn't try to bother to be kind as she added, "Can't share employee records.

With no other options, Fallen left the hotel.

That night, she waited up until midnight to see if she could pop into the dream the instant it turned into Thursday. Fenn had gone to sleep long ago at 10, exhausted from practice. When the clock flipped over to 12:00, she closed her eyes.

She woke at 6 am and realized she had been dreaming of Thomas, but the regular weird, out-of-context kind of dreaming. Thomas had been more of a blob. And the hamster that had been her kindergarten's pet was there, too. Nora had been in and out as well.

But, of course, the hyper-real, gorgeous, inside-a-painting type dream she was hungry for with Thomas had never happened in the early hours of Thursday before. She tried again to reassure herself. They had the whole day ahead of her.

Yet it had been a week since she'd felt his arms around her. Her desperation humbled her as got out of bed. And it choked her up when she realized she finally had something in common with her mother—the feeling of waking up in need of another hit more than anything else.

She went downstairs for Fenn and made him eggs and toast before he was picked up for school by an older teammate with a car.

The frustration Fallen had woken with continued throughout her day. She tried falling asleep everywhere. She went for a few laps around the block to tire herself out with no success.

She waited. She imagined. She brushed her hair out. Then she put on the black dress again. She wanted to greet Thomas in something other than her hotel uniform.

She waited. And waited. The clock was her punisher. She tried lying down again, arms crossed like they would be in her coffin someday, she assumed.

The afternoon dragged on. Fenn was home after practice and had a paper to work on that he'd apparently left to the last minute. He closed his door and played music while Fallen continued waiting.

But she couldn't get to Thomas. It was room 514. Of course it was. She'd known it the moment Orbit gave her Thursday off. Why else would he have done so? Because of him, she was missing being wrapped in Thomas' arms, and it was devastating.

Missing Thomas was what she did, but missing him on the day supposed to bring her joy was the worst.

And then it hit her—if she was missing him, he was missing her. He would have no idea why she wasn't there. That took the breath from her lungs.

Fallen stood. It was 10:38 pm. She'd spent the whole day waiting, and now she felt an urgency she couldn't contain. It came at her in a tremendous rush. She had to see him.

Fallen tossed on a denim jacket and black flats with the dress and ran. She took time to lock the door so Fenn would be safe and hopefully not notice she was gone. She went as fast as she could to the hotel, holding up her long skirt the whole time. When she arrived at the back door, she was thrilled to see it had been propped open by a smoker. The supply closet was also open for the night crew, so she slipped in, finding it empty. She went to her cart and lifted her master key, sneaking back out once she had it clutched in her hand.

Fallen rushed down the hallway and took the stairs up to the fifth floor. She didn't have her watch on, so she wasn't sure how much time her trip here had taken. After opening the door to 514 and closing it behind her, she thought to pull the antique desk over to the door, bracing it in such a way that she hoped would ensure complete privacy.

If there were a fire, she'd be a goner if she was still asleep. But she could already feel a blessed weight against her eyelids. She crawled onto the bed, the black silk of her dress spreading out to cover the white bedspread.

She closed her eyes and felt the rush of being transported. She opened them as quickly as she could and sat up in the woods, right where she'd first met Thomas. Sure enough, the campfire ring was still in place, though the embers were black and cold.

She sat on one of the logs and felt dejection. She was too late. This wasn't going to work. Orbit had won. He had taken the night with Thomas away from her. It was such exquisite pain. She wondered if he knew what he was doing by denying her this pleasure.

The sun was coming up in the dream world. Dew glistened on the plants. Birds sang to welcome the sun and dispel the night. Fallen touched the tips of her shoes together and tucked her hair behind her ears.

Her skin needed his. The warmth from holding him was like nothing else.

And then she heard it—or she imagined it: a soft echo of her name.

Fallen stood and spun, searching for him. Her name was getting louder.

"Here! I'm here! Thomas?"

And then he came crashing through the woods at a breakneck pace. She jumped up and down, waving her arms.

He almost looked like he was running from something. Running for his life.

Her smile dissolved as she forced herself to look past him. She didn't see anything.

Thomas grabbed her hand and pulled her with him. "Come with me, love. Come quickly."

He half dragged, half pushed her, depending on the obstacles they encountered. When they'd run until she was out of breath, he pushed her against the thick trunk of a huge oak. He met her eyes and held a finger to his lips, telling her without words to be quiet.

Whatever they were running from, Fallen knew she should be scared. But all she could think about was Thomas—the dynamic, exquisite details of his chiseled jaw. His muscles were wickedly defined. He scanned the area over and over, listening intently.

Fallen fisted her hands in his white T-shirt, lifting it enough to see the strength in his stomach. She used the shirt as leverage to pull his face closer.

Maybe he was mad?

Maybe he was going crazy.

But she would play into his mania if that's what it cost to be near him. He still watched for something, strung tight with anticipation of a danger she couldn't see. He kept his finger on his lips to remind her to be quiet.

She kissed it instead, turning her head slightly so she could nibble up the side before licking the tip.

That brought his considerable attention to her, like he was seeing her for the first time. He took her face in his hands and kissed her deeply. She covered his hands with hers, thrilled that he was ready for the affection she desperately needed.

She took her hands from the front of his shirt and placed her fingers underneath it, sliding them to his back.

If he didn't want to talk, she would be okay with that. She had other plans for his mouth anyway.

She'd picked up her dress, determined to sink to her knees, when she heard it too. A definite cracking of twigs and underbrush caused by something big. Thomas slid his hand around her waist and drew her close, reaching for his waistband with his other hand, then mouthing a curse.

Thomas was used to having a weapon, that much was clear. But instead of being scared, she was angry. Her time with him was not supposed to be spent running from an unseen danger.

And it didn't have to be. She hugged him hard and pictured a different setting. When she opened her eyes, she clung to Thomas in her bedroom. It wasn't the ocean, it wasn't a four-poster bed, but she was selfish, and this was her ultimate goal: to have Thomas in her world.

He opened his eyes and shook his head. "Clever Fallen. My sweet dream girl. Just change the setting. I was worried about finding you. I was late. I'm sorry I was late. I had to be up all night, and when I went to bed I was scared. Is it okay that I was scared? To think that you were by yourself. That I would miss this time with you? It means everything. You're everything. Is that too much? Am I too much?"

He overwhelmed her with his feelings and his racing thoughts, and she could only smile and steal kisses from him. "Same," she murmured, laughing a little. "It's the same for me. Same."

"Tell me where we are." He sat on her twin mattress and opened his arms to her.

She sat in his lap and stroked his hair. Fallen looked around. Her room was basic, but some of her things were missing—her cell phone, its charger, her clock-radio...

"A version of my bedroom, which is super lame." She touched his face, feeling his scruff, watching him take in her space. "I was late, too. The hotel I work in, I was off today, and I tried to see if I could dream you here, in my room, but I couldn't."

"What did you do?" He ran his fingers over hers before taking off her jacket while she talked.

"I broke into the hotel." She wrinkled her nose. "In hindsight, I should be more careful. If I get fired, how will I get to you? I've been looking everywhere. I can't find you when I'm awake." She straddled him, kissing his lips between her words. "I just want you in my life. How can I get more you? Once a week is going to be the end of me."

"Dream girl, once a week is going to be the end of me, too. Does it feel like a click for you? When I see you, I feel a click in my chest, and then I finally have a hole filled. I've never felt like this before." He twisted with her on him, laying on his back and pulling her to his side. They were nose to nose this way. "Did I put that dress on you?"

"No, you didn't. It was in my real world, and I wore it to room 514." She tried to burn the image of him in her bed into her memory. It was a mistake, she realized now. This night would give her memories, but the loss of him would be much more tangible now that she'd seen him here.

"Room 514? That's funny. I stayed in a room 514 once too. I remember because it's my mother Lucy's birthday—May 14th. Before—" And then the white nose invaded. They covered each other's ears.

She watched his face, thinking about that detail. Out of the corner of her eye she saw more of his bicep. As he covered her ears, his shirt had revealed the inside of his upper arm.

It was her name.

She reached out and touched it as the white noise tapered away.

"For you. So you know, and I know, you're real." He kissed her fingertips where she traced the letters.

"Thank you." She burrowed into his chest, treasuring the feeling of his arms around her.

"You're real, right? I mean, I've been telling my friend about you, and he says I'm just battle-weary, that I'm making you up." He put one hand on her hip, running his other palm up and down the outside of her thigh.

"I'm so real. And waiting for you. And wishing for you." Fallen waited for him, and he didn't disappoint as he took her declaration and turned it into touches.

Thomas went for her zipper and slid it down quickly. He languished kisses on her mouth as he helped her shimmy out of her dress, freeing the buttons up top on his way. He kissed her neck and the tops of her breasts.

"How much time do we have left, Fallen?"

"Not enough. Not enough." She went for his belt. This wasn't how she wanted it to be for him, for their first time, but she was urgent to claim him. To be a release for him. To give him something to look forward to.

They moved from testing to frantic, each discarding the undergarments in the way.

"Fallen."

"Thomas."

She sensed his hesitation and ended that by angling her hips to take him.

"You're sure?" He was inside of her, but had stopped.

She took control from underneath, accepting him deeper and deeper until she had the pleasure of watching him lose himself. A feral look bloomed in his eyes, and she sunk her fingertips into his shoulders.

"More."

And then they became one. One purpose. The fireworks in her heart for him detonated. His arms held him strong above her, and she turned her head and bit his forearm lightly.

"Damn it." He was struggling too, to stay inside her, to make it magic, but she wouldn't give him the luxury, not knowing when she would be forced to wake up. His furious pace only allowed her to hang on. Her breasts heaved with every thrust, and his hands eventually had to take hold of her. He was rough now, forgetting himself, forgetting how big he was, how much weight he had, but Fallen accepted him with a welcome shout.

This, she wanted this with him so much, letting him into her body. To be this connected felt like a prayer answered. She wanted to be sore from him. She wanted to remember him, make him hers so when they met in real life, they would know each other like this.

"Oh my God," she gasped.

With his pace, she knew he must be close, so she locked her legs in place and insisted on having him inside when he reached the peak of his pleasure. She watched as the pain of climax rocked through him, treasuring the sight of him.

He was cursing and saying her name, and it felt like victory.

Thomas moved to her side and cuddled her in. "I'm sorry."

"Please don't apologize. I got what I needed. When we do it

again, we'll take more time, but I can feel my eyes getting heavier."

She kissed his chin as he kissed her forehead.

"I loved that. I hate that we can't stay here."

His hair was wet at the temples from their exertions. She kissed his tattooed bicep that he'd slipped under her head. He reached past her and nabbed something from the side table.

He lifted her arm and showed her his intentions. She nodded her approval. With the pen he signed his name, pressing enough to ink, but not enough to hurt her. Then he drew a heart.

"For our first time."

"Of hopefully hundreds," Fallen added. Each blink was a test of endurance, trying to keep him in her field of vision. "What was chasing you? Before?"

His voice was slurred, but he answered. "Lad. He had a gun. He didn't see me, but I saw him. All that mattered was finding you."

And with that, she felt the rush of leaving him. She woke up with his words echoing through her mind. She fully expected to see Lad in 514 with her. When she realized she was alone, she was relieved. And then tremendously sad.

She gathered her dress and crawled off the bed, her heart still slowing down from sex with Thomas.

She stopped and covered her mouth as it broke into a wide smile.

Him.

She'd had him.

Fallen moved the antique table out of the way of the door, remembering to straighten the comforter before she left.

Her walk home was freezing. It was getting much colder, and she wasn't dressed for it. She wasn't dressed for anything, except the perfect thing she'd just experienced. She let herself into her house and ran to her room. In her head she knew

Thomas wouldn't be there, but her heart was a spiritual thing, hoping anyway.

She opened her door, holding her breath. The room was exactly as she'd left it. Her heart crashed, like the stupid, wishful thing it was. Fallen tossed her jacket on her desk chair. She walked in and sat. The things that had been missing in the dream were present now. She ran her hand over her bed. Calling their experience a dream seemed to diminish it somehow. It was as real as this moment. Thomas' comment about being battle-weary weighed on her mind. Did he mean that literally? As she glanced in her dresser's mirror, something caught her attention; she stood slowly and walked toward her reflection, holding out her arm. It was backwards, his name in the mirror, so she looked down.

And there it was. Thomas' name and a heart. On her arm in real ink. Tears clouded her eyes.

He was real. He was real.

He was real.

12

INKED

When Fallen woke up Friday morning, she looked at her arm for the longest time, ignoring her alarm. This was something that couldn't be explained away. She'd watched him do it in the dream, and now it was here. And it was on her right arm. She could never write neatly with her left hand.

It had been Thomas. That gave her peace. As crazy as it all felt, the man she was head over heels for was a person. That mattered.

When she finally got ready for work, she let herself think about the scarier part of the dream's revelation—that Thomas had been running from Lad. Could he be even more a danger to her than she'd realized? Was he stalking her in the dreams as well?

Luckily, her work uniform covered the doodle from Thomas, because she was not planning on scrubbing it off anytime soon. And knowing Mr. Orbit, if he saw it, he would make her remove it.

On her walk to work—moving a little more quickly than usual—she had a thought. She wanted to make his signature permanent. Because her newest fear was losing it. It validated her feelings and reminded her of his adoration. She toyed with the idea while she walked, finally finding a purpose for the tattoo parlor she passed by every day.

When she slid into her place at the meeting, she was happy to see that Desta was back. The woman didn't look sick...well, aside from her ever-present cough. Melanny seemed far more relaxed this morning, and Fallen figured out why when she announced that the crew could stop doing their extra lobby chores because Mr. Orbit had gone. Fallen was grateful to be standing against a wall so she didn't actually swoon from the relief.

Even the housekeepers from 8 and 9 couldn't get her spirits down with their snide comments about Fallen not being protected by her sugar daddy any more. Fallen waited for Desta after she got her cart. The older woman made her way back to the door, assuring other employees she was fine.

They pushed their carts together toward the elevator and were left by themselves as everyone else got in the elevator first.

"Are you feeling better?" Fallen asked quietly after the birdcage had rattled away.

"Better my ass. That man made me take the leave." Desta shook her head and pouted.

"Mr. Orbit?" Fallen was surprised. He'd seemed to talk to Desta nicely. Maybe she'd gotten the wrong impression.

"Yes. Mr. I-am-so-important Orbit."

Fallen held open the elevator door as Desta loaded in her cart.

"Can you stop by later and talk about room 514 with me?" Fallen watched the woman's face carefully.

Desta's left eye twitched before she answered. "Yeah. I'll stop by." She pushed her cart out into the hallway.

With that, Fallen reset the elevator to take her one floor up to level five. Today she would find out what was going on in that hotel room. She hoped that would help everything make sense. As she pushed her cart down the hall to start at room 501, she noticed activity in front of 514. The maintenance guys were involved, talking back and forth loudly with the room door open.

She entered the first room and began cleaning, now wondering all over again what the hell was going on.

The workers bustled back and forth in room 514 for a good two hours. Fallen toyed with the idea of popping into see what they were doing, but she had a feeling that's what Mr. Orbit wanted her to do, so she stayed away and remained wildly curious instead.

Desta came down, smelling of smoke, when Fallen was beginning in room 507. The maintenance men had just packed up to leave, one of them stopping to apologize about the mess they'd left in 514. She'd told him it was no problem, but now she worried that somehow they'd taken the magic connection out of the room.

Desta unpropped the door and let it close behind them. Fallen was startled, but smiled when she saw that Desta had grabbed a sheet from where she'd set it on the desk.

"Why don't we start with you telling me what you want to know about 514?" Desta snapped open the linen with a practiced wrist before lifting the sheet high and watching the corners land perfectly.

Fallen pointed. "Show off."

Desta laughed and then coughed.

"Well, first, it's been empty the whole time I've worked here. No one stays there, even when we're crowded. Orbit told me it's a memorial to his parents. And just now the maintenance guys were in there doing something, and I have no idea what." Fallen tucked in her side of the bed.

Desta stood and put her hands on her hips. "Well, that's interesting. Very interesting."

Fallen waited.

Desta sat in the desk chair and leveled a hard stare at Fallen. "Not too long ago there was a girl who cleaned this floor for three years. But since then we've had lots of turnover. I'm not sure if you're a quickie or a long termer. I think the jury's still out. But 514 always plays a part in that."

"Did the other housekeepers experience things in that room?" Now Fallen felt a little scared. Why were they in and out so much? Was Thomas the man they all saw in their dreams? Jealousy raged through her.

Desta took a while to answer, like there was a battle inside of her. After a resigned sigh, instead of answering the question, she asked one.

"Do you love him?"

"What? Who?" Fallen played dumb.

"The man you meet when you dream." Desta was quiet; just her raspy breathing animated the room.

"You know about the dreams?" Fallen grasped the mattress so she would stay upright.

"Intimately." Desta lifted a brow.

"Really?"

"You have to keep this between us. I'm never supposed to talk about it, but there's a spark in you, lady. I feel like you can handle the truth of it all. Well, the truth of what I know." Desta reached over and started to wipe at dust on the TV stand with her hand.

"I'm ready. I don't think you can shock me." Fallen touched the spot on her arm that had been inked by Thomas.

"I started working here at 45. I'm 70 now, so that was 25

years ago. Has it been that long? I guess it has. Time moves quick; you gotta pay attention to it."

Fallen tucked her legs up underneath her.

"At first, like you, I cleaned the fifth floor, including room 514, which was always empty. One day I fell asleep on the job, and I had a dream of my Burt. After that, once a week I got to be with this amazing guy—the man who was made for me. And it wasn't enough, but we made it work. I started smoking because I wanted to have the smell around to remind me of him. He loved his cigarettes. That would sound crazy to anyone else, but not to you, does it?" Desta paused.

Fallen shook her head. It didn't sound crazy at all.

"Thought not. It wasn't too long into our relationship—maybe six months?—that Mr. Orbit's dad sat me down one day. He was the owner back then. See, the family has owned this hotel, and quite a few others, for a real long time." Desta seemed to look for approval to continue.

Fallen waited, afraid to breathe.

"Well, I was surprised to find out he knew I took naps in 514. When he asked me about it that day, I confessed. But instead of being angry, he encouraged me to continue. Which was odd. I took him at his word, though, and kept up my routine. I loved Burt too much to stop anyway. I wanted to see him, and I couldn't make it work anywhere else."

Fallen was completely absorbed by what Desta had to say—almost like one of the dreams. She wished the current Mr. Orbit was a little more like his father and had just encouraged her to continue her naps without the charity balls or bed making.

"How much time did you get?" Fallen asked.

Desta's sad smile gave her a sinking feeling.

"Fourteen years. For 14 years I had my Burt once a week. And then one day I went, and he wasn't there. I was desperate. We were never able to tell each other much about our real lives. So in the end, he was just gone. I don't know if he died or something changed or..." She shook her head. "For another year or so I dreamed and tried to find him, returning to all the places we'd been together. We had a little house over there, all decorated. In our time we lived a whole 'nother life."

Desta looked misty for a moment. "When the things he'd imagined started to fade, I didn't have the heart to keep going. It was too painful."

"I'm sure." Fallen recalled the moments she'd been in the dream without Thomas. She couldn't imagine the abrupt end of a 14-year relationship.

"Since then, there have been lots of girls working this floor, and some have napped in the room, though not all of them. And they each stayed on for varying amounts of time. Some last a week, some last a few months, and occasionally someone lasts longer. I have a ton of theories, but nothing solid. The girls are always secretive. Several have just stopped coming to work, so I don't really know what happened. Did they figure out something I couldn't and learn how to stay there full time? I don't know if I'll ever know."

"I'm sorry for your loss." Fallen meant the sentiment from the deepest part of her.

"Things changed when Lad took over." Desta shook her head. "Instead of just respecting the room and letting it live, he wants to claim it. He wants the true love for himself, so he's been interfering, as near as I can tell. And it's affecting him."

"How do you mean?" Fallen felt like her head might explode with questions.

"Well, he's tried napping in there himself, but it doesn't seem to work. Instead he's become obsessed with the women who work on this floor, especially the ones who dream." Desta leaned forward. "He was married to one of them, but then she divorced him." Desta waited to see Fallen's reaction.

"He seems a little obsessed about me." Fallen twisted her fingers together.

Desta nodded. "Is the man you dream of your true love?" she asked.

Fallen thought about it. She thought about how much she longed to see Thomas' face. How crazy she felt, needing his arms around her. Was that feeling manufactured somehow in the hotel? It was impossible to know. She just spoke the truth she felt.

"If true love hurts more than this does, I don't want any part of it." She touched Thomas' name again.

"That sounds about right. How can something that makes you so miserable make you so desperate to have more of it?" Desta started coughing again. After a moment, she stood. "I have to get back to my rooms. I have a ton of suspicions, but now you know all my facts."

"Desta?" Fallen stood too.

"Yeah?"

"I feel crazy. Is it really happening? Is he in this world? Can I find him?" She crossed her hands over her heart like she could protect it.

"It's real. And as far as the rest of that goes, you need to ask Lad's ex-wife. Just a rumor, but I think she's neck deep in her happily ever after."

Desta closed the door behind her, and Fallen sat back down, trying to absorb the avalanche of information.

When Fallen had entered room 514 to clean at the end of her day, the only change she could identify was an added security camera. She was troubled by the new technology and mentioned it to Desta on the way out to her car.

"Don't worry, muffin. I got you. Just clean it real nice, okay?" Desta patted her on the shoulder before getting into her car.

But it was hard not to worry because Thomas was never far from her thoughts. What if their work in the room had changed her ability to dream there? What if being watched ruined it—along with being terribly violating.

As Fallen arrived home, she found Nora walking out of the house, carrying the jeweled bag with the swag from the charity ball. It seemed she planned to start her weekend off with a bang.

"What do you have there, Nora?" Fallen pointed at the bag.

"You got these pretty gifts. I was just going to take them to show my friends."

Fallen closed her eyes for a moment. Luckily she hadn't shown the watch to Fenn because she'd intended to save it for his graduation. When she looked again, she saw Addiction shining back at her from Nora's eyes. It would use every dirty trick in the book to get money for booze.

"Give me the things back, please." Fallen knew it was a pointless battle, but she had to try anyway.

And then the excuses came. The denial. The anger. The bargaining. Finally, Fallen had had enough.

"You take the watch. And give me the house key you took from Fenn. Then you can leave."

She watched as Addiction hemmed and hawed, weighing the instant gratification against the long-term benefits of having a key so it could steal and manipulate Nora's children in the future.

When Fallen closed the door, she had the bag and tiara and

key. Despite their fight, Nora had claimed she would bring back the watch someday soon. She was just borrowing it for a while.

Fallen tried not to feel the betrayal too deeply. The worst part would be explaining to Fenn that Nora was not getting on the wagon anytime soon.

For the next few days, Fallen checked her email almost daily, getting to the library just a few minutes before it closed. She was tempted to check on the hotel computers, but she saved that option for absolute emergencies. She thought constantly about all Desta had told her, but she'd asked no more questions. Although she and Desta passed each other at least every morning and afternoon as their shifts started and ended, she had asked for a few days before they discussed 514 again. Fallen had felt guilty then, realizing that Desta was delving into painful memories to counsel her.

She made it a point to clean room 514 without looking at the camera. Uneasiness slipped down her spine whenever she was in there, knowing Mr. Orbit—or someone else—could be watching her from somewhere. It was an unwelcome addition to her anxiety about whether or not she'd still be able to see Thomas next Thursday when she tried to dream.

On Wednesday her rooms had been easy to tidy during the mid-week lull at the hotel, so after work, she finally had time for all the errands she'd been wanting to do. First she logged in at the library and found a return email from Mr. Orbit's ex-wife.

Fallen,

Please pardon my tardiness in replying to your email. It's a difficult topic for me, and my husband has begged me to leave it alone. But I need to share with you what I learned. I want to help lift the burden of being separated from the one you love from your shoulders.

We will need a good meeting spot—crowded, hard to listen in on so we can talk.

~Ellen

Fallen typed back that she would be at Fenn's football game against Poughkeepsie High School on Saturday evening, so they could meet in the stands with the home crowd. She would be there anyway, and her time off was limited, so hopefully that spot would be what Ellen needed it to be.

As Fallen left the library, she found the email had heightened her hopes for getting to Thomas. Or getting him out. However it would work. She just needed the room to still be working after whatever Orbit had done.

After the library, she stopped at a pawn shop and offered the man at the counter the charity ball tiara. He pointed out that the bag was worth something as well, being covered in real gold glitter and a few gems. As he worked out the price, she looked in the case. Sure enough, a watch that looked suspiciously like the one she'd been planning to give Fenn was up for sale.

Fallen left the place with $200 cash and a guilty heart because she planned to use some of the money just for her. But nothing could stop her from visiting her next destination. She finally entered the tattoo studio she'd walked by many times on the way home. She'd been keeping Thomas' ink dry in the shower, so it had only faded a little, but she wanted to make sure she would never lose it.

For $50 she had the signature inked in place forever, along with the small heart. The pain was crazy on that part of her arm, but for a reason she'd have trouble explaining to others, it made her love for Thomas real by immortalizing the miracle of the pen ink, which had transferred with her over to the waking world.

When she went to bed Wednesday night, her tasks complete, she pictured two things: Thomas' face and the unblinking eye of the security camera in room 514.

13

BREAKER

Fallen had bandaged Thomas' name and put on the required cream. She'd expected some regret when she woke the next morning, but she felt only exhilaration at the thought of showing Thomas what she had done to honor him—and relief that it would never wash away.

When she got to work, Desta waggled her eyebrows from across the meeting room, so after the staff was dismissed, they lingered in the supply closet.

"I've think I have a plan for you." Desta pulled out her cell phone.

"Thank God. Because I have no idea what to do." Fallen leaned closer.

"Well, the layout of 512 is exactly the same as 514. Let's go there together now. You open the door, and we'll recreate the angle of the security camera and snap a picture of what it sees."

Fallen perked up. This plan had merit. "Then I can run down to the business center and print out the picture…"

Desta nodded. "At the end of our shift, I'll flip the breaker, and you can go in and tape the picture to the ceiling."

"Then all Orbit sees is the undisturbed room?"

"You can go have a nice nap, unmonitored." Desta flashed her a knowing smile and fought off another bout of hacking cough.

"You're brilliant!" Fallen hugged the woman, yipping as her tattoo hit Desta's shoulder.

"What'd ya got there?" Desta nodded toward her inner arm.

Fallen debated showing her what she'd done. But this was Desta... She rolled up her sleeve and pulled back the dressing.

She whispered, "His signature."

Desta's gaze was alarmed as she snapped it from the mark to Fallen's eyes. "He was able to do this?"

"Well, not the tattoo, but he signed my arm, and I just had the artist follow the lines, so it would never fade." She recovered it and readjusted her sleeve. Maybe it wasn't a great idea to show her.

"This is bad. Maybe you shouldn't do the dream any more." Desta started straightening her cart nervously.

"Why? I thought it was a nice message from him to me here." Now she felt a bit defensive.

"It's just...the room has been acting weird. And this is more proof of that. There should be no crossovers. I don't know what Lad has... You get the white noise, right?"

Fallen nodded.

"When you're treading on topics that could affect the past or the future, the noise stops your communication." Desta bit her lip. "It's a safety feature."

"What?" Fallen was thoroughly confused.

"It's just sometimes you're not in the same time period as your love. You're not meant to learn things that can affect how history happens." Desta started rolling out her cart.

"That's some trippy crap. Are you telling me Thomas could be from the future?" Fallen felt like she was frozen to the ground.

"Or the past." Desta nodded.

That was scary. Fallen felt small in the face of something so huge. Thomas could be living before or after her?

"Come on. We still have to do work or we get fired." Desta waved at Fallen until she took action, grabbing her own cart and following Desta to the birdcage. "And watch yourself. Not all cameras are as obvious as the one in 514."

Fallen took her advice and focused on small talk as they rode up to the fifth floor.

Inside room 512, Fallen stood on the desk to replicate the view she imagined the security camera in 514 had. She took four photos in total. Desta made the phone disappear as Fallen hopped down.

"You know what? I'll print the pictures. I think the less out of the ordinary you do, the better." Desta looked determined.

"You're sure? I don't want you to get in trouble."

"It'll be fine. No one will even see me, and as for the rest of this plan we've concocted, we have to throw the breakers from time to time for a lot of different reasons. I'll say I thought there was a leak by an outlet. That's one of the perks of being old. Everyone assumes you're a little off."

Desta helped Fallen straighten the bedcover, both of them subconsciously programmed to clean.

"I think Burt's gone," she added softly after a moment. "I assume he's gone. But part of me hopes the room just ended our communication, and he's still alive. When you're over there, keep an ear out for him, okay?"

Fallen nodded. She could ask around in those groups of blurry people, if she ever got to be in one again. Desta wished her well and promised to meet her in the hall outside 514 at 3:50 pm to give her a thumbs up or not.

Fallen knew it was reckless to try to meet up with Thomas again. But she also knew she didn't have a choice. He was worth the risks.

She spent her day thinking about what Desta had said—that

Thomas could be from another time. She realized what a delicate, hoping version of love she felt for him now that the already insurmountable circumstances of dreaming were complicated with the suggestion that her present might not be his as well.

After her lunch break, Fallen checked in with Melanny, hoping for information on when Mr. Orbit would be back.

"I'm just covering the fifth floor this week, right?" Fallen put a confused look on her face.

Melanny exhaled as she looked over her glasses at Fallen. "I swear I could just sing 'Row, Row, Row Your Boat' and the same information would be conveyed." She put down her pen. "Until further notice, no extra cleaning. The visit from Mr. Orbit is over."

Fallen nodded, assured that she would be alone in the room.

As she turned away, she heard Melanny mutter, "You should know—you're the one sleeping with him."

Fallen turned back to her and said, "Pardon?"

Melanny shook her head. "Nothing. Talking to myself."

Fallen wanted to fight back, but more than that she wanted access to 514 until she could find Thomas. Which required being employed at the hotel. She swallowed her indignation and went back to work.

At the appointed time, Fallen met Desta in the hall outside 514. The woman gave her a hidden thumbs-up as she passed her a printed picture, with little bits of tape ready for the ceiling in front of the camera. Fallen pushed her cart into the hall and pretended to wind her vacuum cord.

Official policy said there were to be no carts in the hallway after check-in time, but everyone skirted that one.

Fallen let herself into the room and pulled her cart in behind her. She didn't bother to throw the bolt, or move the furniture, both of which she fully intended on doing as soon as the picture was affixed.

When the power went off, she climbed the antique desk and soon had the picture in place. She said a silent prayer that it would pass for the interior of 514. She should have been more careful and scoped out the exact location of the pillows and chairs. She would next time—if she got a next time. Right now she focused on *this* time.

She hopped down from the desk just as the lights blinked back on. Fire extinguishers beeped as they came online again. Now Fallen secured the room to her liking and felt her body rejoice as the otherworldly exhaustion began to creep from her toes up her legs. Fallen stretched on the bed, reviewing her mental checklist. She'd let Fenn know she'd be working late, so he wouldn't worry. She briefly regretted not bringing a change of clothes. All she had here was her uniform.

But it was only 4:00pm. So much Thomas time until midnight and the end of Thursday. She closed her eyes and let the rush take her.

Not knowing where she would wake up was always disorienting, but Fallen tried to be prepared so she wouldn't panic. This time, instead of waking up in a place she'd been before, she opened her eyes sitting at a gorgeously set table. Everyone around her was dressed for a black tie event. As she glanced around the room, an intense gaze locked on hers.

Mr. Lad Orbit sat across from her at the table.

Her cheeks immediately flamed with guilt and fear, and Lad's gaze stormed at her. His eyes were wild, before closing halfway. He held a steak knife in his fist, and the glimmer of silver captured her attention for a moment. When she dropped her gaze to her lap, she noticed she was still in her uniform. Shame joined her emotions as the other women at the table could pass for princesses in their elegant gowns.

She swallowed hard and felt a foot tapping against her Payless Velcro sneaker. Lad was trying to get her attention. When the tapping became urgent, she looked at him.

"*Smile,*" he mouthed.

She did so, but halfheartedly until she saw a familiar form in waiter's garb walk in with a tray.

Her smile burst through now, matching the way her heart soared at the sight of Thomas. She had worried for a moment that it might only be Lad in this dream.

She glanced back to find Lad enraged that she was smiling at Thomas.

She tried her best to take her eyes off of him. A chill on her décolleté alerted her to an outfit change, and she looked down to see a strapless gown with diagonal check details and a black wrap. It instantly made her feel more at ease, and a little proud, in the group of finely dressed people.

Over her shoulder, a silver tray was presented. Thomas' voice was love in her ear.

"Now you fit in," he murmured. "Better, you shine."

She took a champagne glass and nodded politely. Lad continued to watch her.

He grabbed the champagne glass already in front of him and stood, clanging it with his dessert fork. The chime echoed throughout the dining room and caused a ripple effect through the others at dinner.

"Ladies and gentleman! Please, can I have your attention? Please."

The people in the dream had sharper faces this time, but something was still a little off.

Thomas set down his tray on a table by the door before turning back to her. She watched as he moved closer to one of the huge French windows and looked through it. He must have liked what he saw, because he reached up and unlatched it.

Thomas met her gaze and mouthed, "*Go to the bathroom.*"

Lad had been going on about choices and life and soul mates. She pushed her chair out. Leaving while he was mid-speech was probably poor form, but she was wasting time that was supposed to be spent with Thomas.

As she stood, Lad gestured to her. She was careful to hide her tattoo with the wrap as the attention of the room focused on her. She wanted Thomas to see it when they were alone.

"So all that to say…" Lad turned to her with a strange look in his eye. "Fallen has agreed to be my wife."

Wild applause met the announcement. Fallen bit her lip as Lad accepted hearty handshakes from the men next to him. The lady next to her stood and embraced her.

"Where's the ring?" She looked pointedly at Fallen's empty left hand.

She began to explain that there'd been a mistake as Lad worked his way around the table.

"She doesn't have one, Jane. Not yet." He slid to one knee in front of her and grasped her hand. "To a strong forever." He slipped the large, square engagement ring on her hand, holding it fast when she started to pull it away.

"I'm sorry, Lad. I just don't—"

He interrupted her with a kiss, clutching her to him like a life preserver in a storm.

She pushed at his chest, and the ice bucket thrown over them was a physical shock. Lad abruptly stepped away and brushed at his now-soaked tuxedo jacket. Thomas set the empty bucket at their feet.

"So sorry, miss. Please come with me, and I'll take you to a powder room. I'm sure the event coordinator has prepared for this kind of problem." Thomas put his hand on her lower back and pointed with two fingers at the exit.

Thomas beckoned another waiter over. When he was close, Fallen realized she could see him quite clearly, right down to his eye color. He was older and watched Fallen with great interest. She couldn't help but think of Desta's Burt. This one would be about the right age…

"Sir, please see to it that the gentleman gets a fresh jacket. We can't have the happy couple catching a chill on their big day."

Fallen watched as Thomas gave Lad a cheesy wink. In an instant, Lad looked ready to explode, but Thomas was already escorting her into the hall. "Miss, please step this way."

She couldn't take her eyes off him. He was strong and in control. He seemed to anticipate that she would be distracted, so he helped her navigate the hall crowded with servers. He nodded to others before taking her in a roundabout way to the window she had seen him unlatch.

If there was something sexier than watching him get them out of the building and away from Lad, she'd never seen it.

He slipped out of the window and landed on a small roof, the only safe place to climb out from the second-story ballroom. She leaned out of the window as he turned to her and smiled. The moonlight highlighted him as he motioned for her.

"Jump. I'll catch you." He held out his arms.

Fallen looked over one shoulder then the other, seeing only servers and no sign of Lad. She turned and sat on the sill, pulling her heels close as she spun to dangle her feet out the window.

He didn't have to tell her twice. Fallen was 100% ready to jump out of windows to be with him.

The sensation of falling took her breath away, but before the fear could fully form, his arms were locked around her.

She gasped a bit at the impact, but he was already setting her on her feet. He jumped off the small roof and Fallen looked at the side of the building. It was massive. It seemed the panes of windows went on forever.

She could see a figure outlined in one, the chandeliers behind him giving his silhouette blurry edges.

She knew it was Lad, even though she couldn't see his face. She turned and jumped again, and again Thomas caught her.

They began running to the road, and she had to hold up her long dress to keep from tripping.

Thomas laughed about their getaway while pulling her along. When they'd gotten around the bend, he pulled her behind a tree and kissed her before she could even catch her breath.

"Okay, it seems Lad's taking quite an active role in these dreams. I'm going to think of a place I haven't been in a long, long time to take us. Maybe we can evade him for a while?" Thomas drew her into a hug and closed an eye.

Fallen put her hands on his chest, wanting to feel his heartbeat under her hands. The rustle of his clothes, the dimple in his cheek when he smiled—all these details she wanted to catalog to prove to herself, yet again, that he was real.

"Okay. I did it," he announced. "We have a little hike. I want to take you to the treehouse my brothers and I built when we were kids."

Fallen gave her outfit a makeover, sad to see the stylish gown go, but glad she wasn't wet anymore. Then she tried to take off the ring Lad had put on her finger. She tugged and tugged, but it wouldn't budge. She gave Thomas a pleading stare. He put her hand to his mouth and kissed her palm before flipping it over.

"You have to be gentle with yourself." He used the utmost patience to slowly wiggle it from her finger, helping her finally get it over her knuckle. He held the ring out to her.

Fallen took it and chucked it behind her like a bride would her bouquet.

Thomas laughed and pointed in the distance at a tree. "I just found shelter so I can ravish you without interruption."

She'd pictured a slab of plywood as a floor with a matching one as the roof, but when they drew near the tree he'd pointed out, she saw that it contained a rather impressive structure.

The treehouse had a doorway and windows, and an old-fashioned ladder leaned against the trunk.

Thomas helped her up, following close behind her as she took the steps in her pedal pusher high-waisted jeans. She'd topped them with a red checked button down tied at her middle over a white tank. When he'd spoken of a treehouse, she'd gotten a picnic vibe and dressed the part. Her high ponytail swung as she climbed up to the lofted wooden house in a huge oak tree.

Thomas climbed in behind her and offered her his hand as she got to her feet.

"This is cute." She loved seeing a part of his childhood—anything to make him more real.

Thomas patted the wall, running his hand over the names carved there.

TOM
EDDIE
JOHNNIE

"God, I wonder how they are today. I miss the hell outta them."

She came closer and stepped into his space as he wrapped an arm around her. She ran her finger over the names as well, lingering on his.

"How old were you guys when you made this?"

"Oh, I was about thirteen. That would make Eddie fifteen and Johnny twelve. Johnny made us laugh, but he was no goddamn help—always cracking jokes and setting up pranks. He'd take the ladder down all the time. And Eddie and I would threaten to beat him up if he didn't put it back. He would say, 'If I put it back, you'll beat me up then, too.' And he was right. We would. They can both fight well enough now. I hope it helps them wherever they are."

Fallen wanted to ask about them, but the words wouldn't come. Luckily, Thomas continued.

"All three of us serving at the same time. Ma could barely handle the news, still torn up from my father's death. She thought for sure that fate was done with her, you know?"

Fallen saw worry and sadness pass over his face. She hugged him. He kissed her forehead and hummed a bit.

Was he at a loss for words like she was?

Then Thomas started to talk. "It had been ten years since Dad's heart attack, the night we decided."

Fallen imagined a pile of fluffy blankets and pillows on the floor. She stepped away from him, and he sat down so she could curl between his legs.

"We knew she'd take it hard," he continued, "but one day when Ma was at the salon, getting her hair done, the three of us discussed the need to do our duty. We couldn't have the conversation without looking at the portrait of our father in his dress uniform over the mantel. We wanted to make him proud—or at least the memory of him proud, but I couldn't imagine the cost for our mother. Still, we agreed that day to enlist."

"My baby brother was a smart ass," he continued. "He just said, 'Ladies love a uniform' while he waggled his eyebrows. And Edward was practical as usual. His plan as for us to spread out in the different services, try to stay alive that way, as it really seemed like war was coming. 'I'm Army,' John said then, like he was calling dibs for the passenger seat in a car."

Thomas shook his head. "I wanted to follow in Dad's footsteps, too. The thought of going to war was terrifying, but also I couldn't imagine doing anything else. All of the neighborhood guys were signing up. I wanted to be a patriot as well. How little I knew about where I was headed. I hate the war but love my country. My parents always kept the flag out and taught us to respect it.

"Then Eddie pulled an envelope out of his pocket telling us he'd already enlisted in the air force. It was just a few weeks until he was scheduled to report. That news had been the first piece of mail he'd received at his new place. John told him he knew a guy who could get him to Canada in a heartbeat.

'I heard Canada's fake,' Eddie told him. 'Like unicorns and your last girlfriend.'"

Fallen laughed and nodded for Thomas to continue. Pretending they had all the time in the world felt luxurious.

"I told him if he was going, I was going. I figured if I killed any of the enemies, there might be one less headed for my brother.

Then John pointed out that Ma was gonna be busted up about it. But we all knew it was coming. And so did she. The military is a family legacy, or so it seems."

Fallen was desperate to ask where the war was. Was he still at war? He did seem to hate where he came to her from. The fighting must be awful.

"But enough of that. I'm here with you." Thomas lay back in the pillows, and she wiggled over so she could put her head on his shoulder. "Tell me about you. What's your day like at the hotel?"

Fallen looked at the ceiling. She'd thought she would just jump on him, feel the things her nerve endings were daring her to feel with him, and that desire was there, of course. But to talk without judgment, to really know him, was amazing.

"It's hard. I mean, it doesn't sound anything like what you've got going on. I'm not struggling to survive, just to keep things right for Fenn and keep a look out for Lad. He hasn't been at the hotel for a week or so now, and it's a relief not to see him—other than just now, when you saved me." She peppered his cheek with kisses before continuing. "My mom came back around. I thought I was going to be able to have some cash, but she took it. For a second I thought she was coming back to me, and to Fenn, to help. But she was just using us again." She sighed. Instead of feeling weak for complaining, her chest felt lighter having him to confide in.

Thomas tucked her closer, and she threaded her leg between his—like she'd do if they had a sleepy Saturday morning to waste together.

"Booze can destroy people." He shook his head. "I'm sorry it has a hold on her. Tell me, what did you want to do before you started taking care of Fenn? What will you do when he's pushed off on his own?" Thomas stroked her hair with his fingertips.

"A teacher. I like kids, and I like handing out tests and new pencils." She flipped to her stomach and regarded him. "When I was little I would sit and write out ten of the same worksheet, line up my toys in rows like they were in a classroom, and pass out their pop quizzes. Then I'd have to answer them all and decide how advanced each toy was. One of my brother's teddy bears failed every test." She ducked her head when he started laughing.

"I bet you were adorable." He put his knuckle under her chin and encouraged her to lift her head. She rolled back over and settled against his shoulder.

"I don't want to be adorable. I want to be impossible."

"How do you mean?" He kissed her forehead.

"I want to be impossible for you to forget, impossible for you to keep your hands off of." She leaned up for a kiss.

"You're my impossible then. Have no fear." He tenderly reminded her he was her impossible, too, with his lips.

She put her hand against his stomach and snuggled in. "This is my spot. Right here. With you—it's home."

He swallowed before talking to the ceiling. "My heart was like a fist. Where I am? It's not a place you plan to survive. I've been there for years, and it's not about skill; it's not even about luck. You get strapped into a machine, and fate's driving. You can't get out even if you want to. So you submit to it. You harden your soul. You get ready to die."

He shifted, rolling on top of her. She sighed in contentment. Being beneath him made her feel safe and secure.

He kissed her lips, then the tip of her nose, before continuing. "But with you, it's like my heart's opening up, and I'm terrified to feel, after all this time. Yet I don't have a choice. No matter where I am, I draw your face whenever I get a scrap of paper."

He laughed a little. "We found a puppy, and I named it Fallen, just so I could say your name over and over. The guys think I'm crazy—such a strange name for a dog. But I don't care. I'm gasping for you every moment I'm awake. And I'm making choices to keep me alive through the week."

His eyes searched hers. "What if I'm not as tough as I was in the beginning? God, I hope no one is affected by my distraction with this. But in the end there's you. Only you. Do what you have to to get back to me when you're awake. You have to. I need you more than air, more than life right now. The softness of you, the tenderness in your eyes when you see me. I'm trying to force fate to throw me in your direction. To hurl me at you somehow. I don't know if it will work. But I'm praying for it."

Fallen touched his face, then his neck. "I will do everything I can to find you."

And then the time for talking ended. As he pushed forward with his hips, she tilted her chin up. This was what she wanted from him, from now.

Thomas had a flicker of a smile as her imagination added small tables with candles to the treehouse. She wanted to watch him so she could re-envision each motion over and over until the next Thursday. The desperate need to stay with him almost choked her, but she let it pass, forcing herself to be in the now, with him.

Thomas sat back, straddling her. She ran her hands up and down his thighs, but it seemed he had no intention of rushing this time. He untied her checkered top, and then paid great attention to her nipples with his thumbs through her tank top. Desire for him flooded her, and she watched his eyes darken. He added slow, nipping kisses to his fingers' teasing. He was in no hurry.

She tried to convince him by pulling gently on his dark hair and bucking underneath him, but he just nodded.

"You, dream girl, are going to feel every bit of this. I've been doing this to you in my mind all week."

He nipped at her mouth and then added his tongue. She frowned.

"No. Don't be sad. In my imagination this week you were either smiling at me or begging me." He took her left hand from above her head and kissed the bare ring finger. "Me and only me."

"I'm past smiling and on to begging now." She tried to keep a frown on her face, but he started to tickle her.

Then, with a lifted brow, he pulled her tank top down, almost to her nipple and used his tongue to remind her where she really wanted him.

"Thomas."

And with that his lips were on her, no clothes separating the intimacy of his mouth on her breast. She inhaled as he revealed her other breast and rolled the nipple between his fingers, pinching it just enough to make her arch her back.

Fallen wriggled under his touch, forgetting herself and calling his name. Thomas took his mouth from her breast and put it on hers, whispering for her to be quiet. The protector in him brought forth another petal of lust in her. She would have a bouquet by the time he was done with her.

He stood and stripped off his T-shirt with a masculine maneuver that made every muscle in his chest more defined. She growled a little.

He paused taking off his pants. "Careful, Fallen. I can barely stop myself as it is. Don't push me over the edge. I have so little control."

Now she did smile. Watching him lose control had been her

favorite part of their last dream together. Instead of a warning, she heard a dare.

She reached down and unbuttoned her jeans, wiggling out of them and sending her panties with them off to the corner. Fallen bit her lip and motioned for Thomas to come to her.

He held his hands in two tight fists, looking almost ready to fight. She scrambled to her knees. He shook his head at her while she unthreaded his belt.

"What are you doing?" He didn't stop her, but she bet he looked at the wrong end of a gun more nicely than the glare he was aiming at her.

"Tasting?" It was a question, but she knew what she wanted to do. With her two previous boyfriends, anything sexual had been awkward. But here, with him, it was elegant. The forest played them a symphony sourced right from the evening. Crickets and wind rustling the leaves made their love song. The self-conscious thoughts from reality didn't follow her here. She only had confidence. The way he looked at her body as she freed him from his pants, stopping to help him with his boots, was empowering.

She felt him lean over her as she worked on the knot in his laces, running his hand over her bum and palming her in places that made her stop and groan.

He shifted and popped the boot off without undoing the laces, and then he wore just skin.

She sat back on her heels and let her gaze clothe him in appreciation. "You are exquisite." She wrapped her hand around him.

He took a quick inhale as she ran her fingertip over the end before responding, "That's what I was going to say to you."

She smiled, but her reply left her as she took him in her mouth. He was hot and smooth, and she loved the way his muscles tensed with every new place she found to lick, nibble, and suck.

"Enough."

He said it with such force that she was shocked. She looked up at him, lips still wrapped around him.

"No. Not this time. Last time I was too fast. Not this time."

He pulled away from her and got to his knees. She wasn't sure how, but in an instant she went from kneeling to lying on her back with his tongue pressing hard and fast against her as his fingers entered.

It was intimate and so quick that Fallen was at the brink of an orgasm before she was even prepared. She tried to squirm away, but he held fast to her. One of her legs was over his shoulder, the other held open with his strong forearm. She couldn't get away if she tried.

As she tensed, she told him, "I'm about to...about to..."

And then he growled against her, the vibration taking her away. The crash of complete bliss was soul shaking. All pretense of being quiet was lost as she shouted and shuddered. She felt like she pulled a muscle in her chest as she came, and yet he increased the friction, adding to her already impossible peak.

"For me. That's right. Come for me." He'd removed his mouth to demand things of her and used his fingers to bring her compliance.

Twice he built her passion to the point that it fell like a curtain, draping over her. Her throat felt rough from her shouts.

He kept a massaging hand between her legs, grinning from ear to ear. "God Bless America."

She'd lost all modesty and urged him up, forcing him to cover her with his body. There was so much of him. She loved the way he smelled, and as she licked his shoulder, the way he tasted.

She felt him near her thigh, persistent in his own need. "Come inside," she offered.

He pressed all the way into her and then stilled.

She grabbed his shoulders and encouraged him, opening her legs wider. "Go so hard that I can still feel you next week."

Her words snapped the leash he'd been on, and he bucked into her wildly. He proved his strength and stamina, taking from her but never forgetting her breasts, biting and sucking, or her pleasure, slipping a hand between them.

The sight of his strong biceps holding him up, the strain in his neck as he hit her in a splendid place inside over and over, was the definition of ecstasy.

She gently bit his forearm before running her hand over her tattooed name.

She remembered her present to him, her keepsake from his hand. She pulled herself up, and Thomas didn't miss a thrust, kneeling and helping her straddle him so they remained connected. She took off her tank top and shirt, and Thomas reacted as if he were seeing her breasts for the first time, burying his face in them. As he turned his head to get a breath, he must have opened his eyes, because in the next second he stilled.

"This is still there?" He pointed to his inked name.

"It will be forever. I had it tattooed in place." She held his face and touched her forehead to his.

He gave her his intense look before taking her by the hips and moving her up and down on him. This was what being cherished felt like. She leaned backward and grabbed her breasts, pinching the nipples hard. As the passion became uncontrollable, he shouted her name, holding her in place with one hand and rubbing her with the other.

They came together, his orgasm lasting so long that he started apologizing between twinges of what he had left.

She could feel him inside her, like a heartbeat. She pulled her muscles tighter, letting him know she was well pleased.

Eventually he rolled to her side, propping up on his elbow.

To be naked with him, seeing him satisfied and sunny was a tremendous thing.

He put a hand on her breast before letting it drift to his name. "I can't believe you did this. You were able to recreate my signature?"

"No, it stayed. It was still on my arm when I woke up. And that's when it became my most treasured possession." She touched his chest, his throat, and skimmed his face. "I wish I could have a picture of you."

He caught her fingers when they coasted close to his mouth and kissed each one of her fingertips. "I draw you every time I get a chance. Sometimes it's in the dirt with a stick." He went back to her breast, setting her hand free again on its trek to memorize him. "But I can't capture you. Every time I forget how lovely you are. I can't get it perfect."

He kissed her again, and she responded. How could she ever live without this? She wanted to ask him where he was, why—anything so she could wake up and contact him. But she couldn't speak. All she had were tears that rimmed her lashes and a prayer that he would tell her on his own.

"Don't cry, my pretty Fallen. This. What we just did here? It will be the light in my darkest goddamn hour. Memories of time with you are my sanity."

She felt the dreaded heaviness in her lids and saw the droopy look on his face as well.

"I've never dreaded something so much as I do this feeling that takes you out of my arms." He cuddled her in close.

She touched her name on his arm, and he traced his signature on her skin.

When she knew she had just a blink or two left, she had to tell him. "I love you."

He hugged her even tighter, and as her lids sealed shut, forcing out the tears, he whispered in her ear, "I love you so much."

And then he was gone. .

14

WAKING, AGAIN

Fallen squeezed her eyes shut when she felt the rush of being pulled away from Thomas. If she refused to open her eyes, he wouldn't be gone.

But his heat was gone. That beautiful *thump thump* of his heart under her hand was missing.

They were just getting started. They were new together. With resignation, she opened her eyes. The loss of him was visceral. She felt sick. The only thing that could compel her out of the bed was the fear of being caught. Judging from the darkness in the room, she had pressed the hell out of her luck. She stood in the room for a moment, catching her breath and wondering exactly where Mr. Orbit might be—besides in her dream. Did that make him nearby in this realm as well? Just what were he and this room capable of?

Fallen was at least thankful that the darkness would aid her in removing the picture that had let her take her nap in privacy. But as she prepared to retrieve it, she looked around the room and realized she'd made a mistake. The little lights on the smoke detector and electronics had been an oversight. The picture did not include the lights. Fallen crawled up and took the picture down, all the while feeling like that was another mistake. She hadn't been careful enough.

She tried to stay out of the camera's view as best as she could after that, but opening the door let in a slice of light. She cursed herself and dragged her housekeeping cart out. Flipping the power on and off on every Thursday would be obvious. Too obvious. This was just the best she could do, and maybe none of it mattered anyway. Maybe Orbit knew exactly what she was up to, because he'd been up to it too.

She let the door shut behind her. Fallen put her cart away and braced for the cold. On her freezing walk home, some of her anxiety burned away. She grinned at the thought of Thomas' proclamation of love. She loved him, and he loved her back. It was a beautiful free fall until she framed it within the impossibility of their situation. He was at war. He'd said as much, so there was no denying it now. But which war? And where?

Yet even in the face of all this, her heart couldn't be fully dissuaded. There was something to what burned between them. She felt it.

In the morning, Fenn woke her instead of the other way around.

"We both have, like, four minutes to get out the door!"

Fallen sat straight up in bed, her notebook and pen still in her hands.

"Shit. Wait, what do you mean?" Luckily, she was still in her uniform. Or unluckily. "I didn't make you a lunch. Or me."

Fenn grabbed her hairbrush and her purse. "I have to be at

school early to get in time in the weight room. It's for football. C'mon, let's run!"

Together they pounded down the stairs. She plucked out a knife and a plate, and he used his football skills to toss her the stuff she needed from the cabinet across the room. She snatched bread and then peanut butter out of the air. He grabbed water bottles and plastic bags and stood next to her. As soon as she had the sandwiches made, he bagged them up. She went to the fridge and took out the two remaining apples, handing him the nicer one for his sack.

They put their coats on together, and she locked the door behind them. A friend honked for Fenn, and he grabbed her arm.

"Quick, if we go fast we can drop you off."

Fenn jumped in the passenger side and clambered over the seat. Fallen slid in behind him and slammed the door.

"You two look like that house was on fire."

Fenn introduced Fallen as the driver backed down the driveway like they were in a getaway car.

"Mitchel, this is my sister, Fallen. Fallen, this is Mitch. He drives too fast anyway, so don't feel guilty if he gets a ticket." He patted Mitchel on the shoulder. "Can we swing by Hotel Revel? Fallen overslept. You're going to have to floor it, though."

Mitchel smiled wide and hit the gas.

"Oh my God." Fallen fastened her seatbelt across her chest as the tires made a squealing noise that no doubt painted the road with rubber.

Fenn laughed. "Don't kill us, dickhead. We've got the spaghetti dinner tonight."

Mitchel took his eyes off the road to give Fallen an elaborate onceover. Before she could demand that he look at what he was doing, Fenn hit him in the back of the head. "That's my sister, not a girl. Do not even think about her."

Mitchel gave Fenn the finger while scowling at him in the rearview mirror.

Fallen tried to break the awkwardness by changing the topic back to dinner. "You need me to pick something up for you to bring tonight?"

Fenn shook his head. "Nah, we're good. Coach loves to do this. You coming on Saturday to our game?"

Fallen nodded. "I wouldn't miss it. Amazingly, I'm off on Saturday."

Mitchel drove up to the front of the hotel's elegant doors. "Here you go, Fallen."

She thanked him and reminded them to drive safe to school, but she didn't think they were paying attention. Her brother was busy crawling over the seat while punching Mitchel.

"Don't you even think about looking at her ass," he yelled as Fallen closed the door.

She turned and hurried inside, shaking her head. She slid into the meeting and listened to Melanny give out orders in a dull monotone that made Friday feel more like a Monday. Desta lingered as Fallen clocked in, and they walked to the supply closet in silence, though Fallen was almost buzzing with the need to chat.

Finally, in the elevator Desta told her to come up with her to start, so she could go over a new way the hotel was folding towels. Once they were tucked into a vacant room on Desta's fourth floor, the woman nearly exploded.

"Did you see him? Did you see Burt?" Her eagerness gave Fallen a glimpse of a much younger version of Desta.

"I'm not sure. I wish you had a picture." Fallen sat on the unmade bed. Desta seemed too anxious to sit.

"You and me both." Desta grabbed the room's pen and notepad. She stuck her tongue out to one side and started to draw. Fallen stood and watched over Desta's shoulder.

It became clear very quickly that Desta had no formal training in portrait art.

When she was finished, she held it up. "Well, that doesn't look right."

Fallen squinted, and Desta shook her head.

"He looks a little bit like Cookie Monster," Fallen offered.

Desta busted out laughing in a way that was contagious. They were both so stressed, the emotion took them over. It was quite a while before they could do anything other than gasp and wipe tears from their eyes. And Desta had to cough, of course.

Fallen touched the horrible drawing. "Maybe just describe him to me."

Desta nodded. "Much better idea. Well, he's tall, about yea high." She went to her tiptoes and held her hand above Fallen's head. "And his eyes are the softest brown. His nose is pointy, but not like a witch—regal like. And he likes to whistle. All the time he whistled while we walked. He could really keep a tune. Gray hair, not a lot of it. And he loves to smoke. Does that help?"

She looked so hopeful that Fallen was torn about telling her about the older gentleman she'd encountered at the dinner. It would get Desta's hopes up for sure. Fallen couldn't imagine going without seeing Thomas for years and years. What if she was wrong? What if Burt had died after all?

She took a chance and described her encounter with the waiter. "But he wasn't whistling. And your description is sort of general. I don't want to hurt you..."

Desta nodded. "Girl, I've been hurting since the last time I saw him, 12 years ago. I can take a little hope. It'll help me get through the day."

"I'll look for him every time; I promise." Fallen went to the other side of the bed and started to help. "Is there really a new way to fold towels?"

Desta rolled her eyes. "No, baby. You can keep doing it the way you were. You wanna tell me how it was? With your guy?"

"I'm scared. He's at war, and that has to be such a contentious place in time." Fallen picked a pillow up off the floor and fluffed it before setting it on the bed. "But the dream? It was amazing. He's amazing. I've never felt so…"

She was at a loss to name exactly what Thomas made her feel.

Desta supplied it for her. "Whole."

Fallen nodded. That was perfect. Thomas made her feel whole.

Fallen went about the rest of her day as usual, and as she was leaving for home, Desta hailed her in the parking lot. She got into the passenger seat of Desta's car after she unlocked the door. The heat was on full blast, though it wasn't very warm yet, and Desta lit a cigarette. She spoke around the act of inhaling and exhaling her vice.

"I just got a text from my friend. I do a few housecleaning jobs on the side to make extra cash. My friend does too, and she's moving out of state, leaving a fairly sweet deal. Adelaide Benson—I'll drive you past the house if you want—her family pays for a housecleaner twice a week. It's a cherry of a job because she's a neat freak. The visit is more to make sure she's got her heat on, and that she's doing okay. Sort of like a wellness check. She's in her nineties, and for the last few years she's been suffering from a bit of dementia. A housecleaner dropping by for $50 an hour is a lot cheaper than a nurse for her. I think she pretty much lives in the present—doesn't remember a lot about her past. And her kids don't visit her much. They all live somewhere else. But anyway, you go in, snoop around and check out her fridge, make sure she has hot water—that kind of thing. They pay you for two hours twice a week. Tuesdays and Saturdays. You want it? I'll recommend you to her."

Fallen was already nodding. "Are you sure? I don't want to take a job from you."

Desta shook her head. "No, baby, I've got too much to do already."

"Then yes. Absolutely. Thank you. Assuming I can walk there, that would be great."

"Well, buckle up, sweetheart. I'll drive you by." Desta finished texting and pinched her cigarette between her lips as she maneuvered the old car out of the spot.

This unmonitored alone time with Desta was too tempting. Fallen had to ask at least a few things of the only person she knew who understood being in love with a dream man. What if something happened to Thomas and he disappeared like Burt had? She needed all the information she could gather.

"How'd you do it? All these years without Burt?" Fallen watched Desta take another drag before she responded.

"I don't know. Minute by minute at first. And barely making it at that. I looked and looked for him. That's the hardest—not knowing what happened to him, why we couldn't find each other any more. Then hour by hour. Then day by day. There's not really a choice in the end, I guess."

She put her blinker on and turned toward Fallen's neighborhood. "I think maybe I'm good at hoping. That's why I take such good care of the hotel. In my way, I'm making sure I don't give up on what's happened to me there."

"You've had no other guys? No kids?" Fallen looked out the window.

"I was married once, a long time ago. But I was young. It didn't last long, and we didn't have kids. After that I went on a few dates here and there, but after Burt there was just..." Desta started coughing.

She didn't have to finish the sentence. Fallen could do that for her. *There was no one else like him.*

"Did you ever figure out where in time Burt was?" Fallen fiddled with a stray thread from the car's upholstery.

"Here and there I picked up hints from what he said, when the noise wasn't trying to blow our ears out. I think maybe he was from the 1920s—just the way he worded things, and some of the clothes he wore when we met up. He was in construction, I think. But I never was too sure. That's the hard part, when the men are from before technology." Desta brought them to a stop as a yellow light turned red.

"I'm pretty sure Thomas is at war, like I told you earlier," Fallen said. "Wherever he is. We do get the white noise, but sometimes he tells me things without really meaning to, I think." She shrugged and then clenched her fists. "I want to fight for him, but don't know how to do that."

"Well, getting information from him is something. Pay close attention to what he's wearing. That seems to be something they can't figure out how to hide. Whoever's in charge of that whole thing." Desta waved a dismissive hand.

Fallen felt like they both should be more interested in that aspect of their dream lives. Who was governing the censorship?

"Does being in a dream protect Thomas in his awake world?" Fallen felt a spark of hope.

"I don't know, sweetheart. If you had asked me thirteen years into my relationship with Burt, I would have said yes. It had seemed that way. But then he faded, and everything I believed in changed." Desta took her glasses off and cleaned them with the hem on her skirt.

"That's understandable…and terrifying," she added after a moment. And speaking of terrifying. "Was Mr. Orbit ever in any of your dreams?"

"No. No one was ever in the dreams with Burt and me. Well, that's not true. There were be others, but they didn't seem to matter. Like, I couldn't see them real good. Does that make sense?" Desta turned down a block Fallen knew well. The extra job would be amazing if it was this close to her house.

"Yeah, I wish Mr. Orbit wasn't there in mine. He seems possessive." Fallen watched the houses carefully. Trying to pay attention while talking about the dream world was hard.

Desta stopped in front of a small, neat house with tan siding, and her face looked pale when Fallen turned toward her. "You've seen Lad? When you're dreaming?"

Fallen nodded. "What does that mean?"

Desta shook her head. "I really don't know. Maybe I'll try to ask him sometime."

"Oh, I don't think that's a good idea at all," Fallen nearly shouted. She calmed herself. Desta surely knew much more about all this than she did, but it was hard to know who to trust.

"Maybe not," Desta said, staring at Fallen for another moment. Then she seemed to remember herself. "Okay, here's the place, according to my friend anyway." She motioned with her cigarette.

There was a buzzing and Desta took out her phone. "Well, girlie, looks like they're interested in you. Can you do a phone interview with Adelaide's daughter this evening?"

Fallen couldn't help but smile. "That sounds great!"

That money would be great for her and Fenn, and such easy work as well, though she felt nerves bubble up at the thought of an interview.

"Okay. You live close enough?" Desta looked at her over the top of her glasses.

"Yeah, for sure. I'm, like, two blocks that way."

Desta offered to drive Fallen home, but she wanted to walk it to see exactly how far it was. After hammering out the details of the time and getting contact info for the call with Adelaide's daughter, Fallen thanked Desta profusely, got out of the car, and plotted her route home.

Later that evening, when Fenn was studying in his room, Fallen called Adelaide Benson's daughter, Marquette, to discuss the available position. The woman was very businesslike, explaining that all the supplies Fallen would need were kept at the house, but that the true focus of the job was Adelaide's well-being and safety. Fallen would need to contact Marquette immediately if there was a problem or anything seemed off with her mother. Fallen agreed to be diligent about checking in regularly and spending some time with the elderly woman. After just a few questions about her background and experience, Marquette officially offered Fallen the job.

They exchanged email addresses, and Fallen promised to set up a MoneyPal account for payment since Marquette lived out of town. She hung up the phone hardly able to believe her luck.

15

FOOTBALL AND EX-WIVES

On Saturday, Fallen woke up after ten in the morning and felt gluttonous but refreshed. She tried not to think about what she'd be doing at the hotel right now. Anyway, her new job with Adelaide would be from 4 to 6 today, and after that she'd go to Fenn's game under the lights at 8. If she rushed through her house chores, she could get a few hours of research in before going over to meet Ms. Adelaide.

Fenn woke up even later than Fallen and was obviously pumped about the game. He happily scarfed down the grilled cheese sandwich she made for him before she headed out to the library. She wanted to talk more with him and felt guilty about skipping out until he mentioned he was going to practice in less than an hour.

After telling him about her new job, she wished him luck, promised to see him later, and locked the door behind them. She had to stop herself from running all the way to the library. Her fear about the war Thomas was fighting was always with her, but she was determined to channel it into action. Today she would see if searching for the name *Lucy McHugh* and researching wars the US had been involved in would turn up any additional information about where, and when, Thomas could be.

She remembered the look on Desta's face when she'd mentioned Lad being in her dreams. That worried her a little. She'd thought of the room just as a doorway to Thomas, but there was a whole other world there. And these days visiting it might be like riding an untested roller coaster without a seatbelt if things were happening that surprised even Desta, a 14-year veteran. But what could she do? Stopping wasn't an option. Pushing those worries aside, she opened the glass door to the library.

She was thrilled to see that it wasn't too crowded so they wouldn't yet be enforcing the half-hour computer time limit. If she wasn't kicked off, she could get in a good two and a half hours of searching before she would have to leave.

S craps of paper littered Fallen's station when she finally logged off. She'd attacked the problem from every angle she could think of, but ended her session without any uplifting information. Lucy McHugh didn't seem to have much of an online presence. The clothes Thomas wore in the dreams had held promise, but had yielded the soul-crushing realization that time was a definite issue. She'd compared his khakis and T-shirts with the images on a website that showed US military uniforms through the ages. Thomas' looked like standard issue from the Vietnam era or earlier. So the Thomas she met in her dreams was not living in her current, modern world.

As Fallen walked to Adelaide's house, she thought about ways of learning more about Thomas during the dreams. It would help to know the state where he lived, his birthdate, and where he was in the world. But she knew all those questions would be drowned out or would fail to come to her mind in the first place while she was in the dream.

When she looked up, she was surprised to find herself on her new client's block. She'd been in a daze the entire walk over. Fallen approached the neat house Desta had showed her and knocked on the door loudly, thinking of the elderly woman's hearing.

A small lady with a swirl of gray hair in a bun on her head opened the door. She had gorgeous blue eyes and lips dotted with pink lipstick.

"Hello, dear. Are you here to clean?" She put her crepe paper-skinned hand on Fallen's wrist.

"Yes, ma'am. I'm replacing your previous housekeeper. I hope I'm not too early." She stepped in and looked around. Desta hadn't been wrong. She would be hard pressed to find something to clean. "I'm Fallen Billow. I work at the Hotel Revel as a housekeeper, and I also live just a few blocks over with my brother. Thank you so much for having me in your home. Would you like to show me how you like to keep things?" She held out her hand for a formal shake.

"Fallen? What a unique name. I'm Adelaide Benson." She accepted Fallen's hand into her own and covered it with the other as well. It was as close to a hand hug as you could get. "Pleasure to meet you."

Fallen liked Adelaide right off the bat. She had such a light about her. The brief tour of the tidy house was sweet. Adelaide loved pictures of her family and had them grouped on the wall. By the end, Fallen knew each of Adelaide's children, grandchildren, and great grandchildren's names. It made her sad to think of Desta's comment about the family not stopping by much anymore, when the matriarch had such obvious love for all of them.

Reasons for the family's concerns about Adelaide's mental

health became clearer when she showed Fallen for the third time where she kept her broom.

Fallen offered to vacuum right away, because Adelaide said the machine was too heavy for her to move around. While making sure the carpet showed the stripes of a fresh sweeping, Fallen peeked to make sure the outlets weren't overloaded. She checked that the woman's windows were locked as she went through with a duster. When she wiped down the already sparkling fridge door, she opened it to run the cloth over the accordion-style rubber that helped keep the box closed and checked that the contents were good. Everything looked fresh.

The time went quickly, with Adelaide following behind and chattering pleasantly. After putting away the supplies and hanging the broom on a hook, Fallen promised to be back on Tuesday.

After she stepped out, she listened to make sure the door lock clicked into place.

She made her way home, freshened up, and put on an extra layer under her jeans and sweatshirt so she could stay warm at the football game.

On her walk to the school, she let her mind sift back through the information she'd learned that afternoon. Thomas was living somewhere in the past. But that didn't necessarily make their love story impossible—just a bit unconventional. The fact that he was at war, however, was more troubling. If his world was full of danger, he needed to get out of it as soon as possible. Fallen tried to keep her hopes in check, but her heart raced. Learning more from Ellen now seemed even more essential than it had before.

Fallen wasn't the first at the field, but she was early enough to get a good seat on the bleachers. She rubbed her mittened hands together until she saw her brother. He spotted her in the crowd and pointed as she waved. The team started to warm up.

The spot next to her creaked as someone sat down. She didn't pay attention until a cup appeared in front of her. She almost shrieked when she turned and met Mr. Orbit's eyes instead of Ellen's.

"I'm sorry. I don't drink coffee." She held up a hand to ward off his gift.

"It's hot chocolate. Do you drink that?" He held one for himself in his other hand.

She nodded and took it, mumbling her thanks. Her hands shook despite the heat of the cup. Having him next to her turned her stomach and put tears in her eyes she was desperate not to shed.

"Are you back for another visit at the hotel?" she asked. Every muscle in her body was strung tight. He seemed more sinister every time she saw him—asleep or awake.

"No. Just passing through. Always checking on things." He sipped his drink.

Fallen just continued to warm her hands. She was surely not going to drink something he'd had access to while she wasn't watching.

"He's looking good out there." Mr. Orbit pointed with his pinkie at Fenn, who tossed the football back and forth with Mitchel, the crazy driver.

"He knows how to play the game, and he's a hard worker." She moved away to give herself some more personal space.

"Never messes with the rules, I bet. Never takes a break on the company dime." Mr. Orbit sipped his drink again.

She didn't answer, but she heard the threat in his words. He wasn't talking about Fenn anymore.

She wanted to pour her hot chocolate on his crotch more than anything. But she refrained. He controlled her link to Thomas, Fenn's link to football, her job—so much. How had this happened?

Orbit pulled a box out of his trench coat and opened it. Inside was the watch Nora had sold to the pawn shop. Fallen looked from the watch to his eyes.

"I had a visit from your mother at the hotel earlier today." He tilted his head.

Fallen felt sick. "I'm sorry."

"She walked a long way to talk to me. And she was very regretful that she'd sold your watch. Told me a whole story about how she wanted to get the money back to you."

Fallen set her cup between her feet and hugged her body. "Could you tell if she'd been drinking?"

He nodded. "Yeah. The bottle of wine in the paper bag was kind of a tip off."

"I'm so sorry." She wanted something else to say, but she had nothing.

He shook his head. "Don't feel like you have to apologize. My father was a drunk. A functioning one, but a drunk."

Fallen looked at his face. He gave her a weak shrug. "Amazing he could run a multimillion dollar company while blasted off his ass most days."

"Nora's not functioning any more." Ironically, they finally had something in common.

"I noticed." He stopped her before she could apologize again. "No, I really mean it when I say you don't have to apologize. I think for my dad it had to do with the family business. I think he wanted something else out of life. Just a guess, though. He wasn't a touchy-feely type. We didn't talk much."

For a moment, Mr. Orbit was candid and real. Fallen was shocked into silence.

"I grabbed this back from the pawn shop, so you could have it again. I suggest you hide it."

"Well, I thought it was hidden before." Fallen sighed sadly. "I couldn't possibly take another gift from you." She held up her hands.

"I hope you will. This might be the first nice thing I've done in a while. Positive reinforcement and all that." He offered it to her again.

She took it in her mittened hand, thinking of Fenn and his graduation someday. It would be a wonderful thing to give him, but every time she saw it on her brother's wrist, would it make her feel the uncomfortable way Mr. Orbit made her feel?

"Thank you." She watched Fenn move to huddle with his team.

"I fear I haven't approached my interest in you the correct way. Have I frightened you?"

Fallen hesitated before looking at him. It was impossible to know how to answer. If she said no, he might keep it up—the pictures, the stalking in room 514, not to mention their strange dream-world relationship. But if she said yes, what would he do with that information?

She decided silence was the safest and shrugged.

"You don't have to say anything." He pulled out his phone and took his glove off to open up his pictures app.

Fallen winced as he began pulling up the photos and deleting them one at a time. She looked over her shoulder to see if anyone else was looking. He had made good use of his zoom feature.

Seeing how many he had took her breath away. Last in the lineup was the one of her on the bed, terror in her eyes.

"You know what? If this is you trying to date me, you have for sure gone about it the wrong way." Her temper had taken over. She heard a warning voice in her head, but this man was a bully.

He slipped his phone back into his pocket. "I can see that." His lips became a tight line.

"I just want to do my job. That's it. I didn't ask for any of the rest of this." She tossed up her hands and accidently knocked over the hot drink at her feet.

When she bent over to pick it up, he snaked his arm around her waist.

She sat up quickly and gave him a hard look. "What did I just say?"

He looked around her. "Shh. It's my ex-wife. I need you to pretend to be happy for a few minutes."

"Mr. Orbit, seriously." Fallen had had enough of his bullshit. She went to stand, but he pressed both hands on her hips to keep her in place.

"Just another minute." He tracked someone over her shoulder.

Fallen turned to see Ellen moving through the section, though she didn't seem to be looking their way.

"Let go of me, or I'll scream."

"You scream and you're fired." The glimpse of humanity she'd seen in him was gone.

She put her head down, hating herself.

"Just lean into me now. That's a good girl. Snuggle up."

Orbit put his arms around her unyielding body. She didn't do as he asked, but she didn't make a scene either.

"Ellen needs to know what she's missing."

He seemed to say this more to the demons in his head than to her.

Fallen waited him out while he smiled, which she didn't reciprocate, and patted her back as if their embrace was mutual and enthusiastic.

"There—she's found a seat. I should have remembered that her stepson plays for Poughkeepsie." He let go of Fallen, and she shifted even farther away. "That wasn't so bad, right?"

She ignored him and turned toward the game. She began fantasizing about Thomas bounding across the field, leaping into the bleachers, and punching Mr. Orbit's lights out.

"Listen, I have to go, but know that I'm here if you want to talk about your mom. I understand." He patted her shoulder, and she flinched.

When she didn't respond further, he got up and left. She felt tears in her eyes again. He was going to make this impossible. Fallen wiped her nose and put a hand on her chest. She couldn't quite take a deep breath. Being around Mr. Orbit felt like being locked in the truck of his fancy car while he drove her who knows where. She would have to compromise a lot to see Thomas. But she knew her heart wouldn't let her make any other choice.

After she got her nerves under control, she focused on connecting with Ellen. Though now she wondered if it was too big a risk. She wouldn't put it past Orbit to be sneaking around, watching her.

Fenn was on the bench to start the game. Fallen picked up the mess of her cup and sidestepped her way out of the bleachers, finding a trash can to toss it in. She took the opportunity to look all around, remembering that Ellen had on a red jacket. In a sea of blue shirts and scarves supporting the home team, the red jacket was easy to spot.

Ellen met her gaze like she'd been waiting for it to happen. Fallen watched as the woman excused herself from the man beside her and began to walk toward the building.

The bathroom seemed to be Ellen's go-to meeting spot, and Fallen followed her at a distance—though she wasn't sure why she bothered. If Orbit was peeping from somewhere, he would know they were up to something.

Ellen smiled like they were good friends as their eyes met in the mirror. Another woman was also washing her hands, so Fallen played along.

"I heard your son plays for Poughkeepsie?"

Ellen responded, "Why, yes, he's number 33."

The hand-washing woman left, and Ellen checked the stalls. "We're alone."

When she turned back toward her, Fallen took in her earmuffs and tall boots. Ellen looked elegant and like she had money for days.

"I've been checking my email for a response." Fallen folded her arms.

"Are you with him? I saw you two hugging." Ellen folded her arms as well.

"Are you jealous? Is that what this is about? Because I honestly have too much on my plate right now to deal with that." Fallen edged for the door. Maybe the woman had nothing to offer and the best thing to do would be walk away.

"Understand this: I'll never be jealous of that man in my life." Ellen stood straighter. "He took things from me that I cherished. I'm just grateful I outsmarted him. And I want to offer you some hope. I just have to know that I can trust you."

Fallen thought she saw compassion on the woman's face. Ellen unfolded her arms and pointed in the direction of the bleachers.

"I found my true love here, while I'm awake. We're together every day now. But it was a fight, and Lad did everything he could to prevent it from happening. It was worth it, though. My husband is worth *any* fight." Ellen made her leather-gloved hands into fists.

Fallen recognized Ellen's determination; it was reflected in her heart as well.

"Joe and I were an anomaly. People who dream in the room aren't usually able to meet in person." Ellen looked nervously at the door. "And I never want to risk what Joe and I have. But I think technology is the downfall. Before the internet, people weren't able to track each other as easily."

The bathroom door opened to admit an older woman. "Ellen? There's a Joe waiting for you outside. He asked me to tell you Lad's car is in the parking lot?"

"Thank you. Very much." Ellen looked at Fallen. "Just keep at it. Don't stop looking. I'll try to send more emails if I can. I just don't want Lad to know that we talk—that could put both of us in danger. Please be as discreet as possible. Good luck."

And with that, she left the bathroom. Fallen waited a moment to give her a head start, then returned to her seat in the stands and tried, without much success, to focus on the game.

Fallen used Sunday to get groceries and clean the house. There was laundry to be done. She also hid Fenn's watch again, loosening a board in her closet this time and adding some Elmer's glue that did a damn good job of keeping the wood from rattling around when it was touched.

In the afternoon she and Fenn did yard work together, and Fenn told her he'd seen their mother downtown, walking hand in hand with a man. When he'd waved, Nora had turned her back. Fenn had rationalized this as their mother just not seeing him, but Fallen had darker thoughts of Nora not wanting Fritz to meet her kids—or maybe even know she had any. Fenn said Nora had looked pretty clear, their code for not completely intoxicated, but Fallen cautioned him to not get his hopes up. She told him a version of what Mr. Orbit had said about the visit from Nora at work because it seemed to be the only way to help him understand her current state.

As usual, he managed this news better than she'd expected, and they had a nice dinner of homemade pizza after they had cleaned up from working outside. Fallen felt like the day had been well spent.

On Monday, Desta was absent again from work. Fallen walked behind maids 8 and 9 and heard them wondering about it. Apparently Desta's attendance record was legendary, so this was unusual—and a bit alarming. Fallen wondered if Desta was ill or if Orbit had "suggested" leave for her again. She had things she wanted to ask Desta about Ellen. Could he have anticipated that? And she was also eager to report about her experience with Adelaide. She just plain missed the only woman at work she thought of as a friend.

Instead of any chatting, Fallen cleaned four extra rooms on Desta's floor, but she couldn't bring herself to skip 514 to save time. She had to be in the place where she found her gateway to Thomas, even if right now it was closed.

After dusting the desk, Fallen picked up the antique mirror to shine the front. When she caught sight of herself in the reflection, she squinted. Just past her, she thought she could see something—a moving picture like a tiny television set in the top left corner. It sure looked like Thomas... And then a little brown puppy came bounding over. The man picked up the dog and rubbed its head before looking in her direction. She wondered if he could feel her watching him.

And when she blinked, all of it was gone. The mirror held nothing but her reflection. Maybe she'd made it up in her head. She'd used her imagination to drum him up because she missed him so much. Fallen hugged the mirror to her chest before she remembered the camera watching her. Then she shined it again and set it back on the desk. All she really wanted to do was tuck it in her cart and take it home to stare in it. Instead, she finished her routine.

As she walked home and then made dinner for Fenn after he got home from practice, Fallen thought about the mirror. She'd have to pay attention to it when she fell asleep on Thursday to see if it did anything. She remembered seeing a flash of light in it once or twice when she was transitioning from the dream place.

Tuesday, she saw Fenn off to school—or to the weight room, actually—and scooted off to work. She was pleased to see Desta had made it when she arrived, but the woman looked a little worse for the wear. Seems her sick day had been legit and not Orbit-induced.

"How's it going?" Fallen gave her a gentle pat on the shoulder.

"Doc wants me to quit the cigs." Desta huddled over in what looked like a painful round of coughing. She kept one hand on her mouth and the other in the center of her chest. "But I ain't no quitter."

"I know." Fallen gave her a half smile. She appreciated Desta's dedication to the hotel and, in a twisted way, even her smoky testament to Burt.

"Did the doctor give you anything for the cough?" They arrived at the supply closet and Fallen helped Desta pull her cart out. Someone had refreshed it before Fallen had a chance to, and she looked at the housekeepers for 8 and 9. "*Thanks,*" she mouthed, and they nodded. Their concern for Desta had been genuine, and it was a relief to see that maybe they weren't completely evil.

"No. Just told me to add honey to my tea and take some painkillers for my chest. He's trying to get me to start with the e-cigs, but that feels like cheating a little on Burt." Desta gave Fallen a broken look. "It'll get better as the day goes on. Think I'm just fighting something off."

Fallen decided to follow Desta to her floor and do the four rooms she'd worked on yesterday to make the woman's day a little lighter.

8 and 9 had already started on their share of Desta's rooms, but Desta fought them all when she realized their plan. Eventu-

ally they each agreed to do only three rooms and let Desta do a few of her own.

Fallen was happy when she finished her allotment in about the same amount of time as 8 and 9. She was getting better at her job. They all crowded into the birdcage when it was time to go up to their own floors.

"Damn. Desta looks rough," 8 tisked. "I don't like her color. It's all, like, gray and shit."

9 agreed. "Desta, she's the real deal. Did I tell you about when my kid was in the hospital? It was before you were hired. I thought I was fired for missing so much work."

8 nodded. "Yeah, you told me. Ol' D did your rooms and logged you in so you'd get paid."

9 shrugged. "When a woman helps you with your child? That's a good person. She didn't even know me yet either."

8 snorted as the elevator stopped on five. "You're lucky about that. If she'd known what an asshole you are, she never woulda helped you."

9 grabbed the spray bottle of water off her cart and squirted 8 as Fallen pushed open the gate and pulled her cart forward.

As she stood in the hallway, 8 addressed her like a person, for possibly the first time ever. "It's good, you helping Desta. She needs a friend. Nice lady."

"Thanks, you too. And I agree. She's an open heart." Fallen waved as she maneuvered her cart down the hall.

"Later, rookie," 9 called as the door closed.

Fallen shook her head and allowed herself a sigh of relief.

After a few more hours of work, she took a lunch break to see Desta, whose color did look much better now. She asked Fallen about the new job and seemed happy to hear Adelaide was such a sweetheart.

With the extra rooms she'd added on, Fallen's day ended too late for the library, especially since she was due at Adelaide's again, so checking her email for word from Ellen would have to wait until tomorrow.

Adelaide answered her door with a smile, and she followed Fallen around the house as she did her neatening and checking all at once. When Fallen was done putting the cleaning supplies away in the closet, Adelaide offered her a cup of tea. Fenn wouldn't be home for a bit, so she didn't see the harm. Plus, assessing how the woman moved around the kitchen was probably a good idea. She was no elder expert, but making sure Adelaide could operate the stove and turn off the burners seemed like a good place to start.

Adelaide was adorable company. She loved to talk about flowers and the music she'd liked when she was younger. She repeated herself a bit, but other than that, she was delightful. Fallen shared a few heavily edited versions of her Thursday dreams with Thomas. The older woman was an active listener and smiled a lot when Fallen said the word *boyfriend*. Saying it made Fallen smile too. It was nice to talk to someone and confide in a safe place about her out-of-the-ordinary love life.

After a nice cup of tea, Fallen helped carry the teacups to the sink and took over the washing. Adelaide fussed but eventually allowed her to do it. Fallen commented about how delicate the cups were as she dried them, and the older woman launched into a description of her antique collection.

Fallen excused herself and left soon after. Fenn's ride was just pulling up as she stuck her key in the door at home. He looked exhausted. They had cereal for dinner and watched their favorite competition show before going to bed.

Wednesday was another day without Desta, and Fallen talked to 8 and 9 about it. They decided to take Desta a meal. Fallen had to do math in her head to make sure she could swing it. Friday would be payday, for both the hotel and her new job with Adelaide, assuming she got to her email in the afternoon, so she could make it work. She passed 8 all the cash she had, and 9 promised they'd stop by the store and then deliver the food after work.

Fallen went in and out of 514 two times more than necessary, pretending to leave something behind, but the mirror wasn't doing anything peculiar. By the end of the day, she doubted she'd ever seen anything at all. Still, she began to feel butterflies on the eve of seeing Thomas.

When she got there after work, the library was crowded with seniors taking a computer class, so she had to wait for something to open up—giving her only a half hour to check her email before closing.

She started with the money, because it was the most pressing, though she hated to put off anything that had to do with Thomas. Fallen set up her Moneypal fairly quickly and had an account ready to go when she logged into her email. There was a message from Ellen. It had no salutation, just a tidbit of information:

Choose somewhere you can barely remember. It might be harder for him to find you that way.

The *him* had to be Lad. Fallen read the words twice before the lights flashing overhead sped her along. She emailed Marquette and gave her the Moneypal account information, thanking her again for the job and privilege of spending time with her mother.

She hit send as the librarian gave her a warm smile.

"Thank you! This is great that you have computers. It really helps."

The lady nodded and waited as Fallen made her way out the side door. She didn't get time to research, but tonight, she got to have the fluttering in her stomach and a heart pounding with expectation.

Too bad she also felt a spike of worry as she considered the possibility that Desta might still be sick. And then a stab of guilt that she seemed more concerned about Desta being at work than the woman's health. But if anyone knew how desperate she felt about her weekly encounters, it was Desta.

Fallen calmed herself with the knowledge that the woman would likely do everything she could to get to work tomorrow. And that meant tomorrow she would see Thomas.

16

BLACKOUT

Fallen wore makeup to work on Thursday, and she'd brushed her hair until it shone before carefully winding it into a bun. When she saw Desta across the morning meeting, a wave of relief flowed through her, followed by a chaser of concern because Desta looked awful. Fallen traded worried looks with 8 and 9. After getting the normal business from Melanny, the three followed Desta as she went to retrieve her cart.

"Thank you for the food, but you girls need not fret about me. I'm an old battle ax. Just want to use up all my sick time." Desta stopped to cough and needed the wall to stay upright. "And don't you be cleaning my rooms either! None of you get it right."

8 and 9 gave her hell and said they were each doing two rooms and that was that. Fallen waited while they left, and was about to tell Desta she'd do two rooms too when the woman stopped her.

"I had to be here for that blackout? Right?"

Fallen smiled. "Thank you. I can't tell you how much I appreciate that you'd even think of that. But if you need to be at home, getting better, that's okay. I'll still find a way there, and I'll keep looking for Burt."

Desta frowned. "Baby, between you and me, there's no getting better."

Fallen stepped into one of the empty, messy hotel rooms, pulling Desta gently in with her. "What do you mean?"

"It's cancer." Desta shrugged.

"Oh, Desta, I'm so very sorry." Fallen hugged her.

"No, don't you worry. I knew what I was doing. All these years. After I stopped seeing him, it was a means to an end." Desta patted the pack of cigarettes in her pocket.

"What about Burt? What if I can find him? You have to try to get better, right?" Fallen knew a lot about alcoholism, but nothing about the disease Desta was facing.

"Let's get you into 514 today, nice and safe. We'll worry about the rest later." Desta gave Fallen a soft smile.

They coordinated a time, and Desta handed Fallen a contraption to stow in her cart. She'd attached the room picture to posterboard and inserted tiny lights for the smoke detector and TV connections. They connected to a battery pack on the back. Desta also handed her some sticky utility hooks.

"You gone high tech on me!" Fallen inspected the apparatus.

"I improved it a little. Hopefully this will work for a while. I've got a dollhouse collection, so I just needed to be a little creative. Plug the battery in and pop these command hooks up, and we'll have rigged a government-level sabotage here."

Fallen hugged Desta again. "Thank you."

The day was a dragging thing, and Fallen felt like her heart was beating in her throat as she rushed through her rooms. Just before lunch, she had a nice distraction by way of a left-behind plush llama in room 510. Fallen brought it downstairs just as Melanny sent her an urgent message. The llama's owner was rather distraught about its absence. Fallen helped Melanny text pictures of the llama enjoying his wait for the little girl near the gym and the candy machine. Assured that a tearful reunion was coming—the family hadn't gotten far—Fallen went back upstairs.

At the appointed time, Desta came through, popping the breaker again. Fallen took a bit longer than she'd intended getting the hooks in place, even though she'd pre-peeled everything. When the picture was finally hanging and the room lights came back up, it looked a little askew, but the miniature lights were on. Fallen looked at the time. 5pm. Seven hours with Thomas.

She lay on the bed to wait for the heaviness. Like a cloying drug entering her bloodstream, Fallen welcomed the false sleep with her lips curved into a smile.

The rush was next, and then she opened her eyes. The first thing she saw was her hand, and the sparkling diamond Lad had put there last time. She noticed the music next. A peppy, timeless dance beat came from the stage. As she raised her head, Lad's gaze was unfaltering on her from across the room. His attention was a jolt to her nervous system. He had a smile for her, but his eyes were angry.

Her blood ran cold for a moment, but she urged herself not to panic. So far she seemed to have some semblance of control during the dreams, despite Lad's attempts at manipulation. They'd always outwitted him, but it was unnerving that he managed to be everywhere, in all her worlds.

Why couldn't she just be alone with Thomas, not playing these games? Not constantly afraid? The dancing people around her were far clearer than usual. Lad was still across the room, but seemed to be making his way over to her.

She looked around to find there were no windows and only two doors. The clapboard room had a shabby chic feel with blue decorations. A large chalkboard on an easel read *Best Wishes Lad and Fallen* in careful handwriting.

An engagement party.

Her engagement party.

Lad was a stubborn guy. She yanked on the ring, but it wouldn't come off. She glared at him as he smiled over someone's offer of congratulations.

She looked for Thomas but couldn't find him among the crowd. She looked down at the slice of cake in front of her. Vanilla with strawberry icing. She stood on her tiptoes to get a better look at the men dressed in shirts and ties sitting at round tables with pristine white tablecloths. Then she noticed the older man seated across from her.

She took a chance and called to him. "Burt?"

He searched her face. "How'd you know my name?"

"Desta told me." Fallen reached her hand in his direction.

"My Desta?"

But that was as far as their conversation went. When Fallen looked up, Lad was still coming toward them.

"I'm sorry; I have to go." Burt stood and melted into the crowd.

Fallen wondered why, but filed the encounter away to tell Desta about.

There was still no sign of Thomas. Would this be the time he didn't make it?

Her stomach dropped.

Oh God, maybe he hadn't made it through the week. He was at war, after all. She hated the thought of it, the word, and everything it made her feel.

Then a huge crack split the air. Everyone turned to see the source of the noise, and the door cracked and splintered. The band stopped playing, and the door flew open.

Thomas had anticipated the kick back and stopped the door from hitting him with an open palm. He wore his usual uniform, and his hair was messy. It almost covered one eye. He found her immediately like he'd known where she would be standing.

She put her hand over her heart as relief flooded her. He was alive. He was here. She smiled at him, so ready to see him, be near him.

He stalked across the room, the guests rushing out of his way like he might be dangerous. The determined look on his face would be scary to others.

But not to her. Not now. He knocked tables over to get to her—just flipped furniture out of his way. Silverware clattered, and strawberry icing splattered on dresses.

He showed no sign of caring.

Fallen stepped around the table so there would be nothing between them when he got to her. She could see Lad closing the last of the distance, but Thomas made sure he was in front of Fallen first.

She put her hands on Thomas's back. The warmth she felt soothed her. Real.

"Step out of the way. That's my fiancée."

Lad was either very foolish or very brave to stand up to the man protecting her right now. Thomas was a warrior. The way he held his body was a warning. He reached behind his back to grasp Fallen's hand and give it a comforting squeeze. She moved closer and rested her head on his back. She hated that their time together was being wasted.

"I'll have you know she entered this contract of her own free will," Lad said. "She does a lot of things of her own free will that you have no idea about."

Fallen slipped underneath Thomas' arm to see how far dream Lad was planning on taking his threat.

He reached into his pocket and held out a photo. She looked at her feet in shame. It was the picture from the bed, when he'd made her kneel on it.

Thomas threw the picture on the ground, where Fallen's gaze was holding.

Before she could vocalize her apology, Thomas stepped

away from her and punched Lad right in the face. The man went down like a he'd been turned off from the inside.

Gasps and shouts went up, and the crowd switched from watching to actively trying to participate in the fight.

Thomas seemed to be already ahead of them, an exit plan set up in his head. He pulled her with purpose toward the second door in the room. He tried the knob, and it was locked. The crowd seemed unsure what to do, and Burt was nowhere to be found as Thomas set Fallen to the side and began breaking down the second door.

Fallen used the time to pile toppled tables behind them to slow the mob. She heard the crack of the door giving way and turned to find Thomas' hand. He wrapped his arm around her waist instead.

"Hop," he commanded, and she did. He lifted her over the broken remnants of the door, and then they were off running. They'd gotten to the end of the parking lot when he whirled her close to him, wrapping her in a hug.

"Think of somewhere for us while he's unconscious." Thomas seemed almost frantic.

"Um... I don't, I haven't..." She wracked her brain for somewhere good. "I think if we go somewhere we just barely remember, it might be harder for him to find."

Thomas nodded. "Plus I knocked him out, so that will give us a head start." He kissed her.

She closed her eyes and moaned. "Don't ask me to think when you do that."

He kissed her forehead. "That's my problem. All I can think about is your naked body, and that's not helping us. You do it. Come on, baby. I know you can."

She centered herself and forced everything else from her mind.

A walk. A walk she'd taken so long ago—she was maybe ten? It had been fall, and the lush sunlight made the trees look like their colors had been dappled on with a paintbrush. Mostly golds, but some reds as well. It had been the most perfect fall day when she found the old church, or at least that's what her young mind had dubbed the skeleton of the building, which was all that remained.

So marvelous. And now, as a grown woman, she had decorated it with white sheers over the openings where the windows once were. It had no roof, but plenty of nooks and crannies for little white candles. Maybe some late blooming ivy threaded through the beams where the roof used to be? And a bed. With Thomas, she always needed a bed so she could lay next to him and whisper secrets, feel his hot breath on her neck.

"Congratulations," he told her as she opened her eyes.

She looked only at him at first, but then their setting came into focus. Perfection. The dream had reincarnated the crisp splendor of that day so long ago. The meadow surrounding the church had piles of the dry, colorful leaves as if a groundskeeper had been there to tidy up.

She wore a short white swing dress and thick thigh-high socks for warmth. Her brown boots ended just above her knees and she'd given him jeans, a white T-shirt, and a black leather jacket.

"I wish I could take a picture of you, with me, right now." She touched his face and remembered the horrible picture Lad had showed him. She took her hand away, sure he would think less of her now.

He seemed to read her mind and put her hand back on his face. "Dream girl, I know what you look like when you want to do something. And I remember you telling me about the pictures he made you take. In that picture Lad showed me? You weren't happy. Are you okay?"

"He's persistent in my awake world, too. But dealing with him is worth getting to see you." Fallen turned her head and kissed his palm. "Please don't let him take any more of our time together. It's precious."

He nodded and hugged her closer, kissing the top of her head. "This is beautiful. Nice work."

She pushed away from him and walked to the nearest leaf pile. "I'm sure I could do better, but this picture came when I asked for one, so it'll do."

She spread her arms, turned, and tipped backwards into the pile. The multicolored leaves fluffed into the air, trickling down around them as he dove in to lie on top of her.

"I love the smell of leaves." He nuzzled her neck for a bit, and she cradled his head to her chest.

"I could hold you forever. Just like this. I'm so happy with you." She threaded her fingers through his thick hair.

His voice rumbled against her chest. "As soon as I can, I'm going to take the pictures I draw of you to all the pairs of eyes I can find back home. I will find you, Fallen. You've got this unique name and perfect face. It shouldn't be too hard." He lifted his handsome face to look at her.

She wished she were able to sketch him too. "You broke down a door to get to me."

"I'd break down every door in the world to get right here. With you. Right now." He slipped underneath her, pulling her body on top of his.

He stopped for a moment, wiggled off the ring Lad had installed on her hand, and tossed it as far as it would go. She had leaves caught in her hair and started to pick them out. He grabbed her hands.

"No. Don't. They look like a crown with the sun behind you like that. Just kiss me." He hugged her closer, and she didn't fight him.

Kissing him was exactly what she wanted for this moment. In the long week between this Thursday and the next, she would remember him just like this: her lips against his while his hands explored her body. He reached her ribs, and his touch tickled, so she sat up and giggled. Mischievousness glinted in his eyes, and he went for that same spot with more purpose.

Fallen grabbed two handfuls of leaves and tossed them at him, scurrying away from his determined hands.

He was behind her faster than she could run, scooping her up and tossing her over his shoulder in a maneuver that made her feel intensely feminine.

"Want to check out this church you built?" He spanked her bottom, and she kicked her feet.

"Yes. A lot."

He tickled her again as he carried her up the old stairs before putting her down on her feet and pulling her back against his chest. She loved how it had turned out. The shabby, whitewashed wood was comfy and welcoming. The white sheers billowed, and the open roof allowed the leaves making their descent to enter, landing with gentle pats. The center roof beam supported the candlelit chandelier that hung above the bed.

It was extraordinary. She turned in his arms to look at his face again. His jawline was so sharp, it could sell perfume. He'd be a model, maybe, when she found him. She had to remember to flip through magazines. Thomas' cheekbones were the kind a camera would love, playing with the shadows and his scruff to make a spectacular art piece.

His broad shoulders were strong as she ran her hands across them. A flicker of a memory came to her as she enjoyed the sight of him.

"The puppy—the puppy you found… Is it brown?"

He lifted an eyebrow. "Yes, she is. How'd you know?"

But Fallen was at a loss to remember how she knew that fact, and why she'd wanted to ask. She couldn't find it anywhere in her mind.

"Your profile." He tilted his head and ran his fingertip from her forehead down the slope of her nose, gently passing over her lips before tapping her chin. "I never do it justice. Lovely. You were meant for silhouettes and cameos."

She kissed his finger when it passed over her lips again.

"Am I a brute for wanting to skip the talk? For wanting to have you naked so soon into our dream?" His nostrils flared as he seemed to hold himself back.

She shook her head. "You've waited long enough."

Fallen loved that he'd said it was *their* dream. At least they had that to share.

She pulled her leafy hair off her neck as he unraveled her scarf, sniffing it quickly before tossing it aside. He took to his knee and unzipped her boots. She held herself steady using his shoulders. When he was done, he turned his face and ran his scruff against her wrist.

"You can leave these on." He ran his hands up her calf until his fingertips danced along the edge of her thigh-high socks. She smiled to herself, happy he was pleased with them.

She held her arms above her head as he grasped the edge of her dress, pulling it off as he stood. He tossed it near her scarf on the ground. Thomas bit his lip when he saw her black satin bra edged in lace.

"So tempting." He touched the seams, and she arched her back like a cat, desperate for more.

Fallen twirled so he could see her matching black panties.

Then his hands were all over her, as if her skin demanded his. Magnetized, with just a bit of bite to his grip, he let her know he was as near frenzy as she was.

She stopped him by stepping away. "You." She stepped back to him, to take control. "Now you."

Undressing Thomas made her heart pound. To see him, just for her, simultaneously vulnerable and strong made wanting him inside her more than sexual. She wanted him inside so she could keep him safe. Keep him real. Keep him near.

Her hands roamed unabashedly. His ass was glorious, and

she grabbed it because she could. He pulled her knee up to his hip and pushed himself against the satin there. He leaned down to kiss her and backed her up at the same time, lifting her gently when they got to the side of the bed. She spread her legs and welcomed him between them.

"This." Thomas paused to search her face. "You make the long days in between worth it."

And then there was no further discussion. He put his lips on her, and she was far, far, gone in him, lying back so she wouldn't fall. He slid her panties to the side as one finger joined his mouth in bringing her pleasure.

His other huge hand found her breast and pushed the lace out of the way so he could pinch her nipple.

It took her no time to fall over the edge he'd brought her to. Loud and desperate, she called his name.

Before she could offer any of her own talents, he flipped her over and set her on her knees.

"Okay?" he asked.

"Harder," she responded before he was even inside of her.

A string of curses spilled from his mouth, and she tossed her hair to urge him on, holding on to the bedspread as he rocked her. She went from bracing herself with her hands to resting on her elbows, changing the tilt of her hips to accept him more deeply.

She felt the delicious pain of heat across her back, which sent her pleasure to another level. She pulled away, spun, and crawled over him. As she licked up his chest, she saw what had caused her pain. The wax from the candles above had dripped onto their skin. She pushed him to lie flat on his back. She mounted him and tilted back as she began to rock, the wax now painting her chest, along with his.

When he came, he tensed and hollered, and she did the same, feeling him pulse inside of her. He raked his fingertips over the drips of now hardening wax and teased yet another wave from her before pulling her up to his chest and rolling over her to protect her from the wax now falling in a steady rhythm. He stood and blew the candles out. Then Thomas slowly peeled the wax from her chest, stopping to run his tongue over her nipples. When she was clean, he lay beside her.

Fallen found her spot, putting her head on his shoulder. They rested in the quiet for a while before she said, "Tell me something about you."

She carefully peeled the wax from his arm.

He looked down at her. "Let me catch my breath. Tell me about you."

He played with the edge of her hair, pulling a leaf free.

"There's not much to say. Keeping things on track takes most of my time. My mom's not going to change. I don't think she'll ever be able to on her own, and I don't have the resources to help her."

"But Fenn's doing great, right?" Thomas rubbed a gentle pattern on her back.

"He is. I just want to be ready for the future. I want to make sure he has a safe place to land, if he ever needs to get back on his feet for any reason. And I'd love to make enough money that I can give Nora support without having her steal from me."

"I think that's a great plan."

"But finding you—that's what I need right now." She kissed his chest and wrapped her fingers in his, letting his heart beat against their palms.

"Don't forget, you want to be a teacher. Make sure that happens." He gave her a look before releasing her hand and hugging her closer.

They held each other like that for a while, in their roofless church as fall leaves tumbled down on them like blessings.

"Now tell me something. Just anything to think about until next time. Does anything worry you?" Fallen turned on to her stomach.

"Tell you what, before you, I'd stopped worrying. Because I'd stopped caring. I mean, lots of the guys have girls they want to get home to, but I didn't. Not until you. And now getting to Thursday is all that matters. I made it through all my time on this planet without falling in love. I've enjoyed ladies, mind you, but no one has ever caused me to fixate on the curve of her hip for hours in a portrait before—like my life depended on it. You've made me grateful for my next breath."

His devastating blue eyes were soft on her, and his words touched her soul.

"Tell me about something that made you laugh," she whispered, kissing his bicep.

"Oh, okay. Let me think." He propped up on his elbow so he could run his hands over her back and bottom. "Um…you're distracting me."

"Tell me something good, and I'll dance naked for you." She wrinkled her nose.

He bit his lip and rolled his eyes. "How about when me and my meathead brothers decided to make the mountain we live on into a giant sledding path?"

She nodded. "Sounds good."

"Well, we were in high school, and we'd just had a huge blizzard. Like, almost two feet of snow and giant drifts. So we dragged our sleds and skis to the roof of the house—it's two stories, mind you—and we patted down a path that went all the way from our roof through all the neighbors' properties down the mountain, across a road, and over some giant rocks. And then we tromped back up the hill and started wagering who could do it the fastest.

Johnny ran in to some girls and told them to follow, and he had them time us. I had on the skis, and Eddie and Johnny were on the sleds. We took off like a bunch a dummies. And the whole damn time, it was drizzling. But did we pay attention? No way. There were girls to impress. So we got started and right away, we knew we were in trouble. It was too fast. The whole track was now covered in ice, and we went flying down the mountain.

Johnny just laughed his head off, screaming about kissing our asses goodbye. Eddie started praying out loud, and I was just trying not to run headlong into a tree. But did any of us stop? Hell no. Because we'd rather be dead than lose. Bunch of idiots. So we almost died going across the road—barely missed two cars and a truck that couldn't stop." Thomas stopped to laugh out loud.

Fallen took a guess. "Because of the ice?"

"Oh yeah." He nodded, sitting up. "And then the girls were waiting at the bottom. Their eyes were huge when we came down that mountain faster than three rockets. They were diving for cover, Eddie was still praying, and Johnny laughed so hard he damn near pissed his pants. I was mostly trying to figure out how to stop us, because there was a sheer cliff coming. You see, we hadn't really put a ton of thought into stopping. Just figured we'd taper off at the end. Instead we picked up speed. So I stopped trying to stop myself and jumped in front of my brother's sleds. They ran over me—both of them—and we came to a halt inches from certain death."

Thomas rolled over to show Fallen his scars. "These are from their sled rails.

And then Johnny starts singing a crazy song about how these girls are going to have to tell Ma her three stupid sons have fallen off the mountain. And he has the worst singing voice in the world, but he gets all of us laughing so damn hard—the girls included. What a day."

Fallen wiped tears from her eyes while she laughed. The story itself was hilarious, but the delivery was everything. He radiated pure joy.

"That's incredible," she said. "You saved them!"

"Not to hear them tell it. Both of them always say they were about to do some real incredible daredevil stuff in mid-air if I had let them go off of the cliff."

"Your brothers and cliffs." Fallen thought of the cliff-diving demonstration he'd given her on their second date.

"They're trying to get me killed, the two of them." Thomas eyed her chest. "Tit for tat?"

Fallen wiggled her shoulders to make her breasts sway. She scurried off the bed before he could grab her, but soon he had her around her waist. They went from playful to heated together as he brought her back to him. As she locked her fingers behind his neck, feeling his readiness for her against her back, her lids started to feel heavy.

No. No.

His hands cupped her breasts, promising more pleasure.

They could still be skin to skin while she had time left, so she spun in his arms. They could still be mouth to mouth. She crashed into him, climbing him as he settled himself into her, desperate. It couldn't be over yet. Not yet. He filled her as he rested her against the empty window frame, hands everywhere as they tried to hold on to each other. The sheers whipped around them. They were a tempest for each other.

"Stay with me." She could hardly talk as her lids began to weigh on her, prevent her from watching him.

"Dream girl, make it until next Thursday. Please."

She felt his fingers dig into her hip as he teased one last orgasm out of her. She got one more glance, just a snapshot of Thomas, his muscled chest working for her, the look of love so etched on his face that it changed who he was.

And then there was blackness.

Fallen woke as the orgasm shuddered through her. Alone in room 514.

17

SAFE

Fallen stayed on the bed in 514 until the last of the warmth from his fingers bled from her skin. Then she dragged herself upright and neatened the comforter behind her. Her feet felt like cinderblocks. Next Thursday seemed even further away than last time.

She looked at the mirror, and a light flashed. Fallen rushed to it when her dusty mind remembered she'd gotten a peek at Thomas through there.

Sure enough, she watched as his eyes opened with a start. The little brown puppy sat at his feet. As he started to fade, his face crumpled into a sob, and his hands, which had just been touching her, curled into fists. But in the next moment, his heart-wrenching sadness became an expressionless mask. He moved quickly as the puppy flinched. Was it a gunshot? A bomb?

She couldn't know because the mirror went back to reflecting only her face—nothing of his.

Fallen sat on the floor hugging the mirror for long enough that her legs went numb, and she had to get up slowly, letting the blood rush back into them before they supported her. She set the mirror back where it belonged with a heavy hand.

She used her flashlight to remove the hooks and the picture from the corner—banking on Mr. Orbit's inattention at that very second to make her escape. It was a ridiculous risk, but what choice did she have. Plus, he'd been there in the dream—with a photograph he'd taken of her—so any doubts about whether the two worlds intersected for him had been put to rest. He had to know what she was up to on Thursdays. But he was a master of the mind game. He gave away nothing.

Fallen sighed. Racing her mind around in circles did nothing for her. She needed to get home. She'd left her cart in the supply closet this time, so all she had to do was sneak out with the picture under her coat.

Outside the hotel, the biting wind stiffened her resolve. She would find Thomas. They were meant to be together. Just to sit next to him and hold his hand would be worth it, to see his sparkling blue eyes and not have to leave. She turned this over and over in her mind, and it burned in her like fuel, keeping her warm as she walked.

Finally she stumbled into her house, closing the door behind her and locking it after her long walk. Then the light in the living room came on, and she looked into the worried face of her brother.

"Fenn, why are you up? You know I'm late on Thursdays." She hung her keys on the hook by the door and shuffled her coat and the picture into the coat closet under his scrutiny.

"Are you drinking?" Fenn looked older than his nearly 17 years when she turned toward him, startled by the question.

"No. No! Why would you ask that?" Fallen smoothed her uniform skirt.

"Because you're acting like an addict. You're distant. You come home at odd hours." He folded his arms over his chest. "What's in the closet? Liquor?"

"It's nothing. Nothing to worry about. It's…" She stepped aside instead of fighting him when he came forward and took out her coat and the contraption Desta had made.

He was clearly confused. "What are you into?"

She took the poster board and battery pack out of his hands and hugged it. "It's just something from the hotel. Something I need. I'm not drinking. I'm not like Nora."

He looked from her face to her arms cradling the photo. "If you say so." He turned, crossed the living room, and started up the stairs. "I just hope you're safe."

Fallen looked at her white-knuckle grip. He didn't understand. She hadn't explained. But Fenn was just a kid. He couldn't understand how important getting to see Thomas was to her.

She wasn't addicted to room 514. She was in a fight between time and the past and her boss…

She sighed as she decided to take the photo with her to her room to hide it where she kept Fenn's watch.

Addiction was her mother's problem, not hers, she assured someone—possibly herself.

Friday was a lonely day, and Desta was missing again. 8 and 9 exchanged disappointed looks with Fallen after the morning meeting as they trudged up to take care of Desta's floor. After a quick parley in the birdcage, they determined no one had spoken to Desta, so they would call after work. Fallen wanted to tell her about Burt. After the lunch break, 8 told Fallen she'd left a message on Desta's phone but still hadn't talked to her directly.

At the end of the day, Fallen was exhausted, but she ran

through her last two rooms to get to the library before it closed. She had just a few minutes there before she was going to be asked to leave.

She put her time into researching when the United States had implemented the draft. The brothers had enlisted, but they'd seemed to know war was coming. However, the draft had been policy for decades—nothing specific enough to be of much help. She also quickly checked her email, but had nothing from Marquette or Ellen.

As the librarian showed her the door, Fallen decided to track down Ellen for a personal visit on her next day off, as email wasn't a great way for them to communicate. Not that their time talking in person had gone that well either... Still, this gave her something to focus her energy on, which helped. Thursday was so very far away, with days and days where things could go wrong in between.

Fenn had been out with Jessica on Friday evening, but he was up early to see Fallen before she left for work. He seemed subdued as she made him scrambled eggs for breakfast, and he refused to take the bait when she teased him about promoting his study partner to girlfriend status.

"I like her, but...I don't know. I don't know what you want me to say."

He seemed frustrated, so Fallen backed off, assuring him she knew matters of the heart were complicated.

"So, if you had anything you needed to tell me, you would, right?" Fenn asked as he downed his orange juice.

"Yeah, if I did. Which I don't." Fallen put her lunch together as her brother picked up his dishes and put them in the sink.

"You're sure about that?" He gave her a look that haunted her. It reminded her of how she'd felt every time she found alcohol hidden in the house when they were younger.

"Fenn, I'm here. I'm making things work. If I have to come home a little late once in a while—I'm sorry. But it's not like you can't stay alone."

"Listen, I know you see me as a kid, and that's fine. But I grew up in this house, too. I know stuff. And I know that you either have a new boyfriend or you're getting into something like what Mom's into. And if that's not true, please correct me. You've been here for me, and I'm going to be here for you. It's not a one-way street."

Fallen's cheeks felt hot with the embarrassment. Fenn had been taller than she was for so long, she'd forgotten to notice he was becoming a man. But she still wasn't ready to share everything with him. This wasn't regular stuff—not like promoting a study partner to girlfriend.

"What I want most is for you to get a shot at this football thing," she told him. "You've got talent, and that can take you places. I wish it wasn't such a struggle every step of the way, but that's our situation. Once we have you in college, I can figure out what to do next. But until then, there's just not much in my life to talk about." She tried to smile, to make him believe her. "And I do trust you. I'll come to you if I need help. But the housekeeping thing isn't that hard, and I really like Adelaide, my client on the side."

Fenn still looked skeptical. "So you're just working all the time? Nothing else?"

Fallen sighed. She had to give him something. "I do have a crush on someone, and that's why I'm out late on Thursdays." She looked at her fingernails.

"I like that better than the other option. When do I get to meet him?" Fenn put his hand on her shoulder.

She looked up at her brother's sweet face and told him

something she really wished were truth. "It's complicated. Maybe soon."

"Okay. But just know I'm ready to beat everybody up." He gave her a cheesy smile.

"Save it for the field, LeBron." Fallen smiled back.

"That's basketball." Fenn shook his head, his shaggy hair animating the gesture.

"Same difference." Fallen smiled at her brother. "All right, I have to get to work. I have to stop at Adelaide's after I'm off at the hotel, but I'll make it to your game tonight."

Having Fenn think she spent her Thursday nights at a man's apartment seemed safer than the truth. But lies had a way of building up. And she didn't like the way the lies she'd heard from Nora over the years now seemed to echo in her head.

Adelaide met Fallen at the front door when she stopped by after finishing up at the hotel, as if she'd been waiting for her arrival.

"Hello, dear. Come in, come in."

Adelaide's house smelled a little funny. But the woman's swirl of gray hair was perfect, and she had her lips dotted with pink lipstick. Fallen started her inspection right away, looking first in the kitchen.

One of the stove's electric coils was red hot, and the dial was set on high. But as far as Fallen could tell, Adelaide wasn't cooking anything.

"Ms. Adelaide? Were you fixing something to eat?" She pointed to the stove and watched as confusion slipped over Adelaide's face like an executioner's hood.

"I don't think so? I mean, I had an early lunch, and it was a sandwich." The older woman began to fret, knotting her hands together.

Fallen switched off the dial and began to wipe down the already spotless counters. Marquette had insisted that Fallen message them if she noticed anything. The stove being left on was clearly a problem.

Adelaide sat down hard at the kitchen table. "Oh, no."

"What's wrong?" Fallen had a good idea, but she sat down to find out for sure.

"My kids aren't going to let me live here anymore. They told me I was one more mistake from getting sent to a place that could care for me." Adelaide dabbed at her eyes.

Fallen couldn't imagine how hard it would be to set rules like that with a loved one. And then she thought of Nora and how she was locked out of their house. Perhaps she had better insight than she thought.

"Your family sounds like they want the best for you." She covered Adelaide's hand with hers.

"You're going to have to tell them? Aren't you?" She looked downright petrified.

Fallen bit her lip. "Marquette did ask me to email."

"Do you have to? I mean, we've done well so far. I love my house. And here I know where everything is." She looked at Fallen with pleading eyes.

Fallen glanced at the stove and back to Adelaide. What a horrible death, being burned in a fire. She wouldn't be able to live with herself if this woman was injured because she'd decided to go against the family's wishes. "I never want you to be hurt."

"I understand. You'll do what you have to. I mean, we could make a deal that I only use the toaster? We can unplug the stove. The toaster has a timer; it won't run past twenty minutes. I never make anything that takes longer than that. I use the microwave a lot. Please?" Adelaide attempted to smile.

Fallen didn't respond, but instead got up to inspect the toaster and the oven. She could drag out the stove and unplug it, but if the family stopped by, they would see that precaution. She remembered Desta saying the family didn't come around a lot. They did all live out of town. Maybe she could check in with Desta on Monday, see what she thought of adapting the stove to help Adelaide stay in her house longer. Though she could certainly still hurt herself with a multitude of other things.

Fallen rested against the counter. Adelaide looked at the table while she awaited her judgment. Fallen felt supremely unqualified to make this decision. She decided to buy some time.

"Listen, let's unplug it for now, and I'll drop by in the evenings to check on you. Does that sound okay?"

Adelaide smiled softly before adding, "Well, certainly my children will pay you for the extra time..."

Fallen understood what she meant. If she was logging extra hours, they would want to know why. Hence telling them about the oven.

"No, that's not necessary. Your house is close to mine—we're neighbors. It won't take but a few minutes to check in at the end of the day, and I'd like to say hello, just to be neighborly, if that's okay with you?" Fallen watched as relief spread across Adelaide's face.

"Yes, thank you. Thank you so much."

Fallen tried to feel good about the plan, but part of her felt sneaky. As they chatted, she went through the needless motions of cleaning, making sure everything else she could think of was safe for Adelaide. They covered the weather, Adelaide's honeymoon with her second husband, and the latest with Fallen's boyfriend, "Tom." Fallen was surprised to realize the age difference really didn't matter; Adelaide had started to feel like a real friend.

Fallen bundled up for the game and arrived a little before kickoff, settling in the bleachers with a pennant on a stick she'd borrowed from Fenn's wall. It proclaimed her a devoted White Plains Panther.

Next week would be an away game, which would be far too tough to attend, so Fallen was determined to be the world's best fan while she could. She plastered a smile on her face, while inside she worried Mr. Orbit might show up again.

When there was still no sign of him about twenty minutes into the game, she relaxed some and waved her pennant. Fenn hadn't started, but now he was in. The crowd chanted his number a few times after good plays.

The cold game ended in a win for the Hillsdale High School Raiders, but Fenn still waved at her before running back into the locker room with his team. She smiled to herself as she walked out of the stadium and walked home.

Mitchel honked his horn when she was about halfway there, and she climbed in next to Fenn for a ride the rest of the way. She convinced him to drive by Adelaide's house and pointed it out to both boys.

"If you ever think of it, just come by here and make sure the house is still standing."

They both agreed and then circled the block to drop her off. Fenn was off to the after-game party at the quarterback's house, so she waved goodbye and let herself into the house.

Alone, she neatened the house and paid the bills while Fenn was out. This gave her more latitude for colorful swearing. Tomorrow would finally be her chance to look for Ellen. She decided to make the hike to the mall and use a display computer to Google her since the library was closed on Sunday. She had a great starting point with her previous marriage to Lad Orbit, and her stepson's football team might be another way to track her down.

Fallen got ready for bed and lay down, tracing Thomas' name on her arm. She closed her eyes and willed herself to dream of him, though he wouldn't truly be there.

Fallen woke in the middle of the night as Fenn arrived home. She listened for a moment before flipping over and committing to the rest she needed. But she couldn't help missing Thomas now that she was awake. The image she had of him being startled in the mirror ran through her mind. It was terrifying to think about how many things could happen to him at any moment. Each day they had together was a miracle, in so many different ways. It was a long time before her eyes slid closed again.

In the morning, she let her brother sleep in and did only quiet chores around the house. As she brought the trash out to the driveway, she caught sight of her neighbor's recycling pile. The sports page of an older local newspaper was on top, and it had a picture from Fenn's football game. Fallen snatched it up and flipped through the article as she walked back inside. She could see the back of Fenn's jersey, so she decided to clip the picture and put it on the fridge as a surprise for him. As she snipped around the picture, she noticed the caption. Poughkeepsie number 33, the one Ellen had said was her son, stood front and center, about to catch the ball. The reporter had helpfully noted his name: Van Mendo.

Fallen stuck the picture to the appliance with a magnet and

found the phone book she was amazed they still actually delivered.

She located a Mendo listing in the white pages that included an Ellen and realized she'd found her mark—no trip to the mall required. The Mendos' address was in a fancy part of the county, but with a bus and a bit of walking, Fallen could get there. She wrote a note telling Fenn she'd be out for the day and did just that.

After Fallen knocked on the intimidating front door, she touched her tattoo of Thomas' name. She had to find out as much as she could.

Ellen opened the door, but her welcoming smile slid off her cheeks as she regarded Fallen.

"Did he send you?" she looked past Fallen—for what, Fallen didn't know.

"Mr. Orbit?" Fallen asked. "No, of course not."

"Yes, Lad. Come in. Quickly." Ellen pulled her inside the well-appointed house, closed the door, and slid the lock into place. "How did you find me?"

"I looked in the phone book." Fallen's eyes wandered over the opulent foyer.

"I forgot they still made those. Tell me why you're here." Ellen folded her arms in front of her.

"You know what? You contacted me first. I wouldn't even have known who you were or thought to bother you. But your sporadic contact and vague hints and warnings are wearing thin. Are you going to help me, or what?" Fallen was shocked at her boldness, but time was running short.

Ellen looked uneasy before nodding. "Okay. Okay. You're not wired or anything? Or here on behalf of Lad?"

Fallen bit her lip and gave her head a brief shake. "I swear I'm not with him. He just likes to make it look that way. He takes pictures of me when I bend over in my skirt. And I can't tell him not to, because he owns the hotel that happens to be the only place I get to see the love of my life."

"That sounds familiar. I'm sorry you're going through this." Ellen waved her toward the spacious kitchen.

Without meaning to, Fallen began cataloging the places in the room that would be the worst to clean: the tops of the cabinets, the intricate scrolls in the crown molding.

Fallen sat across from Ellen at the table in the eat-in portion of the room.

"Can I offer you coffee? Or wine? I think I need wine."

"It's lunchtime." Fallen knew she sounded judgmental, but she heard alarm bells in her head when people relied on alcohol.

"Yes. Good. I was afraid it was too early." Ellen went to the counter and opened a bottle of red. Fallen declined a glass.

"The room," she said instead. "Is your husband the man you met in your dreams?"

Ellen looked around before nodding. "He is. But no one knows that except for me, my husband, and Lad. And now you."

So it *had* been done. Hope made Fallen's heart soar.

"Tell me how you did it. I need to do it too." Fallen leaned forward.

"My husband—the man who was with me at the football game—has warned me never to talk about it. But he doesn't know what this does to a girl. Doing what I needed to with Lad to get to Joe?" Ellen's eyes were liquid chocolate and flickered with an embarrassment Fallen recognized. "It makes you doubt your intentions."

Fallen nodded. But empathy wasn't what she needed most. "How did you get to him?"

Ellen tapped her French manicured nails on the tabletop. "When I started at the hotel, I was homeless. No one knew, of course, because I was creative with how I presented myself. But I was vulnerable, for sure. Then Lad—he was 27 at the time—paid so much attention to me, I actually thought he cared. He took me out, and I believed we could work. It would be like a rags-to-riches story. *Pretty Woman* and all that." She stopped and ran her hand through her hair. "He took me on some dates, sometimes providing me with the only meal I had all day. He took some pictures of me, of course, but since we were dating, I told myself it wasn't a big deal. When he asked me to marry him, I was surprised, but flattered enough to say yes. He wanted me to keep working at the hotel, though. I never understood why until a few months into our marriage. Then the woman who'd been cleaning the 5th floor quit, and Lad moved me there."

"She just stopped? Had she been dreaming in 514?"

"I don't know for sure. I didn't know anything about 514 then. But Desta stopped of her own free will. You could too, if you wanted to." Ellen paused until Fallen shook her head.

"I can't stop."

"I understand."

There was a moment of silence as the women acknowledged each other. Desperately in love with a man stuck in your dreams was a unique problem to have.

"Then it was my turn, and I soon discovered what can happen in room 514. Lad had been grooming me for it. I know that now. It wasn't enough that I had married him. He needed me to choose him over the person the room had for me... Or he wanted me not to dream while I was in there, like him. I don't know. He never would say. But either way, that's not what happened. Instead I met Joe."

Ellen's eyes were tender as she looked at her wedding band. "You know, real love is such a stunning, quiet revelation. Until it happens to you, you think it can be forced, created somehow. Or that what you have is good enough. Lad still thinks he can make it happen. That, and he's not entirely stable."

Fallen nodded.

"The truth is, Lad *hates* room 514. It took his parents. It drove them to their death. They each wanted turns in 514 with their dream loves. In the end, they shot each other there. Lad found them. He was just a teenager."

"That's horrible." Fallen had chills, thinking about how much time she spent at the scene of a crime. "I guess that's why he wants it left empty as well."

"Before they started using it, his parents used to let guests stay in the room. And sometimes it was just a regular room. Not everyone dreams there—the room evaluates the person somehow. But then after a few people dreamed, an intense competition developed over staying there. Lad's parents got a little greedy and jacked up the room rate, but they still had plenty of takers. They had a good racket going, the two of them, and for a while, I think they were happy.

"During that time, they had Lad and hired Desta to be his nanny. She loved that little boy, and he loved her. There are pictures of him and her all over his house. Then when Lad got too old for a nanny, they gave her a job as a housekeeper on the fifth floor. They wanted to keep tight control over room 514, you see. Things had gotten out of control. There had been more than a few suicides and a lot of broken hearts over what went on in that room. They closed it off to the public. But Desta still went in there to clean, and at some point she started to dream. Then one of Lad's parents—I don't know who was first—started visiting the room, and when the other found out, they started stopping in too. Eventually they both dreamed of someone else, and things went horribly wrong.

"I don't know if it was jealousy or longing for their soul mates, but they killed each other over that room. And then

Desta watched as Lad became an orphan at 15 years old, not to mention inheriting the hotel business and management of that crazy room. She was determined to make his path different from his parents', and different from her own as well. She was in deep with the room by then, I think. She made sure she remained in charge of cleaning the fifth floor, and she kept 514 closed. And she urged Lad to find interests outside the hotel, maybe even think about selling it when he came of age.

Desta did all she could for that man. But not long after he turned 25 and assumed legal control of the business—13 years into her dream relationship with the love of her life—Lad rebelled. He said it was his hotel, and his life, and he would do with them as he pleased.

With everything in him, he thinks that if he can find someone to love him, choose him over the person the room has matched them with, that will avenge his parents—and maybe even shut the room off."

"Why doesn't he meet his own girl in there?" It seemed like an obvious move.

"The room chooses who dreams. And Lad never does." Ellen took a long guzzle from her wine glass. "Lots of people don't. I was not the first girl he'd brought in to work the fifth floor. None of the others had dreamed, and that made Lad uninterested in them. I think I was a Hail Mary pass. Marrying me first was something new for him."

"So am I another Hail Mary?"

"Maybe. I'd hoped he would move on after what happened with us, but it seems he can't let it go. He just keeps trying and forcing and manipulating. I think if he could distance himself from the hotel and room 514, he would be much better off."

Fallen's mind was blown. It all sounded like a fairy tale, but she knew it was true. She knew the feel of Thomas' arms around her.

"So you beat the room?"

Ellen finished her wine and poured more. "After a while, Joe and I started sharing information. We whispered to each other in places only we knew."

"So you could avoid Lad?" Fallen asked. "In my dreams I'm engaged to him. He's always trying to find us, keep us apart." Fallen watched as Ellen's face fell.

A man stepped out from the hallway and scared them both into gasping. It was Joe, Fallen realized as soon as she was able to breathe.

"He's in them now? Ellen, what did I tell you? You need to stay out of it." He coaxed her out of her chair and hugged her.

"Wait, what does that mean?"

Joe answered for Ellen, who looked terribly upset. "Lad was never in our dreams. But to pass information that can be heard over the noise, you have to outsmart it." He shook his head. "Lad said he never could dream in the room at all. If you're seeing him, he's found another connection somehow, and he's changing the way the dreams work. That gives him a lot of power. He could choose to affect the course of history, as well as the relationships created in the dreams. Who knows what he might be capable of doing."

Fallen felt panic grip her—though less for the fate of the world, and more for the fate of one man. "So how did you find each other here? Please? I love him so much. He's at war; he's not safe." Fallen stood as she implored the couple.

Ellen patted Joe's chest. "In my dreams I had visited Joe in the past, but not the too distant past. I realized he could be still alive in my present. Lad and I were married then, so I used his money to buy a private detective who found Joe. He's older than I am now, but we're able to be together." Ellen touched Joe's face.

"I thought my dreams were crazy, so many years ago." Joe shook his head. "I eventually talked myself out of them when Ellen didn't appear. I got married and had my son, but the relationship didn't last. Even if my dream relationship hadn't been real, I knew love could be so much more. My wife and I divorced, and I raised my son. When Ellen arrived at my door many years later, it was like a bomb hit me. Everything came rushing back in an instant, and I was grateful."

The doorbell rang. Joe gave Ellen a wary look. "You two, wait out of sight."

Fallen and Ellen stepped behind the doorframe as Joe accepted a bouquet of black roses from a delivery man. As he closed the door, he pulled loose a card.

He gritted his teeth as he handed the card to Ellen. "This is what I was talking about."

Please don't let my ex-wife taint my future wife's opinion of me. ~Lad

Joe gave Fallen a hard look. "Listen, best wishes with everything, but you have to leave right now. He's watching you or us or both. We don't want any trouble."

He escorted her to the door while Ellen dabbed at her eyes with a piece of paper towel.

"Thank you for what you shared," Fallen told them.

Ellen nodded as the door closed.

18

YOU ARE NEEDED IMMEDIATELY

Fallen made pancakes for Fenn on Monday morning as a surprise, to give his week a good start. After sending him off to school and starting her walk to work, she returned to her ongoing mental task: processing what Ellen had told her. And what Desta had shared. She had to keep all these secrets, but surely somewhere within them there were common threads, something that would make sense. It seemed unbelievable that an old hotel would have a room in it that caused time travel and located true love matches across the ages, but Fallen only needed to look to the tattoo on her arm to know anything was possible.

Desta was absent from work when Fallen arrived, which alarmed her until 8 and 9 shared that she was recovering from bronchitis and enjoying the quiet. After that Fallen tried to set her desperate questions for the woman aside and give her time to heal.

She had to continue the effort on Tuesday, as Desta again stayed home, but at least Fallen had Adelaide to visit with after work. The older woman needed some help with closet reorganization, and they'd talked about tackling the attic next. Fallen was happy to have something to do, and Adelaide's happy chatter helped pass the time as well. She was a walking, talking history book, and as close to a friend as Fallen had right now. She tried not to think too much about that. She'd started telling Adelaide about Fenn's games and hopes, and a little about Nora, too. Adelaide not as delicate as she seemed, and shared some of her own memories of loved ones battling alcoholism. It was nice to have a kindred spirit.

On Wednesday, Fallen couldn't resist going back to Ellen's house after work. She refused to live being paranoid about Mr. Orbit all the time. But a For Sale sign on the property greeted her when she arrived, and when she peeked in a window, the interior of the house was barren. The flowers from Lad had changed a lot for Ellen and Joe, it seemed. What did that mean for her? Fallen realized she had no idea what he was truly capable of—and no option to up and disappear like these two had.

On Thursday—finally Thursday—Fallen was thrilled to see Desta standing near her cart as they assembled for the morning meeting. She listened as Melanny went through the assignments and acknowledged that Desta was back, which was surprisingly human of her. As soon as they were dismissed, Fallen was by Desta's side. As they walked down the hallway, she asked how Desta was feeling.

The answer was an edited summary. "I'm fine."

Fallen had so much to ask her, so many questions about her absence and the new details she'd gathered about 514, she thought she might need to write it all down. She was just about to explain that when Desta went to her knees, then fell over on her side.

"Help! Help!" Fallen knelt next to the older woman, who started to cough, and then her eyes rolled into her head.

8 and 9 abandoned their carts in the birdcage and ran over. Fallen worked on instinct and thought Desta's problem might

be a lack of air. She always seemed to struggle to breathe after a coughing bout.

Fallen rolled Desta to her side and pounded on her back, hoping to loosen up her airway. Desta's glasses fell off.

9 checked for a pulse, and 8 fumbled with her cell phone as she dialed 911.

"She's alive." 9 reported. "You know what?" she added to herself. Then she jumped up and ran down the hallway.

Fallen focused on Desta. Her lips were blue. She probably needed CPR. Fallen didn't know how to do it. She pounded on the center of Desta's back again, and the woman coughed. Fallen felt relief flood through her.

9 returned with a woman dressed in her pajamas with a stethoscope hanging around her neck. She immediately began checking Desta over.

"I saw the medical bag in her room when I cleaned," 9 explained. "I hoped she was a doctor."

Pajama lady was composed as she assessed Desta. "I'm a surgeon. Good observation. Okay, you two help me. We're going to prop her up against the wall."

While they maneuvered Desta together, Fallen offered what she knew about the woman's background.

"She's a heavy smoker and was recently diagnosed with cancer."

8 and 9 gasped.

Fallen bit her lip, wondering if that was information she should have kept quiet.

But then the paramedics arrived, and Desta came to, trying to send the help away before falling unconscious again. Fallen pocketed Desta's glasses to keep them safe.

They hustled her downstairs, and even though it was Thursday, Fallen insisted on riding in the ambulance. Melanny reluctantly agreed that she should go.

Fallen watched out the back window of the ambulance,

trying not to think about the growing distance between her and room 514, as well as the relentless passing of time. When she looked back at Desta, the paramedics had cut open her shirt to access her chest, so Fallen turned around to give some privacy.

Fallen made quick arrangements with Fenn for him to drop by to check on Adelaide and explained that she would be at the hospital with her friend.

Hours later, after hovering in the waiting room and being updated on Desta's condition with alarming infrequency, Fallen was invited to go in to see her. As they walked, a nurse explained that Desta had fluid on her lungs as a complication of her cancer. She had a drain in place now, which sounded painful.

When Fallen entered the room, Desta was conscious, thank God. Fallen held her hand. She set her glasses next to the bed.

"Oh, thank you. What time is it?" Desta whispered.

Fallen looked at her watch; it had been a long day. "11:20."

"You have to get back. To the room."

"There's no time. It's fine. I'll go next week when you're better." Fallen looked around the room at the monitors. "You have medical insurance, right?"

Fallen knew she and Fenn didn't have any, and she wondered how much a trip like this cost, let alone having cancer.

Desta shrugged. "I'll manage. Don't you worry about me." The talking brought a painful bout of coughing.

Fallen looked at her feet and felt guilty asking questions when talking was obviously a challenge.

There was knock on the hospital room door, and Fallen stood to answer it.

She found Mr. Orbit there, with flowers, a very anxious face, and a fading bruise below one eye. "Is she okay?"

Saying nothing, Fallen turned to face Desta, who watched her intently. "It's Mr. Orbit. Are you up for a visit?"

Desta nodded.

Fallen opened the door. "She has trouble talking, but come in." She stepped to the side and allowed him to go past and take her chair.

He was tender with Desta, kissing her forehead and fussing over her flowers until they were propped on the side table. "I told you it was too soon to come back to work."

Fallen leaned against the wall, interested in the dynamic between them. Had Desta really raised him?

She patted his hand and made the okay symbol with her hand.

Mr. Orbit whipped a pen out of his pocket and flipped over a pamphlet to the blank side. After he dragged the eating table on wheels over, Desta was able to write answers to his questions.

Her breathing sounded wet. Desta was in trouble. Mr. Orbit asked a few questions about her care before deciding to go to find the doctor. As the door closed behind him, Fallen didn't hide her confused look. Who was this kind human being?

Desta wrote and then twirled the paper to face Fallen.

Go. Go now. Lad will stay with me he won't be at the camera.

"I can't leave you here with him." Fallen shook her head.

Desta picked up the pen again.

He won't bother me. I'm ok. Go!!!

Fallen patted the woman's shoulder. "I saw Burt," she told her, wanting to offer comfort. "He knew your name. I'm going to try to get to him again."

Desta smiled, but made frantic hands at Fallen. When Fallen

came near, Desta put the paper she'd been writing on in her hands.

Fallen understood. She tucked the paper into her bra and grabbed another pamphlet for Desta to write on. She slipped out of the room and turned the corner at the end of the hall just as she saw Mr. Orbit and a doctor appear at the other end, headed back to Desta's room.

She tried not to think about the ultimate end of Desta's disease, and instead focused on getting back to the hotel. If she could make it in time, perhaps she'd not only see Thomas, but have a chance to learn more about Burt.

As she left the hospital, Fallen noted the clock above the exit doors. 11:40 pm.

Only 20 minutes left. She had to hurry. She dove into a cab that had just dropped someone off. It would cost, but her dream was waiting.

She tried not to lean forward as she waited for red lights that took forever. She kept her eyes on the clock. It was 11:54 when she paid the cab driver and ran up the hotel's service entrance, grateful for the master key she still had in her pocket. She took the stairs, which seemed crazy, but the birdcage moved too slowly.

Thomas.

Just to touch him, just to know he was okay after seeing him flinch in the mirror.

Her heart pounded in her throat as she made it to the door of 514. She inserted her master key, and it gave her trouble at first. She could only guess at the time now. Maybe four minutes had passed?

Thomas.

Her eyes brimmed when she slammed the door open. Even just a kiss. To see his face.

The clock in the room read 11:59 as Fallen threw herself at

the bed, willing the darkness to claim her, waiting to feel the rush.

She looked at the clock despite her wish to keep her eyes tightly shut. 12:00.

"No! No. Please, I can't have missed him." Her tears fell.

There was no rush. The feeling her body equated with love was absent. But a flash of light caught her eye.

"Of course. The mirror." Fallen scrambled from the bed and picked it up.

At first she saw nothing, and then Thomas took shape for her. He opened his eyes and shook his head. Disappointment was evident on his face that the relief she felt at seeing him was instantly replaced with regret.

Another whole week.

She watched as he moved the sleeve of his white T-shirt and touched her name. She touched the mirror, wishing he could tell that she saw him. The brown puppy wiggled itself up the rough-looking blanket on Thomas' cot.

He petted the dog's head while it tried to lick him over and over. She watched him take a deep sigh.

"I love you, Thomas McHugh. I'm so sorry I missed our date. Stay alive."

He showed no sign that he heard her.

He reached under his cot and pulled out a folder stuffed full. He sat up and moved the puppy to the side. As he flipped through the papers, Fallen saw herself. His drawings—her face, her hand, her eyes, her body. Her name.

Just before the mirror faded, she watched him cover his face with his hands.

Fallen sat back on the bed and hugged the mirror.

She'd missed him.

She missed him.

It took Fallen an hour to get off the floor and return the mirror to its rightful spot. How would she survive the horror of missing Thomas? Seeing him in the mirror just made things worse. Or maybe it was better, she told herself.

She walked home numb. The cold combined with the pain of missing Thomas and her worry about Desta was a changing kind of experience. It brought the low-level panic at which she lived each day—worrying about her mother, worrying about Fenn, wondering how to make a life for herself—into sharp, crushing focus right at the center of her chest.

When she got home her brother was waiting for her, sitting on the couch with his arms crossed.

She didn't say anything as she hung up her coat and took off her shoes.

"So that's it? No phone call? Nothing?" he asked. "Is your friend okay? Miss Adelaide was fine when I went by to check on her."

"It's Thursday. I thought you knew I'd be late. I'm sorry. And my friend is...I don't know. Thanks for asking." She rubbed her arms as the skin prickles kicked in. She should call him more. It felt a little like another job to do, and then she felt guilty about feeling that way.

"This guy? The one you're seeing? Is there a reason he doesn't come around any other time of the week? Is he married?" Fenn stood.

He was worried. She could see this from his point of view now, at least a little. She was the only adult he had that made sense. She was usually practical. She had nothing in her life to be frivolous about, after all. It must be unnerving to see her stressed out and despondent over Thomas, particularly since he didn't really understand why.

"This job just takes a lot out of me. It's going to be okay. Nothing is out of hand. I'm paying the bills. You're getting fed." She tried to step past him, and he moved to block her way.

"Is it your boss? Mr. Orbit? Because he seems like a nice guy."

"How would you know?" Warning alarms went off in Fallen's head. What had her mother said? What had Orbit done now?

"He comes to some of my practices." Fenn tilted his head.

Orbit's stalking was tiresome. What exactly did he think he was going to accomplish?

"I'm sure he seems nice to you. But no, like I've told you before, I'm not involved with him." Fallen took her ponytail holder out and slipped it over her wrist. "Thursdays are going to be late, and I can't stop that. Tonight I'm especially late, but like I told you, today another housekeeper had to go to the hospital. She needed me there. She doesn't have any family." Fallen crossed her arms too.

"I'm sorry to hear that," Fenn said immediately. "And I understand why you went. I just wish you could let me know."

Fallen felt like the child in their relationship as Fenn held out his arms. She waited a beat before walking into his big hug.

He smelled good, she noticed. She crossed deodorant off of the grocery list she had in her head.

"Thanks," she finally said. "How was your day? Who are you playing this weekend?" Fallen patted Fenn's arm as she stepped back.

That was the perfect question as he slipped right into talking about football. The coach had made some comments that led Fenn to believe he might start some games soon.

"That's great. I hope he picks a home game for that. I'd love to see you." Fallen went to the kitchen to make the sandwiches for the next day's lunches, but Fenn had already made them.

She thanked him, and he nodded.

"I checked with Mitchel, and his parents can give you a ride on Saturday to the game," he added.

"Oh, tell them that would be great."

Fenn nodded again, but rather than turning to go to bed, he focused on his right foot and kicked at the tile in the kitchen.

He definitely had something he needed to discuss.

"What's up?" Fallen asked.

"Mom stopped by tonight."

"Is she here?" Fallen looked around for any signs of Nora. She thought immediately of Fenn's watch in her room.

"No. She couldn't stay, but she mentioned that she'd been clean for a few days and wanted to come back home. I told her I had to talk to you. The guy she was dating told her she has to move out...so, you know—it's hard. I don't want to see her on the streets." Fenn shrugged.

Fallen nodded. "Agreed. But a few days clean is not really very long, you know? We've got things working pretty well here, and I'm not about to let her destroy that."

Fenn crossed his arms. "We can't just give up on our own mother. Alcoholism is a disease, you know."

It had to be two in the morning, and she was too worn out and heartsick to have this argument. Nora brought chaos and crisis into a household. Fallen would happily make room for her mother, but Addiction was the one who wanted to move in. Still, she opened her mouth to appease her brother.

"I'll try to find her after work or on my day off and see what's going on."

Fenn finally smiled a little and went upstairs to his room.

Her heart felt like a waterlogged rag doll as she went through the motions of being Fenn's big sister. Missing Thomas was a spike through her soul. After a quick shower, she made sure all the doors were locked and extinguished the front porch light. Her resolve hardened as she looked out into the night.. How many rock bottoms had it taken before Fallen was able to ban Nora from the house? Nora would always be a challenge for her, but she wasn't about to give up and allow that chaos back so soon.

Upstairs, she curled in her bed and waited for sleep to take her. Her exhaustion made it a quick transition.

On Friday, 8 and 9 helped Fallen with Desta's floor, and Fallen went to the hospital to check on Desta after work.

When she knocked on the door to her room, Desta called, "Come in!"

She was clearly feeling better. "Great to hear your voice," Fallen said as she entered. "How's it going?"

Desta had a vase of flowers by her bed, and her lips weren't a scary blue anymore.

"Better. Thank you for coming to see me. Did you make it in time yesterday?"

Desta's eyes were eager. Fallen tossed around the idea of lying just to tell her about Burt some more, but she decided on the truth, because the truth was what she wanted from Desta as well.

She shook her head. "I didn't make it."

"I'm sorry," Desta said. "That's my fault."

"Don't be silly," Fallen said. "You did everything you could to help me! It will be fine. I'm just glad you're feeling better. Who are the flowers from?" she asked, trying to steer the conversation to a happier place.

"Lad." Desta nodded while looking at them.

His name opened a door for Fallen. "That's nice of him. He seemed very concerned about you. Is he still here?"

She shook her head.

"So, he's paying for your stay?" It was an invasive question, but Fallen had a hunch. And no more desire to play games. Who knew when Desta might disappear like Ellen and Joe had.

Desta nodded. "He feels like he owes it to me."

"And why would that be?" Fallen asked innocently.

Desta hemmed and hawed for a few sentences as if seeking a plausible explanation, but when she finally locked eyes with Fallen, she seemed to settle into the actual narrative.

"I raised him, Fallen. I raised him as if he was mine. His parents—they were caught up in the room. And he was just this towheaded little guy playing with his cars. He needed love, and I had so much love to give."

Fallen nodded.

"You don't look surprised." Desta lifted her eyebrow and started to cough.

Her cough was a conversation stopper. Fallen brought her water and tried not to wince when she saw how painful the spasms appeared to be.

The woman needed a moment to recover her breath, and talking seemed like it was asking too much. In the interim Fallen supplied what she knew and explained how she knew it. Desta didn't look too surprised either.

"I know the hotel is a huge part of your history, and that room gave you your true love," Fallen said. "But it sounds like Lad was also a love in your life. You've done a lot for him."

Or at least she wanted to believe that was true. She still wondered why Desta had made it seem like she had no real ties to Lad, and why she hadn't warned her about the room—or about him.

Desta shook her head. "We all do what we can to get by. I

saw the room break his parents. You see, they rented that room, and people either got hooked on a love that couldn't be in real life, or they didn't dream but would set themselves up to someday be someone else's dream come true." Desta coughed again.

A thought hit Fallen like a thunderbolt. "Wait. You mean Burt spent time in the hotel at some point? And because he didn't have a dream, he became part of your dream?"

Desta nodded while coughing.

"And Thomas? He stayed in the room, too? At some point?"

Desta's eyes were sad, but she continued to nod.

Fallen refilled her water.

As they waited for Desta's coughing bout to taper off, Fallen tried to put that new information in her puzzle of a mystery.

Desta picked up her narrative, as if she knew each word was a valuable resource Fallen desperately needed. She told her of the loss of Lad's parents and her desire to protect him after he'd been orphaned, to keep him away from the room.

"I couldn't get rid of it it—but I could be there and clean. I kept Lad away from it as much as I could, and once a week I would get Burt. Every day Lad could grow up a little more."

Desta touched at a tear that was caught on her bottom lashes. "I wanted him to fall in love the real way—in the world outside the hotel. But he's obsessed with the room, and so angry. After he was old enough to run the business, we had a fight. I'd lost my Burt somehow, so I stopped going in 514 to dream. Lad started putting new girls he'd chosen in there. He'd try to date them, but it never worked out. Then he got married, and I thought he was finally going to go on and live his life, but instead he sent his poor wife in there too. You know how that ended…"

Desta sighed. "He can't figure out why the room never brings him a love, and I don't really know either. He doesn't dream in 514, but he's stayed in there—against my wishes—so I've always thought he might end up in someone else's dream. You said you see him in yours, but he's obviously not your match." She shook her head.

"He's trying to be," Fallen said softly. "He's pursued me there from the very beginning. He acts like we're a foregone conclusion, like he owns me. He keeps putting an engagement ring on my finger." She sighed and looked up to find Desta looking horrified and wringing her hands. Fallen covered them with her own, soothing her.

There was so much to comprehend about all of this, but at the end of the tale, Fallen had only this exhausted looking women who had dedicated her life and happiness to a little boy who was frittering away her sacrifice.

"He's been hurt and angry and alone for so long that I don't think he truly knows what love means, or what it requires of him." Desta patted her hand in return.

"And yet you let me go in that room and straight into his sights? Not to mention knowing it might doom me to love a man I couldn't have? Do you regret that at all?" Fallen hated to grill Desta in her hospital bed, but she had to know.

"I'm a bit of a desperate old lady myself, I guess," she said. "It's no excuse, but I didn't realize how far Lad had gone with things. I just wanted to find my Burt. I knew I had cancer, and you seemed nice—I knew the room would pick you. The love I had with Burt, that you have with Thomas—would you ever give that up? Despite how much it hurts?" Desta looked up pleadingly, her lips more blue than when Fallen had entered

"No. I wouldn't. It's a gift and a curse though." Fallen stood. She needed to get back to the house and get started on Fenn's dinner.

"All love is." Desta offered.

She leaned over and gave the woman a kiss on the cheek.

She refilled her water and promised to tell 8 and 9 she was doing better.

A gift and a curse.

19

PICTURES

Fallen woke Saturday morning and called to check on Desta in the hospital. Unfortunately, the woman's endless coughing forced Fallen to hang up to avoid putting her at unnecessary risk. Maybe she could take a bus to the hospital for a visit after work and her check-in on Adelaide. But she'd have to hurry to make it before the football game. She wished for the millionth time that she had a car.

After a tiring, but uneventful day at work, Fallen walked to Adelaide's house that afternoon, as had become her daily routine, except the few times Fenn had done it for her, like yesterday. There'd been no more instances of burners on, but Fallen was starting to worry she might have to tell Adelaide's daughter anyway. Adelaide seemed to be repeating herself with greater frequency.

When Fallen arrived, she found Adelaide waiting, chipper and happy. Everything was as it should be, and she proudly showed Fallen how she'd made lunch in the toaster.

"Great job." Fallen gave her a careful hug.

The thought that this sweet lady could be hurt made her feel even more guilty. Maybe it was time to email Marquette, even if she didn't get to keep the job.

Adelaide seemed to have a little project going in the living room with photo albums scattered over the coffee table and couch.

"What are you working on?" Fallen asked as she ran a rag over the clean end table, peeking at the plugs along the wall while she did so.

Adelaide motioned for Fallen to sit on the floral sofa before taking the spot close by. "Dusting off my pictures," she explained. "Just looking through, remembering. My second husband, God rest his soul, always insisted on going through the pictures and talking about the people in them. He felt like it was good for our memories."

A look of slight confusion came over Adelaide's face, and she stopped talking. "Was I making you dinner?" she asked. "I think I was."

Fallen shook her head. "No, Miss Adelaide, we were looking at your photos."

Adelaide gave her a blank look before smiling sweetly. Fallen exhaled. This wasn't going well. It was time to let Marquette know.

Adelaide began to neaten the open photo albums, and a black and white picture fell from one the yellowed plastic pages. It landed upside down under the table, and Fallen had to sink to one knee to retrieve it.

When she turned the photo over, she was glad to be already on her knees because the sight of him in her awake world would have for sure knocked her to the ground.

Thomas.

It was a picture of Thomas.

Fallen felt her eyes fill with tears, and she set down her duster to touch the image with her finger. Maybe she was making sure it wasn't a mirage.

"He was handsome. Dapper in his uniform." Adelaide tapped the photo with her slightly bent index finger.

It took a few seconds for Fallen to remember how to turn air into words.

"Who is he?"

"So handsome." Adelaide gave her another puzzled look. "My second husband, God rest his soul, always insisted on going through the pictures and talking about the people in them. He felt like it was good for our memories."

She took the picture from Fallen's hand and tucked it back into the album.

Fallen was too stunned to do anything but watch as Adelaide stacked the albums on the coffee table.

When she stood to fuss over a different task in the kitchen, Fallen unstacked the books and flipped back to the picture of Thomas. With her phone, she took a snapshot of the front and the back of the picture before slipping it back in place.

She did the rest of her chores in a bit of a haze. She wanted to ask more of Adelaide, but her memory didn't seem to be firing entirely correctly today. She didn't want to upset her, so after finishing her duties, she slipped out without saying another word about it. Just seeing the photo was almost more than she could absorb anyway.

On her way home, Fallen had to stop and look at the pictures she'd snapped. She cursed her shaky fingers because Thomas' face was blurry. She flipped to the back of the photograph and studied it a moment. It hit her slowly what she was looking at.

Not his name.

Not his rank as an officer.

It was a birth year. And a death year.

1920-1945

Fallen stumbled when she realized she finally had information on Thomas: how his life was defined. A birthdate and a death date. So much was contained in that brief mathematical description.

How did he die?

At the thought of the word *die*, a sob escaped her and she sat on the sidewalk.

"No. No. No."

The details she'd collected about wars crashed over her. WWII had been mostly concluded by 1945. Maybe that date meant something else in this case. Maybe the span of 25 years meant something totally different. Maybe finding her love's picture with two years on the back with a dash in between was just a different hallmark. Maybe he'd left the service in 1945…

The cold made her get up. Routine made her put one foot in front of another.

Reality set in. She was in love with a dead man.

When she got home, Fallen was grateful for the empty house. She closed the front door quietly behind her.

She clutched her phone in her hand and walked straight to her room, leaving her jacket on and her horrible sneakers in place.

She crawled under the blankets, not bothering to put on a light. She looked at his face—static in the blurry picture; no color, but it was him. Her tears made the picture even more stained.

Fallen wouldn't find him in her waking world like Ellen had Joe, no matter where she searched. Maybe a gravestone. That's all she could hope for.

An hour later, Fallen dragged herself up because she had to be there for Fenn. He'd set this all up for her. Despite her fatigue and the fact that her brain was swimming in emotions churned up by the photo of Thomas, she put herself together for the event. After a hot shower, she made sure to put her work uniform in the wash.

As planned, Mitchel's parents picked her up for the drive to Mahopac High School, and she was relieved that Mitchel's father drove more slowly than he did. However, she parted ways with them soon after arriving when it became clear that Mitchel's parents planned to highlight their game-watching with pom poms and coordinated cheers.

From a quieter spot a few rows away, Fallen watched for Mr. Orbit—or even Ellen. Luckily, she just got to watch Fenn play, and for a moment here and there, she almost forgot the tragedy that had unfolded in her brain. She wasn't a font of fabulous football knowledge, but she could tell how wild the crowd went after Fenn completed a play. She even saw a group of girls in the stands with Fenn's number painted on their cheeks.

Mitchel's parents were also very complimentary on their way home. Fallen managed to smile, thanked them for the ride, and let herself into the house.

Her soul was a wasteland. Maybe there was sense to be made of this world. Maybe there was some purpose for all this. But Fallen was far from finding the desire to seek it out. She looked at her phone picture until the device ran out of power. She didn't roll out of bed and plug it in until Fenn came home the next morning.

Over breakfast she listened to him talk about a football boot camp his sponsor had already paid for that would be held during the Thanksgiving break at the end of the month.

After a little while, he seemed to notice how down she was and asked her about it. But Fallen shook off explaining things to him. There was no rational way to describe where she was emotionally and why.

Fallen took a shower instead of talking any more after hearing him mumble about girls and hormones. She stayed in there so long that the water heater ran out of warmth. She dressed in her favorite old sweatshirt and soft jeans with boots that had holes in the bottom. She put black socks on and hoped the raggedy state of her footwear would be less obvious.

After she pulled her hair back, she curled up on her bed again, looking at Thomas. God, she wished she hadn't flipped the picture over. She would give anything to drain her mind of the knowledge she now had.

Around lunchtime Fenn asked her if she minded him running out to a friend's house before dinner and the team meeting at his coach's tonight.

Of course she didn't. He was busy with the team, and the coach loved to make huge pasta dinners. That affinity was a huge help to Fallen's food budget.

Not that food mattered anymore. Not that anything mattered.

The only thing Fallen could think to do with herself was see Thomas' face. Seeing Thomas' face in pictures would ground her. Give her an anchor. Prove that her feelings were real. She left quickly, once she decided, going to Adelaide's with the hopes her memory would be better today and they could reminisce over the photo albums again.

FOR ALL THE EVERS

Adelaide welcomed her as always, but Fallen hadn't been in the house two minutes before the doorbell rang. Adelaide answered the door with a smile, and without hesitation, while Fallen stood off to the side. The older woman didn't check to see who was at the door before opening it. Another strike against her independence.

A well-dressed woman embraced Adelaide and seemed slightly surprised before she smiled at Fallen. Adelaide took the woman's coat, hanging it in the front closet. Fallen held her duster awkwardly before introducing herself.

Marquette Jones, Adelaide's daughter, greeted Fallen and explained her role as the family's emissary. Adelaide went to make tea, and Fallen winced as she tried the stove a few times before switching to the microwave to heat up the water.

Marquette lifted an eyebrow at Fallen, who nodded sadly at the unasked question. Yes, the stove was off. And yes, the reason Marquette feared was correct.

After two cups of water were steaming, Adelaide went about making the rest of the snack. Fallen went through the motions of tidying up. She was desperate to page through the photo albums for more pictures of Thomas, though that project was likely off the table for now.

After Marquette had her snack and tea, she kept up the small-talk banter Adelaide seemed to be enjoying. Fallen could see her hopes for more time with Adelaide's photo albums were not going to realized, and since today wasn't an official cleaning day, there was really no reason to stay, but she found herself dragging her feet.

When it became too awkward to hang around any longer, Fallen poked her head into the kitchen to say goodbye. Marquette insisted on walking her out, which Fallen understood would be their chance to speak openly.

Marquette didn't even try with small talk. She crossed her arms in front of her and looked Fallen up and down on the front porch before asking, "Why did you unplug the oven, and why are you here on a Sunday?"

Fallen tucked her hands into the pockets of her coat. "About that…"

"I'm all ears. I'm very interested in why the most important part of your job—keeping us informed—you failed to do." Marquette squinted.

Fallen waited a beat, trying to convince herself the woman wasn't being combative right off the bat.

When Marquette had nothing else to say, Fallen offered her observations. "You hired me over the phone. I have no background with elderly clients, which you knew, and I didn't want to jump the gun. And before you judge me, understand that I stop by every day to check on her, even Sunday. She's doing okay, but she's been scared you and I would have this very conversation. The last few days, though, she's forgotten a few things that do warrant some communication between us. I promise I was planning to let you know." Fallen took a breath and waited.

Marquette's demeanor became less confrontational, and she let her hands fall to her sides. "I didn't realize…"

"I figured as much. This can't be easy. No one wants to take away her independence. But of course she has to be safe. I was going to recommend that you come in person to visit her."

"I thought maybe you hid the fact that she was having trouble so the paycheck would keep rolling in. I know you're in the neighborhood." Marquette couldn't seem to stop herself from laying the guilt at Fallen's feet, with an extra helping of noting she was broke on top. The neighborhood was in a serious decline. And Fallen fought every day to keep a place in it for her and Fenn.

"Maybe don't assume the worst of everyone," she said with a shrug. "Maybe go back inside and be with your mom." Fallen started down the front walk.

"Wait. I'm sorry… I just, I know I should have stopped this sooner. It was just easier…"

Fallen took a few more steps toward the sidewalk.

Marquette called after her, "Will you be back on Tuesday?"

Fallen shook her head, turning. "I'll be back tomorrow to say hello to her. Like usual."

Back at home, Fallen had barely hung up her coat when there was a knock on the door.

She opened it hesitantly. There were so few people she wanted to see on the other side.

Nora didn't say hello, but she searched Fallen's face with her gaze as if she cared how tired she might be. Fallen shook her head; she knew what Nora really wanted—and it wasn't to make sure her daughter was getting enough sleep. She sighed and stepped to the side. Nothing good would come from letting her mother into the house, but her heart had a tough time sliding on the boxing gloves.

"You all right, Fally?"

Fallen knew Addiction would try anything to get what it wanted, but pulling out the nickname Nora had used for Fallen as a child was a low blow.

"I've been better, Nora. Life has gotten a little more depressing even than usual these last few days. And now I'm trying to decide which angle you're going to try to use to get money for alcohol when what I'd love—not that you care—would be to brag about how great Fenn did at his football game last night."

Fallen's phone rang in her purse, and she answered it quickly, keeping her eye on her sticky-fingered mother while she listened to Fenn ask if she was feeling any better and remind her he was on his way to his coach's basement with the rest of the team for dinner.

She assured him she was fine, and then Nora took the phone with grabby hands. She started in with the accolades and peppered him with questions like she cared about his answers.

Eventually Fallen gave her the universal sign for wrap it up. She wasn't running a phone booth, and every pre-paid minute had a price. She took back her phone the moment Nora hit the end button, before she could start searching it for information.

As she turned to put the phone away, Nora grabbed her wrist.

"I need to be honest with you. This is such a bad time for me. I really need to get a little relief. I tried. Honest to God, I tried to stop all at once, but then Fritz dumped me, and I wanted to get my full-time job back and help you with the mortgage, and Fritz was cheating on me, and—never let them cheat on you, baby. This is what happens. Men use women. Get the best years of your life, and then they leave you, and you can't trust anyone, and I can stop, and I will stop as soon as it make sense. But now is not the time, and I've followed you. I know you think that old bat two streets over is your new mother—is she replacing me?"

Fallen walked to the stairs and sat on them, putting the phone to her forehead. Being in Addiction's sights was exhausting.

Her mother rattled on—anything to get what Addiction wanted. False gods. Lies. Promises that had no meaning.

"Nora."

Her mother continued, seeming to speak louder since Fallen's eyes hadn't yet registered any compassion.

"Nora."

"And I'll tell you something else, I'm the only mother you're ever going to get—"

Fallen stood and stepped close to her mother's traitorous

face. How dare it be such a part of the good memories of her childhood yet hold no comfort for her now?

"Mother." Nora fell silent when Fallen used a word she hadn't in months. Maybe years. "I'm taking care of myself and Fenn. That's all I can do. You need a program or something, but I'm just hanging on by the skin of my teeth. I can't take your problems onto my back, too."

Her mother started to interrupt. Fallen held up her hand. "You need to focus this considerable determination to get what you want on someone else. Not me. And not Fenn. Like I told you before, this house is closed to you. I'm closed to you. He's closed to you. My money is not for you. I don't know how many different ways to tell you this without actually picking you up and throwing you out of here."

A second knock on the door stopped Fallen's monologue. She wasn't getting anywhere anyway. Addiction's desperate fire had such a firm hold on Nora; Fallen's presentation of reason and logic was as pointless as washing dirt out of cotton candy.

"Come on, Nora. You can answer the door on your way out." Fallen made an elaborate gesture to encourage her mother to follow to her direction.

Reluctantly, Nora opened the door, and then her demeanor changed again. Fallen could tell from the flirtatious sway of her mother's hips and the breathy hello that Mr. Orbit was on the front door step before she saw him.

He gave a self-depreciating chuckle and stepped over to look at Fallen from around the door. "Ladies, I hope I'm not interrupting."

Her mother went all Scarlett O'Hara on his ass. "Absolutely not. My daughter and I were just discussin' some female topics, you know—getting our hair done and such."

That wasn't even how Nora talked.

"I'm sure." Orbit couldn't have been more cordial.

They both turned to look at Fallen when she sighed and interrupted their performance.

She saw it then—the resemblance between Orbit and Nora. Desperation had quite a grip on both of them. Each sought answers from her. She had nothing left to give either of them.

"Well, I'll leave you two to it," Nora said, suddenly willing to go. "Don't stay up too late. Hey, little girl, where's your brother tonight?"

"I'm not telling you where Fenn is so you can go hit him up for money."

Nora stumbled at her harsh answer. "Well, I just…"

Her cheeks flushed, and Fallen felt a flicker of remorse. Mr. Orbit offered her mother his hand, and she padded down the front steps.

Fallen watched with her arms folded in front of her.

Orbit leaned down and whispered to Nora before slickly passing her a bill. Nora first pretended she wouldn't take it, and Fallen swallowed her own protest. If Mr. Orbit wanted to turn his money into alcohol, that was his choice. At least Nora would leave Fenn alone for tonight.

The transaction complete, Nora patted Lad's arm and then hugged him awkwardly. But she was on the move now, desperate to get to a bar or a liquor store, so there was no lollygagging. Fallen looked at her feet so she didn't have to watch Addiction get what it wanted.

Mr. Orbit's shoes shuffled against the cement as he climbed the front stairs. Fallen a watched as the tips of his fancy leather loafers almost drew close enough to touch her worn boots.

"I tipped her for helping bring about your show-stopping face," Orbit explained, inadvertently adding fuel to Fallen's emotional fire. She hated being his pawn.

"She'll use every dime to drink until she passes out. Which takes a lot nowadays."

She pegged him with a hard stare just as he reached up,

maybe to touch her face. Her words seemed to put his hand in his jacket pocket instead. He changed topics rather than apologizing like he should have.

"I heard Fenn did great last night."

She left the silence between him. From one battle to the next.

"Desta's not doing very well," he offered after a moment.

And that was the one topic that could break down the hasty wall Fallen had built and drag her from the depth of one sadness to another.

"What? I just saw her the other day. What did the doctor say?"

He looked into the distance above her head. "Maybe a month left. Her cancer is aggressive. Now's a good time for hospice, but she has to decide if she wants to go home for care or if it's better to stay in the hospital."

Fallen held the door, feeling herself lose a bit of steam.

Orbit reached out again, and Fallen noticed his hand shaking a bit. "I'm sorry—I should have delivered that better. I just…I just came from the hospital. And I'm not sure what to do next."

Fallen shook her head.

This man was the most frustrating part of her dreams and the scariest part of her waking days. She wasn't letting him get her alone with this sadness.

"I understand that your relationship with Desta is complicated. I recommend making the most of your time with her," she said. "I'll visit her tomorrow after work. Thank you for understanding that I need privacy as my comfort during this difficult time." And then Fallen closed the door on him.

She breathed out and almost laughed at her amazingly coherent dismissal. She leaned against the door and waited for more knocking or a crash of glass—expecting his temper to get the best of him. But instead, his retreating footsteps were followed by the sound of his fancy car pulling away.

Fallen silently thanked Desta for all that she'd shared with her about Mr. Orbit and room 514. Poor Desta. And poor Burt. Would they find their way to being together again?

And how in God's name would she manage to see Thomas again if her partner in crime was so very sick?

Fallen looked to the ceiling. She had to power forward. That's how she was built. When life tossed insurmountable challenges at her, she put her head down and made things work. There was no time for wallowing, only action. Thomas needed her to be his dream girl, Fenn needed an adult that could provide, and Desta and Adelaide both needed a friend. She would be all those things.

20

POSSIBLE

Getting a hotel room clean was starting to be something Fallen didn't have to think about. She'd developed a routine that made sense and hit all the essential spots. This came in handy, because she had to go over to see Adelaide today, if only to save face. Fallen shoved her obsession with the photo albums as far down as she could and focused on potential things to say to Adelaide. Who knew what Marquette had told her after Fallen was gone. She had put a serious smack down on that woman yesterday. The anxiety it should have caused her hardly registered.

But when Fallen managed to trudge over to Adelaide's on Monday afternoon, she found no one home. She wondered how possible it would be to break in and steal the photo album that held Thomas' picture. Then her mind started turning. Adelaide had to be related to Thomas. Had she been his wife?

Anything was possible.

Nothing was possible.

Fallen jotted a quick "I was here" note on the back of a receipt from her purse and tucked it in the screen door.

She'd showed up, and that had to count. She vowed to reach

out to Marquette again, but right now there was another moment she needed to be present in. Fallen rode the bus to the hospital and sat next to Desta, holding her hand while she slept. Desta might not have a family to send her positive energy, but she had people who loved her, and Fallen considered herself one of them.

Ellen had gone. Now Adelaide was missing. She'd failed to connect with Thomas last week. Numb from so much loss, and bracing for more to come, Fallen had arrived at work on Tuesday, put her head down, and done her job. She and the others didn't have to pitch in on Desta's floor anymore because there was a new hire who seemed to know her way around a cleaning cart pretty damn well.

The word today had been that Desta didn't want visitors; she was just too weak. This left Fallen completely adrift. Only Desta understood her crazy situation and its emotional toll. Though they hadn't spoken, Fallen had felt better after sitting with Desta last night.

No one mentioned Mr. Orbit, though she'd watched his Jaguar drive past her on the way home last night, and she was fairly sure it had just passed her again as she turned toward Adelaide's. Marquette had still not returned her email or the voice message she'd left, and Fallen's heart lurched as she saw Adelaide's house dark and quiet, with no response at the door for the second day in a row. Fear raced through her as she considered the possibility that Adelaide had been injured, but looking through the windows, she could see nothing out of the ordinary.

On Wednesday Fallen made sure to speed through her

rooms so she could get over to see Desta after work. She didn't care what "the word" was; she was going to be a good friend. She took the bus and noticed Lad's fancy car in the hospital parking lot when she arrived.

How could she get him to leave her and Thomas alone in the dream? Their time together was short—if she could even get to the dream this week. And would Thomas still be there? Had he already passed away?

All this was so completely nerve-wracking that she had shoved her concerns away inside her head just to function. When she got to Desta's floor, visiting hours were almost over. The nurse checked the list and found Fallen's name on it, so she was waved through to follow the woman's quiet shoes down the hallway. As they approached, she heard a distinct voice coming from Desta's room. Mr. Orbit droned on until the nurse interrupted him as she opened the door and announced Fallen. He stood and nodded at her.

Fallen thanked the nurse and leveled Orbit with a stare. The loss of Thomas, the loss of everything, really, made her bold.

"I finished all my work—if that's what you're thinking." She looked from him to Desta.

The woman was strapped into an oxygen mask with an IV dripping something into her arm. The veil of pain around her almost shrouded her eyes. Fallen felt her hard shell soften.

"Oh, Desta." She walked over to squeeze the woman's hand gently.

"I'll leave you two to it. I need to stretch my legs." Orbit walked out, but managed to put his hand on her lower back as he passed her.

Desta pointed to the chair.

There was a lot Desta didn't have to say. Her hand had been cold. Her lips had a blue tinge. Even her skin was suffering from the lack of adequate oxygen in her system.

Fallen's hopes of getting any advice or information from

Desta also ran out of oxygen. Every breath was a struggle, and that was a fight she couldn't add to, not even for Thomas.

But Desta pulled the mask away from her mouth and clearly had a message to give Fallen. "Don't...tell Burt...about this... About me."

Fallen felt her eyebrows lift in surprise. "But—"

Desta's ragged breath made Fallen's hands itch to cover her face with the mask again, let her get some air.

"No death... Only forever."

Desta replaced the oxygen mask, but it was a bit askew. Fallen stood and adjusted it for the exhausted woman.

"I hear you," she assured her. "It's okay. I think you and Burt will be together in the next life. You know what? I know you will. Everything happens for a reason—and this, me and Thomas? It was a way to let you know Burt was still waiting."

Desta nodded. And her eyes grew sleepy.

Fallen kissed her forehead and carefully covered her cold hands with the thin hospital blanket.

Orbit returned to the room. Fallen didn't have to see him to know he was behind her. He had a force like a black hole, an energy that drained everything else around him.

She turned to face him, and he looked past her.

"Nice to see her calm. She's been agitated."

Fallen put her hands in her pockets. "She needs a warmer blanket; her hands are cold."

"It's part of what she has going on. I have an electric blanket over there, but we can only use it a little. She's having trouble regulating her temperature." He shrugged. "I wish I could do more. She's like family to me."

Fallen squinted at him. He let this woman clean hotel rooms when he was clearly rich enough to take care of her. "You should have let her just live in one of the rooms. She could have bossed us all around."

She watched his temper flare before he tilted his head, acknowledging her point.

"There's a lot of things I should've done differently, Fallen. But sometimes you have to let people have their way a little. Can't keep the reins so tight. Desta loved her job. Maybe you assume too much." He folded his arms in a way that plumped up his biceps.

Was he trying to intimidate her? She was over it. Over him and all his posturing.

"To each their own," Fallen said. "I'll visit her on Friday."

She stepped around him, and he grabbed her upper arm, which she hated. "If she makes it until then."

"I have a demanding boss. So I'll do the best I can." She stepped backward as she yanked her arm from his grasp.

She walked past him and his words ran cold over her spine.

"You working tomorrow?"

Fallen looked over her shoulder and waited for his gaze to move from her ass to her eyes. "Damn straight."

He nodded. "Well, I'll see you then."

Fallen flipped her ponytail and left the room in a way she hoped looked commanding.

He got off on threats, but she had very little left to lose.

Fallen's hands had trouble braiding her thick hair for work on Thursday morning. She made Fenn's lunch on autopilot. Her mind was occupied with a steady stream of questions. Would she see Thomas today? Was he dead? What would Mr. Orbit throw at her next? How long did Desta have?

It would be a crazy day. Her devastated heart trembled. Her imagination was pretty much pissing its pants.

Fallen logged in at work and listened to Melanny's lackluster team talk while keeping an eye out for Mr. Orbit. Of course, even if she didn't see him, he could be watching from somewhere else via the cameras. Fallen made small talk with 8 and 9 in the birdcage on the way to her floor. After she mentioned seeing Desta, she couldn't answer any of 8 and 9's questions about her without tearing up. The two women embraced her awkwardly.

When 8 reached in to her pocket to offer Fallen a tissue, a broken, bent fork fell out.

She scurried to pick it up and hid it like it was contraband.

"What's that for?" Fallen wanted to move the conversation away from Desta's health—it was hard to put in a day of work thinking about her pain.

8 winked at Fallen. "It's my 'I need a nap' fork."

"What does it do?" Now Fallen was truly puzzled.

"Girl, I made this after watching a YouTube video. If I need a nap or maybe to spend a little extra time with a maintenance guy, I slide this in the room's lock and nobody can get in, even if they have a key."

Fallen must have looked desperate because 8 offered it to her. "Do you need a nap today? You look hyped-up as shit."

Fallen nodded, trying not to appear too eager. The answer to her dreaming problem today was clicking into place.

"You can keep that," 8 told her. "I've got a couple."

Fallen nodded. "Thanks." This would ensure her privacy in 514 above and beyond the furniture she liked to put in front of the door. Orbit couldn't get in, if he was here and searching for her.

Still, throughout the day her resolve shifted. While she wiped dirty mirrors clean and vacuumed up crumbs, Fallen longed to have hope. Maybe she could change the past. If she could just figure out exactly when Thomas had died and how, maybe she could tell him, and he could avoid the deadly situation.

After using her iPad to send down an updated list of rooms ready for guests, Fallen approached 510. Just two more rooms until 514, and still no sign of Mr. Orbit. She stepped inside and tried out the broken fork lock. It seemed to work.

She left it in place as she cleaned, and put it back in her pocket as pushed the cart to the middle of room 512. Today 512 was super neat and only took her half the time a messy room would have.

Then came her moment to go into 514. She centered herself, resolving to find out whatever she could about Thomas and his circumstances. She half expected to hear Orbit's grating voice as she entered the room, but it wasn't there.

First, she cleaned everything. Then she brought her cart into the room and doused the lights. After letting her eyes adjust to the dark, she was able to make her way over to the desk. She worked quickly, putting the picture in place for the camera.

Once that was set, she used the broken fork to create her DIY security system. Finally she felt like she would be secure—at least on this side of things.

She stretched out on the bed, her eyes already starting to close, which made her heart race—a barrage of feelings that had once been foreign to her body, but now felt so welcome. She would see him. Maybe. Hopefully. *Please*. Nothing was guaranteed.

When Fallen opened her eyes, she was seated in a church pew. Towering stained-glass windows surrounded her, and the carpet held the faded scent of incense.

Lad was holding her hand, and he smiled when she met his gaze.

The man seated in front of them was talking about marriage and commitment, looking at them intensely.

Fallen tried to pull her hand from Lad's, but he had a firm grasp. She could feel a ring on her finger.

"So, this is our last counseling session, and unless either of you crazy kids has any questions, it looks like we'll have a wedding next week."

Lad stood and held out his hand to the priest. "Thank you, Father O'Hannan."

The priest looked at her as she stood as well.

"And you, little lady, I know you're not much for talking, but you will at least have to say 'I do,' at the ceremony."

He joked, but Fallen covered her mouth with the one hand she was allowed to have possession of. She looked at her feet, seeing the horrible Velcro sneakers. She looked back up at Lad when he cleared his throat, and the priest was gone.

"Do you remember these dreams when you're awake?" she asked him. No use pretending anymore.

"Fallen, you crack me up." He smiled again, his eyes unreadable. "Yes, it does feel like a dream world. You are a dream come true." He patted her hand. "How about we go out dancing—and then practice a little bit for our first night as man and wife?" Lad bit his bottom lip as his eyes slid over her chest. "I'm due the service since I forgave your dalliance with that solider. I mean, we can't pretend you're a virgin, right? But your wanton ways have come to an end."

And then Lad's hands were all over her—grabbing her ass, sliding over her breast for a hard pinch.

She grabbed his hands and pushed them to his sides. "No."

"That's fine. You want the payoff to be on the big night. I get it. Just don't forget your wifely duties." He smiled, but his eyes were mean.

Fallen decided playing into his fantasy might be the best way out.

"I'm leaving for my bachelorette party in a few minutes. You're off to your bachelor party, right?"

Lad seemed delighted at the change in her demeanor. He liked his delusions stroked, apparently.

"Yes. All the guys. And I promise you're my number one. I won't cheat on you like you cheated on me." He came in for a kiss, and she offered him her cheek.

"You should go now." She pointed to the door.

"Okay. I'll meet up with you after, though." He walked back up the aisle and waved over his shoulder.

It worked. Whatever weirdness this dream was, and however Lad controlled it, she was still in charge of some things too.

She looked around the empty sanctuary. The side door seemed like the best choice; she didn't want to go out the same door as Lad.

She pushed open the heavy wooden door and spilled out into a sunlit field. The tops of the long grass held little puffs of wishes and wheat. She shielded her eyes and looked for Thomas. He came around the corner of the building, and she felt all the tension leave her. He was alive.

They had urgent things to talk about, so much she had to mention, but in an instant, her mind became a sieve. There was just Thomas. He was searching for her. To be the goal he sought, to see his excitement and relief that matched hers was exactly what heaven was made of. She ran to him, but his long legs were much faster than hers. He picked her up and whirled her into a hug. She inhaled his scent.

"Fallen."

"Thomas."

She kissed him on the lips that she'd stared at for nights at a time. They'd been blurry then, though she couldn't quite remember why. It was as if her memory had been jammed. Thomas set her on her feet and ran his hands from her hips to her jaw. His gaze as he felt her shape could start and end a million wars.

It was him. And her. Finally. Finally together.

He changed her outfit as they hugged again. She glanced down to see a glamorous red and white dotted dress with a huge skirt. The top had pearl buttons and a v-neck, with what felt like a little pop collar.

He now wore a deep blue suit and tie with a matching hat. He looked a little like a gangster. He motioned toward their transportation, which he'd obviously thought about ahead of time. He was a genius, and she told him so. The gorgeous, cherry red convertible looked a whole lot like a PT Cruiser. If they were moving, surely they'd be harder for Lad to locate.

"Welcome to the Ford Deluxe. It matches your dress."

He walked her to the passenger side and held open her door. She slid in and made sure his side was unlocked. She needn't have worried. He hopped in over the door and flashed her a grin fully loaded with dimples and bright, white teeth.

"Wanna go for a ride?"

She nodded, amazed at how handsome he was. "Yes. Take me away from all this." She waved her hands at their surroundings.

The engine came to life, but seemed to have a permanent sputter.

"Is this a car you own?"

"I did. I sold it when I enlisted. I miss her. Not as much as I miss you, though. Get over here." He patted the leather seat next to him.

She slid over and cuddled into him. The scent of him, the heat of his hard body, and the feel of his arm around her shoulders sent a wave of ecstasy into her brain.

She tilted her face to his, ignoring the driving he managed with one hand. "I'm so free with you."

He looked at her, glancing back at the road from time to time. "I know what you mean."

He started to hum, so she laid her head against his chest to feel the vibration.

"Tell me." She touched his jaw, running the back of her hand over the hint of dimple. "Tell me what'd it be like to be your girl. Your real girl."

"That's easy. I think about it all the time." He kissed her fingertips as she outlined his mouth. "I'd kiss you—like this—" He nudged her forehead with his chin until she angled her lips in the right direction, and then he kissed her. The car stayed on the road, so she assumed he kept his eyes open, but his lips tasted delicious.

Just the simple things, the small details—she couldn't take them for granted. They had to last her a whole week. Maybe her whole life.

He ended the kiss with smaller kisses before finishing his statement. "I'd do that all the time. And with my friends? I'd have you sit in my lap just to make them jealous. Every night I'd drive to your house to kiss you goodnight. Until we were married, and then? Then I'd kiss you all night and good morning too."

She covered her mouth so she wouldn't sob. She wanted this world he painted in her imagination. "More."

Thomas nodded and gave the car more gas. "I'd take you to the movies. And then we'd have a milkshake. And I'd dance with you in the moonlight."

Fallen nodded. "Let's do that. Take me to the movies."

Thomas tilted his head and nodded. "Let's."

Three turns later, a classic theatre appeared, aglow in lights with a sign proclaiming *Double Indemnity* as the evening's show.

She waited for him to open her door, because it was a date after all. They strolled across the parking lot under the stars. The gravel crunched under their feet. Thomas pulled open the shiny silver and glass doors, and the scent of popcorn hit them, though there was not another person to be seen.

"Popcorn," he breathed. "It's been forever since popcorn."

Fallen let go of his arm and walked around the counter. "What'll it be, sir?"

He leaned on his elbows and looked her up and down. She added a little kick that tossed up the hem of her dress.

"I'll take popcorn and the gorgeous lady." He lifted his eyebrow and gave her a slow smirk before pulling his hat off his head and putting it over his heart.

Fallen grabbed a red and white box and scooped out the fluffy corn to fill it up.

She turned and took the first piece out, holding it for him. He pretended to snap at her like a tiger, and she laughed. In an instant Thomas vaulted the counter and had her up against the popcorn machine—mixing her laughter with a surprised shout. He wrapped his arms around her waist and brought her flush against him.

"Tell me more about our date," she asked while looking at his lips.

"Well, I'm so charming that she lets me touch her. Lets me do whatever I want."

Fallen batted her eyelashes. "She sounds a little fast."

"It's okay—it's only because she's crazy about me." Thomas touched the end of her nose.

"Now *you* tell *me* about this date." Thomas swirled her away from the machine and lifted her to sit on the counter

She liked this better because they were eye to eye. She pulled him in and whispered her imaginings in his ear.

"Well, the girl, she wishes for him. All the time. She imagines what it would be like to spend a whole day holding his hand. And she would show him off. And no other guys would dare come near her—because her guy? He's just so tall and intimidating. Like Superman. And he keeps holding the doors and smiling at her a lot."

She looked in his eyes. There were so many colors there—pale blue, deep gray—highlighted by a dark circle.

"She would let him take anything he needed from her, because she needs it too."

Fallen flipped her hair out of her face, and Thomas leaned close and planted a kiss on her exposed throat.

He whispered in her ear, a sensitive spot for her. "He needs her so much." He nibbled her earlobe before touching the tip of his tongue to it.

She grabbed his tie and pulled until his lips were on hers again. She scooted forward so he was safely between her legs. She ran her hands down his chest, unbuttoning the suit jacket as she went, letting her hands rest on his belt buckle.

"Come, beautiful girl. Let's go to the movies." He grabbed her ass and held her aloft. She snatched the popcorn bucket as she slid down his body. Thomas strolled with her on the thick, red carpet. He pretended to talk to an attendant who wasn't there and handed him make-believe tickets.

"He says theatre number two for us."

She blew a kiss in the direction of the ticket stand, and Thomas narrowed his eyes. "Are you flirting with him?"

She winked at the spot before turning back to Thomas. "Ex-boyfriend. Just want him to know what he's missing."

Thomas frowned and turned away from her, very thoroughly miming beating up someone, complete with ventriloquism of the high-pitched squeals of his "victim."

Fallen laughed so hard she had to squat down on her white high heels. When he saw how hard she was laughing, he added a few more kicks.

"Okay, that'll teach him a lesson." Thomas pretended to dust off his suit jacket before offering his arm to her.

"Thank heavens I'm well protected." She waved at her face like she was overheated by his masculine display.

He rubbed his lips. "No worries. I'll keep you safe."

She tried to look at the floor before the uncertainty showed in her eyes, but he didn't miss a thing.

"What's wrong?" He stopped in front of the gold-etched doors that kept the flickering screen just beyond.

"I just wish I could keep you safe, too. War scares me." She bit her bottom lip and searched his face for answers he couldn't give her.

He gave her a sad smile. "I love that you want that for me."

Fallen insisted on another kiss, and Thomas went slow with her, like he had all the time in the world. The wasteful kiss was a tender one. Eventually he escorted her to theatre #2, his hands tracing over her back possessively.

Fallen held tight to his arm because she sucked at walking when she couldn't take her eyes off the sharp angle of his jaw and his blinding smile.

The empty theatre was already dark, the black and white film flickering on the screen. Thomas picked out a middle row and stepped to the side to allow her to choose one of the overstuffed, deep red seats. He sat next to her and slung his arm over the back of her chair as easy as breathing. She held up the popcorn, and he leaned low to take a piece from the bucket using only his tongue. He smiled at her while he crunched.

"This stuff is heaven. I've missed it."

Fallen crossed one leg over the other before putting her head on his shoulder. Low, sweeping music played as the characters acted out their drama in what looked like a grocery store.

She closed her eyes and concentrated on the heat of Thomas' shoulder against her cheek, the gentle thump of his heartbeat, which she could just barely hear. The popcorn box tumbled from her hand as she moved to grasp his crisp shirt in her hand.

"What's wrong, dream girl?" He covered her hand with his, kissing her forehead and hair.

Fallen didn't want to cry; she wanted this memory remain the perfection it had been a moment ago. She shook her head and buried her face, inhaling his cologne.

Her mascara bled onto his shirt, staining it. She spied it as she peered through her blurry lashes. "I'm sorry. I made a mess of your shirt."

"I love whatever marks you leave on me, Fallen. Tell me." He ran his hand across the back of her neck.

"You already know." She didn't have to explain. This moment with him—the stolen gorgeousness of being together—it was cruel to have it be so brief.

"To have happiness this complete where I am is better than heaven."

He ran his fingertips down her cheek.

She nodded against his chest and changed the subject. "Do you know what's happening in the movie?" She glanced up at him, the screen flashing in his pupils.

"Nope. Never seen it before. You?" He lifted an eyebrow.

She shook her head. "I think it would be a lot better if you were naked."

A slow, lustful smile spread across his face. "Agreed."

Thomas stood and held out his hand. She wrapped her fingers around his, pulling herself out of the chair. Their feet crunched on spilled popcorn as they walked through it to get to the aisle.

He took charge as soon as her high heels reached the carpet, lifting her in his arms with a clear intention. Fallen used her levitated perspective to look closely at his lips. She tasted them with the tip of her tongue. Her heart had been scrubbed raw, and his attention was the salve.

Theirs was a reckless love. But it didn't matter. He adjusted her mid kiss and sat her on the stage near the screen. Now she was taller than he, which was unusual. She took the opportunity to unbutton his shirt while looking at his face.

"So elegant—you should be on all the big screens." He ran his hands up and down her thighs, pulling her skirt up higher with the each pass.

"So handsome—you could be a rock star."

He looked puzzled for a second until she opened his shirt and ran the palms of her hands over his chest. He traced the edge of her white-laced panties with his thumbs. She inhaled and held her breath. Having him so near where she wanted him tested her patience. But she didn't want him to think she only used him for the way he made her feel. Still, the moan she exhaled gave away her deepest feelings.

"Lay back. Let me see you." Thomas pulled his shirt the rest of the way off. She admired his tattoo, rubbing her name trapped in ink on his forearm as she followed his directions.

He must have found something to stand on, because he scooted her bottom over, and then he could reach her. He took off her panties and kissed her thighs, murmuring about the softness. The soundtrack of the movie was louder this close to the screen, so she couldn't hear a lot of what he said, but his eyes told her.

And then he was her everything. This part could never be faked or imagined. His fingers and tongue and breath were inside her. The friction and adoration had her panting for him. He took her over the edge quickly. She locked her legs behind his neck, and he had to struggle to get out of her grasp.

When she was spent, she let her arms drop to either side. He lifted himself up onto the stage, and she looked at him hazily.

"Are you okay, baby?" He eased down next to her.

"So much more than okay." She wanted to touch him but hadn't the energy after the rush he'd given her.

His self-satisfied smirk made her blush and bite a smile at the same time. He unbuttoned the front of her red and white dress slowly, but nimbly for such large hands. He spent his time looking at her breasts like they were just for him, pushing the lace out of the way to get to her nipples.

"A masterpiece. You are every piece of art in the world poured into one tiny package." He took the job of keeping her nipples peaked very seriously; when his hand found one, his teeth were on the other.

She kissed the top of his head, the rush for him filling her again. She wrapped her arms around him and gently put his cheek flush against her chest. He sighed. As he relaxed against her, she felt his need and knew it was her chance to lavish attention on him.

Fallen whispered, "Lay on your back, solider boy."

"I had other, very detailed plans." He lifted to look at her. His sparkling blue eyes were the color of midnight at the very edge of a full moon. The flecks of silver there were the stars.

"I need to put you in my mouth. Can I do that?" She fluttered her eyelashes at him.

He blew a curl of hair off his forehead. "I do believe that would be sensational."

He rolled off of her, but held up a hand when she tried to crawl closer. "But I think you have to be naked. Totally. I have to see you in just your skin like my life depends on it."

Fallen stood and took off everything but her thigh highs and white heels. Thomas rested on his elbows, his delicious body stretched out like an invitation.

"Spin for me. Hold up your hair."

She did as she asked, then turned to peek over her shoulder.

"Stop."

He sat up as she froze. She watched him get to his feet like the athlete he was. Easy. Strong.

But it was the artist in him that touched her and murmured to her. "The way your shoulders move…right here, at the center of your back." His touch was feather light. She felt chills race to follow his touch. "And this?" He touched the lowest part of her back. "These two dimples? I'd kill just for them."

She laughed a little.

"This part of your thigh…" He bent at the waist and touched her just above her stocking. "…might be the softest thing on earth. Except inside you. Inside you is pure perfection." He grazed his fingertips over her ass and reached into her from behind.

She panted and lost her balance. He put his other hand on her stomach, keeping her steady as he pushed lower to find the place between her legs that had already given him her soul. He rocked her like this, pumping in and out, watching her carefully as he brought her to the edge again.

"Stop." She put her hands on his forearms. "You. Only so much time. I need to do this for you."

Ever the gentleman, he stilled his hands, but she had to pull them away from her body.

Fallen held on to his arms as she took to her knees. This is what she wanted him to have. The flashing screen highlighted him in front of her as she tugged on his pants. There was pure masculinity in the way he divested himself of the last barrier between them.

Him. All of him. The power she felt as she treated him to everything she could imagine or dare with her mouth and hands was addictive. Everything about him was what she needed.

And when he was just at the edge, when he was ready, she pulled away.

He groaned at the loss of her.

"Now let me ride it."

She watched him swallow as he knelt. She pushed on his chest until he lay back. And then she was his predator. She let her hands and mouth find every secret he had. And when she didn't want him to wait one second longer, she sat astride him. Fallen used her passion to give him everything he needed.

She reached between his legs as the veins in his neck corded and hugged him from the inside. His growls of pleasure made her work him even harder until he begged her to stop. Fallen leaned forward and kissed his chest as he hugged her to him.

"Dream girl, that was…"

She finished his sentence for him. "Everything."

The deep breath they took together was a promise.

Fallen stayed on his chest until his heart slowed to a resting rate.

Thomas sat up and hugged her to him so they could be face to face.

She tried to etch his cheekbones into her memory. He seemed to be doing the same.

"How are things where you are right now?" she asked.

"A mixture of great and horrible. We've had a wave of good news that the war may be ending—but not in the place where I'm fighting. Not yet. We're hopeful, but where I am? It's really bad right now. Lots of enemy strongholds. The land mines are everywhere, and there's no way of knowing…"

He stopped himself. "I don't want to talk about that now, here with you. My Fallen."

She nodded but really wanted him to continue. He'd gotten out so many details about without being interrupted. That could be helpful for finding him in the waking world. Suddenly Fallen knew she had to tell him something. It was at the tip of her tongue, but the words were too blurry.

"Tell me about you. How's the job?" He rubbed her shoulders and cupped her boobs when she had a chill.

"It's hard to give you an update when you're still inside me." She rocked her hips back and forth and gave a gentle swirl.

"Temptress. Tell me. About you." He closed his eyes and seemed to relish her small movements.

"The job sort of sucks. My friend is sick, so she's not at work anymore. And my only other real friend is a 90-year-old woman with memory loss. Lad is funding my brother, my mother continues to struggle and bring her chaos around at the worst possible times, and I'm barely ahead of the bills. Seriously. I've gotta cut back on something, but in 2016, a girl without her cell phone is pretty much considered dead. It makes everything much harder—"

She stopped talking as his eyes widened.

"2016?"

The gravity of what she'd told him hit her like a sack of bricks. She'd revealed her when.

"The future?" He moved his hands from her breasts to her cheeks. "You're in the future?"

She nodded against the pressure of his fingers, afraid to say more, afraid to somehow break the loophole they'd found.

The flashes from the projector danced on his skin. She looked at him with intention, hoping he'd take the hint and tell her when he was from.

"That's a long time away from here. That's a real long time away from here."

"But is it possible? Could you be where I am?"

She watched his mouth move as he did the math. He rolled his eyes and shrugged. "I guess. Maybe."

She exhaled the relief that flowed through her. "Oh, thank God. I was scared I was too far forward."

"You pretty much are, dream girl."

Her mind clicked into sharp relief, and Fallen tossed caution to the wind. "When were you born?" she asked. "And where? How old would you be?"

But she didn't get to hear his answers because the back door of the theatre slammed open.

Thomas reacted before she could think. He had her behind him as he faced Lad straight on—in the nude.

She clutched his sides and teetered a bit on her heels. Their clothes were scattered everywhere.

"We don't want any trouble," Thomas said to open the conversation.

Fallen peered around her love. Freaking Lad. And just when she'd finally been able to share some information with Thomas —not to mention actually remembering something she wanted to ask him. She sighed impatiently, but the gun in Lad's hand sobered her. She had no idea if they could die in this dream world, but she wouldn't allow his weird fixation on her to hurt Thomas.

"You're naked with my fiancée. I think all you want is trouble," Lad seethed. He leveled his gun at Thomas.

Fallen stepped out from behind his solider, despite his desperate attempts to keep her shielded. She was banking on her nudity stunning Lad enough for Thomas to do something. He always seemed ready to fight. She covered up as best she could with her arms and hands.

"Lad, you have to understand; I never said yes to your ring. When I arrive here, it's just on my finger every time." She watched as Lad's eyes raked up and down her form.

"You're naked." He swallowed visibly.

"We all are under our clothes." Fallen watched as Thomas inched away in her peripheral vision.

"Now you want to be a wise guy? I'm here to provide a life for you, Fallen. And I find you with him?" Lad re-pointed the gun at Thomas, who stilled.

Upping the ante, she held her hand out to Lad, revealing her breasts in the process. His jaw opened slightly, and his aim wavered.

Her soldier knew what the hell he was doing. Before Lad even could figure out how to put pressure on the trigger, he was face down with Thomas' knee in his back. "Close your goddamn eyes," Thomas demanded, removing the gun from Lad's hand. "You don't get to see her like that."

Fallen scrambled for her dress and stepped into the shadow just below the screen to pull it over her head and button it up. She stepped back into view as she did up the last button to find Thomas putting the finishing touches on the binding he'd arranged for Lad with his own shoelaces.

Thomas stood up, as Fallen walked over with his pants in her hands. She stopped near Lad's face and pulled Thomas down for a deep kiss.

"Thank you. My hero," she said in an exaggerated voice. Thomas rolled his eyes. He was still adorable.

"This is not the way a gentleman acts. She's mine." Lad yelled, trying to be involved in the confrontation from the floor.

Fallen watched as anger and disbelief crept onto Thomas' face. "You can't own a person, dickhead."

She tugged on his arm. "Come, we don't have time." Suddenly she could feel how tired she was. Their passion or maybe the adrenaline from having the gun pointed at them seemed to have masked her growing sleepiness.

Thomas pointed at Lad. "You're not engaged. Not to her."

Together they walked quickly up the aisle, the end credits scrolling across the screen just before they hit the door.

Fallen staggered as they got to the lobby. Exhaustion made her feel drunk, all of the sudden.

"Let's get to the car." Thomas scooped her up when her legs went out, which had to be a feat of strength because his own legs were shaking. He dropped her in on the passenger side.

She rested her head on the seat and watched him struggle to get in the car.

"I can't drive," he said, his words slurred.

She wanted to say, *it's okay*, but her lips were numb. She was able to flop her hand between them, and he covered her fingers with his.

"Sleep. Sleep now so I know you go first. I don't want you here with..." He trailed off but glanced to the theater where they'd left Lad tied up.

She wanted to say she loved him one last time, but instead she closed her eyes like he wished.

The rush and swirling disorientation descended fast. Maybe the universe was angry because they'd broken the rules for their time together. She felt herself hit the bed with a bounce.

Fallen gasped, happy to be able to move her lips but instantly missing the warmth of Thomas' hand on top of hers. As soon as she could control her body, she rolled out of bed and went to the mirror. She saw Thomas sit straight up, seeming ready for a fight. His puppy perked up as well. He put one hand on his heart and the other on the dog's head before the image flashed away.

Fallen methodically undid her precautions as her memory slowly returned. She hadn't told Thomas about his death year. She hadn't even thought of it. After she slipped the picture off the ceiling in front of the camera, she put it back into her cart again. She slipped her broken fork into her pocket and thought of Desta. She hadn't seen Burt at all this time.

Now for the big moment. Creaking open the old door to room 514 at 12:30 on Friday morning took more courage than Fallen believed she had for a moment. But the hallway was empty. She was relived to get her cart all the way down to the maintenance closet without seeing a soul. Fallen refilled her cleaners and set up her cart for the next day.

"You know, I've noticed a pattern. On Thursdays." Melanny's voice was actually welcome.

"You're here late," Fallen commented. "I was in 514. No one stays there, and I kept my cart inside." She took her jacket from its hook, hoping the action hid her shaking hands.

"Well, Mr. Orbit is at the hospital with Desta, so he has me working as his secretary."

Melanny seemed to feel very important.

"Which you should know since I still think you're boning him."

"I'm not, though if that was any of your business, *you'd* know." Fallen zipped up her jacket. "I clocked out a long time ago. You don't have to pay me overtime. I apologize for keeping you up." She hit the doors, but Melanny followed her.

"Why are you in that room so much?" The manager gave her a hard stare.

"It's warm, and I'm tired. I have two jobs, and I still struggle to keep the heat on at home." Fallen decided her pride could take the hit.

She was surprised to see compassion on the older woman's face. "All right. Fine. But don't do it again."

Fallen nodded, knowing her agreement was a lie. She would be back next week, and she had so much to do between now and then. There had to be a way to save Thomas from his fate.

21

FOR DESTA

As usual, coming to work on Friday felt so unimportant when she'd just been with Thomas. Though she worried continually about his well-being, this week that stress would compete with her resolve to be ready with information she could share on their next encounter, questions about how Mr. Orbit would treat her, and the pain of preparing for life without Desta. When she entered the meeting room, 8 and 9 looked up with sad eyes.

"It's a matter of hours, they say, for Desta," 9 murmured. "We're going to the hospital after work. You wanna bum a ride?"

Fallen swallowed hard before nodding. The morning meeting was subdued, and she couldn't even look at Desta's replacement. Although she'd only been at this job for a few months, so much had happened to her here. And it all came back to Desta. She was the spine of this place—holding everything together properly—as well as its heart.

Fallen threw herself into her work and cleaned her floor as well as she possibly could. It was a way to grieve a bit—she made the rooms shine for Desta.

Room 514 got a lot of extra attention, and Fallen took a

long, hard look at the antique mirror. She contemplated taking it home with her, but when she saw nothing but her own eyes reflected back at her, she set it down. It wasn't worth getting busted for stealing it. The camera was still there.

She ran the dust rag over the headboard of the bed, paying attention to the deep grooves in the wood. She heard a tiny click, and the air suddenly felt different. Even before he spoke, she knew she wasn't alone.

"Thought I'd find you here."

Fallen stopped her dusting, her knees on the pillows with the rag in her hand. She heard the door click closed, sealing her in with him.

"Yeah, just making things clean." Fallen shuffled her knees backward off the bed and dragged her skirt down.

"You really love this room, huh?" Mr. Orbit ran a finger across the dresser.

He was dressed down for once—jeans and a white sweater. He looked younger.

Fallen straightened the comforter rather than answer.

"No answer? That's okay. Desta isn't responding anymore, either. But before she stopped communicating, she asked to see you. I'm here to give you a ride."

Fallen nodded, gathering up her cleaning tools and looking over the room. As she tried to inch past him to put her tools on the cart, he captured her by the shoulders.

"Can you look at me?"

It took a minute to summon her courage and remember she needed to obey in this case. She preferred ignoring the connections he thought they had.

"You're very pretty. Did you know that?" His steely eyes combed her face like he owned the deed to it.

"I don't have a lot of time to think about that. I'm busy trying to survive." She bit off her words.

Orbit nodded as if he understood before lifting a knowing eyebrow. "I could make your life much easier."

"I'm not sure that's how things work, Mr. Orbit. I may be struggling, but I'm in charge of my own life."

"Are you? You able to give that talented brother everything he needs to succeed?" He tucked a loose strand of hair behind her ear. "Struggling and succeeding are two very different lifestyles, Fallen."

It was tight wire to walk. Was Mr. Orbit able to remember what happened in the dreams? He had to, didn't he? Yet he never acknowledged a thing... What was he planning?

"What time do visiting hours end?" Fallen stepped to her right until he let her shoulder go.

He sighed. "We can get in at any time. This is goodbye now."

Fallen took the opportunity to prop open the room door with her cart before she straightened it. She wanted no opportunity for Mr. Orbit to take another picture while she bent over.

"It's so sudden." Fallen took one last glance around the room and saw a few more things she would have liked to straighten, but she would have had to walk past Mr. Orbit to do it, so she decided to leave them be.

"She's been sick a long time—just good at denial. I'll miss her terribly."

She waited for him to leave the room with her, but he turned and faced the view out of 514's expansive windows.

Fallen sorted her cart again. She didn't want to close the door. She associated this room with Thomas, and having Orbit inside seemed like a desecration. He suddenly seemed to think there was time to waste, but Fallen was worried about getting to Desta before it was too late. She needed to tell her Burt loved her.

"I hate this room," Mr. Orbit said suddenly. "It's come between me and everything I've ever loved."

Fallen cleared her throat.

"I've often thought of burning it down. Wouldn't that be the most freeing thing?" He peeked over his shoulder, but seemed to look right through her.

"Love perseveres. Even if you burn it to the ground." Fallen watched his eyes focus on her again like he'd just remembered she was there.

"Yes. I'm sure it does." He brushed off his jeans like he'd gotten them dirty. "Shall we go?"

Fallen pushed the cart out of the room and felt relief when he stepped into the hall with her.

Just then the birdcage stopped at her floor with 8 and 9 inside.

Fallen pointed to the women and told Mr. Orbit. "I've already made plans to go to the hospital with these ladies. Are you going now? I'll see you there."

She walked quickly toward the other maids and heard him huff behind her.

"Yeah. I'll see you there."

Fallen couldn't believe her luck—until she saw him re-enter 514 as the door closed to the birdcage.

The ride down the elevator with 8 and 9 was awkward, but at least neither of them would try for a kiss.

"Are you with him or what?" 8 asked. She kept her eyes forward when Fallen looked over.

"No. He just expects stuff from me, and tries to make it look that way sometimes. It's very confusing. Not sure how it got to be this way." Fallen grabbed her cart's handle so hard she could see her white knuckles.

9 nodded. "You're not the first. You might not be the last. That man? He's crazy. Like, he seems normal, and a little hot, right? At first. Then you realize his train doesn't pull all the way in to the station."

Fallen bit back her smile.

"I see you, girl. You're laughing. It's okay. We'll keep an eye on you. Desta fancied you."

9 patted Fallen's shoulder, and she let her smile come through.

"Desta also fancied Orbit, so there's that." 8 gave Fallen a look that told her the jury was still out, as far as she was concerned.

Downstairs they settled themselves into 8's car, which she drove like a maniac. Fallen's heart was racing by the time they parked in the parking lot at the hospital. Fallen thanked them for the ride but explained that she'd get home on her own. She encouraged them to go ahead to see Desta without her.

Fallen wanted to say goodbye to Desta alone. She went to the gift shop and looked around. The flowers there were pretty but wildly expensive. It seemed pointless, too. Mr. Orbit had said Desta wasn't communicating anymore.

She'd read that hearing was the last sense to go. She hoped Desta would still hear her when she said goodbye.

Fallen decided against a present and was headed out of the store when she ran into 8 and 9.

"We're all done. Be prepared, though. It's sad." 9 gave Fallen a tissue from the pack she'd been using.

Fallen took it with thanks and used her time getting up to Desta's hospital room to try to control her emotions. She'd never been at someone's deathbed. Watching her own mother kill herself with alcohol didn't count. That was a slow progression.

But lung cancer was vicious. That a woman who'd had opinions and a sense of humor and a light in her eyes with love in her heart could be reduced to…

Fallen opened the door, and there was a silence. A desperate wait. It was hard to find Desta through the tubes and various devices helping her. She was barely in this life anymore. A nurse sat in the armchair.

"What's your name?" she asked.

Fallen felt like they should be whispering, as if they were in church or at a funeral.

"Fallen."

"Thank goodness. She wanted to see you. I'm going to step out to give you privacy, but this button here?" She showed Fallen a red button on a clicker that Desta was clearly not pressing anymore. "It'll alert me."

"Okay."

Fallen's unease must have been visible because the nurse smiled. "Just talk for a little bit. Tell you're here."

With that, the nurse left the room, leaving the door open.

Desta was such a cougher; it was crazy to be in a silent room with her.

Fallen sat in the chair.

"I'm here, Desta. It's me, Fallen."

She looked at the woman's pale face. The connection that made falling in love with a dream guy seem sane was fading away. She chided herself for selfish thinking at Desta's darkest hour.

"Last night was Thursday. And it was a great dream," Fallen told her. "I know Burt loves you."

Fallen wondered if she was laying it on too thick; her time with him had been so brief in past dreams.

"I made sure to tell him how good you looked, and that you had saved a place for him in your life here. He said he loves you very much."

Fallen looked from her hand on top of Desta's wrist to the woman's face and saw her eyes fluttering open.

"Hi. Yeah. It's me. Burt loves you. And when you leave this life, I think you get to stay on the dream side. That's what I think."

Desta's eyes were bloodshot, but Fallen could swore they focused on her. Fallen filled the moment with words.

"And I think Lad's going to be okay. You saved him too, Desta. You did good work. It's all fixed."

Fallen patted her hand again and maintained the eye contact. She might have been imagining it, but she thought Desta had nodded a little bit.

Desta exhaled loudly into the mask and closed her eyes, resuming her shallow breathing. Fallen wanted to bury her face in her hands and cry, but she worried Desta might open her eyes again. She stood to leave quickly, pressing the nurse's button on her way out.

When she stepped into the hallway, Mr. Orbit was leaning against the wall. He was easily within earshot of the whole one-sided conversation she'd just had with Desta.

The nurse patted Fallen's arm on her way back in to sit.

Mr. Orbit looked devastated. Fallen didn't know what to say —or if she should say anything.

"She really loved me," he mumbled.

Fallen nodded as he shook his head. "You should get in there and sit with her."

His shoulders dropped as he did as he was told.

Fallen hurried to the elevator. She had no idea what grief would do to him. Would his grip on reality slide even further when Desta passed away? Would he be more grounded or more obsessed?

She waited outside for the next bus and was thankful when it arrived before Mr. Orbit came out to leave.

When she got in on Friday night, she was by herself at home for a few hours before Fenn returned from his game. They'd traveled to Purdys, and she just didn't have the energy to get there this time. White Plains had lost, and Fenn hadn't loved how he played, he told her. After getting all the what-ifs out, he gave her an update on Adelaide.

"There were a lot of cars in her driveway today after school," he said. "I hope she's okay."

Fallen quizzed him a little on exactly what he'd seen before he headed up to bed, and she decided to show up for her normal cleaning time after work on Saturday to see if she could catch anyone at the house who might be able to tell her what was happening.

Fallen traced Thomas' name on her arm, thinking about what she'd told Desta—wishing it was true. She wished she and Desta had an entire afterlife to devote to the men of their dreams, but there was no way of knowing whether that was true. Better to focus on this life anyway. She had to warn Thomas somehow. Change the course of his days. She traced the ink again. Maybe, just maybe she could still save him.

Fallen left a sleeping Fenn behind as she headed to the hotel for work Saturday morning, and after a busy day —at least the time moved quickly on Saturday—she bundled up to stop by Adelaide's house on the way home.

When she got there, she recognized Marquette's car. And her soft knock on the front door was answered by Adelaide herself. She seemed very excited to see Fallen, but kept referring to her as "sweetheart" instead of using her name as she took her jacket and hung it in the closet.

Marquette was on her cell phone, rubbing her temple. "Well, until I find out what I've got going on here, I have no idea how long it will take me to get her set."

Adelaide went to the cabinet, but seemed confused when the stove wouldn't turn on as she tried to heat the kettle.

"It's okay," Fallen called. "I don't need a drink. Did you want one?"

"Oh no, sweetheart. I'm just happy to see you. I wasn't sure what had changed. You were coming around a lot... Anyway, now it's nice to see you." Adelaide motioned to the kitchen table and paused to stare at her daughter for a moment before returning to the task of sitting and visiting with Fallen.

While she made small talk with Adelaide, Fallen overheard Marquette talking about the things in the house and how they were going to have to get a junk man out to dispose of almost all of it.

Adelaide winced when she heard the word *junk* again and dropped her voice to whisper her suspicions to Fallen. "I think they're putting me in a home for old people. That's what she's going on about."

Fallen reached across the table and covered Adelaide's hand. "I'm sorry."

Adelaide shrugged. "We all have our time. I'll miss this place." She looked around and teared up a little. When Marquette ended the call, Adelaide visibly stiffened.

"Did you come to help?" Marquette spoke to Fallen as she entered the room. She didn't sound aggressive, just interested.

"It's my usual day, and I like your mother. She's good company." Fallen smiled at her.

Marquette looked back at Adelaide and her face softened. "Yes. That she is. Can I speak to you outside for a sec?"

They left Adelaide sitting at her table and stepped onto the porch.

"I'm sorry I accused you last time. And I'm sorry we disappeared. I needed some time with Mom to really assess what's going to change in our lives. It's hard to accept, for me as well as her, that the time has come to let go of her independence. But it has. And in light of that, I have a favor to ask." Marquette shivered.

They'd left the house without putting on their jackets.

Fallen nodded, waiting. In the back of her mind, or maybe the front, all she wanted was more time with the picture of Thomas.

And more information.

Marquette offered a possibility with her suggestion. "Can you stay here with her for a little while? I have to call a few junk removal places and get her some good suitcases for the move to assisted living."

Fallen agreed immediately, but felt bad that this step for Adelaide would be what gave her an opportunity to get back to the thing she desperately wanted. When they went inside, Adelaide had gotten up from the table and was standing in the living room.

"Don't worry about cleaning; just enjoy the time together." Marquette seemed relieved to scurry out of the house as soon as she had her jacket on.

Fallen pointed to the stack of photo albums that were now sitting off to the side of the couch.

"How about we look at these?" Fallen grabbed the one she was desperate for.

"Oh, sure, sweetheart. My second husband always told me to look at the pictures to help me with my memory."

She tapped her temple with a fragile finger and sat on the couch. Fallen sat down next to her, flipping through the pictures until she found Thomas' again. Thankfully, the loose picture had stayed in the album.

Adelaide took the picture from Fallen's hands and smiled. "This was my first husband's brother Thomas. They looked a lot alike."

Fallen held her breath. Information. It was a lifesaver to her drowning hope.

She exhaled as she asked, "You know him?"

"Oh, no. He was killed in action two years before I met my Eddie. He and Johnny were still so devastated. We lost many boys over there, though."

Fallen knew as much from the dates on the back of the picture. But hearing it confirmed, it felt like her heart had stopped beating.

Fallen opened her eyes to see more Thomas—pages of pictures. Adelaide was explaining how the brothers grew up with their mom after the death of their father.

Fallen nodded. She already knew. She'd heard it from the man himself while she was in his arms.

Her eyes roamed the pages: Thomas with his brothers, all three in swimsuits. Thomas by himself, standing like Superman, looking into the distance. No tattoo on his arm. No sign that what she'd done in her dreams had occurred in his reality.

Adelaide interrupted Fallen's thoughts. "This was three years into their service. All three of them. Last time all three were together as well."

It was crushing to see that moment captured on film. She touched the picture through the crinkly, clear protector.

Adelaide thought for a moment. "You know? Help me with this, will you? I've got a box Eddie kept over there in that wicker chest."

Fallen's hands shook, but she set the photo album on the coffee table in front of her, desperate to see more.

She helped Adelaide move two large afghans to the floor and

watched as she opened the wicker chest. It had been in this house every time Fallen had been here, and she hadn't known.

Adelaide lifted out a photo box with *Thomas* written in all caps across the top. It wasn't heavy, but Fallen carried it back to the couch for Adelaide.

She wiggled the tight-fitting top off, and inside was a treasure trove: letters from Thomas to his mother, to his brothers. Right off the bat she saw the cartoons he'd drawn on the front—his way of making fun of his brothers from a distance. Yellowed papers, a few more pictures. Then something that made Fallen's tears flow freely—a beautifully framed Purple Heart.

She lifted it out of the box and wiped her hand over the glass.

Thomas F. McHugh
Killed in Action
May 7, 1945

Adelaide was still sifting through letters while Fallen's world imploded. She'd wanted more details, yet having them felt awful. She would have just dissolved on the couch, but Adelaide said, "Your name is Fallen, isn't it?"

Fallen managed to nod.

"It's all over these letters. Of course! I'm sorry I had forgotten for a moment. Isn't this the craziest thing? All these drawings Thomas sent to Eddie—they look just like you, the spitting image actually."

Fallen saw his handwriting, the signature she wore on her arm, at the bottom of two letters she could see, and an impeccable drawing of her face from two nights ago. There was even a movie screen behind her.

"Oh my God. He's real. He was here. It happened."

Adelaide touched her on the shoulder. "Are you okay, sweetheart? You look like you've seen a ghost."

"Not a ghost… It's just—I'm Fallen. I'm the girl from that picture."

Adelaide eyes went a little unfocused before she nodded. "Okay. You're Fallen? And you're dating Thomas? I'm so sorry he's passed. Are you just finding out now?"

And Fallen wondered if she had moved into some alternate dimension. That this woman could so clearly understand her dilemma was astounding. She should have really opened up to her weeks ago.

But then Adelaide continued, and Fallen realized what had happened.

"When my Eddie gets home, he'll be happy to meet you," she said. "Your name is all over these letters. Thomas seemed very smitten. He even wrote about getting a tattoo with your name on it."

Adelaide flipped through what had to be ten different drawings before finding the letter she sought.

"Here it is. Take a look."

Fallen took the letter and heard Thomas' voice as her eyes fell to the last paragraphs:

> As you've probably heard, it's bad where I have my guys right now and I don't mean the steamy weather. Hell, you might not even get this letter. Post has been crap. Tell Ma I said hi. I want to send you this picture and when you get home, you can see if you see this name around? She has a real weird name Fallen. I actually have a tattoo on my arm. I'm crazy about her and when I find her, I'm going to marry her let me know. I'll send more pictures.
>
> Love, Tom

Fallen covered her mouth. He was looking for her. Like he'd said he would. And she'd been doing the same thing—just seventy years later.

"Here, sweetheart. You have to take these drawings. Ed will be glad to meet you. It's only been two years since they lost Thomas, but it still feels raw for him."

Fallen nodded, accepting the drawings. Adelaide was lost in time for the moment, and Fallen completely understood the feeling. She wished she could go back to when just finding

Thomas on Thursdays was her most pressing worry. Now she knew for certain their remaining time together was limited. Just *how* limited was the next question.

She looked at the next letter. And the next.

Thursdays. It seemed to be April, rather than October, where Thomas was, but they always met on Thursdays. She went to Adelaide's wall calendar and matched the Thursdays she'd dreamed with Thomas to the dates on his letters. Calculating forward, May 7, 1945—the date of Thomas' death—would be not this Thursday but the next.

Her throat closed up, but before terror encompassed her completely, she realized that the currently slightly confused Adelaide might be able to help her.

"How did he die?" she asked the woman softly. "Thomas—how was he killed?"

Adelaide shook her head. "A hero, my dear, a true hero. He was leading his men through the jungle and after so many years at war, he must have just had a sense about something. He had his men stay back while he went ahead, and he stepped on a landmine. It killed him instantly, so he didn't feel any pain, we hope. But he did save a good number of his men by insisting they stay back."

Adelaide looked around like being in her living room was confusing.

"You were talking about Thomas," Fallen offered.

"Such a shame. Such a handsome guy. No wife. No kids. It's important to never forget that those boys died for us." Adelaide started stacking up the rest of the drawings—either ignoring the resemblance to Fallen or just not seeing it anymore.

She stopped mid pick up and put her hand to her cheek. "I think I'm getting tired. Is it rude if I have a little bit of a lie down?"

Fallen shook her head. "Not at all. Let me make sure you're all set."

Adelaide used the bathroom before coming to sit on her bed. Fallen found another afghan and tucked it in around her.

"Rest now, and thanks for the visit." Fallen closed the door and damn near ran back to the living room. She had no idea how much time she had before Marquette returned, and she needed to snap as many pictures as she could.

She was three letters in when she heard a car door slam and Marquette speaking loudly on her phone. Fallen grabbed her purse and shoved as many of Thomas' letters as she could in her bag, cringing when she heard the crinkling. She hated the thought of any of his words being damaged.

When Marquette entered the living room, Fallen had switched to putting the keepsakes back in the box.

"How is she?" Marquette seemed to be eyeing the furniture like a buyer.

"She's resting. We were looking at her pictures." Fallen put the award on top of the remaining drawings of herself in the box so Marquette wouldn't see them.

"Let me guess, her husband used to tell her to do that to help her memory?" Marquette took a moment and wiped at a tear before adding, "Maybe he should have given her better advice."

"Actually she did great remembering all the details of—your uncle, would it be?" Fallen replaced the box in the wicker basket chest.

Marquette nodded. "Yes. Listen, thank you. I'll certainly pay you for your extra time. Adelaide will be coming with me to move to the apartment in the morning." She walked through the living room touching things. "There's a service coming tomorrow to get this stuff out of here."

"Won't she need her things?" Fallen replaced the afghans.

"The apartment is already furnished. She'll have a roommate. It's near my house, so I can visit her, and she'll be closer to my kids, too. They're all in the area. But this is all five hours away, where we live, so it's just easier to get rid of most of this.

She doesn't really remember it anyway. I'll go through and pull anything of value. I just need a breather before getting into the thick of it." Marquette waved a hand toward the front door. "Thanks again for all you've done."

Fallen nodded, realizing she was just going to have to leave now with what she had in her purse. She considered punching the woman's lights out real quick so she could get the rest of Thomas' things, but she needed to stay out of jail for Fenn and her next Thursday date.

She had one week to figure out how to make sure Thomas didn't step on that landmine.

22

PICTURES

Back at home, Fallen ran up to her room. She didn't take off her coat or her shoes, just plopped on the bed and carefully began extracting what she could from her purse.

First there were three pictures of herself, each signed and dated, which she laid out on the bed. She brushed her hand against the paper and got the chills. Thomas' hand had touched the same place in his waking world. She bent and put her face against it too, imagining his hand there instead. He was a wonderful artist. She couldn't draw more than a stick figure, but the love they shared, and even the ecstasy she'd felt in his arms, was conveyed clearly in the drawings.

The old church decorated with fall leaves was there. And the treehouse too. He'd drawn his own hand in the center of her chest. She could tell he'd done a rushed job of adding a scarf to cover her nipples. She looked right at him in the drawing.

Love. So in love. Carefree too.

She missed him so much.

The last drawing was her wrapped in the curtains that had skirted the movie screen on their last date. She removed her calendar from the wall and matched the days of their dates with the dates of his letters. Her calculations had been correct: he had two weeks left. Well, not quite. According to the Purple Heart, he'd died on a Thursday.

And then Fallen fell into despair. What could she possibly do? Could she change the past? The story of Thomas as provided by Adelaide was incredibly sad and scary. Her Thomas losing his life to a landmine. Never getting home to his brothers and mother. Never getting home to her.

She wept for his lost future, but she was careful to not disturb the papers in front of her. Somewhere in her mind, even as she started to lose it, she knew she had to protect them.

Fallen took time to mourn, to shout, to cry. And then she had to stop. Because she needed a plan, and someone who is losing her shit can't save anyone's life.

By the time Fenn came home from wherever he'd been, she'd dried her eyes and collected Thomas' papers carefully. She would pore over his letters now. All information was potential help.

When she went downstairs, Fenn reported that he'd had a great afternoon playing football with his friends. He asked about her red eyes, and she told him it was a long day at work, that Adelaide was moving to an apartment five hours away, and she thought she was getting a cold. He talked to her for a while and said he'd already eaten when she offered him food. Then Fallen just tried to remain present with him as she bided her time. The letters called to her.

After he hit the shower on the way to bed, she reviewed everything one more time, then loosened the board in her closet and carefully put the documents inside, next to Fenn's watch. She set her alarm for early the next morning, though it was her day off. She would stalk Adelaide's house and watch for the junk guys. Getting the rest of Thomas' things into her possession was all she could think about.

She woke up three times during the night to check on her stash. And each time she read Thomas' letters. Memorizing the words on the page was inevitable, but she tried to pretend it was new information each time.

In the morning, Fallen walked to the grocery store a half an hour before it opened, just to get a look at Adelaide's house. Everything was quiet; Marquette's car was still there.

She waited around until the doors opened at the store, then did some quick shopping. On the way back, when she passed Adelaide's house, things had changed. Marquette's car was gone, and the front door was propped open. Men with 1-800-Clean printed on the back of their shirts carried belongings out to their truck.

Fallen ran home and practically threw the groceries on the counter.

Her brother met her in the kitchen, sleepy. "You okay?" he asked. "You look rough."

She ran a hand through her hair, which she had forgotten to comb. "I'm fine. Well, actually, I'm not. I really need to go for a walk."

"Hey. Is it anything I can help with?" Fenn pushed his hair out of his eyes, and it flopped right back.

She weighed her options. Alone it would be very hard to fight off at the junk guys to take Thomas' stuff—if it was still even there. Maybe Marquette had decided to preserve a few of her family's memories after all. She was probably selfish for wanting more than she already had, but Thomas' life was on the line, and she had to put saving him first.

"Yeah. Actually, remember I said Adelaide's getting moved to an assisted living place?" Fallen gathered her hair into a sloppy knot-style bun behind her head so she would look a little less like a crazy person, even as she felt nuttier all the time. "She showed me some stuff that belonged to a veteran in her family, and I just want to make sure it doesn't get tossed out."

Fenn had started unpacking the groceries, but when he got to the bananas, he stopped to have one like his life depended on it. "You want us to go dumpster diving?" he asked, popping the last of the banana in his mouth.

"It's a little more complicated than that. There's a service there cleaning out everything. I just want to make sure, maybe talk to them..." she trailed off.

Fenn nodded. "Give me a minute to get dressed, and I'll call Mitchel. Having a car might help carry the stuff, yes? Like, how much is there?"

"Just a photo album and a box." She had roped her brother into her delusion. Possibly an addiction. But it was love. And life on the line.

"Still good to have a car," he told her. "Be back in five."

Fallen finished putting the groceries away while she waited for her brother. She pictured the junk truck at Adelaide's filling up and the company swapping it out for an empty one. This made her jittery.

When Fenn returned, she already had on her jacket.

"Mitch the bitch will meet us there. Let's go." He held the front door open.

On the walk he quizzed her. "Why are you interested in this old lady's relatives?"

Fallen wished she could confide in Fenn, but she just couldn't, so she gave him part of a reason that was a little true.

"I just think veterans need to be respected, and I get a feeling from Adelaide's daughter that she might not feel the same." Fallen pointed at the truck as they arrived on her street. "See? I don't even know what's going on there. I'm assuming that everything gets tossed or resold."

The side of the truck read: *Call us and forget about it forever.* Which was fairly tasteless considering the reason they were packing up this particular property.

"Yeah," Fenn agreed. "That would be my take as well. Here's our ride."

Mitch pulled up alongside them and waved as he eased the car to a stop along the curb. They joined him in the car to case the joint.

There was no good moment to run in and raid the stuff, so Fallen just watched the furniture she'd been cleaning regularly get packed into the truck. First came the two bedrooms, then the kitchen stuff, and at last, Fallen saw the living room couch.

"That's it." She interrupted her brother and his friend talking about video game characters to point out the change in the situation. "They're in the living room now. That's where the stuff is.'"

Fallen scooted closer to the front of her place in the backseat, trying to examine everything that came out of the house.

Finally she saw the wicker chest in the arms of a burly moving man.

He set it down in the truck, and the guy behind him brought the afghans that had been on top.

When they started to close the rolling overhead door, Fallen felt her heart lurch. "Oh no! We're too late." Panic raced through her.

"No, wait. They aren't taking the truck. They're going for lunch, I bet. And that last guy was lazy as shit. I'm willing to bet he didn't lock it." Mitchel slouched in his seat as the workers piled into a pickup truck and drove away.

Sure enough, the clock read 12:15. They waited a respectable amount of time before Mitchel pulled up behind the truck and hopped out like he worked for the company.

Fenn's blue jacket did actually resemble the color the moving men had been wearing. Mitchel yanked on the truck's rolling door, and it flew open.

Fallen pointed out the trunk to her brother, and he hopped in and popped it open. Mitchel jumped in as well and held a hand out to Fallen. Under the blankets she found the photo album, and Mitchel grabbed the photo box.

Once they had the things Fallen was desperate for, they hopped out of the truck, and Fenn jerked it closed.

"Oh crap," Mitch announced. "They're back."

Sure enough the moving men had returned, fast food in hand.

Mitch was the coolest. "Just walk. Smile and wave. It's going to be great."

Fallen did her best to wave and giggle when the man on the passenger side rolled down his window to give her a low wolf whistle.

When they reached the car, they didn't bother to put their ill-gotten gains in the truck. They just toted them on their laps. Mitch put the car in reverse and made an unhurried U-turn, despite Fallen and Fenn freaking out around him.

"I told you. I got this. You'd be surprised how looking like you aren't in a rush is a great diversion. And it helps to have a pretty girl with you."

Mitch winked at her in the rearview mirror, and Fenn punched him in the arm.

"You've done this type of thing before?" she asked. What kind of guy was her brother hanging out with anyway?

"Well, no. But I watch a lot of spy movies." Mitch turned the opposite direction from their house. "And I'm going the long way to your house in case they get wise."

Fenn immediately began teasing Mitch, and soon they were going back and forth about which movie spy they should be.

Fallen reached over the seat and lifted the lid of the box on Fenn's lap. Sure enough, Thomas' Purple Heart was on the top.

She closed the lid, but not before her brother saw what was inside.

"They were tossing out the guy's Purple Heart? That's rough."

Mitch agreed, and Fallen felt a little vindicated for her first burglary.

Fallen spent Sunday night flipping through Thomas' things on the floor of her room. Fenn had popped in a few times to see how she was doing, but she was barely able to focus enough to answer him.

With Thomas' letters and drawings and photos spread out in front of her, she felt more connected to him than ever.

Unfortunately, the new resources in front of her also made her aware of the gripping pain his family felt after his death. There was an obituary newspaper clipping with a copy of Thomas' smart-looking military photo carefully folded between the letters from him that were bursting with life.

The telegram from John to his mother notifying her of Thomas' passing was heartbreaking in its simplicity. Fallen couldn't help but imagine his brother choosing the words he knew would shatter his mother. And Lucy getting the notice. Was a telegram always a bad sign? Fallen suspected it was.

There was very little information given about where Thomas had died—some small Philippine island—and nothing on how. So all she had to go on was Adelaide's memory of what her husband had told her. Both John and Ed had been in different countries at the time, so maybe they were wrong, and the story was just rumor. But the date printed on his Purple Heart seemed definitive. Now she just needed to figure out a way to tell him.

They'd gotten away with a lot in the last dream, shared way too much information. If only her memory had worked better…

She filed the papers and pictures away and kept them by her

bed, except for the Purple Heart. She had heard rumors of people selling them online and feared her mother would somehow become one of them. She put the honor with Fenn's watch behind the board in her closet.

Monday morning came all too quickly, and Fallen and Fenn got out the door late. Mitch did a drive by of the hotel to drop her off again, so she just squeaked into the meeting on time. But the sad eyes in the room deflated her, and she knew. Now she knew for sure.

"Desta passed away early this morning," Melanny explained to the subdued room. "Her funeral will be this Thursday. Please plan to attend."

8 and 9 included Fallen in their condolence hugs, and they took the birdcage together to their floors.

Fallen kept a box of tissues with her, because she kept finding tears on her cheeks as she walked through the routine Desta had taught her.

It wasn't until she got to 514 and the end of the day that Fallen remembered seeing Mr. Orbit let himself back into the room last week instead of following her to the elevator to go see Desta for the last time.

She opened the door carefully, and noticed immediately that the camera was gone. The ceiling had been patched, and unless someone knew where to look, they might never notice the variation in the plaster.

As usual, she checked the mirror, and found it was not in the giving mood. So she did her regular, mostly unnecessary, shining of the room in which she dreamed.

She wondered if Orbit had put in a less-obtrusive camera somewhere, and she paid extra attention to the vents and under the tables, thinking of the spy movies Fenn and Mitch had discussed on Sunday.

When she'd finished, she took one last look at the mirror before closing the door and locking it behind her.

Rather than dragging through the week focused only on returning to Thomas' arms, this time Fallen spent time with his letters and drawings, tangible testaments to their dreams and a way to feel his presence every day of the week.

He'd mentioned her to her brothers, always professing that he loved her and was serious about finding her. The small snippets of the war he shared seemed to be aimed at an audience already following new reports closely. She didn't have the responding letters, of course, and she wondered what receiving these had been like for his family. Had they worried he was losing touch with reality? It had to be a concern. The human body and mind could only take so much.

Fallen sorted the papers into happy and tragic on either side of her. She made time to investigate what she now knew—his rank, his platoon. But all she could find about him was the simple, basic entry on the website for Purple Heart recipients.

There was no picture there, so on her second trip to the library this week she uploaded his military picture to provide a face with the name.

By Wednesday night, Fallen still had no good plan for how to communicate his impending death to him. She tried memorizing the date in a sing-song rhythm and using various mnemonic tools, hoping she could trick herself or the dream world into letting her remember.

The other issue was Desta's funeral. She had no idea how to slip out and make it back to 514. Skipping her date was not an option this week, as this would be her last chance to warn Thomas about his death.

Thursday morning, she dressed for work, bringing along a tote bag of nicer clothes for the funeral. She decided to take a simple approach: just claim to be sick and leave. This would be transparent to Mr. Orbit, but she had no other choice. She had to take the risk to tell Thomas.

Fallen arrived at the hotel and learned Mr. Orbit had brought in a skeleton crew from one of his other hotels to keep the Revel functional. The regular staff would attend the service together that afternoon. So after they'd cleaned the most necessary rooms, managed the most pressing tasks, the crew took over, and everyone changed into somber attire.

Fallen got a ride to the funeral parlor with 8 and 9, all the time wondering how she would be getting back. As she found her seat, she marveled again that Mr. Orbit had let the staff come. Truly, though, Desta's job had consumed most of her life —that and a man she dreamed of. Without her coworkers, the room would have been largely empty. There were only a few neighbors and a nurse from the hospital. The casket was closed.

When the proceedings began, the pastor seemed to have known Desta well, which was a comfort. Fallen could barely keep it together when the organ played, and 9 passed her a tissue. She felt selfish as she wiped her eyes. She should've been focused solely on Desta, but more and more, she was also panicking in her head.

Orbit took the podium at one point and read a speech about loyalty and putting the company first, which seemed hollow, considering where they were.

When the service ended, it was almost 3 pm, and Fallen's nerves were shot. She needed to get back to the hotel. She texted her brother, asking if Mitchel might be able to pick her up, and he responded that practice had been canceled due to the rain, so they could swing by. Sure enough, as the doors were propped open, the pattering of rain filled the lobby.

She managed to avoid eye contact with Mr. Orbit by picking

at invisible lint on her skirt. She stepped outside when she saw Mitchel's car approach and didn't look back, even when she thought she heard her name. Rather than joining those who would follow the casket to the cemetery, Fallen would return to the room and keep her appointment with a dream. As sad as it was that her friend was no longer in this world, she knew Desta would understand.

"Hey, I think that guy wants your attention." Mitchel caught her eye in the rearview mirror.

"It's probably my boss. I don't want to talk to him." She put her hand in her hair and pulled it to cover her face.

"No worries, baby doll. I got you." He gave her a cheesy wink, and she almost smiled.

Fenn reached into the backseat to pat her shoulder. "I'm sorry about your friend. Do you want to go home?"

"No. I'd actually like to go back to work, please." She pointed in the direction of the old building when they got to the main road.

"You sure? If I get off for the day, we play." Mitchel was flirting with her, she realized. She wouldn't have noticed if not for the murmured threats from her brother in between every word.

"Desta loved the hotel. I feel like I need to pay my respects there—just some quiet time in her favorite room."

Her explanation seemed valid enough, and the boys were respectful the rest of the way, falling silent like they too were in a funeral procession.

When they let her out at the front of the hotel, she told her brother not to wait up; she would be late as usual. Then she thanked them for the ride.

She heard Fenn telling Mitchel that she obviously already had a boyfriend as she shut the rear door.

It took everything in her not to run immediately to 514. She'd tucked her master key into her tote and had the broken fork with her as well. The substitute guy at the front desk just nodded politely as she went past.

In the birdcage, she wondered if she should grab the picture for camouflage, but with the camera being gone, at least as far as she could tell, she wouldn't know where to put it anyway.

So Fallen would go without. She passed two guests on her way and addressed them politely out of habit, realizing only as she unlocked the door that she wasn't dressed as an employee.

Her simple black dress was a steal she'd found for ten dollars two years ago. When paired with her one pair of black heels, she could make it to funerals and weddings without looking out of place.

She slipped off her jacket as she walked in, letting it land on the floor.

Fallen jammed the fork in the lock and slid the broken part through to secure the door from the inside.

It would have to do. And she still wasn't sure she would be able tell Thomas what she needed to. At least she'd made it to spend time with him—unless Mr. Orbit had done something to the hotel room.

She forced herself to stop imagining what he could have had done to the room.

As she sat on the bed and swung her heels up on to the comforter, she touched Thomas' name on her arm. Soon she would see him. And then her gaze fell to the pen on the desk by the pad of paper.

Ink. Thomas' writing had moved with her from world to world. It had been right in front of her the whole time. She already felt groggy as she crawled off the bed and snagged the pen.

She went to write the information on her palm, but thought better of it. She could wake up looking at Mr. Orbit on the other side. It would do no one any good for him to see the message she was trying to convey to Thomas.

She pulled at the neckline of her dress and pushed her bra aside. If she was lucky, Thomas would be the only one to see this part of her.

Forcing her eyes to focus, she scribbled:

KIA May 7th, 1945

And then there was only blackness.

23

CRAZY TALKING

Fallen opened her eyes to see her dress melt into white satin studded with sequins and gems. She ran her hand over it and reveled in its softness on her lap. Then she raised her eyes to take in the room. She sat at a makeup table, and her reflection could have been on the cover of a bridal magazine. Her skin was flawless, and her hair cascaded over her shoulder, swept to the side by an elaborate clip.

Her gown was strapless with a full skirt. A woman entered the room covered in a black lace veil, and Fallen looked down again. This was a wedding, and she was the bride. The engagement ring from Lad had appeared on her finger again, and her throat went dry.

She was getting married to Lad.

Oh God.

And that's when she noticed the writing on her left breast. She pulled her hands to her chest and looked at the reflection in the mirror to see if the woman had seen. It was impossible to tell because her lace veil masked her face.

The woman patted her on the shoulder with a gloved hand

and walked over to fluff a thin, white veil. It was obviously intended for her head.

Fallen could see her handwriting peeking out from under the dress. This was a problem. She couldn't have Lad asking questions about…well, she couldn't bring to mind what it said, just that it was important. For Thomas.

Fallen wanted to see if it was as bad when she stood up. She hiked up the dress as best she could, but it was still visible. The black-veiled woman came over and tisked her.

"You got some writing there."

Fallen gasped, recognizing the voice. "It can't be…"

The woman lifted her veil. "Sure it can, honey!"

"Desta! Desta, you're here!" Fallen threw her arms around her. She looked years younger without her glasses, and her voice no longer sounded like she gargled with asphalt in the morning. "I've missed you so. And I was so sad. Does that mean this is heaven?"

Desta put her finger to her lips. "No, it's not. But I got to make a pit stop here. If you wish for something hard enough, I guess it happens."

"Have you seen Burt?" Fallen rubbed her hands up and down the woman's arms, trying to wrap her mind around this latest crazy turn.

"Not yet, and I don't know how long I have. I gotta find that guy and take him with me! Let's get some concealer on that tit S.O.S. you got there, just so it doesn't call attention." Desta grabbed the stick of makeup necessary for the correction and then looked back at Fallen's face, her thick veil over thrown back over her shoulders. "Girl, you crying for old Desta?" She grabbed a tissue and blotted it under Fallen's eyes.

"Of course. This is a great surprise. I'm happy to see you."

It was surreal to have the woman whose funeral she'd just attended apply makeup to her boob.

"Is Lad here? He was going to the…" And then her brain did the blank-out thing the dream side was famous for.

Desta seemed to understand. "He's not here yet. But he will be. You being here sets him off. Somehow he always knows."

"Okay." Fallen looked at her reflection and the note she couldn't quite convince herself wasn't visible anymore. "I don't want to marry Lad."

"I know, baby. And I'm going to help you as long as I can. Just make sure not to say *I do* to a man you don't love. Remember that. Can you do that?" Desta gave her an urgent look.

Fallen nodded and helped Desta replace her veil as the doorknob clicked and rattled.

They were all set when Lad waltzed into the room in a full tux with tails.

"Ladies." He stopped in his tracks and bit his index finger, looking her up and down.

"My bride. You're stunning. How jealous all the other men in the world will be as soon as you're mine for good. Come here and give me a kiss." He pointed at the floor.

"I can't mess up my makeup," Fallen responded.

The air grew thick and awkward.

"This is really bad luck. Out with you," Desta chided, using a fake accent.

Now that Fallen knew it was Desta, she was amazed that Lad didn't recognize her. But he showed no sign of it as she shooed him out the door.

Fallen waved as Desta pushed Lad into the hall and shut the door behind him.

Desta moved her veil aside once more. "Fallen, I love Lad, I really do—despite all his shortcomings. But I can't let someone else miss their true love story. I hope you guys make it out, like Ellen did."

Fallen wanted to say so much, ask so much, but the words wouldn't come. Instead she hugged Desta again.

"Okay, I'm going to get out there and look for your Thomas to make sure he gets in the building. Good luck." Desta covered her face and left Fallen in the room to pace.

There was a bouquet of hydrangeas on the table by the door. Fallen picked them up. Although they were a ball of tender colors, in the waking world she was allergic to the scent of them. But so far no sneezing here… She checked her dress again and made sure the words were hidden. She'd just decided to take another look to jog her memory when someone knocked on the door.

She tentatively called "Come in," and a huge smile spread across her face when she saw Burt on the other side.

"Did you see her?" Fallen rushed to his side.

"I'm here to walk you down the aisle," he said formally.

Fallen was stunned at his lack of acknowledgement. She had a horrible feeling Desta was in love with a man who didn't recognize what a gift she was.

But as they stepped into the hallway, she realized Lad was within earshot. Fallen took Burt's offered arm and squeezed it.

When Lad nodded and stepped down the hall, Fallen realized they were in a church. Burt took her in the opposite direction.

When they seemed to be alone, she yanked on Burt's arm until he put his ear near her mouth. "Did you see her?"

Burt looked at her like she was speaking another language. "Who?"

Once they stepped into the foyer of the church, Fallen handed Burt her bouquet. "I have to go check for something."

She had every intention of running from the church the second she opened the huge front door. But as she reached for the handle, two tuxedo-wearing men stepped in from the sides.

She was so focused on her escape, she hadn't seen them in the shadows.

"Going somewhere?" the larger one asked.

"I just wanted to make sure my friend arrived," she semi-fibbed.

They shook their heads. "Everyone is accounted for," the other one said. "Now they're just waiting for you."

She lifted her dress and walked back to Burt, who handed her the bouquet again.

The traditional wedding march suddenly resonated through the church, and Fallen didn't even have a chance to take a steadying breath before the interior doors parted to reveal her to the waiting crowd.

Burt patted her hand on his elbow. "Let's go."

Fallen felt claustrophobic as the crowd stood and turned to face her. Some were snapping pictures. There were far too many people—more than she had probably ever met in her life. Lad stared her down with an intense gaze that was tinged with victory. And then he licked his lips.

He reminded her of an alligator. She was his prey.

Fallen looked to the two doors on either side of the altar. They were both guarded by men equally as burly as the ones by the front exit. She had no way out.

Burt walked her the rest of the way. He left her veil in place, but offered a hand to Lad who shook it. Then Burt took her bouquet out of her hands.

Lad held out his hand with a cocky smile. "You're going to love this."

She reluctantly put her hand in his, like it might burn her. Once her palm landed against his, he clamped down on her fingers.

"Gotcha." There was no playful wink. He was literally telling her he felt he'd won.

The minister started to speak their vows almost immediately. No build up.

"Do you, Lad Preston Orbit, take Fallen Billow as your bride from this point forward to have and to hold, for better or for worse, until death does you part?"

Lad stepped closer and gripped her hands to stop her from taking a retreating step. "I do. Until death."

Fallen got chills at his intonation. She looked over her shoulder and then over his. No sign of Thomas.

She might have to save her own damn self right about now.

"Very well. Fallen Billow, do you take this man, Lad Preston Orbit, to be your forever love from this moment in time, for better or worse, until death does you part?"

Fallen felt like she was on the tracks and a train was coming at 100 miles per hour.

No. I can't. I won't. This isn't what I want, *she said in her head as Lad answered for her.*

"Of course she does. I'm a catch." And then he pulled her against him for a biting kiss.

The crowd gasped, and possibly the only thing that could have stopped Lad happened.

A dead woman came back to life.

"Lad, step away from her. You know she doesn't want this."

Lad succumbed to the pressure Fallen exerted on his chest and stepped backward.

He looked past Fallen to Desta. Fallen turned and watched as the woman threw off her veil.

Before Lad could respond, Burt whooped and dropped Fallen's bouquet. "My Desta? You're here?"

And Desta went from angry to delighted. "Burt, you big lug! I've missed you."

Burt hurried around the pew to get to her, almost pushing over the tuxedoed guard protecting the exit door.

Burt kissed Desta like they were alone, and like they weren't a day over twenty.

The crowd in the church seemed flustered, but the slurred emotions on their faces made Fallen wonder if they were on drugs or something.

Lad put his arm around Fallen. "Don't think of going anywhere, wife."

"I never said yes. I never said anything. And it doesn't count if I don't do that," Fallen informed him. She really hoped her words were true.

Lad frowned before pointing. "How is Desta here?"

"How are *you* here?" Fallen grumbled.

Desta pulled away from Burt and touched his cheeks, kissing his chin, then his nose. "Give me a moment, my love," she told him. "Then we'll have forever."

"That's fine, but I'm not letting you out of my sight."

Fallen wiggled out of Lad's arms as the crowd started murmuring.

Desta and Burt crossed over to meet Fallen and Lad.

Lad held open his arms, and Desta stepped into them.

Lad closed his eyes and put a kiss on the top of Desta's head. "Seeing you here is fantastic."

"I know, my boy. It's good to see you too." Desta patted him on the back. "Can you listen to an old woman? One last time?"

Lad looked from Desta to Fallen. "Depends on what it's about."

"I wonder if you can hear me. Or if the part of your mind that's not well any more makes decisions for you here, too." Desta paused and stepped back to look at Lad again. Then she motioned for Burt and whispered to him. He nodded and walked over to the side door.

Desta addressed Lad again. "You've believed your whole life that, one way or another, that room was your destiny—no matter how many times I told you it wasn't, that you had a choice. You still have one. Stop trying to force love, Lad. Stop trying to win something that isn't a contest. Do you see this girl? She doesn't love you. That is not a reflection on you. It just means this isn't right. But you have to be worthy of love, open to give and receive it. When that happens, the woman for you won't have to be tricked into marriage. She'll arrive early and run down the aisle to you."

Fallen felt a new wave of respect for Desta.

"How can you say that?" Lad countered. "Look at what you have with him." He pointed at Burt. "You've conquered death to be together, and you found each other through the room. That has to be superior."

Desta shook her head. "I did all I could to save you from this." She waved her hand around the beautiful church. "Don't get me wrong, I'm crazy about Burt, but not being with him all this time? It was torture. I missed him. I missed being a real family. You can have those things, Lad. You could even have children. Leave that hotel. Sell it. Get rid of it. Never think about room 514 again. Will you do this for me?" Desta hugged him again.

Lad hugged her back. "I'll try, Desta. But I don't think I can live without her."

He turned his gaze in Fallen's direction, and she had never felt more like a piece of meat. She was something he wanted to win, not a person.

"That's the crazy talking, honey. And I don't know if you can fight it, but I sure hope you do." Desta patted his cheek again. "I'm leaving soon. I love you. And I believe in you. Your parents' fate doesn't have to be yours. Let this girl be with the man who loves her. Who she loves." Desta turned, stepped back, and nodded at Burt.

Maybe because Burt was older, or maybe because Desta had some sort of dream mojo, but the tuxedo guard stepped aside and let Burt open the door.

Fallen put her hands on her heart when she felt it lurch at the sight of Thomas.

He was waiting with his hands against the doorframe, and he looked up from his feet straight into her eyes.

Fallen stooped, picked up her bouquet from where Burt had dropped it, and handed it to Desta.

Desta whispered in her ear when she came in for a hug. "Run for it. Burt and I will hold him off. Think of a river with warm rocks and pretty flowers."

Fallen turned and faced Thomas as Lad reached for her. She picked up her dress and bolted for the door. Her veil slid off completely as she moved toward Thomas.

Lad started losing his mind behind her. His inhuman wail echoed in the church, and the pain in his howl brought reflexive tears to her eyes.

Thomas stepped toward her, only to be stiff-armed by the tuxedo guard.

But Fallen knew he would win the scuffle. He was experienced at hand-to-hand combat. He put the man on the floor without even taking a swing.

Fallen again picked up her heavy wedding dress and ran toward Thomas' extended hand.

Lad yelled, "No! She's mine. We're married. We just got married! You can't take her."

Fallen looked over her shoulder and saw Desta and Burt holding Lad by the shoulders and chest.

"Are they okay?" Thomas asked.

Hearing his voice was a balm, even in this tense situation.

"He won't hurt Desta; he loves her." Fallen felt mostly confident of that.

"Let's go." Thomas led her through the door as the tuxedo guy started to get to his feet.

Once outside, Thomas pulled her into a hug. "Take me somewhere, dream girl."

Immediately she painted the scene Desta had described in her head. The genius of the suggestion was revealed when she and Thomas were suddenly hugging in a place she'd never actually been to before. It would be very hard to track them here, she imagined.

"Fallen." Thomas touched her jaw and ran a fingertip across her forehead. "You are beautiful. How dare he try to marry you?"

She leaned into his touch and lowered her lids. "Kiss me."

He kissed her and kissed her and kissed her.

Fallen memorized him with her hands, reassuring herself, as always, that he was real.

"You look gorgeous, but I can't see this dress on you one more second."

Fallen spun to show him the closure of the dress at her back. She soon felt him kissing her bare shoulder as he struggled with what seemed like tiny buttons.

"This will take forever." Thomas told her to brace herself as he took a firm grip on the bodice. He tore it off of her as she laughed and laughed.

He wiggled the skirt down her hips, and she stepped out of the layers of fabric while holding on to his forearm.

She wore a strapless bra and a slip when all was said and done.

"Better." He went to his knee and took her left hand in his. He slid the engagement ring off, yet again. "I've decided the reason this keeps happening is because I never put something here to get in his way."

Fallen noticed he had two rings on his own left hand. "Fallen Billow, my beautiful dream girl, will you take my heart? Please?"

He pulled a shiny silver band from his pinky and perched it at the ready, waiting for her answer.

"Of course. You already have mine."

Thomas looked like he'd scored the winning home run—

young and elated. He slid the ring onto her finger and pulled her to sit on his knee.

"Thank you, love. When I get back home, I'm going to find you in the future. No matter how long I have to wait. Before you, I never thought I would go home. But now I'm going to do my damnedest to get there." He put his hand at the nape of her neck and kissed her again.

"Thank you. This ring is so pretty." She admired his and hers together on her lap.

"I guessed at the size? How's it fit?" He watched for her reaction.

"Great. They have jewelry stores where you are?" As she looked from him to her new ring, she realized it had faint writing on it.

"No. Nothing fancy like that. I made them myself out of quarters. Is that okay?"

Fallen ran her hands through his hair and changed his outfit to jeans and a dark T-shirt. Just something other than his uniform.

"It's amazing. I love it even more now."

"You like putting me in dungarees, huh?"

She felt her eyebrows come together at his funny word for jeans. "We don't call them that anymore."

"What do you say?"

"Jeans."

"That's a person's name," he objected, teasing her.

She tried to tickle him as a retort, but he had the better of her quickly. A white blanket appeared beneath her as he laid her down amidst the grass.

The sound of the river was peaceful and the rocks embedded in it looked as warm as she'd hoped they'd be when she'd painted them in her head. But that was nothing next to him. Her nerve endings begged for the pleasure he could give her.

Thomas began kissing and nibbling her, and she let her hands roam, enjoying the hard feel of him.

She was ready for him, ready to make yet another lasting memory. But when his hand drifted up to her breast, she remembered something wildly important.

"What's this?" he asked as he traced the edge of her satin bra.

Fallen looked down and felt dread. There would be no waiting for each other, no finding each other in the future. She pulled on the edge of the bra and rubbed away the foundation with her knuckle, revealing the words she had written there.

They looked foreign to her at first; she couldn't remember what the message was.

Then he read it out loud once, and then again.

"KIA May 7, 1945."

She remembered then, but her tongue was frozen. All she could do was point to the words and nod, tears coming down her cheeks. She prayed he understood.

"Is this for me?"

She nodded again and wiped at her mouth, begging it to work.

"Killed in action? Me? On the 7th?"

She nodded again and hugged him to her chest, against the words that condemned him to death. Her mind flipped through images of the Purple Heart, the newspaper obituary, and the horrible telegram from John to their mother.

"My girl, no. I have plans for us. For you." He lifted his head and held her face in his hands. "That's too soon." Thomas looked off in the distance before sitting up and pulling her from her place on the blanket into his arms.

She cuddled close to him, putting her face in his neck. She was getting his shirt wet but wanted to be as close to his warmth as she could.

"Well, shit." Thomas rubbed her back. "Do you know how it happens?"

Fallen willed the words to come. "I was told a story. I'm not sure how true it was, but I—"

Their cuddle session was ruined as the sanctity of the river exploded with pounding feet.

Lad was headed right at them.

Thomas scrambled to his feet, shielding her.

"You're breaking the rules," Lad screamed. "You're ruining the room. There is no sharing!" Spittle flew from his lips, and his eyes bugged out.

Fallen grabbed fistfuls of the back of Thomas' shirt, and when he fell, she staggered.

Thomas landed on the ground, and his eyes closed as if for a nap. Fallen fell to her knees to look for an injury as he started to fade away.

"No. No. Don't go." Her hands went right through him as he disappeared.

Lad scooped her up by her armpits, and she was too stunned, watching Thomas leave, to react at first.

Was that it? Was that the last time she would get to see him?

"Thomas!" She shouted his name at the blanket he'd left behind.

Lad tossed her over his shoulder and headed toward the river.

"You little hussy, how dare you break the room? We were going to beat the odds, Fallen."

He tossed her in the river, and it was shallow enough that she could prop herself up on her elbows to breathe. He scrambled on top of her and wrapped his arm around her waist.

"You work for me. I'm keeping you fed. I'm keeping your brother in football. You need me. Why is it so hard to understand that? He's pretend. I'm real." Lad looked down at Fallen's semi-exposed breast, and his eyes widened. He yanked her bra down and pointed at the message she had written on her chest.

He narrowed his eyes and scrubbed at the words like she was a lamp that could make his wish come true.

She curled her shoulders and started to hit him, but every time she did, she slipped under the water. In order to stay above water with his weight on top of her, she had no choice but to let him furiously rub at the skin above her breast.

"Stop. You're hurting me. This hurts me! Lad!" She could only use words now, but thankfully they seemed to work. He stopped and got off of her, helping her stand so she didn't have to struggle to breathe.

"We're in a dream." Fallen pointed at her chest and thought about it being clean of pen marks, and it was. "Just picture something, and it happens."

Lad tried to help her out of the water, but she swatted him away and staggered out on her own. She wrapped the blanket she had planned to make love to Thomas on around her shoulders.

"You can't force love. You can't demand it just because you want it." Fallen pushed her wet hair out of her face.

Lad stood a few paces away and bent over to catch his breath before trying to convince her yet again. "You don't understand. I know what this room does to people. I was an orphan because of it. I just want to get a girl out of it alive."

"That's not true. Your ex-wife is alive," Fallen pointed out just as a crash of lightning and thunder announced dark clouds rolling into the sky.

"Thanks to me," he scoffed. "She was doomed as well. Never think that the room is smarter than I am. I know its tricks. It thrives on pain. I love her. I loved her enough to make sure she could find her dream man. I live without her every day, and sure, the room is happy that I have to suffer, but she got out."

He looked around wildly. "I want to get you out, Fallen. I'm rich. I'm real. You'll want for nothing. Your dream man is a ghost. He dies. He's been dead for seventy years. I think the room is cruel for setting you up with him. You think I'm fighting your love, but I'm not. Thomas is the room. Thomas doesn't love you. The room just makes it feel real."

The thunder and lightning crashed again and again, bolts flying every which way like she'd never seen them in the waking world.

"Look at the sky," he commanded. "This is what happens when you cross the room. It wins, or it kills you. Come back with me. Come here to me. I'm not the bad guy. I'm the prince. I'm the white knight. Come to me, please!" Lad held out his hand.

Fallen was sure about her love for Thomas, but Lad was confusing her. Actions were louder than words, right? Thomas had made her happy and proud. Lad had hurt her, demeaned her, coerced her, and attacked her. Still, something didn't make sense about all this.

"You're confusing me," she told him.

She didn't realize she'd knelt on the ground until she spread out her hands to catch her balance. Darkness descended, and the last thing she saw was Lad's mouth fixed in a straight line as he headed toward her, unbuckling his belt.

24

END GAME

When Fallen woke, she was already clenched in a ball. She totally expected Lad to attack. Instead she looked around to find she was alone in room 514. She rolled out of bed quickly and found the mirror. There was nothing. Nothing. Just her own eyes searching the surface, looking back at her.

And then she caught a glimpse of Thomas waking. He hugged the dog on his lap and patted the cot around him as if he were looking for something. He stood, set the puppy down, and punched his own hand it what seemed like frustration.

And then he was gone.

Safe behind the fork-jammed lock, Fallen gathered herself for a while. The ring Thomas had put on her finger was gone. She'd almost had to marry Lad. She'd seen Desta! And she'd been able to tell Thomas the day of his death…but what was that Lad had said at the end? Thomas was the room? Like it was alive, like it could trick her into loving it.

She glanced around at the four walls where she'd spent so much time. Was there something sinister she'd failed to understand? If so, she still didn't understand it, and what seemed more pressing was the fact that those might have been her last moments with Thomas. What if even the information she'd shared couldn't change his fate?

She had no answers, but when she finally felt able, she freed the broken fork from where she'd wedged it and pulled open the door. Mr. Orbit waited for her with a menacing smile on his face.

"Are we having fun yet?" he asked.

Instantly her guard was up. She covered her chest with her hand, in the process realizing she was going to have bruises from his harsh scrubbing in the dream.

"You have really fantastic breasts. I didn't get a chance to compliment them before."

Fallen kept her foot on the door, refusing to back away like she wanted to. She didn't ever want to be alone in a room with this man again, particularly not this room.

"I'm in love with you, Fallen," he told her, though his tone and demeanor conveyed nothing like love. "I know it's too soon. I just... I can tell." He tilted his head like telling her these things wasn't frightening.

"You don't love me."

"I do. More than Ellen, even. You'll be perfect. I feel alive when you're around. In control." He put his palm against the door.

"You don't know what love is." She shook her head.

"And you do? Is it what you find here? In this room? Don't think I don't know. You're a slut for this room. You're a good girl, Fallen. You don't have to be that way." He put his hand on his chest earnestly.

"I would like to go home, please." Fallen refused to have this argument. He was really having it with the demons in his head anyway.

"I'm a man of means. I can offer a life to you—to you and your brother—that will hit everything on your wish list. I'll tick every box for you. Do you know how many girls would kill for this opportunity?" He held out a hand to her. "Being mine can't be that hard. I'm a great guy. I'm pretty good looking."

"I would like to go home." She locked gazes with him, staying as calm and even as she could.

"You work for me. I'll tell you when it's time to go home." Orbit stepped toward her, but she held fast, even though his every exhale now fluttered her hair.

This man had taken perhaps her last moment with Thomas from her. And now, while she still wrestled with having just told the love of her life when he was going to die, this giant man-child was in her face, demanding things from her.

Fallen Billow got very, very angry.

"You asshole. Get out of my face. Back up. Move your ass and let me out of this room. You don't own me. Stop demanding things from me!" Fallen poked him in the chest. "This isn't how it works. You don't get to buy people with your money and your privilege, you spoiled brat."

He backed into the hallway, eyes bulging and veins in his neck becoming more pronounced.

She let the door to 514 close behind her.

"Why am I locked out of this room when you're in there? What are you doing in there?" He pointed at the closed door and stayed way too close to her.

"Why don't you look at the camera footage?" she taunted.

She was sick of cowering before him. Thomas had one week to live seventy years ago, and even though that didn't even make sense, it was killing her.

"Oh wait, you had the camera removed," she continued. "You're a stalker and a creeper, and I don't want to date you or marry you or anything else!"

He lowered his voice and advanced on her, pulling her against him in the hall. "I removed the camera so there wouldn't be evidence of what I'm going to do with you in there."

She searched his face, his crazy, out of control face. Fighting with him was like trying to fly a kite in a tornado. It would end poorly.

"Let go of me." She pushed him away and stomped on his foot.

"How much, Fallen? Every woman has a panty-dropping price. Tell me yours." He leaned close to her mouth like he wanted a kiss.

She looked down, and when he kissed her forehead the way Thomas liked to do, she snapped. Fallen kicked her boss's boss's boss in the shin, then made a fist and hit him as hard as she could right in the nuts.

The guest room door to their left opened and a man stepped into the hallway. Mr. Orbit was like a wasp's nest Fallen had run over with a lawn mower—lit up with anger and fury.

He grabbed her and maintained his hold, despite the obvious pain she had caused him. She turned to the man and said the only word she needed to: "Help."

The hotel guest moved like holding people who were out of their minds was perfectly normal. His soothing speech made Fallen wonder if he did so for a living.

He wedged himself between her and Orbit, and in an instant she was out of his grasp, finally. Then began Orbit's protests that he owned the hotel and the man was about to get kicked out. The guest agreed that that sounded like an option, but he explained that he couldn't watch a man hold a woman against her will.

A woman came out of the man's room to survey the commotion. "Check on her," he told her. "He was roughing her up."

If the man was calm, his wife was fire. "Oh no he didn't!" she snapped.

She came immediately to Fallen. "Are you okay, sweetness? How about we go downstairs and get some water. Let my husband handle your man. He's really good at it."

Fallen shook her head. "He's not my man. I don't want your husband to get hurt."

"No worries. He's trained. It's part of his job." The woman steered Fallen to the elevator and then out into the lobby.

"You're so kind. To open your door when you hear yelling? That's brave." Fallen felt like she wanted to cry, but she was too numb now. "I guess I'm fired..."

"Do you live around here?" The woman offered Fallen a lobby couch like it was her own living room.

"I work at this hotel. I was at my friend's funeral. She used to work here too." Fallen realized she probably wasn't making sense.

"Does that man you were with upstairs get this angry often?" The woman handed her a cup of water from the hotel's welcome table.

Fallen accepted it with thanks and tried to figure out how to answer the question. Finally she offered, "He's my boss's boss's boss. I work for him, that's all."

"Really?" The woman looked as if she could see the truth of Fallen's situation. "Sweetheart, I think you're in a little bit of shock. Has today been tough?"

"What's your name? You're such a brave person." Fallen felt like this woman's kindness might break her. She was good at taking care of everyone else, but someone taking care of her might be her undoing.

"I'm Trisha. And I think you need a nice hot shower and a long rest. Do you live nearby?" Trisha started looking things up on her phone.

"Yes. I should walk home. You're right." Fallen took a sip of the water and discovered she was so incredibly thirsty she had to chug the whole thing.

"Can I get your address? Or the address of where you're going? I've already ordered a car service." Trisha held up her phone and showed Fallen the app.

"I can't take a car service. I can afford to walk. That's my price point right now." Fallen realized she'd left her purse in room 514 with her jacket. "Crap. I left my stuff up there."

"Can you get into your house? Is anyone home?" Trisha guided her out the front doors. "The car is almost here. The driver must have been right in the area already."

"Yeah. My brother is home. I can get him to let me in." Fallen tossed her paper cup in the recycle bin.

"Well, my husband just texted me that your boss is getting in the elevator now. Let's move you out of here before this escalates. Okay? I've got your ride, don't worry. I have an account with this company. Let me do this for you—from one lady to another." Trisha waved at a fancy black car that pulled up.

Trisha had such a warm way about her, Fallen just had to trust her. She almost stumbled when she thought again of her last moments with Thomas, and Trisha put her arm on her shoulder.

"You sure you're okay?"

Fallen nodded. "It's been—how did you put it? A really tough day. Maybe the toughest yet."

Trisha opened the car's back door. "Hurry now."

She gave the address to the driver and insisted that the fare go on her card. Then she closed the door and patted the side of the car.

The driver took off, and after a moment Fallen looked out the back window to see Mr. Orbit standing in the parking lot. He looked around wildly, but didn't seem to see her.

Fallen turned back and slumped in the seat. Trisha had bought her time, but Orbit wasn't done with her by a long shot.

With vigorous knocking Fallen was able to rouse Fenn from bed. When he opened the door, she shoved him back inside and had it locked behind her before she saw any hint of Orbit's fancy car.

Seeing Fenn's face made her want to just give up. He could obviously tell she was a goddamn wreck.

"What's going on? Did someone hurt you?" His eyes bugged out a bit.

Fallen shook her head, but slid down the door and sat on the floor. "I think I've ruined everything."

Fenn sat across from her. "What's wrong?"

Ironically, it was the stubble on her brother's jaw that made her tell him. He wasn't a kid anymore. And she would never be able to make it so his mother wasn't an alcoholic. All she could offer was herself.

It came out in a torrent. She edited the parts about the dream world, but she told him the essence of what had her torn: she didn't know where her boyfriend was, her friend's funeral was sad, and her second job was also sad, not to mention now over. And, her boss's boss's boss kept trying to push her into being with him and had even mentioned marriage.

Her brother listened in a way that made her think he would be a great husband someday. He absorbed what she told him with his whole body, but didn't judge her on any of it.

"The worst part is, he's your not-so-anonymous sponsor, and he's really mad at me now. I should just date him. He's rich as sin." She trailed off and played with the hem of her dress.

That wasn't the worst part. She'd told Thomas when he was going to die. That was the worst part.

Fenn couldn't have been sweeter. He went on and on about how they could work together, and he could get a job. She smiled at him, but in her heart she just wanted him to have a regular, happy life.

And then she had a thought that made her stand up straight. She hugged Fenn, thanked him for the talk, and zipped up the stairs.

If her warning to Thomas had worked, the papers in her closet should be different. If she'd affected the past, the newspapers proclaiming his death wouldn't have that information anymore.

She closed her bedroom door and yanked open the closet. As supportive and amazing as Fenn had been, she needed to see this alone.

After pulling out the documents, her eyes scanned the pages as she felt her hopes crash to her feet. The clippings were all the same. Thomas F. McHugh died on May 7, 1945.

Fallen crawled into bed with her favorite picture of him. He had his hands on his hips, wearing a bathing suit. She refused to believe he was some sort of manifestation of the room. Thomas was real—his eyes, the sparkle in them when he was bringing her to orgasm, the shouting when he got to his own, the way his fingers felt as they traced her collarbone around to her shoulder and down her spine.

Fallen fell asleep looking at his picture and wishing she knew his fate.

The weekend was a slow blur of torture. Fallen called in sick on Friday, too fearful to face Mr. Orbit since he'd officially acknowledged his dream self and officially started acting really crazy. On Saturday morning, her purse, cell phone, and coat were in a package on her doorstep with Trisha Vandella written in the return address. That was enough to persuade her she'd be best served spending her Saturday away from the hotel as well.

She took a long time writing out the thank you. After her phone had charged, she was shocked to find she had no voicemail firing the hell out of her. No texts from Lad, no drive bys. Nothing.

On Sunday, since she was off anyway, she went shopping for groceries but bought sparingly. She had no idea how much longer she could hold on to this steady paycheck, so she needed to make what she had last.

On Monday, she knew she dared not hide any longer, so she steeled herself for whatever lay ahead at work. She arrived to find the parking lot nearly empty—only staff cars filled a few spots. But the morning meeting was packed with every employee. Even the essential people that ran the front desk had left their posts.

8 and 9 welcomed her back and asked how she was feeling, but they shrugged when Fallen asked what was up with the hotel. No one knew.

Mr. Orbit walked into the meeting ten minutes late and wearing the most expensive suit Fallen had ever seen. He also wore aviator glasses and didn't remove them as he addressed the employees.

Fallen couldn't see his eyes assessing her, but she could certainly feel them.

"Ladies and gentlemen, please take this as the hotel's two-week notice. Except I'm closing this location effective immediately."

The shock was a wave through the room. Fallen felt her mouth drop open but closed it quickly when she saw him smirking.

"You'll all receive one month's pay—which is more than generous—to support you as you find alternate employment. In the lobby I have some specialists to assist those of you with medical benefits and retirement plans. Any questions?"

No one moved or breathed. They were shocked. Fallen knew she was in a staring contest with Mr. Orbit.

She raised her hand.

"Ms. Billow?"

"Is the hotel going to be sold? Hasn't it been in your family for years?"

"We built it in the 1920s, but that's neither here nor there. It's mine to do with as I choose. And no, I don't plan to sell it. Any other questions?"

Fallen straightened her shoulders and lifted her chin. "You couldn't even wait until Desta was cold in the grave to destroy what she loved?"

The other employees murmured and gasped, and there were a few muttered curses.

Orbit ripped off his sunglasses, revealing bloodshot eyes. He pointed at her. "Don't you dare talk to me about her, you slut."

8 and 9 were ready to go. "Oh no. That's too far, you stuffy rich—"

He put up his hand. "Go into the hall." He delivered this order to Fallen like he was the president on a TV show.

8 and 9 locked eyes with her as she left. She nodded, trying to reassure them. Nothing could really hurt her now. Fallen pulled her hair out of its ponytail as she walked through the crowd to the hall. Defiant.

Orbit slammed the door behind him as he stepped into the hall with her.

She turned and faced him.

"How dare you say that to me? To *me*? You of all people know what she meant to me."

"So to honor her you're putting everyone out of work? How does that even make sense?" Fallen crossed her arms in front of her.

He tried to move closer, and she backed up. She wasn't letting him touch her again.

"Come here to me, Fallen. I'll open the hotel right back up if you come up to room 514 and make love to me." Lad opened his suit jacket dramatically.

"No. You don't put this on me. You don't give me impossible choices. You've held my brother against me, my poverty against me. But I'm not playing your games now. I don't screw for money. Or for jobs." Fallen took another step backward when he tried to advance.

"Have it your way. I'm tearing this hotel to the ground. And I think I'll make sure it goes down on a Thursday. How'd you like that, Fallen?" His shaking hands were in fists.

"I need one more week," she said, keeping her voice even. "That's it."

"What will you do to get that week, Fallen? How low will you go? What's rock bottom? You certainly aren't trying to be my friend."

There was no use telling him he wouldn't know a friend if one hit him in the balls.

Fallen looked at her feet. Thomas had one more Thursday, maybe. It was a crapshoot. What time was he killed? What time could he sleep? She had just a few days left to find out anything else she could about his actual death.

"I'm not having sex with you," she told him.

"Save these people's jobs, Fallen. Say yes—and get in my car." He tented his fingers and tilted his head.

She considered it longer than she should have. But then she pictured Thomas. He would hate that she'd compromised herself to get more time. She would find another way. Becoming a concubine for this man was not the answer.

She shook her head and took another step back. "I'm done with this. I'm done with you."

"Fallen, you'll regret this." Orbit narrowed his eyes.

"No, I won't." She considered him one more time. "I hope you find peace. Don't punish others because you didn't get your way."

She kept her arms around herself and made her way through the front lobby, past the stations set up to help employees make sense of the sudden change in their lives.

She didn't turn when she heard him raging behind her. Her walk home was a sad one. She noted how crisp the sky was. Maybe she was going crazy. Maybe that's what all of this was. How could something as mundane as a housekeeping job turn into time-traveling love? Or the manifestation of a malevolent room as a person—which she still didn't believe.

Orbit's Jaguar roared past her when she was a few blocks from home, but she refused to look at him, and thankfully he didn't stop.

When she entered her empty house, she went upstairs to look at pictures of Thomas and cry a little. Or maybe a lot.

On Tuesday, Fallen spent all her time at the library, jumping from computer to computer to extend her research time as much as possible.

The research was eye opening and heartbreaking. The Pacific theater included thousands of islands. She found accounts from men who should have crossed paths with Thomas, and perhaps even known him, and she scoured their words for any trace of her tall, dark-haired dream man. The day of his death had been 24 hours before the Allies accepted Germany's surrender, and six days after Hitler's suicide. Could he have known the war was almost over, even though the focus of his fighting was on a different enemy?

Her heart cried when she got home and double-checked the dates on the telegrams announcing his death. The one to Thomas' mother had not been sent until May 29. She must have celebrated the war's end with the rest of America and imagined having all three of her sons home soon. The note from John had come on June 9.

She rocked herself to sleep that night, still with no plan to save him.

On Wednesday, she went back to the library and ransacked the shelves of books on World War II. She took pictures of some passages, but the truth was, none of them gave her any idea *when* on May 7 Thomas had been lost. Would he sleep? Would she get one more chance to try to warn him? Try to beg him?

That evening, after ravioli with Fenn, she finally told her brother that she'd been fired from the hotel—well, actually that the hotel had closed as a way to fire her, along with everyone else. Fenn was concerned for her, and for her boss's boss's boss's state of mind, but assured her she would find a better job soon. He even joked that without her paychecks, they might never see their mother again. Fallen wondered whether deep down he believed that to be a blessing or a curse.

She didn't sleep on Wednesday night, her room littered with the priceless evidence that Thomas had lived and died seventy years before. In the morning, she knew she had to go to the hotel and try to get into 514. The building was still standing, and Fallen didn't want to regret not trying for the rest of her life.

After Fenn went off to school, she arrived to find locked front doors and lots of no trespassing signs. She still had her master key, but she was pretty sure it wouldn't be just that easy to open the back door anymore. In her tote she had her broken fork and a hammer. It seemed like a crude way to break a lock, but it also seemed the most effective.

Fallen scoped out the area and then circled around to the

back door. She saw no one around, so she started whacking away at the lock. Her efforts were loud, but she didn't stop.

She was yelling at the damn padlock by the time she found the sweet spot and it finally gave up. She slipped off the chain threaded through the handle on the back door and then used her master key.

Inside, she pulled off her hood. She'd borrowed her brother's black hoodie and paired it with leggings and black boots. It was as close to a ninja as she could get. She took the stairs, because although the place seemed like a ghost town, she had no idea where Mr. Orbit might be—in the building or watching his cameras. She couldn't dwell on it because breaking and entering a hotel was probably punishable with jail time. And Orbit was watching today; he had to be. He knew Thursdays were special.

Just the backup generator lights came on when she flipped the switches. Fallen was still a little amazed that Lad had gone this far—was it just to spite her? What was he going to do with this place? Thinking of all the canceled reservations and people out of work made her sick to her stomach all over again.

Her key opened the door to room 514. The room smelled musty, and without the heat it was also chilly. The windows had condensation on the inside. Fallen hurried to set up her broken fork security system, and she took the hammer with her as she climbed onto the bed. The comforter felt slightly damp. The place had only been truly empty for two days, but large buildings must need climate control more than she'd realized.

The sleepiness took her quickly, like she'd slid a needle under her skin to instigate the feeling. After the blackness coincided with the rush of movement, she opened her eyes again.

She was still in room 514.

Panic engulfed her. Maybe once Thomas was gone, there was nowhere to go. Today was the day, after all. But she didn't have the hammer now, so that tipped her off that something had changed.

She sat up and saw that her broken fork lock was missing as well, so she got off the bed to slide the door open. The hallway was empty. She felt a chill skitter up her spine. Something was different. Off.

"Thomas?" She whispered at first, but then she shouted. What did she have to lose? She waited a moment and heard footfalls on the staircase. She had nowhere to hide, except back in 514, so she just waited.

The fire door from the stairway opened slowly. Fallen fully expected to see Lad, but instead Thomas walked through. As soon as he saw her, he ran toward her.

Relief took her legs out from under her. She knelt on the ground as he rushed in her direction.

"We've got to hide, dream girl." He helped her to her feet and backed her into room 514, closing the door behind him.

"You're here. I was scared." She touched his face and felt the scruff there.

Thomas gave her a distracted kiss. "He's coming."

"Who?" she asked, but really didn't need to. It was always Lad.

Thomas looked through the peephole. "I don't see him yet."

"How did you know to come here?" She ran her arms over his. She had to tell him something important.

"I stayed in this room once before I was deployed, and I always remembered it. Five-fourteen is my mother's birthday, remember? I just had a hunch I needed to check it out." He finally seemed to focus on her. "Fallen, I was scared I wouldn't get to you in time. Before..."

He kissed the hell out of her then, his hands everywhere. She hugged him tightly until a knock on the door startled them both.

Thomas steadied her and put his index finger to his lips. He looked again and frowned. "It's not him," he whispered.

"What?" Fallen took a look herself. At first she just saw

brown hair, but then the woman's face came to the peephole. It was Nora. "Mom?"

She pulled open the door before Thomas could stop her. Nora all but fell through the doorway. She reeked of booze.

"Nora, why are you here?"

"Did you know my daughter is dating a millionaire? He's going to fix everything." Nora's slurring was on par with the worst benders Fallen could remember.

Shame washed over her as Nora gagged in what had to be impending vomit. Fallen couldn't look Thomas in the face as she dragged Nora to the toilet just in time.

"This isn't right," Thomas said from the bathroom doorway. He faced the bed so Nora could have some privacy. "Last time you knew the woman at the wedding, and this time your mom is here. Except for Lad, we've never seen people we know before."

Fallen pulled her mother's hair out of her face and tucked it in the back of her grubby shirt. She ran a washcloth under the sink to put on her mother's forehead. Then she heard the sound of Nora's body hitting the floor.

"Crap." She set the cloth down, and Thomas helped her pull her mother off the floor.

"It's okay, let me," he said as he hefted Nora onto the bed.

Fallen fussed with the blankets to prop her mother on her side and slid the wastepaper basket near her head.

Once Nora was situated, Fallen hugged herself. "I'm sorry you have to see this. It's my worst nightmare."

Thomas pulled her to him and hugged her. "Shit."

"What?" Fallen looked at his face to find it paled.

"Well, if this is your worst nightmare…" Thomas' voice drifted off.

She felt the rush of being transported, standing this time. She clung as hard as she could to Thomas.

When their feet had settled, she opened her eyes to darkness, warmth, and incredible humidity.

Thomas finished his sentence, "...then I'm afraid we'll be taken to mine."

Fallen looked around and saw palm trees and unfamiliar foliage.

Thomas was instantly on alert.

"Where are we? Where's my mom?"

"I don't think your mom's here. This is a battlefield. The one place I never wanted to see your pretty face. Thomas touched her cheek for a moment before pushing her roughly behind a tree.

It took a minute to realize the popping she heard in the distance was gunfire. His eyes scanned the surroundings like the veteran fighter he was.

"I can't believe this is happening. I need to keep you safe." Tension corded his neck and clenched his jaw.

"Listen. Listen to me." Fallen touched his bicep so he would hear her. "Let's fix it. Together. Let's go to the lobby of the hotel we were in. Do you remember it?"

"What if I go and you stay here?" he whispered. "No." He pressed himself against her as a gunshot sounded closer to them.

"We have to try. It's just a dream here. It's okay. Come with me. Hug me. Dream with me. The front lobby. It has the red chairs and the gold-framed mirrors?" At least she hoped they'd been there when he'd stayed at the hotel.

He finally looked down and nodded at her. "Let's try. But if you get stuck here, lay low. I will find you."

She nodded back and kissed him, thinking of the lobby she'd had to clean so much getting ready for Mr. Orbit's first visit.

The uneasiness came, and she opened her eyes to look into Thomas' stunning blue ones.

"It worked," he assured her.

They were sitting together on the floor, but Fallen could see that the lobby had all the modern touches it shouldn't have. They'd gone back to the abandoned hotel, not the one Thomas had stayed in. Out the front door she saw her brother and Mitchel pull up in the darkness. Fenn began banging on the glass.

"That's Fenn."

Thomas shook his head in disbelief. "He looks like you."

"Fallen, answer your phone," Fenn yelled.

"He wants you to answer your phone?" Thomas looked confused.

Fallen stood, and Thomas steadied her elbow. She locked hands with him before she hurried to the revolving door. She pushed on it to get to Fenn, but it wouldn't open. "Help me, can you? It's stuck."

He pulled her away from her struggle. "Fallen."

"What?" Why wouldn't he help her? Fenn was right there, and Mitchel was pointing to the side of the building. She couldn't understand what he said.

"I can see through them. Can you?" Thomas pointed out the door.

Fallen looked, and he was right, Fenn was transparent. "Oh my God. Is he okay?"

Fallen went for the emergency door instead. She heard Lad's laughter and whirled around. Thomas pulled her into his arms.

Lad was transparent too. "I think the room is slipping." He leered at her. "Because I can see you just a little, maid."

He lurched for them, and his hand went right through Fallen's stomach, as if she were made of air. She felt nothing, but Thomas pulled her away anyway.

He kissed her again, despite Lad's rage all around them.

"Something's happening," Thomas whispered. "Your mom, your brother, now him. Maybe it's my time. Now." He ran his hands from the top of her head to her shoulder, lifting up the ends of her hair to sniff them.

"No." Fallen shook her head. "I've wanted to tell you so badly. It's a landmine."

There was a loud hiss. Lad's mouth was still moving, and in her peripheral vision, she saw Fenn and Mitchel take off in the car.

"Can you hear me?" she asked Thomas, touching his lips, then his ears.

He nodded.

"Your brother's wife said you led your men down a path, and because you went first—we lose you." Her heart sighed with relief as he nodded.

"And my men?" Thomas picked up her hands and kissed her knuckles. Lad literally walked between them, but he was fading —just a mosquito, just noise.

"They made it. You saved them." It was like being dipped in ice-cold water when she watched him nod.

"Good."

"Good? What the hell? You can't do it. Just stay back; don't go. Okay? Stay alive. For me. Make it back to me." Fallen covered her mouth as he shook his head sadly.

Around them the lobby went white. No more fanciful pictures to play with in their imaginations.

Thomas pulled her in again, kissing her head. "Dream girl, I'm a solider. Those are my men. That's my job." His eyes were teary.

"Don't close your eyes. Please, stay. Just stay." Fallen held on to him as tightly as she could.

He tilted her face toward his, lips smiling but eyes sad. "I won't. I can't stay."

"You can." She climbed up him until he held her, her legs wrapped around his middle. "I believe we can stay here. Just don't wake up. Don't go back." She ran her fingertips down his handsome face. "I know what's going to happen. I'm begging you. And I've never begged anyone for anything. Ever. Please, Thomas."

He put his forehead against hers. "I'm going to miss you." His eyes teared up a little, but his determination shone through. "So, so much. Forever."

Her own tears were free now, coasting over her lips and into her mouth. She wrapped her arms around his neck and spoke against his mouth, the salty emotions painting his lips as well. "Love me enough to stay."

He shook his head infinitesimally, refusing to break the contact. "Don't say that."

She had to play dirty. He was her everything.

"If you loved me, you'd stay." She gripped his wide shoulders.

"Dream girl." He sighed his nickname for her for one last time. "I love you enough to die for you."

She panicked in his arms, hearing the finality. "No. No. No! Please. No."

He held her closer as she struggled to get away. If she didn't say goodbye, he couldn't leave.

"Stop. Don't. Be still." He set her on her feet and stroked her hair from the crown to where it ended at the middle of her back. "I need this. This one moment with you. It makes me brave." He began to nod. "It's happening. It's going to happen. I can't desert them."

His voice sounded less commanding. He was scared.

They weren't going to get to have this life together, but she could try to help him with his death.

"Okay. Okay." She wiped her tears, centering herself with a

strength she hadn't possessed until this very second. "Look at me."

They looked into each other's eyes. Despite all she had done—the hoping, the praying—it had come to this. He began to fade, his lids getting heavier.

"Remember this. Remember us," she told him.

He put his arms around her. She made sure they maintained eye contact.

He's leaving.

Superhuman strength welled up in her as she focused instead of dissolved.

"Know that I love you more than time." She kissed his lips, his nose, his lips again.

"What if I'm a coward…in the end?" He voiced his unspoken fear.

"I swear on this, on our love—I know you will be remembered only for your valor."

She'd seen his Purple Heart. His legacy was bravery.

"Dream girl."

He grew quieter; this was how it went, the way it ended in all her waking nightmares.

The pain of not saving him would crush her soul.

"Yeah?" She put her hand on his heart, feeling it thump against her hand.

"Live. And that flag?" Even in his last moments, pride and commitment.

"It'll fly every day." Her heart performed a wedding here, in this place, only to that piece of material instead of to him.

"Love. Don't give up on that." He held her face and kissed her.

Beneath his gentle lips, she couldn't lie—even if he wanted her to. "There's only you. There will only ever be you."

"Okay." He ran his knuckles along her cheek and jaw. "Yours

is a face worth fighting for. Don't worry. I'll make your future safe."

"When I die, I'll come here. I'll find you."

Thomas nodded. He was almost gone now, barely in front of her.

She wanted him ready for battle on the other side.

"I love you forever, Fallen." He was just a ghost of a shape.

"You give them hell, Thomas McHugh." She went to her tiptoes as he took his last kiss.

In the wisp of his silhouette, after the kiss could go on no more, she sensed his stunning blue eyes on her, like she was his talisman.

"I'll love you for all the evers I get." She blew a kiss, and the wisp of him washed away with the sentiment.

Then he was gone. She'd sent the man she loved to his death.

A sound as close to the soundtrack for hell as she'd ever heard ripped though the quiet. It wasn't until she put her wrist to her mouth, blocking her airway, that she realized the noise had come from her.

She bent at the waist, hugging her middle as she gasped.

Was it now?

Was it now?

Was he dying right now?

She cried herself to a prone position, and desolation found her like a rogue wave.

It had all been for nothing in the end.

A little while later, when she felt the heat, she opened her eyes. She was awake, back in her world, and it was on fire.

Engulfed in flames, Fallen felt a small hope. In death she could see him again. In death she could triumph.

She dropped the hammer and noted the broken fork. Her mother was nowhere to be found. She scrambled off the damp bed in room 514 and grabbed the mirror. Mr. Orbit was banging on the door and screaming her name, but she couldn't be bothered with that now. She grabbed the edge of the moist comforter and used it as a filter against the smoke.

Beyond her reflection, she watched someone shaking Thomas awake as he reclined against a tree. His men, the ones he was so protective of, filled him in about something. She watched the mirror as intently as she could.

"Don't," she told him. The comforter dropped from her mouth. If he was going to die, so should she.

Orbit continued banging on the door to room 514. He was corporal enough now to exert his force on the wood. It didn't matter.

Only the mirror mattered.

She touched Thomas' moving image.

Don't go.

Please.

I warned you.

I fixed this.

I saved you.

Thomas, save yourself.

He listened to the urgent words from his fellow soldiers. Tears blurred Fallen's vision as she watched her love stop the man in front of him to take the lead as they traversed the hidden, tropical wood. Thomas kissed the quarter ring on his hand and armed himself. Her ring had not made it back with her.

She knew she was growing faint, the smoky air burning her throat.

Still she forced her eyes to stay open. She would be with him until the end, even if only remotely.

Thomas held out his hand, and the men trailing behind him stayed back. The look on his face was resignation, like he'd expected this all along.

Fallen could tell when the landmine detonated because of the way his men reacted, the shockwave knocking them back. Then white smoke fogged the mirror.

Fallen passed out holding the piece of glass to her heart.

25

REST IN PEACE

Fallen remembered holding the mirror, but she didn't remember getting to the lobby. She was still hugging, but her arms were around a person now, not metal and glass.

She looked down at familiar hair. Thomas.

Her heart rate raced, and she struggled to sit up, keeping his head in her lap. She ran her hands over his middle, looked at his legs. He was perfectly intact. But still.

Fallen ran her hands over his face, whispering his name. "Thomas. Please."

When his eyes fluttered open, she gasp-shouted with joy. "You're here."

His confusion took a while to dissipate, then his reflexes kicked in, and he was on top of her in a heartbeat.

"Stay down!" He took in their surroundings in the lobby. "What happened?"

He stood and lifted her with him.

"I think we died. Maybe. I saw you just before the landmine, and where I was there was so much smoke... But it doesn't matter. You're here, and it didn't hurt." She went to her tiptoes and kissed his distracted face.

When he committed to the kiss, the room went topsy-turvy and Fallen felt like she was tumbling through space in Thomas' arms. They landed with a thud on the bed in room 514. Neither would take their hands off the other.

The mirror lay on the bed as well.

The room was a haze of smoke, and they both started coughing.

"Fallen! I know you're in there! You have to get out. It's on fire. The hotel is on fire." Mr. Orbit was still yelling from the hallway.

"Is my mother here?" Fallen crawled off of the bed, the mirror under her arm.

Thomas jumped up and checked the bathroom. "No. We're getting out right now."

He slid open the window and punched out the screen. "Come here."

Fallen peeked over the sill. The room beneath 514 had a small balcony. The mirror slipped from her arms and landed on the umbrella below, then slid off the building, out of sight.

She looked at him. "I can't."

"You will." He picked her up and set her in the sill. "Hold my arms."

She did as he said, and after he lifted her, he slid her down the building. Her knees banged against the wall. "You're coming, right?" she asked.

Thomas was all sergeant when he looked at her. "Bend your knees," he ordered. And then he let go.

Fallen screamed as she hit the balcony and crumbled. She rolled over and looked at the open window above her. Smoke streamed out of it.

"Thomas!"

Fallen had watched him die once today; she wasn't about to

do it again. But as she got to her feet, she realized she didn't have her key anymore. It was in the tote upstairs.

Before she could form a plan, she saw Mr. Orbit dangling out of the window above her. She stepped to out of the way, and he landed and rolled.

"Jump!" Fallen pulled Lad out of the way.

Thomas' tall frame landed the most gracefully of the three. Fallen sighed, but Thomas shook his head.

"We've got to run. This place is about to be engulfed."

"I started the fire on the fifth floor," Lad offered helpfully.

Fallen tried the sliding door. "These are always locked." She looked over the side. The next balcony was on the second floor.

"Maybe we have time." Thomas grabbed a metal patio chair and threw it through the plate glass. He kicked away the shards at the bottom of the frame and stiff-armed Lad when he tried to run through.

"Ladies first, asshole." Thomas entered the smoke-filled room behind Fallen.

She went to open the door, but Thomas stopped her and felt it first. "It's okay," he said. "Let's try."

He opened the door, and they ran down the hallway with Lad behind, limping a bit.

"Wait for me!" he howled.

"No," Fallen said as she pulled Thomas toward the fire door.

His crazy ass had started this fire, so he was on his own. She focused on getting Thomas out. After taking the stairs as quickly as they could, Thomas checked to see that Lad was still descending.

Something crashed loudly outside the stairwell.

"Keep going." Thomas and Fallen ran the rest of the way to the ground floor, and she pulled him through the hallway door.

"That one has a padlock!" she yelled, gesturing to the closest exit. "We have to go out the way I broke in!"

Fallen and Thomas got to the side door in time to see the lobby's ceiling collapse on itself.

Lad appeared and headed toward the padlocked door. Fallen yelled for him, but the roar of the destruction drowned out her voice. She grabbed a metal pole from where it was propped by the door. Desta had used it to hold the door open when she smoked.

When they made their way out, the fresh air almost hurt. They both coughed violently.

Fallen heard Lad banging on the door that was chained closed. She went to the lock, eyeing the structure. She had to try. She couldn't listen to a man burn to death, even if he was the worst asshole in the world.

She started in on the padlock with the pole. Thomas took it from her, swung hard, and the lock burst free. Fallen pulled the lock off, and Lad crashed through.

Thomas kept the pole and pulled Fallen to him. "We've got to clear out. Now."

Lad limped behind, and they all increased their pace when they heard an explosion. They were two blocks away when the first sirens wailed.

Fallen hugged Thomas as they continued to cough. He tossed the pipe at their feet.

Lad leaned over to spit on the sidewalk. When Fallen could get a good breath, she began to yell at him.

"You crazy bastard, you're marching right down there and tell-ing the cops what you did. You almost killed us."

"Who is he?" Lad pointed at Thomas.

"The man who saved your sorry ass twice—when it was the last thing you deserved." Fallen started coughing again.

Thomas motioned for Lad to come closer as if he had a secret to tell him.

Lad inched forward.

Once he was in distance, Thomas hit Lad with an uppercut

that lifted the man off his feet. The left hook Thomas planted on Lad's cheek resulted in an audible crack. Lad sunk into a boneless puddle on the sidewalk, bruises appearing already.

"Never touch my girl again." Thomas stood up and tucked Fallen under his arm.

Fallen pointed at it the police cruiser in the distance.

Lad seemed too weak to run as Thomas greeted the officer. "This man here started the fire in that place."

The policeman said, "Is that so?"

Lad didn't even try to deny it. "That room has caused so much trouble. I just wanted to be free of it."

Fallen shook her head.

"I didn't want you to die, Fallen. That's why I was there, bang-ing on the damn door." Lad stood and put his hands behind his back like the officer asked, words slurring from his facial injuries.

"And you two were in there because?"

Fallen didn't have a great answer as to why she'd been five floors up in a closed hotel. Lad answered for her. "I gave her per-mission to get a mirror from a room. I just didn't think she'd be here today."

Fallen looked at him warily, but nodded.

Everyone paused to watch as five more fire engines pulled up to the scene.

"I own that hotel," Lad said, his voice stronger now. "Tell them to let it burn. There's nothing worth risking their lives over."

"You don't say… Let's get you in the car and start running some information. There was an ambulance dispatched. You two should check with them real quick. Your cough sounds like smoke inhalation, and it's more damaging than you think when you're all hyped up on adrenaline. We'll need you to give your statements once you're able." He pushed on Lad's head as he sat him in the backseat.

Fallen cuddled into Thomas' chest as she realized what she had.

"I stole you." She turned his head to face hers. "I stole you from time."

Thomas nodded solemnly before kissing her fingers. "You sure did."

A little while later, Fallen closed the door to her room and looked at Thomas' strong back as he inspected the interior.

"Everything's really different." He ran a hand through his dark hair.

That was an understatement.

"I'm sorry." She clicked the lock. "I know you'll figure it all out. I'll help you. But not just yet." She smiled at him.

"I remember this room from the first time I got to have you." He turned and smiled back at her.

"We were in such a rush. Time's not our enemy any more—although Fenn will be home from school in a few hours." She unbuttoned her jeans and shimmied out of them, kicking them aside.

"Oh." He bit his bottom lip, looking at her legs.

The hunger in his face and the way he clenched his fist made her want to take off another piece of clothing, just to get his reaction.

"Not everything's different." She pulled her sweater off and piled it on the jeans.

In her simple white panties and bra, she waited for him. She tucked one foot behind her calf and hugged her middle, feeling real-world forward with him all of a sudden. Their dream world had once been the only place where she didn't have inhibitions.

"You are very different. Like an angel." He took her bait, thankfully, and closed the space between them. His big hands coasted over her exposed skin. She had the chills and a rush of warmth at the same moment.

"Fallen." He whispered her name in her ear as he nudged her hair out of the way before pecking her neck with kisses and tiny bites.

She wrapped her arms around his neck and pressed herself against him. "No fear of drifting off to sleep anymore," she informed the base of his neck.

"Hmm." Thomas pulled her hard against him and let his hands drift to where she pulsed for him. His fingertips pushed into her damp panties. His other hand grazed her lower back and then slipped under her panties. He used both hands on her now, his fingers working from the back and the front in a way that made her knees weak.

As she lost her balance, gravity added to the friction he made, and she came louder than she probably should have—from just his hands.

She was useless now, and he guided her to her simple bed and helped her recline. Her legs spread for him automatically. He went at her through her now see-through cotton panties until she begged for more. What she wanted didn't have a name, just a feeling, and she needed more of it.

Thomas stepped away from her at the cusp of another release to take off his shirt. Fallen propped up on her elbows to watch the slow removal of his jeans.

"You okay, dream girl?"

"More than okay. But I need to be on top of you."

She got off the bed and pointed him toward it. She danced away every time he tried to get closer. Thomas finally shrugged and took the spot she'd suggested. Her man was from the past, but Fallen was about to give him a real future experience.

She took off her bra and panties and joined him on the bed. First, she knelt between his legs and let him know she appreciated his hard work earlier. She got as creative as she could, using both hands and her mouth to his advantage. And when she was sure he was almost there, she stopped and climbed on top of him.

Riding him felt selfish. His prone position was such a visual gift. She lavished kisses on him, biting his nipples and tracing the ridges of his muscles with her tongue before lifting to the top of his want and slamming back down in a way that had him tossing and grabbing handfuls of her breasts.

Taking him to the height of his masculinity made her feel powerful and lovely at the same time. When he was as primal as he would get, she showed him no mercy and hugged him as hard as she could from the inside.

When he seemed as useless as she'd been earlier, she flopped down next to him with her head on his arm. She watched as he caught his breath. She smoothed his hair off his forehead and touched his nose, then his chin. "So handsome."

"You are too much, beautiful dream girl. What was that?" He gestured to the spot above him that she'd just vacated.

"Love." She put her leg over his and pulled herself even closer. He rubbed her back with the arm she used as a pillow. "I stole you from time. From fate. And I'm not even sorry."

Thomas barked out a deep laugh. "You're shameless."

"I hope so." Fallen kissed his bicep and put her hand on his heart. The beat was solid.

Thomas covered her hand with his and winked at her. "Speaking of shameless, look what I found in the pocket of my pants." He dug under the pillow and pulled out the two rings he'd made out of quarters.

He brought her hand to his lips, kissing it. "I realize I'm not supposed to be here with you, but I'm so grateful. I'd like to make sure we start that first forever right now."

He picked up the smaller ring. "Be my girl here too?"

Fallen nodded as he slid the ring on her finger. She insisted on putting the larger ring on his.

He smiled as he rejoined their hands and ran his finger over her ring. "You sure you won't change your mind? What if this old geezer is too stupid to learn all this new-fangled stuff?"

She shook her head. "Not possible. My mind has no say in my love for you. My heart is a serious bully, and she's determined."

Thomas pulled his arm out from under her. "You're saying your brain is against me? Anything else love me?"

She maneuvered herself when she noticed he was ready for more. "All of me. My mind, too. I was trying to be poetic. But maybe you need to remind me about all this love."

Thomas knelt between her legs and looked her up and down again. "Your pleasure is my pleasure."

He was inside her quickly, and she swooned. She wrapped her legs around his waist as he stilled.

"Thank you," he said.

She wrinkled her nose, unsure what she deserved thanks for.

"For stealing me from time. I want to spend all the evers I get right here. Inside you."

"Me too," Fallen breathed. Then he started making all her dreams come true again.

26

FOR THIS EVER

Fallen was napping on my bicep. I was tempted to move her hair out of her face, but left it so she would rest. As real as my time in my dreams with Fallen was, this new place had a solidity to it that just seemed different.

I was trying to process what had happened, going over it step by step. I should be dead. There was part of me that knew that. This world had whooshed forward in such a huge jump. It surprised me how many things were the same.

Fallen's device lit up and vibrated. I couldn't see what was going on. The screen was flashing. It looked like a super small TV. Like the ones I'd seen in the city before I deployed. I looked at her beautiful face. Impossible. She was impossible, yet she was here with me. I pulled my arm out from underneath her carefully, her head hitting the pillow.

I crawled out of her bed and pulled on my clothes. I indulged in the sight of her for a few moments before taking a throw blanket from her chair and draping it over her so she wouldn't catch a chill.

After putting my clothes on, I moved her curtain out of the

way to look outside. Still trees. Still grass. The cars that rolled by were strange. Big. Rounded. Quiet.

I ran my hand over my face. I'd traveled in time. Somehow, this stubborn, brave woman had pulled me seconds before my death into this future with her.

Or I would wake up. I heard the the door downstairs open and my body tensed. I was still ready for the battlefield. I touched sleeping Fallen's shoulders and her eyes fluttered awake.

"You're still here." Her smile was blinding. This woman was very, very happy to see me.

"I am. And the door opened. Is that your brother? I heard keys." I picked up her clothing from the floor.

She grasped her blanket in front of her breasts. "Yeah. Should be."

I held out her bra and she stood to put it on. She had an easy grace about her as she took each item from me. She was blushing a little too, under my gaze. Instead of her black pants, she grabbed a pair of dungarees—wait, no, jeans now.

I heard the footsteps on the stairs and waited until another door closed somewhere else close by in the house.

"Should you introduce me? It's a bit improper to have me up here." She put her hand in mine..

"Improper? I think that was my favorite part." She put her hands on my chest, rubbing a circle pattern there.

After she fluffed her hair a bit, she bent at the waist to see into her dresser mirror. When she stood and I put my hand on her shoulder.

"Ready to meet Fenn?" She clenched her fist. I was betting she was nervous. I was too. Because I shouldn't be here. If this actually was my permanent new reality. She took her little screen device and slid it into her pocket.

Fallen

When I woke from my nap in Thomas' arms. I was still

grateful. Grateful he was here. Grateful we had lived, that he had lived. In the adrenaline rush that was saving lives, right and wrong were clearly defined. Now, he was here and there would be consequences. We had to make things fit.

Thomas was going to have to face the passage of time. A huge passage of time. I was going to have to research things that would be new to him. News to him. Maybe cherry pick the biggest events. The most important of which was his whole family as he knew it passing on.

He'd have to mourn the loss of them all. And the only traumatic event that caused it to happen was meeting me in his dream. Of course, he'd been destined to die—so it was complicated.

I'd never be able to convince myself that saving him was wrong. I couldn't see it that way.

I turned and faced him, going on my toes to give him a quick kiss.

"Fenn's going to be crazy about you. No worries."

I opened my door quietly and pulled Thomas behind me down the hall. I wanted to introduce the two most important guys in my life in a room more formal than my bedroom. Once Thomas and I were standing in the kitchen, I called up to Fenn.

There was no response, so I took out my phone and texted him. His response beeped right through.

K

I looked to see Thomas taking in the world around him. The kitchen obviously had things he was used to. And a few things he wasn't. We didn't have a house phone. We had a microwave. The stove was an older model, but still new seeming, I'm sure, to Thomas. Even the materials around the house—I wondered how many of them were perplexing.

Fenn ducked into the kitchen. Sandy hair flopping in front of his face.

"Oh hey! We've got company."

He strode towards Thomas and held out his hand, easy smile in place.

I introduced them, "Thomas, this is Fenn, Fenn this is Thomas."

My brother's smile got even wider. "So you're the guy that's been on my sister's mind? Nice to meet you."

Thomas shook Fenn's hand and I was proud that I'd taught my brother the greeting. Insisted on it, actually.

I got a peek at the type of man he would be when he patiently gave Thomas the short tour around the house. I pulled together the quickest meal in I could with the small amount of groceries we had on hand. I kept stopping to find Thomas with my eyes, hands in the air if they were messy. His handsome smile in return made my heart flutter over and over.

Three full plates of frittata were hot and ready by the time they got back to the kitchen. Cheese, eggs and noodles made a filling meal. Thomas scarfed it down in a way that reassured me that he was really real.

After dinner, Fenn insisted on doing the dishes. The night was mild, so I found Fenn's jacket and Thomas helped me into mine so we could walk off dinner. He held my hand.

I pulled it to my chest and hugged it. "I'm so happy."

I smiled into his face and he returned it but his eyes were sad.

He offered, "I'm glad."

We walked on my road and then took a less busy sideroad. We could see the stars.

Thomas stopped and tilted his head back. "Well, the stars look correct again. This is real life now, huh?"

"It is for me. This is where I started. I can't imagine what it's like to suddenly be somewhere so different. From the Pacific Theater in World War II to here." I moved his sleeve up and touched my name there.

"It's going to be an adjustment. Do you think? I mean, time wise... that any of my family is left?" Thomas covered my hand with his.

I felt selfish. I knew the answers and he didn't have them yet. But, before I opened my mouth, I realized I hadn't checked on the newspaper articles since he and I had been back. Maybe we had changed time?

I set his heart up the best I could, "It's been over seventy years, Thomas."

I watched his family die in his imagination as his face fell.

"But we have to check the newspapers. It's not unheard of for some people to live into their nineties now. Our population has benefited from longer lives thanks to a lot of medical and scientific advances—I'd imagine, from 1945."

We backtracked to the house. I offered a thanks to Fenn for cleaning up, and he gave me a thumbs up. He was on his phone playing a game or texting—I couldn't tell which one.

Thomas hesitated at the foot of the stairs, "Is this okay?"

I squinted at him and smiled, "Yeah. It's fine. Things are ... different."

He followed me to my room without any more questions, but we left the door open.

I pulled out my collection of his things. After popping up the loose board, I pulled out the box I that held my historical research and stolen documents. As I spread out the yellowed papers and pictures, I watched his face with concern.

Thomas

She had typewritten papers with pictures on them, dated pages with faded writing. I spotted letters I'd written to Ma and John and Eddie. They looked like they belonged in a museum. The folds betraying the very fibers that made up the paper, almost looking like fabric.

The telegram from John to Ma. About my death. Fallen

touched that one just as I read it. The date she had predicted was still inked there. I felt her palm on my cheek. Her thumb rubbed the tear there away.

"My handsome, love. I'm so sorry."

I picked up the telegram. Poor Ma. Poor John. The dates flew into my reality. My death. And then the end of the war. The time between where I was dead and Ma didn't know yet. I hoped she'd celebrated with friends. I thought about the neighbors and their loud parties on Fridays. I hope happiness made a mess out of the block.

And then I had to know. And clearly Fallen was well studied in the information in front of me. "My mother? My brothers? Are they here too?"

My voice was rough, but I wasn't trying to be a tough guy here. Fallen picked out three separate newspaper clippings.

She handed me the first. "Your mom—she passed away in 1969. She was supported her whole life by your insurance money."

I saw a beautiful picture of my mom. Older than when I last saw her. She was holding a little American flag. I could almost feel the agony in her face. I touched it with my fingertips.

"My brothers?"

Two more newspaper clippings.

"Eddie passed away in 1985—heart condition. He and his wife didn't have children. She went on to marry another man."

I closed my eyes and she put her hand over my heart. "And Johnny?"

"Johnny was married three times. He had daughters with his first wife. They are still with us. I've been trying to get in contact with Valerie, his middle child. He passed in 2010."

I brushed my knuckles together. "Three wives? Johnny is such a tomcat."

"Well, they were all at different times. Anything I could find about him was that he was the life of the party. Loved loud music and laughing. So the research shows, anyway."

"That would make Valerie my niece, right?"

"Yes. We can ask her all kinds of questions as soon as she gets back to me. And I'm friends with Adelaide. Her memory is in and out, but I bet she would love to meet you." She waited me out. Letting the information settle in. And she would wait however long it took.

She stopped my hands from the repetitive knuckle rubbing and took them in hers. I gazed at her and through her at the same time. "Whole generations have happened. And I need to…"

My sentence dropped off and she didn't try and finish it for me. There was nothing I could say that would help. She pulled my head to her chest and wrapped her arms around me. When I began to sob, I pulled her in closer. She straddled me and seemed to be trying to absorb my pain.

When I was exhausted, I stopped crying. I felt a bit bad about it, but Fallen was lovely and understanding. I loved her even more. I wanted to see my brothers' graves and my mother's. And I wanted to meet Valerie.

In the morning, Fallen suggested that we go to the local library and see if we could find Valerie first, than maybe she would have the answers as to where we needed to go next. We walked to the library hand-in-hand. I pointed out some of the more unusual cars. I mean, they were all weird, but some were like boats on wheels.

"Those are SUVs. They're gas guzzlers. You should see an electric car." Fallen tucked herself under my arm. "I wish I knew more about them. Maybe we can look them up together."

"I need to see Valerie." She murmured her agreement and we kept on.

The loud noises grated on my nerves. I was jumpy. I mean, when I came home for furlough back in my own time, I was jumpy then, too. But it was even worse now. Maybe it was because trees and grass were the same, but a lot of the houses had just enough stuff I couldn't place or recognize. Time travel, I guessed. Impossible. But somehow...

Like she could read my mind, Fallen spoke up, "I spoke with Lad's ex wife. She used 514 to find her love and he lives here with her now too."

She tilted her head so I could look in her eyes.

"Can we talk to them?"

I placed a kiss on Fallen's forehead. Because she was still here. And she'd saved me even though I was still coming to terms with it.

"They split town when Lad started threatening them." She led me across the street and the door opened when Fallen put her foot on the doormat. The doors swung open all on their own. I pulled her backwards and reached for the gun I no longer had.

She soothed me with a gentle hand. "I'm betting these weren't invented yet for you. But they don't hurt. It senses our weight and that opens the door."

I didn't like it, but Fallen wasn't afraid. I could tell by her eyes, her pupils were even and her breathing was regular. We walked through. The library had books, but there were screens everywhere. People were pounding away on paper thin keyboards.

"Where are the card catalogs?" I was used to seeing the wall of little drawers that kept track of where all the books were.

"Would you believe if I told you that those files were all stuffed into computers now?"

The word computer scratched something in my memory. Maybe something I read in the newspaper? Fallen went up to an empty screen and pulled a chair next to hers. Even the chairs were bizarre. Instead of wood, they were metal and plastic.

Fallen plugged numbers into the typewriter and they appeared on the screen. If she made a mistake, she could easily fix it. It wasn't permanently on the screen. After searching Valerie's name, she was able to narrow down a phone number from a dizzying amount of results.

"Okay. I've got what I need. Did you want to see anything here?" She waved her hand toward the books.

I scanned the room. One shelf had a book about the Grumman F6F-3 Hellcats. It was a fairly new plane that had replaced the F4F Wildcat. It was a history book. After pulling it down and flipping it open, I realized I'd spanned the distance between the computer and the shelf.

Fallen put her hands on my bicep. "You recognize that one?" I nodded. "Maybe we pull a few of these down and have a look? Is that okay?" She grabbed the books that had been on the shelf next to one in my hands.

"Will this tell me what happened to my men? Is that in these books?" My hands were shaking slightly. I held everyone's futures in my hands.

"You were a hero for them. I know that from Adelaide. But we can research the hell out of all of it. It's not like I have a job. We can even take books home and look there, if you want." I wanted to know, but then finding out seemed like cheating on life. "Knowledge is power, they say." She brought me to a low slung brown sofa. "Sit with these, let me call Valerie and see if I can connect with her."

I flipped the pages open. The war, the news—it was now history. Neatly catalogued in between pages. Which didn't seem right, considering I felt like I could still hear the helicopter blades and I had four bug bites on the back of my hand from the jungle I was supposed to die in.

Fallen

He was immersed in the peek at the history that —for

Thomas— probably still felt like future. I had to have a bridge for him. A connection somehow. I stepped into the lobby, where I could still see Thomas and dialed the number I'd found for Valerie.

She answered and I realized I didn't have a plan. Thomas wasn't supposed to be here. How would I explain what I needed from this woman without scaring her? I looked to Thomas and then to the shelves behind him. Newspapers. That was my answer.

"Hello! I'm Fallen and I was wondering if you'd be willing to be interviewed about some of your relatives that were in World War II? My associate and I are writing an article about our fallen heroes." I held my breath.

Maybe it was too crazy a request. People are so private. Thomas leaned forward in his seat, running his index finger over the text there. I hoped for him, said a little prayer as well.

"Oh. I thought you were a telemarketer for a minute there, sweetheart. Are you talking about my Uncle Tommy?"

I could hear music in the background and a man shouting at an Alexa robot.

"Yes, actually. And John and Edward? We're focusing on families that were drafted all at the same time."

I swallowed hard. Something felt right about this woman. That meeting her was the way to go.

"That would be okay. I don't mind speaking to you at all."

I finally exhaled.

Luckily, the address that Valerie gave was only about thirty minutes away and I was pretty sure there was a bus that ran that way. Valerie gave me an email to firm up the details, but we could possibly go the following day.

After thanking her, I hung up. Thomas was gone from the sofa when I looked in his direction. I panicked. My heart was hammering in my throat as I rushed back into the library. He was just a short distance away tucked in one of the stacks. He was juggling two thick books while trying to page one handed through a slightly smaller one.

I rubbed his back. "What did you find?"

His face was pure anguish. "My guys. I found some mentions. But there's very little. "

I took the extra books from his arms so he could get a better grip on the text he now had.

I recognized it as one of the many I'd paged through myself, trying to find out what had happened to Thomas.

"I know, I've been through this one. We can do more research. But I do have some good news."

Thomas closed the book and focused on my lips, like the news I was promising was desperately needed. "Valerie would like a visit from us. So we can ask more about your family."

He tipped his head toward the ceiling. "I can't believe I won't see them again."

I hugged him around his neck as my heart ached. I'd be so lost if Fenn was suddenly gone from my life with no hope of contacting him.

I pat his back and kissed his neck gently. "It'll be okay, Thomas."

And I really hoped I wasn't lying to him.

Fallen and I took a pile of books from the library. I carried them, and she held my elbow as we navigated back to her house. The people we passed gave my clothes the once over. Army issued reversible khakis made me blend in where I had been. Fallen must have noticed as well because when we got back she went looking in her brother's room for a change of clothes for me that were more contemporary.

The pants were a bit short, and the t-shirt tight but I looked more like a current civilian. I was hugging Fallen when there was a knock on the front door. I was half expecting the Police to show up with questions about our role being involved in the fire that took the hotel.

When Fallen opened the door, her demeanor changed instantly. A harder, older version of Fallen pushed into the living room.

"This is your new man? He's a good looking one. What do you do for a living?"

Fallen put her arm around her mother. "Nora, this is Thomas."

"You're Fallen's mother? It's nice to meet you ma'am." When I held out my hand for hers, I could tell her hand eye coordination was off. And then the scent of booze hit me. Fallen had not been exaggerating when she said her mother was an alcoholic. I could see the damage her hard life had on her. Fallen looked soft and brave. Her strength and love for her brother was something I could relate to.

"She left a very profitable relationship to be with you. So I hope you bring something to the table." Nora staggered a little into our handshake. Fallen seemed to anticipate it and caught her mother's forward movement. Fallen used her hip to twirl her mother in the opposite direction. The door was still open.

"Lad's in jail Nora. So I didn't really leave as much as I escaped. You have a place to stay tonight?" Fallen pushed her mother out the door and held up one finger, asking for a minute with her mom in privacy without saying it out loud.

I made my way to the pictures on her wall. They were a just a bit crooked. Fallen was young and Fenn was just a baby in the one that was largest. Nora was there too. Young, pretty and smiling.

The door opened and shut behind me and I stretched my hand out to Fallen. She rushed to me like I might disappear.

"You really know how to handle her, huh?" I pushed her hair behind her ear, pulling her into a hug. She's redirected Nora like a seasoned bartender.

After nodding against my chest she pointed to the picture I'd been admiring moments before.

"You know, I feel like I lost her soon after that picture was taken. Sometimes it's like only the ghost of who she used to be peeks through what she's become." Fallen tipped her chin to the floor. "I wonder if she's gone forever." Then she snapped her gaze to my face. "I'm sorry, was that insensitive? I know it is much more concrete for you."

I traced her spine through her shirt with my thumb. "No, not at all. Actually, I think we have different situations but the same pain."

Her mouth slid to the side. "The irony, huh?"

"Is your mom okay for the night?" I tried to see out the front curtains.

"Yeah. She's got a new man. Well, an ex-boyfriend that came back in to the picture—so she says. Is it weird that when she's like this I don't think of her as my mom? I call her Addiction in my head. And that's the monster I fight."

"You do what you have to to survive and keep Fenn safe. It's got to be right. Your brother seems like a great guy. And you? Well, you're my angel." I kissed her deeply. Her mouth was home. I knew the feel of her bare skin could help me push off all my concerns, at least for a little while. "Speaking of him, do we have some time?"

"Yeah. He's with his friend tonight." She put her hand on my face. I bent my knees and picked her up, kissing her as we ascended the stairs to her bedroom.

Waking up next to Thomas felt like I was winning the lotto. Wanting to see him in my waking world had been my dearest wish, but I think I'd resigned myself to only getting to be with him on Thursdays during brief dream world in room 514. But I was happy to have fallen so wonderfully in love. But now.

This.

I ran the back on my knuckles on his jaw. His smile appeared before he opened his eyes.

When he did finally look at me I had goosebumps from just knowing he was feeling the same way. He snuggled me closer. We had obstacles and heartbreak ahead, locating his family and acclimating him to the present, but at least we had each other.

Thomas and I showered together, and spent way too long discovering each other over and over. We got dried off and dressed, holding hands after I locked the door behind us. We strolled to the bus stop and waited on the bench there. Thomas wondered out loud what his niece would be like.

We did the math and realized that she could very well be retired. After a bus ride filled with explanation about our scenery in whispered hushes we had a short walk to the gated community.

After finding the cute blue cottage that looked similar to the others around it, we matched Valerie's last name with the listing on the Internet. The driveway had two cars and a golf cart parked near the tallest flagpole with a large American flag waving in the breeze. As we watched, a small parade of people came out of the front door. Two of the men helped an elderly lab into the back of the golf cart carefully. We couldn't quite make out the joke delivered by the woman on the front patio that was punctuated uproarious laughter.

Thomas leaned down to my ear. "I'll bet you a dollar that one is John's kid."

I felt my lips curl into a smile. John was the funny one.

After the crew moved out, only two remained on the patio. Thomas and I walked up the path and he stepped forward first, extending his hand.

"A pleasure to meet you, Valerie!"

Valerie had cornflower blue eyes and a classically pretty face. She tilted her head to the left and squinted a bit as she looked Thomas up and down. "Have we met before?"

I came forward and introduced myself to her husband, Steve. A handsome older man that gave Thomas a firm handshake as well.

"No, Valerie. Not yet. But I'm glad that this day has come."

I was a little alarmed, I didn't want Thomas to get us in trouble by tipping his hand that he was possibly her uncle.

Steve and Valerie invited us into their home. It was cozy and they had a flair for decorating. Classy porcelain was mixed in with pictures of her children and grandchildren. We knew everyone's name and ages before Steve could even get drinks in our hands.

Thomas and I both took sips of the iced water. Steve began carrying dirty cups and plates from their party to the kitchen, apologizing, "Sorry for the mess. Our cocktail hour went a little long."

Thomas held his glass up, "Cocktail hour? It's just past lunch!"

Valerie stepped next to Thomas, "Retirement is busy business. We have to start the party early so we can fit more in the day. We're going to the races this evening."

Thomas smiled and turned his body toward her. He was much taller, but Valerie had a big personality.

Valerie wrapped her hand around Thomas' wrist. "What did you say your name was?"

There was suspicion in her face. I watched as Thomas calculated his response.

"Thomas McHugh."

Steve dropped a plate in the sink before turning off the water from the faucet. "Are you related to John McHugh?"

The pause in conversation could only be described as otherworldly. And then Thomas shrugged.

"John McHugh was my brother." Thomas put his hand over Valerie's. "Do you believe in miracles, Val?"

Valerie gave Thomas a comforting nod, like being in her uncle's presence seventy years after his death was not surprising. "I always knew I'd be the one to bring you home Uncle Tommy."

Steve came around the counter, leaving the faucet on to put his arm protectively around his wife's shoulders. He might possibly be harder to convince. I reached over the counter and turned off the water.

Steve narrowed his steel grey eyes. "There certainly is an uncanny resemblance to the pictures we have."

And then Thomas reached down and hugged Valerie, and then grabbed Steve with his other arm. I knew I was witnessing the reason I'd even entered room 514 beyond finding my love. Reuniting this family was destined.

We found out so much about Valerie, John and Edward. Steve had great questions for Thomas about his time served and seemed very knowledgeable about the war itself. We got to see the documents that Steve and Val had saved and laminated. Letters to John. Scraps of paper that had cartoons on them. A music box.

My eyes filled when I saw how much they had cherished his memory—even though they had never met him.

Thomas and I told these two our story. Our unbelievable, rollercoaster of a story. And they heard it. I felt sure that they understood the importance of the need to keep it secret.

I took pictures on my phone, letting Thomas and his niece pose near her Grandfather clock—with a picture of John framed behind them. When the day had gotten late, we promised to stay in touch—there was so much still to discover about John and Eddie. Val and Steve promised to swing by the following morning to my house and take us to the graves of John and Eddie and Thomas' mother.

Thomas and I both marveled on the bus ride home about how cool it was to have people we could trust so quickly. I covered his hand with mine when I saw his expression darken. Tomorrow would be bittersweet. I could tell he adored his niece, but he was reluctant to face gravestones with his loved one's names written on them.

Thomas did the best he could to look presentable with the outfit he borrowed from Fenn. Fortunately Fenn had to dress up for his team on game day, so there was a tie. The only button down Fenn had was white. Thomas said he wished he had a darker color. But it wasn't a funeral, even if it felt like one. The reality of having nothing but our love was proving to be hard on him. Thomas claimed he had nothing to offer me.

Though he mentioned, Well, there was something I tried with John and Edward, but I had no idea if time had been favorable to my idea."

I wore a simple dark blue dress and black jacket. It had faded elbows. Thomas said he burned with the need to provide for me.

After I fluffed my hair from under the collar, he wrapped his arms around me and whispered into the nape of my neck, "Do you know how exceptional you are? That you've been able to provide for your brother and keep your house? At your age?"

I absorbed his compliment and turned it into delight. "Thank you, Mr. McHugh. It's nice to have you notice."

Steve and Valerie tooted the horn when they pulled into the driveway. They'd insisted on giving us a lift when they learned we'd be taking busses to get around.

The ride to the grave sites was far more fun than it should've been. Valerie related tales of her father, John and Thomas told tales from the brothers' childhood too.

More than once, Thomas reached his hand over the seat to hold Valerie's. He commented often that the sparkle in her eyes reminded him of John.

When we pulled into the cemetery, a hush came over the car. Steve brought up little facts as we made our way to the parking lot. That John had had a military burial. That Edward and his wife were buried close by. That Valerie's grandparents were neighbors to his brothers.

Steve and I hung back as Thomas offered Valerie his arm to hold. We made small talk, I mentioned how I was worried about the adjustment for Thomas. Steve assured me that he and Valerie would be a resource. Thomas was family, and by extension, so was I.

Valerie pointed out the gravestones, and Thomas took to one knee next to each of them. When he got to his mother's, Valerie rested her hand on his shoulder.

Steve motioned with his head that we could join them, so I came to kneel in the grass near Thomas. His name was under his parents'.

"She wanted to bring you home. This was the best she could do. I know she can see you now, here, safe. And it brings her mother's heart joy," Valerie offered.

Thomas stood and hugged Valerie. "Thank you for that."

Steve patted Thomas on the back, "Your sacrifice was always honored, by John and Edward too."

Thomas held his hand out to me and I slipped under his arm, putting my hand on his chest.

"Fallen's made this easier. And thank you both so much. For all you've done."

Steve went back to the car and revealed that he and Valerie had brought flowers for each grave. Thomas placed each, sweeping dried leaves away with his hands as he did so.

We gave him a few moments to himself, and from his shaking shoulders, I knew his grief was open in this place where his family rested. Valerie passed me a tissue from her purse, and I met her watery eyes. Bittersweet was the only word appropriate.

When Thomas was ready, he walked with us back to the car.

Our ride home was peppered with more stories. When we were almost home, Thomas broached a topic he'd clearly been mulling over.

"So, I know that Ma was able to use the life insurance I set up—but there was a message I left for John? Do you guys know anything about that?"

I furrowed my brow.

Valerie looked into the distance and then made eye contact with Steve. "Now it makes sense. All those years."

Thomas waited for clarification, but his fist was balled. He was nervous.

"Actually, Edward didn't have any children, but he insisted on putting a huge chunk of his money in a bond for a girl named Fallen. We had no idea what it was about. But we lost those papers years ago. Maybe if we could find his wife's family?" Steve shrugged his shoulders.

"I can help with that. I managed to make friends with Adelaide. I helped her before she was put in the nursing home. She's a sweetheart." I met Steve's surprised blue eyes in the rearview.

Valerie looked less surprised. "That's the brothers up there working together, I think." She pointed at the car roof.

Thomas started to laugh. "I bet you're right. They would work together like that."

His laughter was welcome and his face lit up. I had the start of hope in my chest that we would be okay. Somehow, we'd make it through.

27

EPILOGUE

*F*allen
One year later...

I touched the lace on the hem of my sleeve. Today was the day. I was marrying my dream man, Thomas McHugh. Somehow, we were surrounded by a huge group family and friends. What a glorious year it had been. I adjusted Thomas' mother's bracelet that Valerie had given me to wear. It was simple gold with pearl in the center. I was getting ready for the big day at Steve and Val's. Her daughters and granddaughter were seeing to the small details. Something old, something blue, etc. Thomas was getting ready at Ted and Jo's, a few roads over. The guys were with him, and I was pretty sure Al was playing bartender. Sue was cooking food, and Jean was making rolls for the reception. Larry and Ted and Steve and Val's grandson were in charge of the golf cart processional.

Steve was able to get the retirement communities lovely rec room for our wedding. There were high ceilings and giant chandeliers. The room would be packed with people from all over. Even 8 and 9 were invited. Adelaide knocked gently on the doorframe. She looked adorable as Pam helped her in the room.

"In our family, we had the tradition of braiding hair for the wedding, if you'd like, I could do it for you?"

I agreed and gently hugged the older woman. I was so grateful she was feeling well enough to be here today. Val dragged a chair from the dining room into the bedroom and I sat down carefully so I wouldn't wrinkle my dress. It was a vintage number I found from an antique shop in New York. It had a gentle neckline and a sweeping skirt. The veil had been in the family, both Pam and Debra wearing it at their weddings, and then Valerie in her wedding to Steve almost fifty years earlier.

Adelaide patiently braided my hair. I let her do whatever style she wished, loving seeing her happy smile and her fingers working nimbly. Doing this was a good memory for her, clearly, to relive.

After she was done, Jo got a mirror for me to see the back. It was simple and elegant and perfect. I hugged my matron of honor.

Steve came in the front door, announcing that we we'd be late if we didn't leave right away. Instead of limousines, we had golf carts decorated with white lights and cans on strings trailing from the back. The entire community turned out to cheer me on.

Music played from car radios, Unforgettable by Nat King Cole. The forethought made me tear up. Val handed me a handkerchief. The ceremony and reception would be in the same hall. Jim, Pam's husband had gotten ordained online so he could do the honors.

When we got to the hall, there was a red carpet laid out. It led up to the double french doors. I had no doubt I was doing the right thing—marrying Thomas today. The people I was surrounded by had become so dear to me and Fenn in the last year. Being considered family here seemingly guaranteed that help and laughter would be a given. Steve and Val helped

Thomas locate the money Edward stashed away in my name. Having no conflicts, it moved quickly through the courts—being awarded to Valerie as a direct descendant. They then gave the money to Thomas. The money helped us get a comfortable start and sock away funds to boot. Fenn's college bills have been reasonable because he got a sports scholarship.

Today, Fenn was here in a tuxedo, ready to walk me down the aisle. He looked older and handsome as he walked to my side.

"You deserve this Fallen. Congratulations."

I hugged him hard. I was waiting for my cue to open the doors and walk to Thomas on my brother's arm when a car pulled up the driveway. My heart fell as I saw Nora climb out of the back, thanking the driver. She had a phone in her hand and a car service app open on the screen.

She was dressed up. That didn't matter to me. I didn't want her here, ruining this perfect moment by bringing Addiction with her to my wedding day. I tried to see her eyes. Instead, Valerie stepped between Nora and her direct path to me.

Fenn wrapped his arm around my shoulders as I watched Valerie confront Nora. Valerie had a pretty face and kind smile, but she was the sharpest mind in a crowd. She read a scene and the people in it like is was her superpower.

I wasn't sure what Valerie said, but she had a firm grip on Nora's upper arm. Nora at first tried to look past Valerie, but then widened her eyes and stared at her face. And then slowly, guiltily Nora pulled a flask out of her purse. Valerie took it and disappeared it in her own bag. Whatever was said, Nora seemed chastised.

Valerie turned, smiling at me. "Nora here was just telling me that she'd like to attend your wedding and that she'll be on her best behavior so help me God. But if you are more comfortable with her gone, she'll be happy to wish you well and be on her way."

Like a little group of mafia bosses, Jo, Jean, Sue and Pam surrounded Nora.

My mothers eyes looked wild at their presence. "Um. Yes. I'll watch and clap. I understand I need to be well behaved."

Valerie nodded approvingly and then lifted her eyebrows, "And?"

"And you and your brother are exceptional and deserve every happiness. And that will be the most important gift I can give you today —not making it about me." Nora glanced at Valerie to double check that she had gotten the words right.

Jo cleared her throat, "One more thing?"

Nora bounced her chin up and down. "And if any of these ladies tell me to leave I'll do so immediately."

The part of me that knew my mother's face as peace and happiness was small now, but she was still there. Having my mom here today mattered. If I could truly put worrying about her off my mind, then I could have her here.

Valerie closed the distance between us. "We've got this kiddo. But do whatever makes you happy. We'll support whatever it is."

"Okay. She can stay."

Fenn squeezed me tightly, huge grin in place. It was good for him to see that maybe we had to continue trying. Not for Nora's sake, but for ours. I felt so accepted and protected by my new crew—it felt like lifetimes away from fighting with Nora over bills.

Nora smiled, but looked chastised enough that she adopted an almost shy demeanor. Fenn waved her over for hugs. I was tense until Nora whispered that she'd agree to anything to get to see her baby girl get married. And then I had to take at least some of my guard down. Fenn, Nora and I shared a hug.

The ladies showed Nora inside and Fenn and I waited outside. When we got our cue, (a text from Steve and Val's grandson) Fenn opened the door. And then there Thomas was. I appreciated the size of the crowd, but there was only my love now.

I found Thomas' gaze locked on me and watched him mouth, "Oh damn," when he saw me in my wedding dress. Then he bit his bottom lip.

I felt the rush of butterflies up my spine. Like clicking in the last piece of the puzzle, taking the first step in a fresh snow— our love was the start and finish of an amazing journey.

The vows were tender—though we made a subtle change— promising to love one another For All the Evers we get.

Thomas

I was married. To Fallen. If there was a more beautiful site than her in a wedding dress walking to me I couldn't imagine it. This makeshift family and actual family was overwhelmingly fantastic. I was worried when I saw Nora walk in the the venue, but she was monitored closely by the females in the room. Clearly, she had very strict restrictions to be allowed in.

After we walked down the aisle, to applause and congratulations, there was a brief pause to switch the venue from ceremony to reception. We stepped outside and had some family and newlywed pictures taken by Amanda, a family friend.

I watched as a look of puzzlement came over Fallen's face. I followed her gaze to the parking lot.

Debra and her kids wrangled a van full of dogs and one fairly miserable cat dressed in their finest wedding clothes. There was apparently going to be a petting zoo portion to this wedding as a surprise.

In the melee, a new dog walked in with Debra and the kids. The dog runs straight for me with a big white bow. Fallen was clearly as surprised as I was to see the brown puppy from my time in the war barreling our way. We both fell to our knees and began loving on "Fallen" the dog. The puppy scrambled to my face, recognizing me and covering me with licks.

Fallen started laughing at my amazement. "This dog is probably a wedding present from your brothers and mom and dad."

Todd, Debra's husband, convinces her that the petting zoo is not the best idea, but I insist on my brown puppy staying with us. No one can give us a straight answer as to where the dog had come from, so I decided to take Fallen's suggestion, she was a special gift from my family on the other side. Fallen and I have our first dance with the squirming, licking dog between us. Happy reunions and a party somehow mingle with heaven to make a perfect day.

And forever . . .

Fallen gives birth to twin boys three years to the day after our wedding. Adelaide lives four more years and loves spending time with Fallen and Thomas, and all of Val and Steve's friends and family. She got to meet the twins before she passed.

John and Edward, our sons, and Fallen the dog are always outside making mischief. Fallen loves teaching at the local school and Thomas works at a World War II museum after he caught the attention from staff giving visitors with questions thorough beyond accurate answers.

The money helped us get a comfortable start and sock away funds for the boys and their retirement. Fenn's college bills were pretty light because he got a college scholarship. He gets a degree in social work and counseling. Fenn works in a treatment center for addicts. Nora also works there. The sight of her grandchildren helped strengthen her resolve to work everyday on her sobriety.

We still have a lot of life ahead of us, but I think it's safe to say:

We lived happily *For all the Evers* after.

FOR ALL THE EVERS

THE REAL THOMAS F. MCHUGH

Bronx Sergeant Killed In Mindanao Fighting

Sgt. Thomas F. McHugh

When I was young, I often visited my grandfather, John McHugh. And during pretty much every visit, he would crank up a parade march, hand the always-present American flag to one of the grandkids, and shout out orders in his sergeant voice as we struggled to stay in formation. We all laughed and giggled when he corrected us.

I didn't know we were marching past a picture of his brother until years later.

Thomas F. McHugh was my great uncle, and my other great uncle's name was Ed McHugh. Thomas was killed in action on May 7, 1945. That's the true story. He stepped on a landmine and ended his six years of service to this country. It's a sad story, but it was just a story to me for a long time.

It wasn't until recently that my father and mother showed me a box of keepsakes they had at their house in Florida—important papers, files, and some pictures of Great Uncle Tommy. My father had laminated all the old, yellowed papers to preserve them.

It was stunning to see the telegrams and the newspaper clippings about his death all in one place.

And that got me thinking about what it must have been like for his family. On his last furlough, Great Uncle Thomas took out a life insurance policy for my great grandmother and said goodbye to everyone. He felt his time was coming. When I interviewed Harry Kirby, a Foreign Legion award winner in Florida, he told me all the soldiers were fatalists. So maybe they all did things like that. But to the McHughs, my Great Uncle Tommy was a war hero, and a family one as well. He never had a family of his own, but he provided for his mother long after he was killed.

So here I am, writing romance novels. I've watched over and over as my beautiful readers give their hearts to the characters I create. And I realized that although Thomas didn't have any direct descendants, my great uncle might be remembered with love if I wrote a story about him.

For All The Evers is dedicated to Thomas F. McHugh. When you read this book, I hope you'll think a kind thought about a real man who lived and died for country and family. He was killed on May 7, 1945. On May 8, 1945, the Allies accepted Germany's surrender. My great grandmother did not get news of her son Thomas' fate until May 29, 1945.

This book was also written for my mother and father, who never let a flag fly in the dark.

Please visit my website DebraAnastasia.com for more information on Thomas F. McHugh. You can also post your own stories. I urge you to appreciate our older generations while we still have them.

This book was also written for my mother and father, who never let a flag fly in the dark.

On the cover of this book and behind each chapter header, the handwriting in the image is a photograph of a letter Thomas sent to his brother, Ed. Thomas' actual signature is at the bottom of the letter image embedded at the end of Chapter 21. Words can connect us where time fails to offer the opportunity.

Please visit my website DebraAnastasia.com for more information on Thomas F. McHugh.

XO Debra

ACKNOWLEDGMENTS

Husband and Kids: If not for you I would not be me.

Helena: Purple Lambo

Jessica RO: I can't even explain how much your friendship means.

Tijan: Rainbow llama

Texas K: Thanks for all the Lamaze support on the crapper

Nina: #NinaReadPough

Teresa: I love you.

Erika: I love how you welcome my crazy.

Jillian: You are a star.

Pam: I'll see you on Sunday nights SISTERS UNITE

Christina and Lauren: You girls are my rocks. I love you.

Martha: Thank you for being such a great assistant!

Jen Matera: Still sorry about that Fire book.

Tara S and Meghan: Sweet Jesus. I love you both.

Shannon, Beverly C, Nise, Patti, Alicia, Flor, Michele, Nancee, Daisy, Liv, Seren, and Ruth, Mom and Dad (S&D)

Uncle Ted and Aunt Jo: Your new house looks great on you!

FB groups that offer so much help.

My SWAT Team and the Revenger Group!

Heather Wish, Dina Littner, L.J. Lisa, Roberta Curry, Ramona Johnson, Eve Chin

Lavin, Blair Ackerman, Pam Brooks, Robyn Diebolt, Ashley Scales, CL Sayers, Crissy Maier, An-gelica Maria Quintero and TL Wainwright, Sarah Piechuta , Elaine Turner, Michele MacLeod

Friends, family, readers, bloggers and author friends – Thank you!

SOURCES

Wolfgang W.E. Samuel. In Defense of Freedom: Stories of Courage and Sacrifice of World War II Army Air Forces Flyers, *2015.*

Harry Kirby, WW2 Veteran and French Legion of Honor medal recipient, interviewed July 10, 2015.

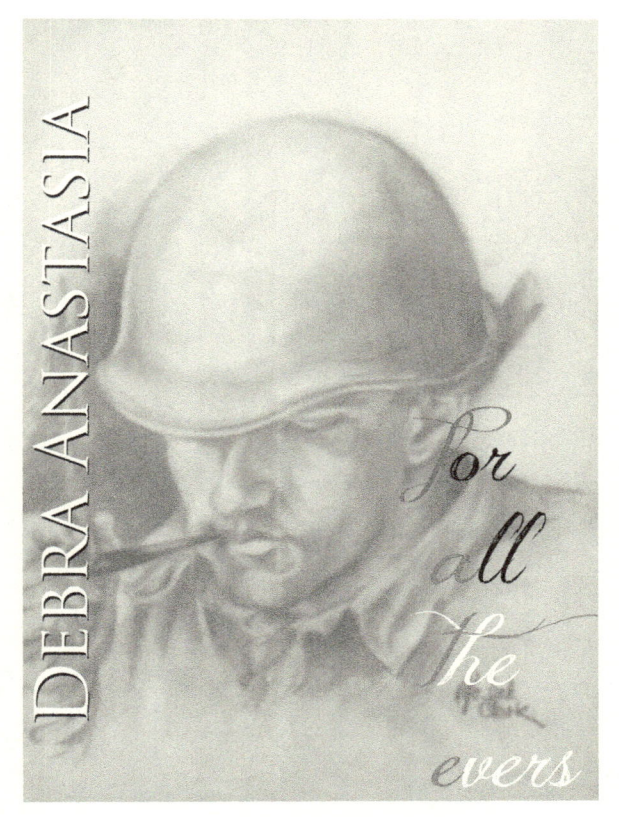

Hand drawn picture Harry Kirby from WW2 *artist unknown*

Jacob Meier. *A Lucky Dogfoot of World War II*, 2003. http://www.24thida.com/stories/images02/Meier_jacob_lucky_dogfoot_book_3a_opt.pdf

SOURCES

The 24th Infantry Division Association
http://24thida.com/stories_by_members/0_default.html
Jan Valtin and Richard Krebs. Children of Yesterday: The 24th Infantry Division In World War II, *2014.*
Tom Brokaw. The Greatest Generation, *2001.*

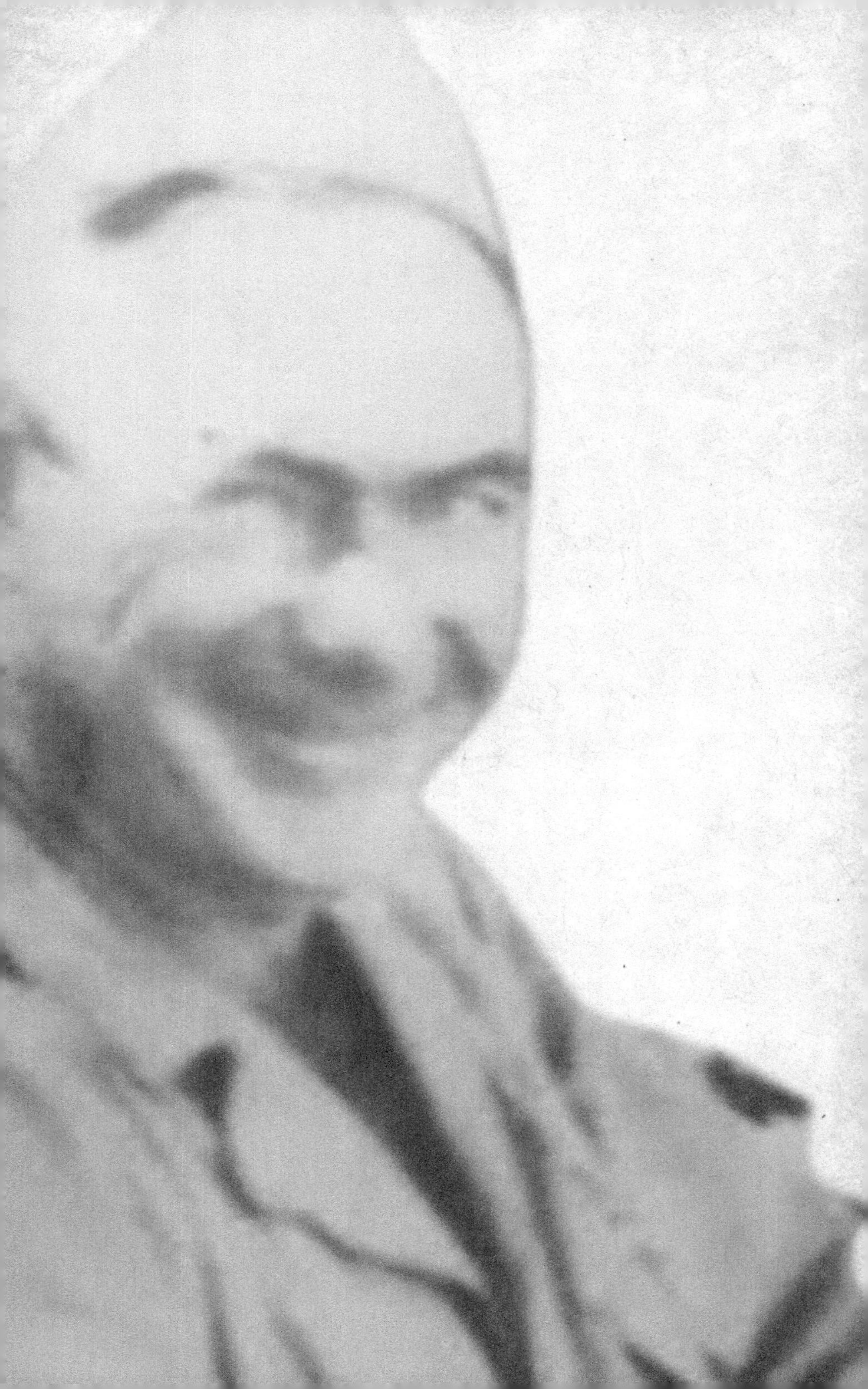

OTHER TITLES BY DEBRA ANASTASIA

WHAT TO READ NEXT...

Angst with Feels:
CRUEL PINK
DROWNING IN STARS
STEALING THE STARS

Mafia Romance:
MERCY
HAVOC
LOCK

Silly Humor:
FIRE DOWN BELOW
FIRE IN THE HOLE

Funny Humor:
FLICKER
BEAST
BOOTY CAMP
FELONY EVER AFTER
BEFORE YOU GHOST (with Helena Hunting)
SANTA'S SUIT SITUATION

Paranormal:
THE REVENGER
FOR ALL THE EVERS
CRUSHED SERAPHIM (BOOK 1)
BITTERSWEET SERAPHIM (BOOK 2)

ABOUT THE AUTHOR

Debra creates pretend people in her head and paints them on the giant, beautiful canvas of your imagination. She has a Bachelor of Science degree in political science and writes new adult angst and romantic comedies. She lives in Maryland with her husband and two amazing children. She doesn't trust mannequins, but does trust bears.

DebraAnastasia.com for more information.

Pretty please review this book if you enjoyed it. It is one of the very best ways to support indy authors. Thank you!

Scan the code below to stay connected to Debra:

tiktok.com/@debraanastasia
facebook.com/debra.anastasia
instagram.com/debra_anastasia

Made in United States
Orlando, FL
16 March 2025